DIRK PITT®: He is th
who lives by the mom
without regret. A gradu
son of a United States
director for the U.S. Na
Agency (NUMA), he is cool, courageous, and resourceful—a man of complete honor at all times and of absolute ruthlessness whenever necessary. With a taste for fast cars, beautiful women, and tequila on the rocks with lime, he lives as passionately as he works. Pitt answers to no one but Admiral James Sandecker, the wily commander of NUMA, and trusts no one but the shrewd, street-smart Al Giordino, a friend since childhood and his partner in undersea adventure for twenty years.

CLIVE CUSSLER: He is a No. 1 *New York Times* bestselling author whose books have been translated into forty languages. With his NUMA crew of volunteers, Cussler has discovered more than sixty lost ships of historic significance, including the long-lost Confederate submarine *Hunley.* Like Pitt, Cussler collects classic automobiles. His collection features eighty-two examples of custom coachwork and is one of the finest to be found anywhere. Cussler divides his time between the deserts of Arizona and the mountains of Colorado.

DIRK PITT® ADVENTURES BY CLIVE CUSSLER

Valhalla Rising
Atlantis Found
Flood Tide
Shock Wave
Inca Gold
Sahara
Dragon
Treasure
Cyclops
Deep Six
Pacific Vortex
Night Probe!
Vixen 03
Raise the Titanic!
Iceberg
The Mediterranean Caper

FICTION BY CLIVE CUSSLER WITH PAUL KEMPRECOS

White Death
Fire Ice
Blue Gold
Serpent

FICTION BY CLIVE CUSSLER WITH CRAIG DIRGO

Dirk Pitt Revealed
The Sea Hunters
The Sea Hunters II

CLIVE CUSSLER AND DIRK PITT® REVEALED

CLIVE CUSSLER & CRAIG DIRGO

POCKET BOOKS
New York London Toronto Sydney

For information regarding special discounts for bulk purchases, please contact Simon & Schuster Special Sales at 1-800-456-6798 or business@simonandschuster.com

An *Original* Publication of POCKET BOOKS

POCKET BOOKS, a division of Simon & Schuster, Inc.
1230 Avenue of the Americas, New York, NY 10020

ISBN-13: 978-0-671-02622-6
ISBN-10: 0-671-02622-4

First Pocket Books printing November 1998

10 9

Front cover illustration by Rick Lovell

Printed in the U.S.A.

Contents

Foreword

"Nobody does it better than Clive Cussler, nobody."
—quote by Stephen Coontz for *Cyclops*

Though I knew that authors rarely resemble their protagonists, I could not help but wonder if Clive Cussler would look like Dirk Pitt when I met him. He didn't exactly. Unlike the hero of his books, Cussler had hair and beard of a pewter gray. He stood tall, but the years had added a few inches to his waist. The blue-green eyes were bright, and he moved with the quickness of a much younger man. His face bore the weathered wear of someone who spent half a lifetime in the great outdoors and gave him the look of an explorer who had just returned from the jungles of the Congo or the icy mountains of Antarctica. It didn't take much imagination to picture him thirty years ago when he might easily have passed for Dirk Pitt's elder brother.

Hailed as the grand master of adventure novels, Cussler is about as down-home as you can get. Although he writes in an incredible office that he built in a Taos chapel style to match his adobe home, he dresses like the neighborhood handyman. He answers all his fan mail by hand, addressing fans by their first names as if they were old friends, often inserting a page from the original draft of his latest book as a souvenir. He's never hired a secretary, and his wife has never had a part-time housekeeper. "She cleans the house before the cleaning lady comes," he explains.

It all goes with the Cussler image of an author who was once described as following the beat of a drummer who was playing in a field on the other side of town. He does things few authors ever attempt. He once bought one of his books back from the publisher. He injects himself into his own stories as did Alfred Hitchcock in his movies, except that Cussler utters dialogue to his hero, who never recognizes him. And he writes wild, far-fetched adventure tales with the same cast of characters. A feat few writers attempt in this day and age.

He and his agent, Peter Lampack, have negotiated book deals with publishers that have been copied by the trade as models of ingenuity. And, unlike all too many writers who peak after one or two books, Cussler incredibly seems to improve. Strangely, he never uses an outline or writes more than one draft of a novel, and yet his complicated plots have hit the best-seller lists in both fiction and nonfiction no fewer than fourteen times.

Relying on his many years of experience as a creative director in advertising, he personally directed the design and layout of the jackets of his books, insisting on the same illustration for the hardcover as for the paperback for the sake of continuity. Instead of the pretentious black-and-white studio portraits that portray most authors on their book jackets, Cussler figured that since the front illustration was in four colors, the author photo on the back might as well be printed in color, thereby adding very little to the cost of the publisher in the print run. He has his own photographer shoot the photo of himself with the Dirk Pitt classic car featured in the book and has his illustrator set the type and do the overlay before sending it to the publisher's production department.

When asked why the photos focus on the car while he stands in the background, Cussler responded, "I'm sure the reader finds an exotic automobile of more interest than me."

What also sets Cussler apart is that he has a genuine fondness for Dirk Pitt. Both Conan Doyle and Ian Fleming hated their protagonists and tried to kill them off but were later forced to resurrect them after an outcry by their reading public.

"He's a likable guy," Cussler says of Pitt. "I doubt whether he'll die so long as I'm alive. Even then, I'm certain my agent and publisher will find some other writer to pick up the flag and carry on after I go to the great beyond. As an adventure hero, Pitt is as timeless as they come. Stories about lost treasure, like a bouquet of flowers to a pretty girl, never go out of style."

Cussler has been called America's Jules Verne, but, unlike the famed French novelist of *Twenty Thousand Leagues under the Sea,* he doesn't sit and write day in and day out. As soon as he sends in the manuscript of a Dirk Pitt adventure to his publisher, he heads for the water and searches for a lost shipwreck. And when he isn't on the rolling deck of a survey boat with his search crew, he collects, restores and maintains a warehouse filled with more than eighty classic cars. Several of the models and makes he owns are driven in his novels by Dirk Pitt. He also collects paintings by Southwest artists for his adobe home, while his office is filled with maritime paintings and models of shipwrecks he and his crew have discovered.

It can be said that Cussler is a man for all seasons. He is certainly in a class by himself apart from most writers I have interviewed. He is genuinely an interesting guy, down-to-earth, approachable, with a Rodney Dangerfield self-deprecating humor. A modest man, he mounts his many achievement awards and certificates on the walls of his office bathroom. Unlike more vain people who display a sea of photographs of themselves standing with famous celebrities, there are only two photos of Cussler to be found in his home or office. One shows him standing in a Star fleet command uniform in the control room of the *Enterprise* amid the *Star Trek* crew. The other has him with feet braced on the mast of a sinking boat while he clubs the shark from *Jaws* with an empty rifle. Both were accomplished with digital imagery. All goes with the personality. Cussler loves to tell funny stories about himself as the butt of comedy in strange situations only he could encounter.

Unlike many successful people, he has been happily married to the same woman for forty-three years. He and his lovely wife, Barbara, match together like a pair of old, comfortable shoes. When confronted with the complimentary titles bestowed upon him by book reviewers and his army of fans, Cussler looks through the blue-green eyes that twinkle, smiles, and says, "That's nothing. When Barbara is mad, she calls me Old Crap."

A cheap man? Hardly. He and Barbara support several charities and school endowments. And, of course, there is his commitment to preserve America's maritime heritage through his nonprofit foundation, the National Underwater and Marine Agency (NUMA). He also gives of himself. In talks with agents and editors about authors over lunch in New York, few are mentioned with the respect of Clive Cussler. Authors whose first books he has endorsed with quotes are in great number. Tom Clancy and Stephen Coontz are among those who received endorsements from Cussler for their first published works.

Clive Cussler writes to his readers. He has written books that are enjoyed by children as young as nine years of age and seniors in their nineties, and by men and women in every walk of life. He is read by presidents, prime ministers, members of the armed forces, housewives, teachers, business executives, construction workers, firefighters, police and even convicted criminals. He is considered the most popular adventure writer of our time because his books and characters come alive and he gives readers their money's worth. The only mystery I can find behind such an intriguing man is that no one has stepped forward to write a biography of him.

Tom Clancy said it best when he wrote, "A new Clive Cussler novel is like a visit from an old friend."

Arnold Stern

Introduction

With more than 90 million copies of his books in print, Clive Cussler has earned his moniker "The Grand Master of Adventure." He has also been called America's Jules Verne. His works are translated into forty different languages, and the exploits of his primary character, Dirk Pitt, are read throughout the world.

In 1996, Cussler branched out into nonfiction, cowriting with Craig Dirgo *The Sea Hunters,* a volume about the exploits of his nonprofit foundation National Underwater and Marine Agency. To the amazement of critics and the publishing community alike, the book reached number five on the *New York Times* hardcover best-sellers list. The introduction of the paperback edition of *The Sea Hunters* gave Cussler his first number one best-seller. He followed up in 1997 with the return of Dirk Pitt in the hardcover novel *Flood Tide,* which opened on the *New York Times* hardcover fiction list at number three, moving to number one the following week, a first for a Dirk Pitt novel.

What, then, does the future hold for the author who has often said, "I envisioned writing a small paperback series; when I started I thought that if I could make ten thousand dollars a year I would be a happy man."

In this, the companion book to Cussler's works, we will examine the phenomenal success he has achieved and look at the evolution of the Dirk Pitt novels. Delving into Clive Cussler's life, we will see how life imitates art and the close ties that are present between Pitt and Cussler. No work about Clive Cussler would be complete without a section devoted to his famous car collection or a concordance listing the characters in Pitt's adventures.

Join me now as we dig deep into the world of Clive Cussler.

—Craig Dirgo

The Reunion

The evening air was brisk, an overture for the approaching cold of winter, when a yellow and green cab stopped at a security gate on the south end of Washington's National Airport. The guard studied the pass that was extended by a hand from the rear window, then handed it back and spoke in an official tone. "Stay on the road. You're in a restricted area."

The driver swung onto the narrow service road that ran parallel with the east-west taxi strip on the southern border of the airport. "You sure this is the right way?" he asked, seeing nothing but an empty field.

"I'm certain," answered the gray-haired man in the backseat. "I've been here before."

"May I ask what you're looking for?"

The man in the backseat ignored the question. "Pull up at that pole with the red light on the top. I'll get out there."

"But there's no sign of life."

"Can you return for me in about forty minutes?"

"You want to stand out here in the middle of nowhere on a cold night for forty minutes?" asked the uncomprehending driver.

"I enjoy solitude."

The cabbie shrugged his shoulders. "OK. I'll take a break for a cup of coffee and come back for you in forty minutes."

The man passed the driver a fifty-dollar bill and stepped from the cab. He stood in the middle of the road beside the pole until the red taillights of the cab faded in the distance. Then he stared at a ghostly building that seemed to materialize out of the night, its silhouette becoming defined against the lights of the nation's capital across the Potomac River. Slowly, the building became physical and recognizable as an old aircraft hangar with a rounded roof. At first glance it appeared deserted. The surrounding land was covered with weeds, and the corrugated sides of the building wore a heavy coat of rust. The windows were boarded over, and the huge doors that once rolled open to admit aircraft for maintenance were welded closed.

The man standing in the road was not alone, and the hangar was not abandoned. At least two dozen cars were neatly parked in rows among the weeds. As he watched, a Lincoln Town Car pulled up to the front entrance door of the hangar, and an elegantly dressed woman exited the car, her door held open by a valet parking attendant.

As the man approached, he could hear the sound of voices mingled with laughter and the music of a Dixieland jazz band blaring out "Waiting for the *Robert E. Lee.*" Before he made his way to the entrance, the man with the mane of gray hair and matching beard paused for a moment, listening to the wave of conversation from inside. Finally, he stepped through the doorway and handed his overcoat to a girl who gave him his receipt. A doorman, dressed suavely in a tuxedo, came forward.

"May I have your invitation, sir?"

The gray-haired man looked at him and said with quiet authority, "I do not require one."

The doorman's face went blank for a moment, and then, as if realizing his mistake, he said, "My apologies, sir. Please enjoy the party."

Then the intruder passed into a scene that he had envisioned in his mind a hundred times and that could only be described in a novel.

Row upon row of beautifully restored classic cars were positioned across a vast white epoxy-sealed floor. Their gleaming mirrorlike paint seemed to fluoresce under the brilliant overhead lights mounted on the girders in the rounded roof. A German jet from World War II and an old 1930s Ford Trimotor passenger aircraft stood parked in the far corner of the hangar. Next to them sat an early-twentieth-century railroad Pullman car and what looked like a small sailboat put together by either a small child or a drunk. The man smiled as he examined a bathtub with an outboard motor that sat on a small platform.

Hanging from the girders and along the walls were antique metal signs advertising gasoline brands, car manufacturers, and soft drinks, many of them no longer in existence. Several red signs with white lettering hung in a row, one after the other, that read, HE HAD THE RING. HE HAD THE FLAT. BUT SHE FELT HIS CHIN. AND THAT WAS THAT. *BURMA SHAVE.*

In another corner of the cavernous hangar an ornate iron circular staircase wound up to an apartment above the main floor where the host lived. The intruder did not make his way up the stairs. Not just yet. There was no curiosity. He already knew every square inch of the apartment in his mind.

Tables arranged in the aisles between the cars were already filled with people conversing as they drank California estate reserve wine or French champagne and dined on the gourmet delicacies from several buffet tables stationed in a circle around an enormous ice sculpture of a Mississippi steamboat that rose from a sea of blue ice with a mist swirling around its paddle wheels. The buffet table featured polished silver chafing dishes and iced platters kept filled with seafood of every variety by a small army of waiters and chefs.

The body of the man hovering around the serving lines was nothing less than colossal. He did not look happy. He was dabbing sweat from his brow and neck as he admonished the maître d' of Le Curcel, the Michelin three-star restaurant he had hired to cater the party. "These oysters you sent over are the size of peanuts. They simply won't do."

"I shall have them replaced within minutes," the maître d' promised before rushing away.

"You are St. Julien Perlmutter." It was a statement, not a question, from the gray-haired man.

"Yes, I am. May I be of service to you, sir?"

"Not really, but I've always been envious of your lifestyle. A gourmand, a true connoisseur of the finer things, the nation's leading maritime history expert. It can safely be said that you're not a common man."

Perlmutter patted his ample stomach. "There are,

however, a few disadvantages to loving good food and drink."

"Speaking of food and drink, may I express my compliments on arranging such an elaborate party? The food and wine selection and table settings are beyond compare."

Perlmutter's face lit up. "I accept your gracious compliment, Mr. . . ."

But the stranger did not answer. He had already turned and began wandering amid the party guests. Unnoticed and unrecognized, he made his way to the bar and waited in line behind a pair of lovely ladies who ordered two glasses of Veuve Clicquot Ponsardin Brut champagne. One was tall, very tall, with blond hair that was almost yellow. She stared from a strong face with high cheekbones and through deep blue eyes. The other woman was smaller, with radiant red hair and gray eyes. She had an exotic quality about her.

"I beg your pardon," he said, looking at the redhead, "but you must be Summer Moran." He shifted his head slightly. "And you are Maeve Fletcher."

Both women instinctively looked at each other and then at the stranger. "Do we know you?" Maeve inquired.

"Not in a physical sense, no."

"But you recognize us," said Summer.

"I guess you could say that I'm familiar with your existence."

Maeve stared at him and smiled thinly. "Then you must know that Summer and I are dead."

"Yes, I'm quite aware of that. You both died in the Pacific Ocean," he said slowly. "Ms. Moran in an underwater earthquake and Ms. Fletcher from the eruption of twin volcanoes. I regret things couldn't have worked out differently."

"Could events have been altered for a happier ending?" asked Summer.

"They might have."

Maeve stared over her champagne glass at him. "This is eerie."

Summer gave the man a calculating look. "Do you think Maeve and I might ever be resurrected?"

"I rarely speculate on future events," answered the man. "But I'd have to say the prospects are dim."

"Then it's not likely we'll ever meet again."

"No, I'm afraid not."

He stood aside as the ladies excused themselves. He watched them move with a feline poise as they made their way through the crowded hangar and thought it was a great pity that he was seeing them for the last time. He stared at Summer and began to have second thoughts.

The bartender broke his reverie. "Your pleasure, sir?"

"What brand of tequila are you pouring?"

"Patron and Porfido."

"Your host has excellent taste," said the stranger. "However, I would like a double Don Julio anejo on the rocks with lime and a salted rim."

The bartender looked at him thoughtfully. "Don Julio is Mr. Pitt's personal favorite. It's also his private stock. Very little of it is exported from Mexico."

"He won't mind. You might say he drinks it because of me."

The bartender shrugged and poured the tequila from a bottle hidden beneath the bar. The intruder thanked him and stepped to a nearby table where several attractive women were seated engaged in girl talk.

"I guess we should consider ourselves lucky," said Eva Rojas, a pretty, vibrant woman with red-gold hair. "Unlike Summer and Maeve, we survived to the end of our adventures."

Jessie LeBaron, refined and lithe-bodied in her mid-fifties, patted her lips with a napkin. "True, but except for Heidi Milligan and Loren Smith, the rest of us never reappeared."

The exquisite Julia Lee, her Chinese features soft and delicate, recalled, "After Dirk and I returned from Mazatlan, Mexico, we both went back to our respective jobs, and I never saw him again."

"At least you enjoyed an exotic and romantic interlude with him," said Stacy Fox, brushing aside the blond strands of hair from her face. "In my case, he didn't even say good-bye."

Hali Kamil, a lovely woman with classic Egyptian features, laughed. "Isn't this where somebody says it is better to have loved and lost Dirk Pitt than never to have loved him at all?"

Lily Sharp, striking and svelte, and the captivating Dana Seagram sat quietly, not speaking, their minds far away, Lily remembering when she and Pitt found the treasures from the Alexandria Library in Texas, Dana when she worked with him raising the *Titanic.*

"It wouldn't be practical for Pitt to have married any of you," said the gray-haired man, breaking into the conversation.

"Why do you say that?" asked Julia Lee as the women all turned and stared openly at the stranger.

"Can you picture Al Giordino coming to your front door and asking if Pitt can come out and play? I'm afraid the scenario would not be acceptable."

Then he smiled and abruptly walked away.

"Who was that?" Dana Seagram asked no one in particular.

"Beats me," replied Lily Sharp. "Nobody I've ever met before."

The party crasher strolled over to a dark metallic blue 1936 Pierce-Arrow sedan that was attached to a matching trailer. A group of men sat next to the trailer. The stranger peered inside at the linoleum floor, the antique stove and icebox. He appeared to be studying the trailer's interior but was in fact listening to the table conversation with more than a passing interest.

A tall, distinguished-looking man who spoke with a German accent pointed across the table to a muscular bull of a man with a clean-shaven head. "Foss Gly here was surely the worst of us all," said Bruno von Till.

A wealthy-looking Chinese man shook his head in disagreement. "My vote goes to Min Koryo Bougainville. For a woman, she made the rest of us villains look like milksops."

Min Koryo, though frail and ancient, still had eyes that burned with evil. "Thank you, Qin Shang. But it cost me a horrible death. If you recall, I was sent hurtling down the elevator shaft of the World Trade Center from the hundredth floor."

Arthur Dorsett, as ugly as any man created, grinned through yellow teeth. "Consider yourself lucky. After Pitt crushed my throat, he left me to be consumed by molten lava."

Foss Gly spread his huge hands expansively. "After beating me with a baseball bat, he jammed his finger in my eye socket clear through to my brain."

Tupac Amaru, the Peruvian terrorist, scoffed. "At

least he didn't shoot off your genitals before killing you in total darkness deep in an underwater cave."

Yves Massarde, immaculately dressed in a white dinner jacket with a yellow rose in the lapel, stared vacantly into the bubbles rising in his champagne glass and wondered aloud, "How could Pitt be even more brutal and vicious than the worst crew of villains ever created?"

The gray-haired stranger leaned between Gly and Qin Shang and said, "It was easy."

Before any of the men could say a word, he quickly resumed his course through the partygoers, moving toward the far wall where an old railroad Pullman car sat on a short section of track leading to nowhere. The gold lettering on the steel sides read MANHATTAN LIMITED. The lights inside had been wired into the main junction box, and the opulent interior was as brightly lit as when the car rolled over the tracks between New York and Quebec. Mannequins were artfully arranged in what was once called the parlor. At one table two men sat as if dining while a porter in a white uniform stood and served.

A distinguished, impeccably dressed man in his seventies sat in a Victorian velvet chair. Next to him on the couch was an attractive woman half his age with ash-blond hair. She wore the uniform of a naval officer, and despite the fact that she was sitting down, it was easy to imagine her standing at a height of six feet.

"I'm sitting in the very same chair where Pitt bounced a bullet off my head," said the elderly man with a British inflection.

"Does he still call you Brian Shaw?" asked Heidi Milligan.

"Yes, but I'm certain he saw right through me."

"He never stopped suspecting you of being James Bond," said Heidi.

The older man reached over, took Heidi's hand, and kissed it. "That will forever be our little secret."

The gray-haired intruder smiled to himself, then slipped away before being noticed.

Inside the old Ford Trimotor airplane, seated in an antique wicker basket chair, a man dressed in Levi's with long blond hair tied in a ponytail peered into the monitor of a laptop computer.

"Surfing the Internet while a party's in high gear?" said the intruder. "That's antisocial."

Hiram Yaeger looked up at the stranger standing in the fuselage entrance. One of the overhead lights was above and to the rear of his visitor, and he squinted while attempting to recognize the face of the man who spoke. The stranger was tall, nearly six feet, three inches, with a slight paunch brought about by age. His hair had grayed over the years, as had the beard covering only his chin. His skin was tanned from the sun. He was probably in his middle sixties, Yaeger estimated, but he looked younger. The stranger wore a faint grin on his lips, but it was his eyes that gripped Yaeger's attention. They were a mysterious blue-green with a light that twinkled from deep inside. The face was that of a man who might have been a ship's captain in a past life, or a prospector, maybe even an explorer.

"Dirk asked me to look up data on a lost ship," Yaeger finally explained. "I could wait until working hours, but I'm not much of a party animal, so I thought I'd get a head start on the project."

"What ship?" the gray-haired man asked.

"The *Waratah.*"

"Ah, yes, the passenger ship that vanished with nearly three hundred people off the west coast of South Africa in 1909."

Yaeger was impressed. "You know your ships."

"The *Waratah* was found by a NUMA South African team several years ago," stated the intruder matter-of-factly.

"No NUMA team headed by Dirk Pitt found the *Waratah* that I'm aware of," said Yaeger.

"Not Pitt's NUMA," said the intruder slowly. "My NUMA."

"Right," Yaeger said sarcastically. He refocused his attention on the monitor, intending to read the information on the mystery ship as he had documented it. But when he twisted around to correct the stranger, the man had disappeared.

Yaeger stood and glanced around outside the aircraft, but his visitor was nowhere to be found. "Nuttier than a fruitcake," he muttered under his breath. "Next he'll claim he found the Confederate submarine *Hunley.*"

The stranger climbed the circular staircase to the apartment that rose far above the hangar floor. He entered and made his way unerringly through the unique nautical furnishings into the kitchen. A small man who peered from owlish eyes through horn-rim glasses was hunched over a large glass dish he was filling with homemade salsa spooned from a mixing bowl. A short man with curly black hair who was built like a beer keg stood over a stove, pan-frying a hamburger.

The intruder nodded at the well-done hamburger and said, "Does St. Julien know about this blasphemy?"

"My friend and I prefer something a little more gluttonous than those fancy tidbits from St. Julien's highfalutin chef," said Albert Giordino without turning from the stove.

Rudi Gunn offered a bag of tortilla chips and held out the bowl of salsa to the stranger. "Help yourself."

Between bites, his eyes watering from the abundance of chili peppers, the stranger said, "You two have known Dirk a long time."

"He and I go back to grammar school," said Albert Giordino, flipping the hamburger between two buns loaded with salsa.

"Al, Dirk and I were the first employees Admiral Sandecker hired when he became director of NUMA," Gunn said as he swished beer around in his mouth to reduce the heat. "We've been as close as bricks ever since."

"You've experienced many arduous adventures together."

"Tell me." Giordino grinned. "I've got the bruises and broken bones to prove it."

"You have enormous respect for him, don't you?"

"Dirk has carried us through some hairy times," said Gunn. "He never fails to deliver. He's a man who can be trusted by men and women alike."

"I'd follow him to hell," said Giordino. "Come to think of it, I already have."

"Your warm friendship is to be admired," said the gray-haired man.

Giordino stared into the stranger's eyes. "Don't I know you from somewhere?"

"Actually, you and I met twice."

"When and where?"

"No matter." The stranger waved a hand airily. "I

wanted to stop up here and find you, Mr. Giordino, because I understand you fancy a fine cigar now and then."

"That I do."

Reaching into his breast pocket, the stranger produced a pair of large cigars and handed them to Giordino. Then, with a curt nod, he exited the kitchen and moved down the stairs.

Giordino studied the cigars, and his eyes widened as his mouth dropped open. "My God!" he muttered.

"What is it?" asked Gunn. "You look like you've just seen the Virgin Mary."

"The cigars," Giordino said vaguely. "They bear the same label as Admiral Sandecker's private stock. How the hell did *he* get them?"

He rushed to the window and peered down onto the floor below. He just caught a glimpse of the gray-haired stranger as he reached the bottom of the staircase and melted into the crowd below.

A short, bantam-sized man with a flaming Van Dyke beard stood staring at a 1948 blue Talbot-Lago coupe with elegant bodywork by the French coachbuilder Saoutchik. He seemed lost in thought.

"Fabulous party," said the gray-haired man.

As if his mind were coming out of a fog, Admiral James Sandecker, the feisty chief director of the National Underwater and Marine Agency, slowly turned. "I'm sorry. What did you say?"

"A fabulous party."

"Yes, indeed."

"A reunion of sorts, I understand."

Sandecker nodded. "You could call it a twenty-year celebration of NUMA and the people who built it."

"You and Dirk have enjoyed a long and illustrious career."

"We've seen our share of disasters and tragedies."

"But you've achieved some remarkable accomplishments."

"Yes, I must admit the trail *has* had its enjoyable moments."

"I wish you many more successful achievements in the future."

"I'm not sure I can keep up with the young people any longer," Sandecker sighed.

"You will. You're in better physical condition than most men your age."

"I'm not getting any younger."

"Neither am I," said the stranger. "Neither am I."

"Forgive me," said Sandecker, studying the stranger for the first time. "But I can't seem to recall your name or where we met."

"We've never met," the gray-haired man said as he motioned to the bar. "I'm going to freshen my drink. Can I bring you back something?"

The admiral held up a half-full glass of tomato juice. "I'm fine, thank you." He watched as the stranger cut through the throng to the bar. *How odd,* he thought. *The guy acted as if we had been pals for years, but for the life of me, he doesn't look the least bit familiar.*

"Another touch of Don Julio anejo?" asked the bartender, remembering.

"Yes, if you please," replied the uninvited guest. He glanced to his side as Senator George Pitt stepped up to the bar. Dirk's father, the senior senator from California, and the gray-haired man were about the same age and could have almost passed as brothers.

"Enjoying the party?" asked Senator Pitt with a cordial smile.

"Especially the people. I feel as though I'm among old friends."

"Have you had a chance to sample the food? The quail pâté and ostrich tartare are excellent."

"I understand you're going to run for your seat in the Senate again, Senator."

George Pitt looked surprised. "That's news to me. I haven't made up my mind yet."

"You will," said the stranger.

"You sound as if you know me better than I know myself."

The man smiled. "I've known you for a very long time, as it turns out. I guess you could say we were both there when Dirk was created."

"My memory is slipping," said the senator, at a loss. "Were you my wife's obstetrician?"

"No, nothing like that." The stranger finished off his drink and set the glass on the bar. "I wish you the best of luck on having your programs passed by Congress."

"Please forgive me, sir, but I can't seem to recall your name."

"In your position you meet too many people to remember them all." The stranger paused to glance at his watch. "Nice talking to you, Senator, but I'm afraid I must move on."

There were two more guests the gray-haired man wished to meet. He found one of them sitting in the rear seat of a 1932 Stutz DV-32 town car. Of all the ladies, Congresswoman Loren Smith was the gray-haired man's favorite. He reveled in her incredible violet eyes and long cinnamon hair tastefully styled in a Grecian coiffure. Loren was exquisitely proportioned with broad shoulders and long legs. She possessed an air of breezy sophistication, yet one could sense a tomboyish daring behind her eyes.

The uninvited guest leaned in the open door. "Good evening, Loren. You look pensive."

She tilted her head, unconcerned that an apparent stranger had used her first name and not referred to her as Congresswoman. She flashed a disarming smile and stared at him.

She recognized me, he thought. *She actually recognized me.*

"How is Mr. Periwinkle?" she asked.

"My burro? Last I saw him, he was running wild with a small herd in the Mojave Desert. I imagine he's a father several times by now."

"You sold the Box Car Café?"

"It retreated under the desert sands."

"This is the last place I expected to meet you again," she said, trying to read whatever was hidden in his eyes.

"I felt I had to be here, so I crashed the party."

"You didn't receive an invitation?"

"I must have been overlooked." He turned and scanned the crowd silently for a few moments before turning his attention back to Loren. "Have you seen Pitt?"

"I talked to him about twenty minutes ago. He must be mingling with the other guests."

"Perhaps I'll catch him on the way out."

"You're leaving so soon? The party is just beginning to get interesting."

He hated to tear himself away from those violet eyes. "I must go. Good to have seen you again, Loren."

"Give my regards to Mr. Periwinkle."

"If I see him, I shall."

She reached out and touched his arm. "Odd, but it feels as if I've known you most of my life."

He shook his head and smiled. "No, it is I who have known you. This will be my only chance to tell you that you have been the girl of my dreams."

He left her in the Stutz alone with her memories and an expression of nostalgia on her face as he merged with the guests and headed toward the door.

When he stopped to retrieve his overcoat, he paused and looked around the floor of the hangar once more, at the wondrous cars, the fascinating people, and wished he could stay longer. There were so many others in the hangar he had known over the past thirty years, whom he didn't have time to talk with. But he realized the illusion was fleeting and time was short. He was about to step out when Dirk Pitt walked in from outside.

"I thought I had missed you," said the stranger.

"One of my guests noticed one of his tires was flat when he arrived, so I changed it for him."

"Saint Dirk to the rescue."

"That's me," Pitt said jovially, "the salvation of lost animals and little old ladies who need to cross streets."

"You wouldn't be Dirk Pitt if you didn't betray a hint of compassion now and then."

Pitt looked at the older man steadily. "Why is it that when we meet I'm never supposed to remember who you are?"

"Because I plan it that way. It wouldn't do for us to become bosom buddies like you and Giordino. Better I make an occasional appearance to set you back on course before quietly exiting stage right."

"I'm not sure I appreciate all you put me through. I have more scars, physical and mental, than I care to count."

"Adventure takes its toll on heroes and villains," said the gray-haired man philosophically.

"That's easy for you to say. I hope I fare better in the next adventure."

"One only knows where the plot will take us."

"Will there be a next time? I hear talk of you retiring."

"The thought has crossed my mind. I'm finding it more difficult to be creative as the years pass."

"A lot of people are counting on us," Pitt said sincerely.

The gray-haired man's face had a sad look to it. It was almost as if he hated to leave. "Good-bye, Dirk Pitt. Until we meet again."

"Good-bye, Clive Cussler. Stay healthy, and never age."

Cussler laughed. "That's certainly something you'll never have to worry about. When we started out together, we were the same age. And now look at us."

They shook hands. Then Cussler closed his eyes. When he opened them again, he found himself standing on the empty road beneath the solitary light pole. The hangar, the people, the cars were all gone, vanished as though they had never existed.

Within five minutes the cabbie returned and picked him up. Pulling the door closed, Cussler settled back into the seat as his mind traveled back over the years to 1965, when he first sat down at a typewriter. He and his friends from the hangar had traveled every corner of the earth and weathered every adventure conceivable. The torment, action and joy they had experienced were legendary. The people they had all touched numbered in the millions. Perhaps it *was* time for a break, he thought. Maybe retirement was not such a bad idea after all.

"Where to?" asked the driver.

"The airport terminal. United Airlines. It's time for me to go home."

Shifting the cab into drive, the cabbie pulled onto the main road leading to the security gate. The harvest moon had risen, and as Cussler turned and looked back, he recreated the illusion of Pitt's hangar in his mind. No, he couldn't retire. Already the plot for the next Pitt adventure was forming in his mind.

An Interview with Clive Cussler

CRAIG DIRGO: Let's talk about your early life for a moment.

CLIVE CUSSLER: I was born in Aurora, Illinois, on July 15, 1931, at 2:00 A.M., a habit I kept later in life when closing bars. I was the only child of Eric and Amy Cussler. My mother liked the name Clive, since it came from a well-known British movie actor of the time, Clive Brook. My middle name was Eric after my father. I'd like to think they never had another child because they thought it was highly unlikely they'd do better, but the truth of the matter was that many families had only one child in those days simply because they couldn't afford to raise more.

It was the depths of the Depression, and Dad was only making eighteen dollars a week. He worked out a deal with the baby doctor, paying him fifty cents a week against the twenty-five-dollar fee for my delivery. After one payment, the kindly old doctor told Dad to forget it, saying facetiously that he would make it up on a rich widow patient from Chicago. Thus, I only cost fifty cents to come into the world.

CRAIG DIRGO: Tell us about your parents.

CLIVE CUSSLER: My mother, the former Amy Hunnewell, was a beautiful dark-haired lady whose ancestors came to America from England in 1650 and settled in Boston. She was born in 1901 in St. Joseph, Missouri. Her father worked for the railroad and later retired to run a fishing lodge and a saloon in Minnesota, wisely selling the latter just two weeks before Prohibition was voted in. Mom was vivacious and humorous and always teasing Dad and me. She also had a creative side that was never fully nurtured but was passed along to her son. She often told of going to a carnival when she was sixteen with her bevy of girlfriends and paying twenty-five cents to a Gypsy lady to tell their fortunes. The obvious question among young girls was: Who will I marry? The Gypsy fortune-teller told Mom she would have a famous daughter. A near miss on that one. As for her husband, the Gypsy said he was tall, dark and in the Army, wearing a gray uniform. Mom and her friends laughed at the revelation. America had just entered World War I, and they all knew that the American doughboys, as soldiers were called then, wore khaki uniforms. Little did Mom know that her future tall and dark husband was born and raised in Germany and was serving in the Kaiser's army on the Western Front. And, oh yes, the Germans wore gray uniforms.

My dad, Eric Cussler, had a tough life when he was young. His father was abusive and didn't want his young son under his feet, so he shipped him off to military academy when he was only eleven years old. When Dad turned sixteen, he served in an infantry brigade as a sergeant, fighting in the trenches on the Western Front. After a leave home, he was promoted to lieutenant and ordered to a hell hole called Verdun. On the march back to the front, British aircraft strafed his column, and he was hit by a bullet in the knee. In the hospital, he developed gangrene and came within an inch of dying. He owed his life to a captured British surgeon who took a personal interest in Dad due to his young age. Because his knee was irreparably damaged and Dad would always walk with a stiff leg, the British surgeon ingeniously operated and slightly bent the frozen knee so that Dad's limp would not be nearly as pronounced as Chester's in *Gunsmoke.* Dad recovered and after the war worked in a bank before attending Heidelberg University, where he received a degree in accountancy. While working in the bank, he made a small but tidy nest egg on the European stock market.

CRAIG DIRGO: How did he come to America?

CLIVE CUSSLER: One of his two sisters had come to America and married. He decided to leave Germany and come across, too. He was almost denied entry into the country when an immigration official considered Dad a potential welfare case because of the injured leg. After a six-day stay at Ellis Island, where he conned his way into the country by claiming to be a piano player, a job where the injured leg would have no effect, he took a train to his sister's farm in Illinois, where he worked in the fields while he learned English. The following year, he moved to Chicago during the Roaring Twenties and experienced exciting times, driving a Stutz Bearcat, making gin in a bathtub, seeing Al Capone on the courthouse steps, finding gangsters' bullet-riddled bodies in the street and finally meeting my mother.

Craig Dirgo: Wasn't your mother in Minnesota?

Clive Cussler: Mom was living in Minneapolis, and while visiting a friend in Chicago, they decided to go dancing. Dad and Mom always claimed they were introduced by mutual friends. It wasn't until they were in their seventies that the truth came out. It seems they actually met when Dad asked her to dance at the Trianon Ballroom to the music of Ted "Is Everybody Happy" Lewis. So it could be said that Dad picked Mom up. This was in 1929. They were married on June 10, 1930, and had me a little over a year later.

As usual, my timing was bad, and I arrived on the same day Dad was laid off his job along with a hundred other workers at Durabilt Steel, a company that made steel cabinets. He moved my mother and me to Minneapolis, where we lived with her parents. My grandfather was making good money working as an engineer on the railroad. Dad finally found a job as a traveling auditor for a company called Jewel Tea that sold coffee and related supplies door-to-door. We moved around the country, living in Terre Haute, Indiana; Louisville, Kentucky; and then back to Minneapolis, where I started in kindergarten.

Craig Dirgo: What happened next?

CLIVE CUSSLER: During the winter of 1937, I came down with pneumonia and nearly passed on to the great beyond. Those were the days before antibiotics, and I lived in an oxygen tent for six days before finally showing signs of improvement. As I began feeling better, the hospital moved an old derelict into the bed next to mine. The police had found him half frozen in an alley. Old Charlie was a neat guy. He taught me card games and told stories no six-year-old should have heard in the days before TV and R-rated movies. One morning, when the nurse came into the room to check on me, I nodded over at Old Charlie and asked why he had turned blue. She gasped, whipped the curtain around Charlie's bed, and within minutes he was whisked out of the room covered by a sheet. When Dad found out an old drunk had died in the bed next to his little sonny boy, he damn near tore the hospital down to its foundation. Boy, was he mad!

Against doctor's orders, he and Mom carried me to their little apartment so I could enjoy Christmas at home. They had sacrificed their small savings to buy me a Lionel electric train complete with a tunnel, a fort with wooden soldiers and a little switchman who came out of a tiny house to swing his lantern when the train went past.

About this time, Dad was offered a promotion within the company that called for a transfer to Chicago. At the same time, there was also an opening in the Los Angeles office if he remained at his present salary level. It was the dead of winter in Minnesota, the snow was piled eight feet high around our apartment and his sickly son looked like death warmed over. He never thought twice. Within the week, we were all in our 1937 black Ford Victoria and headed for sunny Southern California. Dad drove straight south to Texas to get out of the snow and cold as quickly as possible and caught old Highway 66 west into the Golden State.

CRAIG DIRGO: Where did you live in California?

CLIVE CUSSLER: We settled in a small suburban community outside Los Angeles, called Alhambra, where I lived for the next twenty-three years. My inaugural in the first grade was an introduction into the differences between east and west. All my classmates were healthy, tanned Californians, while I was this pale, sickly kid with ribs poking through his chest who looked like an anemic ghost. I recall they laughed at me because I wore short pants when no self-respecting California kid would ever be caught dead in short pants.

I survived and still treasure happy memories from my eight years at Fremont Elementary School in Alhambra. The principal was a tough old bird, rather attractive as I think back now, and well respected. Her name was Mary Mullin. Those were the days when teachers took no crap from their pupils. A number of fathers, including my own, wrote letters to Miss Mullin, stating that if their boys were naughty, she had their express permission to paddle their asses, which she did on numerous occasions. I only felt her wrath twice, as I recall. Amazingly, at my fortieth high school reunion, nearly twenty kids out of my old Fremont grammar school class attended. Friendships were made that are still cherished.

CRAIG DIRGO: What did you do for fun as a child?

CLIVE CUSSLER: I was very fortunate in growing up in a neighborhood where there were six boys of the same age who caused mischief and were all punished by razor straps, belts or switches but were very industrious and creative. From the age of eight until we all entered high school, we built tree houses and eight-room (granted, they were small) clubhouses, dug caves and covered them with boards and sod, and developed entire miniature cities out of mud. In the open fields behind our homes, before the Southern California housing boom in the postwar years, we struggled to move bales of hay from a local rancher's harvest and constructed a huge fort, where we played French Foreign Legion fighting off the raiding Tuaregs of the Sahara Desert. We also built a twenty-foot boat in the middle of a vacant lot and pretended we were pirates raiding the Spanish Main.

I joined the Boy Scouts at age twelve and was a member of the Cobra Patrol of Alhambra Troop Six. My scoutmaster was a wonderful man I've never forgotten. His name was Guy Smalley, and along with my dad, they inspired me to make Eagle Scout by the time I reached fourteen. The camping trips, the hikes, those Thursday night meetings in a log structure built from telephone poles donated by the phone company, they're still with me. Few boys had a finer childhood.

CRAIG DIRGO: What was your first job?

CLIVE CUSSLER: When I was old enough, my father insisted I learn work ethics. My job, if I was to be offered food and clothing, was to mow and trim the lawn every Saturday. We lived on a corner lot, and if you've ever lived on a corner lot, you know how much yard there is to maintain. The trimming was the part I hated. There must have been five miles of sidewalks and flower beds to edge. Even to this day, I'd rather run up a steep slope in my bare feet on pea gravel than trim a yard. I also had to wax Mom's linoleum floors. Remember those? And dry the dishes every evening. All for twenty-five cents a week.

When I became a teenager, Dad raised me to a dollar a week. I wasn't impressed. With the canny mind of a fourteen-year-old, I began doing such a rotten job of taking care of the yard, Dad finally threw up his hands in exasperation and hired a gardener.

Through high school, I worked every chance I got. Getting up at 4:00 A.M. to deliver the *Los Angeles Times* seven days a week for twenty dollars. Selling magazine subscriptions door-to-door. Loading trucks at a laundry. Boxing groceries in a supermarket. Working a dirty job grinding the burrs off the impellers that went inside water pumps. I saved every nickel and dime for that glorious day when I could afford to go out and buy my own car.

CRAIG DIRGO: What about high school?

CLIVE CUSSLER: Except for the extracurricular activities at Alhambra High, I found school to be a colossal drag. Frankly, I hated it. During algebra and civics classes, I stared out the window, blocking out the teacher's lecture while I fired a cannon with John Paul Jones on the *Bonhomme Richard* in his epic battle with the British frigate. Miraculously, I managed to survive four years without an F and, I might add, an A or a B. My report cards, much to the frustration of my self-disciplined and highly intelligent German father, were filled with C's and D's and the usual notation: "Clive seems bright, but he doesn't apply himself."

When fans and interviewers ask me what teacher inspired me to expand my horizons and enter a writing career, they always seem saddened to learn I never had a teacher who saw any potential in a boy who seemed lost in Never-never Land. All they saw was a disinterested student who would probably end out his days working as a farm laborer. I've always thought that education is geared more to students who show a flair of scholarship than those who have an untapped well of creativity.

CRAIG DIRGO: So school was *not* your favorite activity.

CLIVE CUSSLER: Hardly. The early forties were the heyday of California hot rods. When my buddies and I weren't making clowns of ourselves trying to impress girls, we were body-surfing on the beach and laboring over our rods. Buying a car meant more to me than sports. Despite being a competent football pass receiver and baseball hitter, I opted for working until I had enough money to buy a 1936 Ford four-door sedan. Never half as fast as I hoped and prone to throwing rods and breaking axles, it was nonetheless a pretty car in dark green metallic paint with the louvers of the hood filled in, moon ripple disk hubcaps, lowered in the back and touched off with teardrop fender skirts. I poured my heart and a thousand dollars into that car. After I went into the Air Force, Dad sold it for sixty-nine dollars.

My friends and I had a lively time in high school. A few actually had girlfriends, but mostly our love was directed toward our cars. I once bought a big black 1925 Auburn limousine with vanity mirrors and flower vases in the backseat for the grand sum of twenty-two dollars. It was right after the war in

1945, and most of the American public, having coaxed the family car to keep running in spite of the gas shortage for nearly five years, wanted a new car. The used-car market fell through the floor, and old classics could be purchased for next to nothing. For the football games, my motley crew and I would dress up like gangsters, complete with overcoats and old fedora hats pulled down over our eyes, and smoke cigars. My poor parents had once suffered for three years in a vain attempt to make me play the violin, and I took the case down from a shelf in the garage and carried it under one arm as the gangsters supposedly did when concealing their submachine guns. Pulling up to the football stadium in the big black limousine, our gang would rumble through the aisles and up the steps to our seats. The security guards never did catch on to the fact that I smuggled beer and wine into the stands inside the violin case.

CRAIG DIRGO: But you ended up graduating.

CLIVE CUSSLER: Barely. I had so many demerits that to graduate on the stage with the rest of my class, the Alhambra High class of '49, I had to work as a gardener on the school grounds after class for two hours a day. I next enrolled at Pasadena City College. It was a junior college in those days. For no good reason that I can think of, I applied myself and began receiving B's and a couple of A's. My dad almost went into cardiac arrest and demanded to know why I was impersonating his son.

During the summer of 1950, an old school pal, Felix Dupuy, and I took off in Felix's 1939 Ford convertible and toured the country, covering thirty-six states in three months. We slept in freight cars in Boise and Houston, in a bandstand in Vermont, in the bushes directly beneath the Capitol building in Washington, D.C., and under the front porch of a school in Kingsland, Georgia, where the local sheriff arrested us for trespassing. He followed our car into town, where he made us sit in a barbershop because the barber happened to be the justice of the peace. There was the threat of thirty days on the Georgia chain gang until I launched into a speech about the ill treatment two red-blooded American boys received in Kingsland, Georgia, while traveling the great United States. Unintimidated and dubious, but maybe a tiny bit confused, the sheriff and the justice of the peace ordered us to remain in the barber shop while they went over to the post office to see if there were any wanted posters out on us. Once they were gone, Felix and I looked at each other, ran to the car and beat it over the Florida border only three miles away.

CRAIG DIRGO: So after the trip, did you go back to Pasadena City College?

CLIVE CUSSLER: When we returned to Alhambra, we were stunned to find all our friends enlisting in the armed services. We'd paid no attention to the news during the trip and were only vaguely aware of the conflict in Korea. Times were different then, and few boys hesitated to serve their country. Felix and I tried to sign up for flight training in the Navy and Air Force, but because so many college students had enlisted while we were driving the country, flight school had a nine-month backlog. So we signed up with the Air Force and went off to basic training at Lackland Air Force Base in San Antonio, Texas. On the train ride from Los Angeles, along with sixty other recruits, we all became drunk on cheap bourbon that had to be smuggled on board, because we were all under age, and proceeded to sing "Good Night Irene" while breaking out the windows in the club car. When the train reached El Paso, a squad of military police boarded the train for the rest of the trip to prevent another incident.

After basic training, I was sent to aircraft and engine school to become a mechanic. The sergeant who interviewed me for a job classification ignored my pleas for the motor pool. "All you do is change spark plugs," he said, waving his hands airily. "What you want is aircraft and engine school." The Air Force had this irrational concept that if I loved rebuilding old automobiles, I would simply adore maintaining C-97 Boeing Stratocruisers in the Military Air Transport Service. The big difference was that my old Ford flathead V-8 had only eight spark plugs. The twenty-eight-cylinder Pratt-Whitney 4,360-cubic-inch engines that powered the C-97 each had a total of fifty-six spark plugs that required changing all too frequently. After graduating from mechanic school, I asked to be shipped to Europe in the forlorn hope I could visit my relatives in Germany. Naturally, the Air Force sent me in the opposite direction—Hickham Field, Hawaii, to be precise.

Like school, the Air Force and I never really hit it off. If I found an angle to get off work, I used it. My medical records read like an *Encyclopedia Britannica.* I once found a large medical book dating back to 1895 in the back of an antique store. I bought it and began studying the entries. I remember one doctor asking me what my symptoms were. I told him, "Sir, I see purple spots before my eyes, I have hot flashes, the back of my neck has gone numb and I can't seem to bend my fingers."

He looked at me strangely for several moments, then he gasped. "My God, son, it sounds like you have Borneo Jungle Incepus. I want you in the hospital."

Very astute, that doctor. His diagnosis was right on the money. I was impressed he was aware of a disease considered rare even in 1895. After three days of blood tests and warnings to stop harassing the nurses, I was declared fit and sent back to the flight line. That antique medical book was the best investment I ever made.

The final six months of my overseas tour passed slowly but pleasantly. I made many fine friends who remain in touch today. Dave Anderson, a sculptor from Tulsa, Oklahoma; Charlie Davis, a pilot from Chicago; and, of course, Al Giordano, a rugged, sarcastic little stonemason from Vineland, New Jersey, who became the inspiration for Albert Giordino, Dirk Pitt's close pal in all the NUMA adventures. Al is now retired and living in Stuart, Florida.

After roll call, Dave, Al and I, along with Don Mercier, who has since passed away, would jump in our cars, drive around the island of Oahu to a secluded cove and go skin diving. We soon became as tanned as the Polynesians and as agile as the fish we speared. Diving was wonderful in those days. The beaches and coves were deserted, and we had the reefs and the turquoise waters to ourselves. It was then I enhanced my already established love for the sea.

To supplement my meager one hundred and thirty dollars a month as a buck sergeant, I used to buy old cars from the new-car dealers, fix them up and sell them to the troops arriving for service in the islands. Not relishing Air Force life, I bought an airplane with three other fellows, a 1939 Luscombe, and rented an apartment at Waikiki Beach. A 1940 Packard limousine was my transportation to and from the base until I bought and restored a 1939 Fiat Topolino with a little 500cc engine. I sold that car when I returned home and always regretted it. On a return vacation to Hawaii several years later, I found that the car had been converted to a dragster that won several trophies on the local drag strip.

Craig Dirgo: It was about this time you met your wife, correct?

Clive Cussler: I met my wife-to-be, Barbara Knight, shortly before I left overseas in October of 1951. She and I were introduced by a mutual friend, Carolyn Johnston, on a blind date when we attended a football game. They arrived to pick me up at my parents' house, and I sauntered out wearing a leather flight jacket, a white scarf flowing over my shoulders, Levi's, and smoking a cigar. I thought I looked rather dashing, but Barbara took me for some kind of barbarian member of a motorcycle club. She sat as far away from me as she could and spoke only about ten words the whole evening. To me, she looked rather dowdy, and I thought she was the most introverted girl I had ever met. Later that evening, when I walked her to the front door of her grandmother's house where she was living, for some indescribable reason I became carried away and asked for a date the following night. I admit I was desperate. To this day, she can't imagine why her brain refused to function and she accepted.

Saturday night, resplendent in my uniform, I showed up at her doorstep at the appointed time. Barbara opened the door and stood like a radiant vision dressed for an elegant night on the town. We stared at each other for a full minute, unable to believe we were the same two people who had met the night before. What a difference clothes make.

I took her to Hollywood, where we swept into all the jazz joints featuring such greats as Nappy Lamar, Stan Getz, Red Nichols and Charlie Parker. Barbara was only eighteen, and I was twenty, and the legal drinking age was twenty-one in those days. But perhaps because I looked older in uniform and Barbara was so dazzlingly attractive, we were never asked for our ID. We had a marvelous time, stayed relatively sober, and I still got her to her grandmother's house at a reasonable hour.

After I was sent overseas, we corresponded for the next two years, until I managed a flight back to the States, courtesy of the Air Force, for a two-week leave. Incredibly, I arrived on her birthday, and we went out to celebrate. The days flew, and I recall a fabulous two weeks together before I returned to the islands. On the flight back, I made my mind up to marry her and began laying the foundation for courtship. I made Ebenezer Scrooge look like a spendthrift while I saved my meager Air Force pay supplemented by my used-car sales. I sold my share in the Luscombe, gave up my apartment at Waikiki Beach and moved back into the barracks to accumulate a nest egg.

A year later, I flew back to Camp Stoneman near San Francisco to receive my discharge. A civilian again after three years, nine months and sixteen days, I caught an American Airlines midnight flight from San Francisco to Burbank. A couple of fellow passengers took up a conversation with me, asking about my time in the Air Force and what I was going to do when I got home. I recognized the taller of the two as Richard Tregaskis, who wrote *Guadalcanal Diary.* The other was Lowell Thomas. Little did I know I would meet him again in New York thirty years later and receive an honor from the Explorers Club in his name.

At the airport, I found an early-morning bus that dropped me off six blocks from home. I was burdened with so much baggage, I had to drag my duffel bag and diving equipment over the sidewalk the entire trip, arriving at my front door to be greeted by my parents at 5:30 in the morning. Three hours later, with a cashier's check totaling my hard-earned wages over the past three years clutched in my grubby hand, I bought an XK 120 modified Jaguar roadster at a foreign automobile dealership, receiving a nice discount because Dad audited their books.

CRAIG DIRGO: So you returned, bought a new car and went to claim Barbara.

CLIVE CUSSLER: That was the plan. So I drove over to Barbara's house and was shocked to find her going with a sailor stationed on a ship in Long Beach. I guess while I was overseas, it was a case of out of sight, out of mind. It never occurred to me that my goal of marriage was not mutual. And yet, my best-laid plans and sacrifice paid off. The swabbie took one look at dashing, debonair Cussler in his brand-new Jaguar, and he took off for his ship, never to be seen again. Who can blame him? His competition was simply too stiff and uncompromising.

After a four-month courtship, I took Barbara out to dinner, then dancing at the Palladium in Hollywood, to the music of Sonny Burke's big band, then drove to Mullholland Drive, where I proposed. They just don't come any more romantic than me. Barbara, unable to resist my best-laid plans, could only say yes.

CRAIG DIRGO: Do you think it was the Jaguar that swayed her?

CLIVE CUSSLER: Probably. Possessing a mind rigid with practicality, I promptly sold the Jaguar and with the hard-earned cash purchased a Nash Rambler station wagon, a beautiful cherry-wood Magnavox TV with a record player, living-room sofa and chairs, dining-room tables and chairs, a new refrigerator and a washer/dryer. My dad gave us a stove, and I took my old bedroom set. So when we moved into a little duplex on Hellman Boulevard in Alhambra, every stick of furniture was paid for.

Barbara never forgave me. She always claimed she would have cooked dinner on a Coleman stove, eaten on the floor and furnished the place with blankets and wooden crates if I had kept the Jaguar. Barbara must have seen something in me my teachers never did, and she had to have nerves of steel. I know she could have reached much higher. At the time we were married in the Chapel of Roses in Pasadena in 1955, I was making $240 a month pumping gas in a Union station on Sixth and Mateo streets in Los Angeles. You might say it was a case of coming from nothing and bringing it with me. Fortunately, Barbara and I matched together like a pair of old socks. After a honeymoon in Ensenada, Mexico, we set up housekeeping as if we'd been doing it for years. Barbara worked in the personnel department of the Southern California Gas Company, while I filled gas tanks for the Union Oil Company. I didn't finish college because I still hated school and had no idea of what I wanted to be when and if I ever grew up.

Six months later, a longtime friend and neighbor, Dick Klein, who married Carolyn Johnston, the lady who introduced Barbara to me, and I became partners and leased a Mobil Oil station on Ramona Boulevard and Garvey Avenue in Alhambra. No more than seventy-five feet separated us from the fence bordering the San Bernardino Freeway. Between us, Dick and I had less than a year's experience, and I've always suspected the only reason the company allowed us to operate the newly built station was that no other dealer wanted a location that was difficult for heavy traffic to reach. Dick and I, however, saw potential, since it was the last stop for gas before entering the freeway, and it was also in a neighborhood where we grew up and knew many of the residents.

The three and a half years I pumped gas was an interesting milestone toward a writing career. So much happened, I could easily write a book on our experiences. We were held up, burglarized, shortchanged, cheated, fleeced and vandalized. A drunken driver missed the turn and crashed into the station, luckily missing everyone who was working that day. You can bet our insurance adjuster became tired of seeing our faces on a continual basis.

We fought constantly with the company over promotions they tried to cram down our throats, much like fast-food chains do today with their franchisees. We put in ungodly fifteen-hour days. As time went on and we could afford to hire help, this dropped to ten hours a day.

We gave aid to more accident victims than I care to remember. A young girl, who walked her dog past the station every afternoon, used to stop and talk. One afternoon, I looked out from my office and saw her lying in the street after she was struck by a car. Dick and I took care of the dog and made her comfortable until the ambulance arrived. She survived. We rushed to perform first aid for a young boy who was struck on his bicycle. He survived, too. And then there were the injured and dead we helped pull from the mangled wreckage of cars on the freeway. Whenever we saw traffic back up on either the east or west lane, one of us jumped on our three-wheel Harley-Davidson motorcycle and took off with a tool box toward the accident, knowing we might have to dismantle doors to remove the victims. We nearly always arrived before the police and ambulance and helped ready the injured for the hospital. I believe that in the three and a half years we had the station, Dick and I testified in eighteen traffic investigations.

Mobil Oil estimated our station, despite having only two pumps, should sell twenty-six thousand gallons of gas a month. Company estimates were universally inflated to urge their dealers to unparalleled heights. I never agreed with the psychology behind it. Few stations came close to the estimates. Dick and I, however, were promoters. We called ourselves Clive & Dick's Petrol Emporium, bought an old 1926 Chevrolet truck and painted it in company colors, actually using it to the embarrassment of stalled customers when we pushed them into the station with it. We picked up and delivered cars for service with our Harley that the company painted with our name and phone number. Dick talked a nearby tire company into wrapping a hundred used tires which we stacked around the station to make customers think we were a big tire dealer and could offer them discount prices. We dreamed up promotions for free brake adjustments and lube jobs just to sell brake jobs and oil. During gas wars, we painted a big sign with lowered prices—I believe we once got down to 27.9 cents a gallon—and propped it on the old truck next to the freeway.

Within a few months, Clive & Dick's Petrol Emporium was pumping forty thousand gallons a month. We were taking home eight hundred dollars a month and thought we had arrived in fat city. Dick bought a new house and a Ford station wagon. I bought a triplex and played landlord.

You talk about cheap. I was a partner in a gas station. I drove a Volkswagen, and I walked to work. My gas tab averaged four dollars a month.

CRAIG DIRGO: So things were good.

CLIVE CUSSLER: For a while. My daughter Teri was born, and I began to think about the future. Because of our success, Dick and I had hoped either to buy or lease a fleet of service stations and build an empire. But the company stepped in and said no. "You're doing fine with your one little moneymaker." With nowhere to go, least of all up, we told Mobil Oil officials to stick it in their ears and sold out. In keeping with my grandfather, who peddled his saloon in the nick of time, we sold our gas station six months before they closed off Garvey Boulevard to build the Long Beach Freeway. The gallonage at the station soon plummeted from forty thousand a month to eleven thousand. Nothing exists of Clive & Dick's Petrol Emporium. An apartment now sits on the corner we once occupied.

Craig Dirgo: What then?

Clive Cussler: I drifted for a while, selling the *Encyclopedia Britannica,* Lincoln-Mercury automobiles and a newspaper cartoon service to retail merchants. It didn't take a message inscribed with fire on stone tablets to tell me I couldn't sell a glass of water to a dehydrated prospector in the Mojave Desert. If I wasn't the worst salesman in Los Angeles, I was no more than two steps away.

Then I got lucky. I overstated my qualifications and was hired as advertising manager for a plush supermarket at the entrance to Lido Island in Newport Beach, California, called Richard's Lido Market. I've never seen another food store with a comparable style and degree of sophistication. The dream child of a peppery little guy, Dick Richard, the store was quite large for its time, with high ceilings painted a dark blue-green. A maze of spotlights provided the illumination, giving the floor the atmosphere of a nightclub. Richard's concept was to provide the finest-quality groceries possible, and he achieved his goal. No other chain store could come close to matching the superiority of the produce, meats and deli products. If it was imported or gourmet, Richard's stocked it. There was simply no independent food store in the nation like it. Richard's spent large sums of money for advertising and in-store promotions that were unique for their time.

On my first day on the job, I was required to lay out a full-page ad for the week's food specials. I had never laid out an ad in my life. Canny guy that I am, I talked to the man who had formerly held my job but who had now been promoted to store manager. I told him that since he had a distinctive manner of laying out the previous ads, I thought it a good idea if he laid out the next one so I could get a feel for his style. He took the bait and showed me the tricks of the trade. I quickly got the hang of it and was off and running.

Advertising and I were meant for each other. It was all there. A devious mind combined with an industrious talent for innuendo, duplicity and hokum. I had found my niche in life. Within six months, I was winning awards for creative advertising from the Orange County Advertising Club and the Ladies Home Journal National Supermarket competition. I even talked the local newspaper into giving me free space to write a homemaker page. Naturally, the recipes all tied in with the market specials for the week on the adjoining page. We even did a column called Sally's Salmagundi, which meant medley or mixture.

Barbara, Teri and I moved from our triplex in Alhambra and rented a little apartment on the beach in Newport. I'd go body-surfing in the morning before bicycling to my office at the supermarket. In the evening, we'd walk along Balboa Island to the Crabcooker Café for a bowl of chowder. Eighteen months later, we bought a little tract home in a subdivision called Mesa Verde in Costa Mesa, where my son, Dirk, and second daughter, Dana, were born.

I slaved in the yard, building an Oriental pond, a mound with a distorted pine tree, a unique divider between mound and pond, a redwood fence and poured concrete with gravel surface for steps leading to the front door and my backyard patio. I planted trees and an Oriental garden in the front and flower beds in the backyard that curved around the lawn. I constructed a Polynesian playhouse for the kids that was perched on sawed-off telephone poles. The roof and sides were sheathed in bamboo matting with a sandbox under the floor. Yes, I missed my calling as a landscape designer.

CRAIG DIRGO: But you found a calling in advertising.

CLIVE CUSSLER: I enjoyed it. I decided to leave Richard's, and along with a talented young artist, Leo Bestgen, I formed a small advertising agency. We decorated the office with antiques and a huge conference table we bought for ten cents on the dollar from Railway Express because it was slightly damaged by the shipping company. We opened our doors and struggled for several months before paying the rent. To enhance our income—Barbara was home with Teri and son Dirk, who had arrived in 1961—I worked evenings in a liquor store in Laguna Beach. Times were tough, but as a family we still managed to have fun. I restored a 1952 Jaguar Mark VII sedan that was owned by a Hollywood screenwriter and loaned to the director for the movie *Will Success Spoil Rock Hunter?* It was driven by Jayne Mansfield and Tony Randall. I also restored an attractive speedboat whose owner had become drunk on his palatial yacht one night and took the smaller speedboat to shore. He collided with several moored yachts and ran aground before the speedboat sank. He said I could have it for free. So I bought a used trailer, and with the help of friends, grunted and strained and pulled the boat off the beach and hauled it home. I sanded and repainted the hull red, white and blue and repaired the damage. I took out the inefficient little inboard engine and replaced it with a hundred-horsepower outboard motor. On weekends, we'd speed around Newport Harbor, find a secluded beach on an undeveloped island, park the boat and picnic while the kids swam.

Eventually, I sold the outboard and bought an old twenty-six-foot double-ender navy whale boat that had been converted into a fishing boat by a Swedish carpenter who built a deck and a cabin on her. I spent many evenings and weekends remodeling her into a character boat. We all had great times cruising around the bay amid yachts costing millions of dollars. Since the outboard had been named *First Attempt,* naturally the whale boat became the *Second Attempt.* We entertained many friends and business associates on that little boat. I learned my lesson about the old adage of a boat being a hole in the water you pour money into. Except for a little eight-foot Sabot sailboat that came later, she was the last craft I ever owned.

After three years, the advertising agency of Bestgen & Cussler prospered to the point where I could stop working in the liquor store and we could make a livable wage. Leo had a great artistic talent and preferred doing illustrations over laying out mundane ads. After many discussions, we decided to sell our accounts and furniture and close the doors, Leo to go into design and illustration and me to become a copywriter at a big-time advertising agency. Everybody thought we were crazy when success was just around the corner. But it was a case of two young men who were not as interested in money as they were in doing what they wanted to do.

Leo became a successful and respected illustrator whose work can be seen in national magazines, and I went to work during the next several years at three national advertising agencies on Wilshire and Sunset boulevards, gradually working up to creative director. This was in the sixties, the truly creative years for advertising. I was fortunate to work with a number of creative people on accounts such as Budweiser beer, Ajax detergent, Royal Crown cola and Bank of America, to name a few. Eventually, I produced radio and television commercials.

I still enjoyed writing and creating original concepts and transferring them into visual images that sold a product and made everybody happy. It wasn't as much fun as being a slayer of kings and ravager of women, but along with occasional fulfillment, there were incredible pressures from deadlines and campaigns that didn't measure up to the clients' expectations. For every four successes, there was one failure that could result in the loss of an account. The awards for outstanding television and radio advertisements that I won seemed flattering at the time but soon began to pale. Years later, when I earned a living writing books, I put them in a big box and left them for the trash man. They were part of a past I seldom cared to dwell on.

CRAIG DIRGO: So advertising was growing old?

CLIVE CUSSLER: It was. We still lived in Costa Mesa, and it was on those long rides on the crowded freeways between the office and home that I created my best ad campaigns. But by now, the old enthusiasm was fading, and I began to think about other ways to make a living. Unknowingly to both of us, Barbara presented the key.

She would go through cycles, staying home with the kids when they were young, then going back to work, then becoming bored with her job and staying home again. Finally, she found an interesting job working nights for the local police department as a clerk, dispatcher and matron for female prisoners. The schedule worked out very well for the family. She was with the kids during the day, and I took over when I returned in the evening. After fixing the family dinner and putting Teri, Dirk and, by now, Dana, who arrived in 1964, to bed, I faced many an evening with no one to talk to. I was never the type to take my work burdens home with me, so out of solitude I decided to write a book.

But what book? I didn't have the great American novel burning inside me or an Aunt Fanny to chronicle who came across the prairie in a covered wagon. After mulling the idea over in my mind for a few nights, I thought it would be fun to produce a little paperback series. No highfalutin schemes to write a best-seller entered my mind.

Thanks to my marketing experience, I began researching and analyzing all the series heroes, beginning with Edgar Allan Poe's Inspector Dumas. Next came Conan Doyle and Sherlock Holmes and all the other ensuing fiction detectives and spies. Bulldog

Drummond, Sam Spade, Phillip Marlowe, Mike Hammer, Matt Helm, James Bond, I studied them all.

When creating advertising, I had always looked at the competition and wondered what I could conceive that was totally different. I thought it foolish to compete on the same terms with already-famous authors and their established protagonists. Bond was becoming incredibly popular through the movies, and I knew I couldn't match Ian Fleming's style and prose. So I was determined not to write about a detective, secret agent or undercover investigator or deal in murder mysteries. My hero's adventures would be based on and under water. And thus, the basic concept for Dirk Pitt the marine engineer with the National Underwater and Marine Agency (NUMA) was born.

CRAIG DIRGO: So, unlike a lot of writers, you started writing with a definite plan in mind.

CLIVE CUSSLER: Correct. The days of Doc Savage and Alan Quartermain were long past, yet I found it interesting that almost no authors were writing pure, old-fashioned adventure. It seemed a lost genre. After taking a refresher course in English, I launched the first book that introduced Pitt and most all of the characters who appeared in the following thirteen novels. The first book was named *Pacific Vortex.*

When I speak at writers' classes, I usually tell the students they can save many, many hours of wasted time by studying and copying the writing style of successful authors who write in the same genre. Ernest Hemingway often told how his early style borrowed heavily from Tolstoy and Dostoyevsky.

Thomas Wolfe, when he was in the merchant marine, purchased a used copy of James Joyce's *Ulysses,* which came close to being the size of the Manhattan phone book. When sailing from port to port, Wolfe laboriously copied the entire book by hand. Months later, when he had at last finished, he took the three-foot-high stack of paper and threw it off the stern into the wake of the ship. When his stunned shipmates asked why, after so much labor, he had simply cast it away, Wolfe said shrewdly, "Because now I know how to write a book."

Me? I leaned heavily on Alistair McLean on my first two books. I was flattered when critics of my early work said I wrote like him. By my third book, though, I began to drift into my own convoluted style with a myriad of subplots. *Iceberg* was always a sentimental favorite of mine because it begins in Iceland and ends up at the Pirates of the Caribbean in Disneyland.

After completing *Pacific Vortex,* I was about to launch a second book when I was offered an excellent position at a large advertising agency as a creative director on the Prudential Insurance account. This was a lucrative opportunity that paid extremely well, but my wife, shrewd judge of me that she is, circled an ad in the help-wanted column of a local newspaper. The ad was for a clerk in a dive shop that paid four hundred dollars a month.

She said, "You want to write sea stories, why don't you take this job instead."

Odd person that I am, I wasted little time in deciding to decline the $2,500-a-month ad job, which was darn good money in 1968, and walked into the Aquatic Center dive shop in Newport Beach to apply as a behind-the-counter salesman. The owners, Ron Merker, Omar Wood and Don Spencer, looked at me as if I had stepped from a UFO. The obvious question was, "Don't you think you're overqualified?"

Maybe I was, but they were astute enough to see a sincerity behind my application and hired me to work in their Santa Ana store. Although I had dived since my years in Hawaii, I was never certified. Merker soon took care of that chore, and before long Spencer had me acting as dive master on diving expeditions to Santa Catalina. I had many fun experiences with those three fine men that are related in the book *The Sea Hunters.*

After a few weeks, they put me in charge of the store while Spencer was working other duties. I'd carry my portable typewriter with me when I opened the doors in the morning and write at a card table behind the counter when business was slow, usually in the afternoons. A little over a year later, I finished *Mediterranean Caper,* bid a fond farewell to the dive shop and returned to the unscrupulous world of advertising.

Having received nothing but rejection letters on *Pacific Vortex,* most of them printed forms, and with the manuscript of my second book in hand, I figured that now was as good a time as any to find an agent. I've told the following story more times than Judy Garland sang "Over the Rainbow," but here goes.

Working in TV production in Hollywood, I knew a number of people at theatrical casting agencies but no literary agents. Gathering the names of twenty-five literary agents in New York from the casting people, I set about contacting them one by one. Having an idea about the competition and how many manuscripts agents and editors receive in a week—anywhere from thirty to sixty—I wisely concluded that I had to beat the odds somehow.

I bought a thousand sheets of blank stationery and a thousand envelopes and had the art director of the ad agency where I was working design a logo and specify the type. Then I went to a printer and had him print the stationery and envelopes so that they read "The Charles Winthrop Agency." For an address, I used my parents' since they lived in a ritzier neighborhood than mine. Next, I wrote to the first name on the list, which happened to be Peter Lampack, who was with the William Morris Agency in Manhattan.

The letter read: "Dear Peter: As you know, I primarily handle motion picture and television screenplays; however, I've run across a pair of book-length manuscripts which I think have a great deal of potential. I would pursue them, but I am retiring soon. Would you like to take a look at them?" Signed Charlie Winthrop.

I mailed off the letter to Lampack and waited for whatever response without a great deal of optimism. A week later my dad called. "You have a letter from New York."

Peter replied, "Dear Charlie, on your say-so, I'll take a look at the manuscripts. Send them to my office."

Thinking so far so good, I sent off *Pacific Vortex* and *The Mediterranean Caper* and pushed the event to the back of my mind while I worked on a campaign to introduce a new El Toro lawnmower. Two weeks later, another letter arrived from Lampack:

"Dear Charlie: Read the manuscripts. The first one is only fair, but the second one looks good. Where can I sign Cussler to a contract?"

I almost went into cardiac arrest. I couldn't believe it was that easy. I fired off a final letter from Charlie Winthrop telling Peter Lampack where he could reach Clive Cussler. Peter sent a letter introducing himself along with a contract I promptly signed and returned. I threw away the envelopes and wrote the next book, *Iceberg,* on the back of Charlie Winthrop's stationery.

Craig Dirgo: So you had an agent now.

Clive Cussler: It may not have appeared so, but this was a major turning point in my life. Peter taking me on as a client was enough of an inspiration for me to leave advertising and consider life as a writer. Sure, no book was published and no money coming in, but still it was worth a shot. Fed up with Southern California smog and traffic and wanting to change our lifestyle, which now that I look back on it was the only sane thing to do, I sold the boat—thank God I sold the boat and actually broke even—then sold the house, bought a new car, a big 1969 Mercury Monterey four-door sedan, and a tent trailer. After the house cleared escrow, we stored the furniture and took off for places unknown in the summer of 1970.

Teri, Dirk and our youngest daughter, Dana, all in elementary school, were happy to go. It wasn't as traumatic for them to pack up and take off as it might have been if they were attending high school. The whole family looked upon our escape as a big adventure. It struck me that it was almost impossible to starve in the United States. The idea was to find a nice little resort area off the beaten path, where Barbara might find a part-time job and I could drive a school bus between hours spent over a typewriter writing the next Dirk Pitt epic. Naturally, all our friends and relatives thought we were crazy to leave California in those days. As it turned out, we were the vanguard of a mass exodus over the next twenty-eight years.

After a remarkably enjoyable summer, we finally settled in Estes Park, Colorado, a lovely little community at the entrance to Rocky Mountain National Park. We leased an attractive alpine house with spectacular views and took up residence. The kids entered their new schools, Barbara took up housekeeping and I began writing *Iceberg.*

The entire family enjoyed an idyllic life for almost a year and a half. I finished the book but had yet to be published. Peter Lampack tried very hard to sell my books to editors but met with no success. At one point, his bosses called him into a conference and urged him to dump Clive Cussler because it was obvious I was going nowhere. But Peter hung in, bless his heart. He refused to give up on me and kept pushing the manuscripts to editors. He now had two books to promote, *The Mediterranean Caper* and *Iceberg, Pacific Vortex* having been condemned to a shelf in my closet.

Craig Dirgo: What happened next?

Clive Cussler: By now, I had put a healthy dent in my savings and the money from the sale of our house in California. I concluded I had to find a job to tide us over until I could finish another book or Peter found me a publisher with an advance of royalties. I put on my best suit, typed my résumé, put together a portfolio of my work in Los Angeles and knocked on the doors of Denver advertising agencies, having no concept of how bucolic they were. Three agencies had openings for a copywriter, and I wasted no time in applying.

The vice president of the first agency looked over my résumé and portfolio and shook his head. "You're overqualified," he said. "A former creative director from major Los Angeles agencies taking a twenty-thousand-dollar-a-year pay cut to work as a copywriter in Denver. It hardly makes sense."

"It does to me," said I, competing for the congeniality trophy. "You must admit you're getting a bargain."

"Perhaps, but the last thing we need around here is you hotshots coming in from the east and west coasts and telling us how to run our business."

"I assure you that is not my intention. I simply have a wife and three kids to support."

"Sorry, Mr. Cussler. It won't work out."

Incredibly, the next agency director who interviewed me had seemingly memorized the last interviewer's remarks. It was like listening to a recording. He actually said, "You must remember, the last thing we need is for you hotshots from the big cities coming in here and telling us how it's done."

I was sorely tempted to drive to the city limits and make sure the sign said "Welcome to Denver" and not "Pumpkin Corners."

I made an appointment with the last agency for the following Monday morning. Over the weekend, I took my oldest suit, wadded it up and threw it in a corner of the bedroom. Then I revised my résumé *backward,* putting only a few of my newspaper ads in the portfolio, and left the demo tapes of my television commercials in a drawer. And, oh yes, I didn't shave for two days. Properly subdued, I drove to Denver and walked into an agency called Hull/Mefford. I noticed that only one four-year-old local advertising award plaque hung in the lobby.

Jack Hull, an intense and congenial man, went through the paces. He bought my pathetic story of escaping those know-it-all hotshots on the West Coast to move to a friendly climate. He offered ten thousand dollars a year to start, but I jacked him up to twelve. Fortunately, when he called my prior agencies in Los Angeles to verify my employment, all he asked the personnel managers was, "Did a Clive Cussler work there?"

They said yes, and he was satisfied I was genuine. I reported for work the next day and was given an old desk badly in need of varnish next to the restrooms, with an old Royal typewriter and no phone. My creative talents were not exactly taxed. My assignment was to write ads for a real estate client, cartoon captions for a trucking company series and ads congratulating insurance agents for selling their quotas in premiums. None suspected I was once a big executive who wrote and produced national advertising, and I never said a word. Everyone in the office thought I was a real hustler because I was typing from dawn to dusk as if my life depended on it. What they didn't know was that I usually knocked out my workload by ten o'clock and spent the rest of the day writing my next book.

I was driving between Estes Park and Denver, a run of sixty-five miles. The locals thought I was short on gray matter, but after the freeway driving of Los Angeles, I rather enjoyed the scenic trip between city and mountains. The drive soon became old, however, and I moved the family to the suburban community of Arvada just outside Denver, where I bought a tract home on a municipal golf course. Again becoming a slave to the yard, I laid in railroad ties for steps, built a wooden sundeck with stairs and another fence and redwood planters.

Then the day came when the president of our largest million-dollar account, a savings and loan company, notified the head of the agency that if his advertising did not become more creative, he was going to look at other agencies. Pandemonium reigned. I was ignored until someone in desperation said, "What about that guy over by the bathrooms? Maybe he can come up with something."

I was called into the conference room and asked, "We know it isn't much time, but do you think you can create an advertising campaign our client might consider by Friday?"

This being Wednesday, I stared around the table, smiled my best Machiavellian smile and said modestly, "I'll try."

I actually had a campaign pretty well sketched out. I worked around the fact that all savings and loans gave the same interest and premiums to customers. But the one thing people prized was their name. So I created a campaign where the tellers and managers went out of their way to call the customers by name, to read them off the passbooks and memorize as many as possible. The primary idea was to make the savings and loan office a warm and friendly place to do business. I did a story board on a little, mean, old, nasty lady who was avoided like the plague when she walked down the street. Mothers snatched their kids from in front of her, shades were pulled when she passed by and men crossed the street to avoid her. Then, when she comes into the savings and loan, she's treated royally and called by name. Simple, but when properly produced, it proved quite effective.

On Friday, I made my dazzling pitch, the client bought the campaign and I was off and running. With a budget below three thousand dollars a spot, I concentrated on the talent and chintzed on the production. I coaxed Margaret Hamilton, so beloved as the Wicked Witch in *The Wizard of Oz,* to play the mean little old lady. She was a marvelous, talented woman, kind and approachable to everyone, regaling the production crew with stories about the making of *Wizard.* During the camera scenes, when she turned and faced the camera after having a pert little teller call her by name, Margaret's taut, prune face lit up like a Christmas tree. Then I had the famous actor of the forties and fifties, Richard Carlson, do the voiceover. "Just when you thought you hadn't a friend in the world, isn't it nice to know somebody cares enough to remember your name?" Then came the savings and loan logo before the fade-out.

I produced a series of commercials featuring the great character actors Charlie Dell, who was on *Evening Shade;* Mike Mazurki, who played gangsters in the classic movie mysteries; Joey Ross from *Sergeant Bilko* and *Car Fifty-four, Where Are You?;* and little Judith Lowery, who was Mother Dexter on the *Rhoda* show. And last but not least, Ted

Knight, who played Ted Baxter on *The Mary Tyler Moore Show*. Character actors, to my way of thinking, are the finest people in the movie business. They're incredibly cooperative and uncomplaining. They live normal lives and never have a bad word to say about anybody.

While I was producing the television commercials, I was creating a radio campaign for a company called Deep Rock Water. I dreamed up an old guy who lived in Deep Rock's well by the name of Drinkworthy, who spoke with a Maine Downeasterner accent through the versatile voice of Johnny Harding, a Denver radio personality. Deep Rock was still running those ads twenty-five years later. Very quickly, the awards began to roll in for both accounts. Several Cleos and International Broadcast Awards all came to the agency, along with first places at both the Venice and Chicago film festivals. Hull/Mefford was on a roll. They merged with another agency run by two ladies, Mary Wolfe and Jan Weir, added staff throughout the office and began welcoming new clients who walked through the door now that we had gained a creative reputation.

I was raised to seventeen thousand dollars a year, made vice president of the creative department and given a company car, which was all very well and good but left me little time to write books. My little creative gang, the art directors George Yaeger and Errol Beauchamp, along with Ashley O'Neal, our Southern accountant, always had lunch across 17th Street in downtown Denver at an old hangout called Shanners. A terrific waitress named Brenda never failed to have our private booth reserved. I always ordered a tuna sandwich, heavy on the mayo, with an extra pickle and a Bombay gin martini. I really lived high. The only downside was I had no time for Dirk Pitt.

Then my ad world came crashing down.

I was offered a promotion to executive vice president but turned it down because I preferred to remain in the creative end. So the agency heads hired an account supervisor from a New York agency. I doubt whether he could explain it, I know I can't, but when we shook hands as we were introduced, it was instant dislike. To this day, I can't put my finger on it.

He was a corporate infighter, and I wasn't. It took him only three months to get the ear of the bosses. I was called in one day and told my two-hour martini lunches were not acceptable and to clean out my desk. Dumb old me, I thought as long as I did my job and won awards and pleased the clients, my job was secure. I looked up at God and asked him, "God, let me keep my job." And God looked down at me and said, "Why?" I swore then and there I would never work for anybody ever again until my dying gasp.

CRAIG DIRGO: So you're out of work again.

CLIVE CUSSLER: That was about the size of it. Actually, the sacking was a blessing in disguise. I went home, retuned my antennae and wrote *Raise the* Titanic! in one corner of my unfinished basement, and the rest, as they say, is history.

Peter's persistence finally paid off. He found a publisher willing to publish Dirk Pitt for the first time. A little third-level paperback publisher called Pyramid printed about fifty thousand copies, sold thirty-two thousand and paid me the munificent sum of five thousand dollars for *The Mediterranean Caper.* The book sold retail for seventy-five cents.

One Saturday morning, as I was going to the lumber yard for some material to finish the basement, the mailman handed me the mail. I sorted through it and found a letter from the Mystery Writers of America. I opened the envelope and found a printed form letter. Thinking it was an invitation to join the club, I merely glanced at it, then froze and read it more carefully. It was notification that *The Mediterranean Caper* had been nominated as one of the five best paperback mysteries of 1973. My peers, no matter how deluded, thought I could write. I didn't win, nor have I ever been nominated again. But I've always owed the MW of A for that shot in the arm when the skies were gray.

Less than a year later, Dodd Mead bought *Iceberg* for five thousand dollars. I was coming up in the world. They printed five thousand hardcovers and sold thirty-two hundred. To collectors, a pristine book and jacket can now pull as high as a thousand dollars. Even an old copy of *The Mediterranean Caper* by Pyramid can bring three hundred dollars, providing you can find one. I finished *Raise the* Titanic! and sent it off to Peter, who read it, approved and relayed it to my editor at Dodd Mead. A rejection came back within ten days.

Oh, the shame of it all. Rejected by my own editor and publisher. It was me against the world, and the world was winning. Peter sent the renounced manuscript to Putnam, but the editor there wanted a massive rewrite, and I refused to do it. Out of the blue, Viking Press bought it, asked for very few changes and paid me seventy-five hundred dollars. Then strange forces went to work.

An editor from Macmillan in London was visiting an editor friend at Viking and heard about the story. Since, as he put it, the *Titanic* was a British ship, he asked for a copy of the manuscript to read on the plane back to England. He liked it and wanted to buy it. Luckily, Peter had sold *Iceberg* to Nick Austin at Sphere, a small publishing house in London, for, I believe, about four hundred dollars. Since Sphere had the first option, they put in a bid for *Raise the* Titanic! that was promptly topped by Macmillan. When the bidding war was over, Sphere owned the book, paying twenty-two thousand dollars, which was rather a healthy sum for Britain in those days.

A week before, I had pulled off one of my craftier moves. Somehow I got the gut feeling that things were falling my way. I called Peter and asked him if I might get the rights back to *The Mediterranean Caper.* He replied it shouldn't be a problem since it was out of print. He was right. Pyramid signed over the rights without a protest. At that time, Jonathan Dodd at Dodd Mead notified Peter that Playboy Publications had offered four thousand dollars for the paperback rights to *Iceberg.* Peter commented that since it was the only game in town, I might as well play. Again, something tugged at my mind. I instructed Peter, "Tell Jonathan that I'll pay him five thousand dollars for the exclusive rights to *Iceberg.*" Peter thought I was crazy. "Authors do not buy back rights," he admonished me. "It just isn't done in the publishing business. Besides, it's a dumb play. You split the four thousand dollars with Dodd Mead, so it would be stupid to offer them three thousand dollars up and above the offered price from Playboy."

Following my instincts and with a mania to own what's mine, I commanded, "Offer Jonathan the five thousand dollars."

Two hours later, Peter called back. "It's a mystery to me why, but Jonathan okayed the deal."

"How can he miss?" I replied. "He's making an extra three thousand dollars."

Talk about guts. Barbara and I had all of four hundred dollars in the bank. We might have tried to borrow from our folks, but I rightly assumed they would think I was crazy, too. So I took out a loan on our aging 1969 Mercury, and Barbara managed to borrow the rest through her credit union at Memorex, where she worked as a secretary. In my enthusiasm, I whisked off a check to Dodd Mead before my deposits had cleared the bank, and the check bounced in New York just as the momentum began building on *Raise the* Titanic! Jonathan Dodd, being the true gentleman he is, honored the deal when the check finally cleared.

The British interest in *Raise the* Titanic! then boomeranged back to America, with Peter officiating over an auction among the American paperback publishers. Never having experienced a book auction before, I was in the dark until Peter explained the procedure. A floor price is set, and the publishers bid up from that amount, the high bid being the winner.

Craig Dirgo: Were you confident this would finally allow you to write full-time?

Clive Cussler: When Barbara walked out of the house on the morning of the auction to drive to her office, I said jokingly, and I swear to God I truly *was* being facetious, "When the bidding gets to two hundred fifty thousand, you can quit."

At 10:00 A.M. Rocky Mountain Standard Time, I called her at work and told her to quit. Barbara walked right in and gave her boss two weeks' notice. The bidding ultimately went to eight hundred forty thousand dollars, with Bantam Books as the winning bidder. Friends and acquaintances often came up to me and said, "Congratulations on your overnight success."

My reply was, "Yeah, eleven years," the time that had elapsed since I first sat down at that old portable Smith Corona typewriter at a desk in my son's bedroom in that little tract house in Costa Mesa, California.

Later, when the dust from the auction had settled, the management at Bantam was stunned to learn that *Raise the* Titanic! was the third book in a series. Fearful that I would sell *The Mediterranean Caper* and *Iceberg* to another publisher and thereby cut into their sales of *Raise the* Titanic! they paid me forty thousand dollars apiece for both books, with the express purpose of simply keeping them off the market. Fortunately, an editor took them home over the weekend and read them. On Monday, having become a believer in Dirk Pitt, he sold the editorial committee on publishing them both. *The Mediterranean Caper* and *Iceberg* since have gone on to sell many millions of copies around the world.

My first and only review from the *New York Times* was a classic. The reviewer wrote, "If good books received roses and bad books skunks, Cussler would get four skunks." With depth of understanding. This had to be a reviewer who took almost sensual pleasure from his craft. I called Peter and grumbled. "They didn't have to be that nasty."

And Peter came back with the classic reply. "Listen," he said seriously, "when we start getting good literary reviews, we're in big trouble."

He was right, of course. The highly touted literary books seldom sell big-time. My own observation of the self-congratulatory establishment writers is that although they create worldly-wise prose, most of them can't plot worth a grunt.

My favorite sinister review came out of the *Christian Science Monitor.* It took up nearly two-thirds of a page and was very tongue-in-cheek. The reviewer criticized and nitpicked every page of *Inca Gold.* When I reached the end of the review, I broke up in fits of laughter. It seems it had been written and sent to the *Monitor* by the superintendent of sewers for the city of Muncie, Indiana. I've saved that one for posterity.

CRAIG DIRGO: So it would seem at this point you had it made.

CLIVE CUSSLER: Things were better, that's for sure. When the first royalty check came in, Barbara, the kids and I celebrated by buying a new refrigerator and a used Fiat sports car. Then I went back to my corner of the basement and started *Vixen 03,* but not before Barbara and I flew to New York to meet my new editor and publisher. Our arrival in the Big Apple was timely. Peter had just concluded negotiations to sell *Raise the* Titanic! to Lord Lew Grade and Martin Starger of Marble Arch Productions to be made into a motion picture.

To celebrate, Peter and his lovely wife, Diane, and Barbara and I went out to dinner at a restaurant called Sign of the Dove. While waiting for dessert, I turned to Barbara and said, "I think the time has come."

Peter and I had now been together for six years, and he had persisted through all the rejections, believing in me, until we finally achieved a breakthrough. He has always possessed a ton of integrity, and I had been reluctant to tell him about Charlie Winthrop for fear he might drop me. But now I was his biggest client and knew he would think twice before making such a decision. I confessed my scam to get him to read my manuscripts with great trepidation.

When I finished, Peter looked blank for a moment and then laughed himself under the table. When he recovered, he said, "Oh my God. I always thought Charlie Winthrop was some guy I met when I was drunk at a cocktail party."

Peter and I have been together now for twenty-nine years. We have the second-longest-running agent-author relationship behind the thirty-one-year association of Henry Morrison and Robert Ludlum. He is my dearest friend, and since he left William Morris to launch his own agency almost twenty years ago, our only contract has been a handshake. Ninety percent of what I have achieved through Dirk Pitt and his pals I owe to Peter Lampack. He is an honest but tough negotiator who is widely respected throughout the publishing field.

The following year, I finished *Vixen 03* and mailed it off to Peter in New York. Tom Ginsberg, whose family had run Viking Press for several decades, also bought the new book and paid a generous advance, perhaps believing I might become a popular author. Unfortunately, Tom sold Viking to Penguin, a foreign publisher that overturned the old management. Two young hotshots (there's that word again) were put in control and commenced to change the entire face of Viking Press. They alienated everyone in sight. Established authors fled the house, including Judith Guest and Saul Bellow. The new corporate chiefs felt that since *Vixen 03* had been purchased by the previous management, it wasn't their personal property. They sent me out on a book tour with little or no advertising under less budget than Willie Loman had selling neckties out of cheap hotel rooms. Ebenezer Scrooge spent money like a lottery winner next to these guys. They put me on night flights so the airline would feed me. They booked me in cheap hotels. The entire tour was chaos and confusion.

The smart thing after this kind of treatment was to flee the publishing house for another. But how? They had dibs on my next book. A manifestation of Cussler's law is that everybody in their life has accomplished something that will pay dividends eventually. It turns out I had knocked out a silly manuscript on the Denver advertising follies right after *Raise the* Titanic! as a catharsis to being fired. It must have taken all of sixty days to write the farce before I threw it in a closet. The tale was called *I Went to Denver but It Was Closed.* Off it went to Peter, who submitted it to Viking's editors. The rejection was incredibly prompt, and, having satisfied our option agreement, we were free to take the next Dirk Pitt book to another publisher. In this case, it was Bantam, which wanted to get into the hardcover market. They bought *Night Probe!* which I always consider as one of my better plots.

CRAIG DIRGO: So you landed at Bantam.

CLIVE CUSSLER: Luckily, it worked out OK. One day,

as I talked to my new editor about minor changes in the manuscript, he asked where *Night Probe!* came in sequence in relation to the earlier books. I casually mentioned *Pacific Vortex* as being the first book to introduce the characters, but it was never published. He sounded stunned. "What?" he gasped. "There's another Dirk Pitt manuscript out there? How soon can you get it to me?"

By now, since all the books were high on the best-seller list, all the publishers saw were dollar signs. I called Peter and told him Bantam wanted to have a look at *Pacific Vortex.* "Not on your life," he came back. "Publish that rag, and you're ruined."

Curious after not having looked at the manuscript in almost fifteen years, I took it off the closet shelf where it was living under *I Went to Denver but It Was Closed,* blew off the dust and began reading. The story was pretty good. It was just that my early style of writing left much to be desired. I spent about three months rewriting it, then sent it to Peter with instructions to pass it along to Bantam. Peter wasn't a happy camper, but to make me happy, he gave it to my editor, who received it enthusiastically.

Months later, when *Pacific Vortex* was ready to be distributed, Peter said he was going on vacation to Jamaica because he didn't want to be around when the book bombed. I have to give Bantam credit, they did a terrific job on the book jacket, designing a double cover with a circular die cut on the outer one that opened to reveal a diver inside. A week after the book hit the stands and the shelves, I sent Peter a telegram at his hotel in Jamaica. It read, "Screw you, *Pacific Vortex* just went number two on the *New York Times* paperback list."

Not long afterward, I had lunch with the president of Bantam. I revealed that I was happy at last to have all my paperback books under one house and that I'd have taken less money to be there. He looked at me in shock, dropped his fork and muttered, *"Well,* I'll have you know that I was willing to pay more."

One-upmanship lives.

This little conversation came back to haunt me when I turned in my next book, *Deep Six.* After entering contract negotiations, Peter was stunned when the head of Bantam offered less money for the new book than they had paid for *Night Probe!* which was their first hardcover to make the best-seller list and made them a considerable sum of money. Peter told them in no uncertain terms their train had jumped the track. Then they came back with the same royalty payment as before. I knew deep down inside that this ridiculous petty haggling was due to the lunch.

CRAIG DIRGO: So it was time to switch publishers again?

CLIVE CUSSLER: It was time. Peter and I decided to throw the book on the open market. Michael Korda of Simon & Schuster offered a much higher amount than Bantam, and I changed publishing houses.

CRAIG DIRGO: Let's talk about the layout of your books and your habit of featuring your cars.

CLIVE CUSSLER: I've always had fun with the author photos on the books. On *Iceberg,* I was pushed by a deadline, and since I was into diving but living in Colorado, I put on an old wet suit and talked a friend into shooting a black-and-white photo of me from the waist up surrounded by water. What nobody knew was that I was standing in a pond in the middle of a golf course. On the jacket of *Raise the* Titanic! I wore an Irish knit sweater that was about two sizes too large and was taken up in the back by seven or eight clothespins.

It wasn't until *Deep Six* that I began displaying the cars depicted in the books as driven by Dirk Pitt, when in fact they were owned by me. I thought, and still do, that readers would rather see the car while I stood in the background than some enhanced photo of my ugly mug taken when I was ten years younger. When they were doing the cover design for *Dragon,* it occurred to me that since they were printing four colors on the front of the jacket, it would cost them hardly any more to print the back photo in color because it would be on the same print run. You learn these things in advertising.

To make certain the photo is first-rate quality, I've always had Denver photographer Paul Peregrine shoot the photo, while Errol Beauchamp, who owns a commercial art studio, does the overlays and has the type set that reads, "Clive Cussler with Dirk Pitt's . . . year and make of car." All the photos on all the jackets were shot on a lawn across the street from my warehouse. On two occasions, we were lucky because it snowed the night before, allowing the colors of the cars really to burst forth. I damn near got frostbite standing beside the cars for three hours because I couldn't walk around and make footprints. As far as I know, I'm one of the few authors who oversee the print and layout of their book jackets.

CRAIG DIRGO: Let's talk about your cars.

CLIVE CUSSLER: I'm often asked if Pitt and I own the

same cars. In most cases, yes. In the earlier books, he drove a Maybach-Zeppelin and an AC Cobra, which I do not own. He also has a Ford Trimotor aircraft and a Messerschmidt 262 jet fighter that I lack. Unlike Pitt, I own no airplanes. I tried to buy an old Ford Trimotor one time, but the elderly fellow who owned the aircraft wanted two million dollars for it, and I barely had enough to buy the landing wheels.

Nor do I own an old aircraft hangar to store my car collection like Dirk Pitt. My cars are stored in a warehouse near Denver. They are maintained by Keith Lowden and Ron Posey, who operate a restoration business on one end of the building. The cars are taken out and driven occasionally, then stored with all gas and batteries removed.

Beginning with *Deep Six,* I loaned Pitt the blue Talbot-Lago. I blew this car up in the book and was amazed at the five letters I received asking if I really demolished the car. I assured the readers by answering that the car was alive and well and living in a warehouse in Colorado.

I've been a car nut since I was eight and saw my first town car, a body style where the chauffeur used to sit in the open while the passenger was enclosed. The first car in my collection is a 1946 Ford Deluxe that my wife spotted for sale in the front yard of a farm during a Sunday drive. "Oh, look," she said, "there's a '46 club coupe like I had in high school." I turned around and bought it, and my son, Dirk, and I restored it in the street in front of our little house in Arvada, Colorado. I recall using spray cans to primer the body.

When I could afford it, I began collecting foreign

classics and American town cars. The classics, however, have become so horribly expensive to restore because parts are all but extinct. After paying sixteen hundred dollars for a twelve-cylinder Packard generator and another eight hundred dollars just to restore it, I began concentrating on the late-1950s convertibles. Those few short years became an era of huge cars with 300-horsepower engines and tons of chrome, an era we'll never see again. They used to say that when you bought one of those big chrome barges, you received your own zip code. My day-to-day cars are a 1995 Jeep Cherokee in Colorado and a 1959 Austin-Healey in Arizona.

Craig Dirgo: So the car collection is one of your hobbies, and finding shipwrecks is the other?

Clive Cussler: My interest in shipwrecks is another story that is covered in *The Sea Hunters,* in which I tell the story of meeting an old wharf rat in a waterfront saloon who told me, "If it ain't fun, it ain't worth doing." My sentiments exactly, especially since my philosophy of life falls somewhere to the right of whoopee.

Craig Dirgo: Let's get back to the books for a moment.

Clive Cussler: I try very hard to make my books fun and different from those of other authors by introducing the elements of old cars, shipwrecks and, yes, even an old derelict like me. I wrote myself into a brief scene in *Dragon* where Pitt and I meet at a classic car concours. When we are introduced to each other, I couldn't resist inserting a line of dialogue when I look at him and say, "The name is familiar, but I just can't place the face." I wrote the interlude as a bit of fun, truly believing my editor,

Michael Korda, was going to demand it be removed. When he left it in, I was surprised and asked him about it. He said, "I must admit I found it unconventional, but knowing you as an unconventional guy, I thought, oh well, it's pure Cussler."

One time was all I intended, but after receiving three hundred letters saying it was great fun, I became a regular member of the cast. Pitt and I never do recall meeting in the previous stories. We both have lousy memories.

CRAIG DIRGO: What do you like to read?

CLIVE CUSSLER: I remember meeting James Michener when he was in Colorado writing *Centennial*. The fellow who set up the luncheon, Mike Windsor, who knew Michener during the war, asked him jokingly, "Have you read any good books lately, Jim?"

Michener smiled. "Actually, I don't read." Then he explained by saying that he had little time to read fiction, as most of his waking hours were spent either in writing or research. Most writers have been there, done that. When you're in the middle of writing a book, it's almost impossible to read another's tale of fiction. Authors are plagued by people who always ask if you've read so-and-so and seem puzzled when you say no. They can't understand why we have no time for recreational reading.

The only fiction books I try to read in the evening rather than watch TV are review copies sent from agents and editors and written by new, first-time authors. I always try to give a newcomer a helping hand, even though I seriously doubt an endorsement from me would buy them a cup of coffee.

I did have the honor of writing an endorsement for Tom Clancy's first effort, *The Hunt for Red Oc-*

tober, and Stephen Coontz's *Flight of the Intruder.* Clancy called not long after his book hit the top of the best-seller list and asked what I thought of his idea to keep using Jack Ryan as a continuing protagonist in his next novels. All I could tell him with any accuracy was that Dirk Pitt hadn't hurt me, and go for it.

When it comes to writing, it's fun to be different and do things other authors wouldn't think of doing. Overseeing the book jackets, appearing in story lines, using plots that haven't been used before, shying away from the old hackneyed story lines using the nasty Russian KGB and Arab terrorists, old Nazi criminals, CIA conspiracies and military espionage. It's definitely more fun to be original.

I do admit to writing a vague formula.

My first two books were basic potboilers, what I call formula A. This is where the readers walk beside the protagonist from chapter one to the end. In *Iceberg,* I began to drift into convoluted plots or what I call formula B. Now I have subplots going on that Pitt and Giordino are never aware of, even at the end. *Raise the* Titanic! was really the first in the series where I had several plots going on at the same time. The trick is always to thread the needle at the end.

I'm often amused by calls I receive from friends and relatives at all hours who are reading my latest book. The conversation usually goes, "You son of a bitch, I'm halfway through such-and-such a book, and there's no way you're going to pull this off."

Often it's not easy, but I never cheat the reader in the end. My readers mean everything to me. When writing, I frequently ask myself, "What would they like to see at this point?" It's not easy getting inside the head of the public. I learned that in advertising. But you do develop a rapport after a time and know what it takes to deliver a fast-paced story that keeps the book in the hands of the reader at all hours. That's why I've always considered myself an entertainer more than a writer. Many writers try to cram their stories down their readers' throats. Others try to get their stories across on philosophy, on the environment or anarchy in the streets of Copenhagen. I feel my job is to entertain the readers in such a manner that when they reach The End, they feel they got their money's worth. No message, no inspirational passages, no political ideology, just old-fashioned enjoyment.

A Pitt book begins with a basic "what if" concept. For example, what if they raise the *Titanic?* Why? There is something of extreme interest on the wreck. Who could afford the enormous salvage cost? The government. Why would the government spend the enormous amount of money required? They might to perfect a defense system. And so it goes.

I like to create a historical prologue, sometimes even using two, such as in *Sahara.* Then lead the reader through a myriad of plots that usually involve four different sections that take place in different locations and using separate events. The trick is to wind them like a cable toward what I call a successful conclusion. It sounds complicated, but surprisingly the scenario unreels inside my head. I never do an outline, never write more than one draft. For a guy whose wife sends him to the store for a loaf of bread and returns with a jar of pickles, it is truly amazing how I can juggle a multitude of characters and events in my head. The hard part is visualizing ships exploding and sinking into the depths, volcanoes erupting and tidal waves sweeping over the South American jungle, and then translating the fantasy into those little black letters on white paper.

Dirk Pitt has changed through the years. He's mellowed quite a bit. When we first started out together, we were both thirty-six. Now he's hovering near forty, and I'm sixty-seven. I tell you, it *ain't* fair. Fans and media interviewers often inquire if I'm Pitt. I originally made him my weight and height when I was younger. Six foot three and a hundred and eighty-five pounds. His eyes are greener than mine, and he certainly attracts more ladies than I ever did. But then, he hasn't been in love with the same sweetheart for forty-three years, either. We've had other similarities. When I quit smoking years ago, Pitt quit smoking. When I went from drinking Cutty Sark scotch to Bombay Gin, so did he. When I developed a taste for tequila, he followed right along. I suppose there's more of me in Pitt than he cares to admit.

He is named after my son, who came first. Just before Dirk was born, my wife and I fought like pit bulls over a name. She wanted Scott or Glenn, and I wanted Dirk or Kurt. As it turned out, Dirk was born late in the evening. In the morning, I was stepping out of the elevator with a vase of flowers as the nurse was walking past. She stopped upon recognizing me, held up an official-looking piece of paper and said, "Oh, Mr. Cussler, I was just going into your wife's room to fill out the birth certificate."

I quickly grabbed the nurse by the arm, hustled her into the nearest office and filled in the birth certificate before my poor wife had a chance. Good girl that she is, she let it slide, much to the delight of my son and my fans. I can't imagine Glenn Pitt. It sounds like a bottle of cheap scotch.

CRAIG DIRGO: What about Pitt—any marriage plans?

CLIVE CUSSLER: Will Pitt ever marry? Probably not. I find it hard to imagine Giordino coming to Pitt's house and asking his wife if Dirk can come out and play. He's come close a couple of times. Two of the women he was in love with died in the last chapter. He asked Congresswoman Smith, but she turned him down. Pitt does not have great luck with women.

Loren Smith, by the way, came about in an unusual fashion. I was casting for an important female character in *Vixen 03.* I had no problem creating someone with style and elegance. Someone lovely with a quick mind and wit. My hang-up was her occupation. Pitt's women are never harsh, stupid bimbos. They've all made it in the world and carry their own weight. A few days previously, I had won an award from the Colorado Authors League for *Iceberg* and now received a letter with the heading, "From the desk of Congresswoman Patricia Schroeder." She wrote: "Dear Olive, congratulations on winning the best book award from the Colorado Authors League."

All my life, I've been cursed by people unfamiliar with the name *Clive,* who think the *C* is an *O.* Schroeder apparently thought I was a woman and sent her congratulatory note. It had to be female bonding, because I didn't live in her district. But at least I had the occupation for Loren Smith, congresswoman from a district on Colorado's western slope.

CRAIG DIRGO: When are they going to make another Dirk Pitt movie?

CLIVE CUSSLER: People often wonder why I've never sold another book to Hollywood. My response is, "Not after the way they botched up *Raise the* Titanic!" The screenwriting was simply awful, the direction was amateurish and even the editing was pathetic. Only John Barry's musical score and the special effects were first-rate. I'm not looking for a blockbuster motion picture, but I am hoping for a production of quality, more of a classic than a run-of-the-mill car chase with special-effects explosions every five minutes.

I recall seeing *Indiana Jones and the Raiders of the Lost Ark* a year after *Raise the* Titanic! came out in the theaters. I almost cried. The manner in which Spielberg produced a fast-paced, nail-biting adventure was how I had envisioned the Pitt movie I never got.

Peter and I have had many, many offers, but the producers in Hollywood are more interested in the art of the deal than the art of creating a movie with scope and depth. We've turned down many millions of dollars because I refuse to cheat my readers with another sloppy production. I don't need the money that badly. I wish to have script and casting approval, but from what I hear from the studio bosses, that's nonnegotiable. A number of actors have approached Peter about making a deal, but most of them are not my image of Dirk Pitt, or they are too well known. If a big box-office star plays Dirk Pitt, you don't see Pitt, only the star. That's why I prefer an actor who is not well known who can become Pitt, much like Sean Connery became James Bond.

None of the producers and studios gets it. They think any author would sell his soul to have his book made into a movie. Once was enough for me. Actors see a chance to increase their fans; producers look only at the money angle. I've yet to be contacted by a director who has read the books, enjoyed them and asked to sit down with me and discuss how a movie on Pitt should be made. Not a likely event, considering the egos in Tinseltown, but who's to say? Someday someone will come along and sell me. But until then, I'll keep writing about Dirk Pitt, Al Giordino and the NUMA gang and be happy in my ignorance.

CRAIG DIRGO: Tell us about what your life is like now.

CLIVE CUSSLER: Teri raised a family and gave us two terrific grandchildren. Dirk received his master's degree and works as a financial analyst in Phoenix. Dana moved to Los Angeles, where she works in the movies. Years ago, the family began spending time in Arizona when Barbara, Dirk and I began attending the classic car auctions promoted by Barrett/Jackson and the Kruse brothers. After Dirk entered Arizona State University at Tempe, we bought a condo in Scottsdale to enjoy the warmer climate during the Colorado winters. Always wanting a Southwestern adobe home, I looked for two years before I finally found one that reached out and grabbed me. It was slightly run-down, so we remodeled and landscaped the yard, and I built an office off to one side of the house, where I have my library, the ship models by Fred Tourneau and marine paintings by Richard DeRosset of the ships NUMA has discovered over the years.

This has become my domain. I furnished the house in Southwestern furniture and Mexican folk art. When people visit, I'm often asked who did the interior decorating. They seem genuinely surprised when I say it was me. They can't believe that a fiction writer has taste or that my wife didn't have a strong hand in it.

Barbara did, however, get her day in court. For *her* domain, she built a beautiful log house in Telluride surrounded by aspens with an incredible view of the San Juan Mountains. Here I had no say except for structural conversations with the contractor. The home is entirely hers from the bottom floor to the top of the chimneys, comfortable, warm and cozy. We have the best of both worlds, spending summers in Colorado and winters in Arizona. Which brings me to one of the most frequent questions I'm asked: How can someone who writes sea stories live in the mountains and the desert? The answer is that I get my fix by working on the water searching for shipwrecks at least one month out of the year.

CRAIG DIRGO: One last question. What's the best comment you've ever received on the books?

CLIVE CUSSLER: In the words of a lady journalist who did a review of *Inca Gold,* "Loren Smith is the woman we all want to be, and Dirk Pitt is the man we all want."

The bottom line is that readers of all ages and both genders enjoy Pitt because there is a little of him in all of us.

The Clive Cussler Car Collection

1. 1918 Cadillac touring with dual windshields and V-8 engine. Body by Harley Earle. Once owned by Flo Ziegfeld and Billie Burke.

2. 1921 Rolls-Royce Silver Ghost touring with V-dash and windshield. Body by Park Ward.

3. 1925 Isotta-Fraschini. Open torpedo body by Sala.

4. 1925 Minerva town car landaulet. Body by Hibbard & Darrin.

5. 1925 Locomobile Sportif tourer.

6. 1926 Hispano-Suiza cabriolet. Body by Iteren d'Ferres. Driven by Cussler in a race against Pitt in *Dragon.*

7. 1929 Duesenberg convertible sedan. Body by Murphy. Featured in *Flood Tide.*

8. 1930 Cord town car. Body by Brunn. Featured in *Treasure.*

9. 1930 Lincoln V-8 Brunn town car.

10. 1931 Chrysler Imperial limousine.

11. 1931 Marmon V-16 town car. Body by LeBaron.

12. 1932 Stutz DV32 town car. Rebodied to LeBaron design. Featured in *Dragon.*

13. 1933 Pierce-Arrow V-12 LeBaron town car.

14. 1933 Lincoln DB V-12 Judkins Berline.

15. 1933 Cadillac V-12 town car landaulet. Body by Fleetwood.

16. 1936 Lincoln V-12 town car. Body by Brunn.

17. 1936 Avions Voisin C-28 sedan. Featured in *Sahara.*

18. 1936 Packard V-12 town car. Body by Brunn.

19. 1936 Pierce-Arrow V-12 Berline. Featured in *Inca Gold.*

20. 1936 Pierce-Arrow Travelodge trailer. Featured in *Inca Gold.*

21. 1936 Ford Convertible Hot Rod.

22. 1937 Rolls-Royce Phantom III town car (sedanca deville). Body by Barker.

23. 1937 Cord 812 Supercharged Berline.

24. 1938 Packard V-12 town car. Converted from a seven-passenger limousine by Earle C. Anthony.

25. 1938 Bugatti 59C coupe. Body by Gangloff.

26. 1938 Harley-Davidson motorcycle with sidecar.

27. 1939 Mercedes-Benz 540K salon. Body by Freestone & Webb.

28. 1939 Rolls-Royce Wraith sedan. Body by Gurney-Nutting.

29. 1940 Cadillac V-16 town car limousine. Body by Derham.

30. 1946 Ford Club Coupe. First car in the collection.

31. 1947 Delahaye cabriolet. Body by Henri Chapron.

32. 1948 Talbot-Lago Grand Sport coupe. Body by Saoutchik. Featured in *Deep Six*.

33. 1948 Talbot-Lago sedan. Body by Ghia.

34. 1948 Tatra 87 with air-cooled V-8 engine.

35. 1948 Packard Custom Eight convertible.

36. 1951 Daimler Lady Docker DE-31 convertible. Body by Hooper. Featured in *Cyclops*.

37. 1951 Delahaye sport coupe. Carboneaux design.

38. 1951 Hudson Hornet convertible.

39. 1951 Kaiser Golden Dragon sedan.

40. 1952 Allard J2X roadster. Featured in *Shock Wave*.

41. 1952 Meteor sport convertible.

42. 1953 Studebaker Regal Starliner hardtop coupe.

43. 1953 Packard Caribbean convertible.

44. 1953 Buick Skylark convertible.

45. 1955 Studebaker speedster.

46. 1955 Rolls-Royce Silver Dawn sedan. Body by Hooper.

47. 1955 Packard Caribbean convertible.

48. 1956 DeSoto Adventurer hardtop.

49. 1956 Mercury Monterey station wagon.

50. 1956 Packard Caribbean hardtop.

51. 1956 Lincoln Continental Mark II hardtop.

52. 1956 Ford Fairlane Sunliner convertible.

53. 1956 Oldsmobile Ninety Eight Starfire convertible.

54. 1957 Ford Skyline retractable.

55. 1957 Mercury Turnpike Cruiser convertible.

56. 1957 Pontiac Safari station wagon.

57. 1957 Chrysler 300C hardtop.

58. 1957 Austin-Healey 1000/6.

59. 1957 Cadillac Eldorado Brougham.

60. 1957 Cadillac Eldorado Biarritz convertible.

61. 1957 Studebaker Golden Hawk.

62. 1957 Dodge Custom Royal Lancer D-500 convertible.

63. 1958 Plymouth Fury hardtop.

64. 1958 Buick Limited convertible.

65. 1958 Buick Roadmaster convertible.

66. 1958 Pontiac Bonneville convertible.

67. 1958 Oldsmobile Ninety Eight convertible.

68. 1958 Chrysler Imperial convertible.

69. 1958 Chrysler 300 convertible.

70. 1959 Austin-Healey roadster.

71. 1959 Lincoln Continental Mark IV convertible.

72. 1959 Pontiac Bonneville tripower convertible.

73. 1959 Edsel Corsair convertible.

74. 1959 Buick Electra 225 convertible.

75. 1960 Pontiac Bonneville tripower convertible.

76. 1960 Chrysler 300F hardtop.

77. 1960 Chrysler Crown Imperial convertible.

78. 1960 Cadillac Eldorado Biarritz convertible.

79. 1960 Oldsmobile Starfire Ninety Eight convertible.

80. 1963 Studebaker Supercharged Avanti.

81. 1965 Chevrolet Corvette roadster.

Advanced Pitt Trivia

For these questions, you will need access to the complete set of Dirk Pitt novels. The answers are in the back of this book, directly after the concordance.

1. When talking to Summer in *Pacific Vortex* after she uses the word *gangster,* Pitt mentions a famous organized crime figure. What name does he mention?

2. Before Pitt's date with Teri von Till in *The Mediterranean Caper,* he splashes aftershave on his cheeks. What brand of aftershave does he use?

3. In *The Mediterranean Caper,* Pitt doesn't wear his Doxa watch. What kind of watch is he wearing?

4. In *Iceberg,* Sam Cashman works on the black Lorelei jet that attacks Pitt. What is his Air Force serial number?

5. The band on the *Titanic* played an Irving Berlin song that is mentioned. What is the name of the song?

6. In *Night Probe!* Beasley has a secretary who helps him search at the Sanctuary Building for records pertaining to the North American treaty. What is the secretary's name?

7. In *Deep Six,* Yaeger drinks a specific kind of tea. What kind is it?

8. In *Cyclops,* Hagen eats from a picnic basket as he trails Hudson, who has just met the president. At what famous store did he buy the picnic basket?

9. What song is Pitt singing when he leads the Cuban children to a makeshift hospital after the explosion in *Cyclops?*

10. In *Treasure,* name the condominium complex and unit number where Rothberg is staying in Breckenridge.

11. What is the inscription on the coin found by Sharp in *Treasure?*

12. The U.S. intelligence services operate a *ryokan* used as a safe house in *Dragon.* What does Showalter call the safe house?

13. In *Dragon,* Cussler makes a mistake and gives Pitt's mother a different first name from usual. What is the incorrect name?

14. In *Sahara,* Yerli calls Massarde after Kamil dis-

closes a UNICRATT team will try to rescue Pitt, Giordino and Gunn. What is the name of the hotel he calls from?

15. In *Sahara,* it's mentioned that Pembroke-Smyth owns an expensive luxury car. What brand of car is it?

16. In *Inca Gold,* at the concourse in Washington, D.C., Giordino is wearing a T-shirt. What does the inscription on the T-shirt read?

17. In *Shock Wave,* Giordino is wearing a dive watch. What brand is it?

18. In *Shock Wave,* it is mentioned that Shannon Kelsey bought a car with her grandfather's inheritance. What kind of car did she buy?

19. In *Flood Tide,* Sandecker mentions his cigars are hand-rolled by a family he is close friends with. What city is the family from?

20. In *Flood Tide,* as the S.S. *United States* makes its way upriver, the distance from the Head of Passes to New Orleans is listed. What is the distance Cussler lists?

The Dedications

Pacific Vortex: No dedication as such but a foreword by Clive explaining the development of Pitt and the story behind publication of the first Pitt book.

The Mediterranean Caper: "To Amy and Eric, long may they wave." Amy and Eric are the first names of Clive's parents.

Iceberg: "This one is for Barbara, whose enduring patience somehow sees me through." Barbara is Clive's wife.

Raise the Titanic! "With gratitude to my wife, Barbara, Errol Beauchamp, Janet and Randy Richter, and Dick Clark." Clive's wife and friends.

Vixen 03: "To the Alhambra High School Class of '49, who finally held a reunion." Clive's high school class.

Night Probe! "In gratitude to Jerry Brown, Teresa Burkert, Charlie Davis, Derek and Susan Goodwin, Clyde Jones, Don Mercier, Valerie Pallai-Petty, Bill Shea and Ed Wardell, who kept me on track." Some of Clive's friends and acquaintances.

Deep Six: "To Tubby's Bar & Grill in Alhambra, Rand's Roundup on Wilshire Boulevard, The Black Knight in Costa Mesa, and Shanners' Bar in Denver. GONE BUT NOT FORGOTTEN." These are places Clive frequented.

Cyclops: "To the eight hundred American men who were lost with the *Leopoldville* Christmas Eve 1944 near Cherbourg, France. Forgotten by many, remembered by few." For an account of the tragedy of the *Leopoldville,* check your history books or read the chapter in *The Sea Hunters.*

Treasure: "In memory of Robert Esbenson. No man had a truer friend." Bob Esbenson was Clive's partner in his classic car business who died suddenly from a heart attack in 1987.

Dragon: "To the men and women of our nation's intelligence services, whose dedication and loyalty are seldom recognized. And whose efforts have saved American citizens more tragedies than can be imagined." Clive felt it was time to give credit to unsung heroes.

Sahara: "In deep appreciation to Hal Stuber, Ph.D. (environmental chemist), of James P. Walsh & Associates, Boulder, Colorado, for sorting out the hazardous waste and keeping me within acceptable limits." Clive wanted to thank the scientist who gave him advice on the threat of pollutants.

Inca Gold: "In memory of Dr. Harold Edgerton, Bob Hesse, Erick Schonstedt and Peter Throckmorton, loved and respected by everyone whose lives they touched." These are people Clive had worked with in the past locating historic shipwrecks with NUMA.

Shock Wave: "With deep appreciation to Dr. Nicholas Nicholas, Dr. Jeffrey Taffet & Robert Fleming." People who have assisted Clive over the years.

Flood Tide: Acknowledgment, not a dedication. "The author wishes to express his gratitude to the men and women of the Immigration and Naturalization Service for generously providing data and statistics on illegal immigration. Thanks also to the Army Corps of Engineers for their help in describing the capricious natures of the Mississippi and Atchafalaya Rivers. And to the dozens of people who kindly offered ideas and suggestions on obstacles for Dirk and Al to overcome."

The Sea Hunters: Acknowledgment. "The authors are indebted to Joaquin Saunders, author of *The Night before Christmas;* Ray Rodgers, author of *Survivors of the* Leopoldville *Disaster;* and those men of the 66th Panther Division who survived the terrible tragedy off Cherbourg, France, on the evening of December 24, 1944, for their stories of horror and heroism. It is truly an event that should not be swept away in the mist of time." Dedication: "To the men and women who have supported the National Underwater and Marine Agency from its inception. Through the tough times and the fun times, their loyalty has remained solid and enduring. This is merely a partial record of their remarkable achievements. Without their efforts, over sixty shipwrecks of historical significance might still lie on the bottom of the sea, ignored and forgotten for all time. Some ships are gone, dredged out of existence or buried under modern construction. Some are still intact. Now that the way has been shown, we leave it to future generations to recover the knowledge and artifacts that remain of our maritime history. And to my wife, Barbara, for her enduring patience, and my children, Teri, Dirk and Dana, who grew up with a father who never grew up."

Brief Synopses of the Dirk Pitt Novels

Pacific Vortex

Pacific Vortex truly should be considered the first Pitt novel. Though it was published in the time span between *Night Probe!* and *Deep Six,* it was the first Pitt novel Clive wrote. As one of the two manuscripts originally sent to Peter Lampack when Clive was seeking an agent, it languished on a shelf in Clive's closet until he casually mentioned it to his publisher, which at that time was Bantam Books.

Upon learning that there was an unpublished Pitt novel, it was decided to introduce the book in a paperback-only edition. Clive dusted off the manuscript and did a quick rewrite. The name of the villain Delphi Ea was changed somewhere along the line to Delphi Moran, something Clive was still unaware of when it was mentioned to him last year.

Because it lacks the complex plotting and detailed writing of the later Pitt efforts, Clive wrote a disclaimer of sorts as the foreword, explaining that the novel was not up to his usual standards.

An interesting side note to *Pacific Vortex* is that Peter Lampack, Clive's agent, was adamantly opposed to the novel being published. Telling Clive that the novel would be his ruin, he scheduled a vacation in Jamaica to coincide with the introduction. When the novel almost immediately reached number two on the *New York Times* paperback best-seller list, Clive called Western Union and sent an I-told-you-so telegram to Lampack in Jamaica.

The plot of *Pacific Vortex* is straightforward enough. The United States Navy submarine *Starbuck* is lost in the Pacific Ocean north of Hawaii, and though an exhaustive search is mounted, no trace of the wreckage is located.

Pitt is sunning on a beach on Oahu. Noticing a bright yellow capsule in the water, he swims out into the ocean and brings it ashore. Inside he finds pages from the log book of the *Starbuck,* which he then takes to the U.S. Navy base at Pearl Harbor. He hands the capsule and its contents to Admiral Leigh Hunt. As we examine the Pitt novels, we will see the name of Leigh Hunter (or in this case, Hunt) frequently. In real life, Leigh Hunt is a close friend of Clive's. The mischief the two have created together could fill an entire book of its own.

The story progresses as Pitt and the Navy attempt to locate the missing ships and the cause of their disappearance. We learn there is an underwater lair built by a mad scientist. This leads to a climactic scene where the underground city is attacked. Interestingly enough, while saving Pitt, Giordino jams his finger down the barrel of a gun, and it is blown off.

The book is also interesting because it introduces Pitt's one true love, Summer, who is killed in the collapse of the underground city. She is mentioned in later books as an explanation of why Pitt can never again love one woman. In addition, it casts the future direction of the series—as Pitt drives an exotic car—and much of the action is under or near water.

Pacific Vortex, while lacking the more complex plot and deeper character development of the future Pitt novels, is nonetheless an enjoyable read. For the time it was written, the middle 1960s, it has held up reasonably well. It introduces Pitt, Giordino, and Sandecker and mentions Gunn, as well as starting to explore the Pitt formula that will later make Clive famous.

The Mediterranean Caper

The Mediterranean Caper was the first Pitt novel to be published, though it was written second, after *Pacific Vortex.* It was published in 1973 by Pyramid Books and the firm of Sphere Books in London, where it was titled *Mayday!* Reintroduced by Sphere and simultaneously by Bantam Books in 1977 after the success of *Raise the* Titanic! the novel is now published by the Pocket Books division of Simon & Schuster. *The Mediterranean Caper* is interesting from a business standpoint. After the book went out of print the first time, Clive made an unusual move for a writer. Hoping he would have a long and successful career, Clive had Peter call the publisher and asked for the rights back to the novel. The publisher agreed because *The Mediterranean Caper* was then out of print.

The novel, the first of Clive's to be published, was nominated for a Mystery Writers of America award as one of the five best novels of 1973.

The Mediterranean Caper truly starts to show the writing style for which Clive would later become famous. Unlike later books, in which the prologue is in the past, the book starts the tradition of narration at the beginning, rather than dialogue, to allow the reader to settle into the scene being played out.

The novel starts with an attack on Brady Field, a United States Air Force base in Greece, by a World War I fighter plane. NUMA is immediately featured, and by the first chapter, the reader has been introduced to both Pitt and Giordino. Pitt's past is explained. His physical appearance and Giordino's are described. Even Sandecker and his position with NUMA are explored. Clive's tradition of describing planes, cars and other mechanical devices in detail is used to good effect.

The novel is the story of a former Nazi who uses an underwater cavern for smuggling. Pitt, with the help of U.S. and Greek customs officials, solves the mystery and apprehends the villains. Pitt, of course, has a love interest, Teri von Till, who we first believe is the villain's daughter but later find out is in fact on the payroll of the Greek customs inspector. The original purpose for NUMA and Pitt to be on an expedition in Greece was to locate an ancient prehistoric fish called the Teaser. At the end of the story, one is located and later captured.

The epilogue is used to tie together the loose ends of the story as well as introduce the tradition of Pitt ending up with a prize for his efforts. In this case, he receives the Maybach-Zeppelin town car that Heibert owned.

All in all, *The Mediterranean Caper* lays a firm groundwork for the novels that follow. The interplay between Pitt and Giordino is evident, as is the detailed description of planes, automobiles and other modes of transportation for which Clive is famous. If the novel can be faulted, it would be for the tendency to make too many leaps of plot. Instead of allowing the reader to attempt to discover the direction through well-littered clues, this is instead explained by Pitt in the form of dialogue. Still, the novel has held up well, with references to the time it was written few, so it has not become dated. If anything, *The Mediterranean Caper* should be read by Cussler fans if only to understand better the journey the Pitt books have made over the years.

Iceberg

Originally published by Dodd Mead & Company in 1975 and in 1977 by Bantam Books, Inc., *Iceberg* became Clive's first hardcover published. First editions of the hardcover are quite rare, and collectors of Cussler memorabilia find the supply of books limited and the price high. The book enjoyed modest sales success, selling thirty-two hundred of the five thousand printed in hardcover, although reprints have kept it in print to this day.

Iceberg begins with a neat hook: the first paragraph in the prologue is actually what the copilot of a plane is reading, a book within a book. From there, we progress to a Coast Guard patrol plane spotting an iceberg with a ship embedded inside. They mark the iceberg with dye, then fly away toward their base. As they leave, a pair of men climb from inside the iceberg and call someone on a portable radio.

Chapter One finds Pitt piloting a helicopter toward a Coast Guard ship and landing on her deck. As is Clive's custom, he mentions his previous book by having the commander of the ship, when introduced to Pitt, say, "By any chance the same Pitt who broke up that underwater smuggling business in Greece last year?"

The plot features a missing billionaire mining engineer and genius who was involved in negotiations with the United States government. The engineer has built a device that can detect underwater mineral deposits. The theme of underwater mining is also common in future Pitt novels. Pitt pilots a helicopter and an old plane, a Ford Trimotor, which he later buys and places in his aircraft hangar/home. In addition, Pitt's diving skills are on display as he dives on a mysterious jet that had attacked the helicopter he was flying.

The villains in this tale are a group of industrialists who form a plan to take over South America. Clive begins to expand on his writing skill in *Iceberg.* Well-written descriptive scenes include a trip to a restaurant named Snorri's and a showdown with the villains in an Icelandic mansion. Rather interestingly, Pitt is beaten severely in the book, something that would probably not occur nowadays.

A fantastic climax to the book is a scene in which Pitt foils the attempted murder of the presidents of French Guiana and the Dominican Republic at Disneyland. Here the writing truly jumps off the page.

Iceberg is unique for another reason: Clive has the genius engineer undergo a sex-change operation. He later uses this idea in *Vixen 03,* where a shadowy spy we are led to believe to be a man is found to be a woman.

The plotting of *Iceberg* truly begins Cussler's habit of convoluted story lines and high-stakes action. He uses the Cussler "what if" formula to good effect.

Iceberg sets the stage for the next Cussler novel, *Raise the* Titanic! in that it introduces the idea of a mineral important to national defense, in this case zirconium. It is rather unique among the Pitt novels for a very important fact: at no time does Al Giordino make an appearance.

In addition, Cussler has Pitt pose as gay, something rather odd. I doubt that nowadays Clive would have written that into the book.

The novel continues the development of the Pitt novels. It is more detailed with more richly written scenes than the previous effort, and Pitt's personality and motivations are explored more deeply. An interesting side note: nowadays, if Clive makes even a minor technical error, he receives numerous letters setting him straight. In *Iceberg,* at least as it was originally published, Kristjan and his sister Kirsti were described as identical twins—of course, that is impossible for siblings of different sexes. Clive told me he never received a single letter pointing out the error.

***Raise the* Titanic!**

This is Clive's breakout book, where the formula he created for Pitt finally comes together seamlessly. For starters, he uses a prelude based in the past for the first time. The continuing characters are now fully developed. The Cussler "what if" scenario is utilized with great results. And the writing is fast-paced and action-packed. Clive even uses a brilliant surprise ending. The book made him a millionaire, and rightly so. It has stood the test of time and reads as well today as back in 1976 when it was first published by the Viking Press in hardcover and later by Bantam in paperback. The book was serialized in the *Los Angeles Times* as a cartoon strip, and *Raise the* Titanic! was the only Pitt novel to be made into a movie.

The prelude, Clive's first set in the past, describes a man on the edge of madness who is awakened aboard a ship by an undefined noise. Through clues, the astute reader realizes the man is aboard the *Titanic* and the ship is sinking. At gunpoint, the man forces one of the ship's junior officers, named Bigalow, to show him belowdecks. There, the man locks himself in a vault to die with the ship. Bigalow survives.

As the novel progresses, we learn that a top-secret defense project called the Sicilian Project requires a mineral named byzanium, thought to have been mined out of existence. The only traces that might still exist are located on a Russian island. A NUMA oceanographic expedition is used to provide the cover for a mineralogist to search the island. Pitt makes his appearance early and with excellent dramatic effect. As is the case in later works, he appears larger than life as he saves the mineralogist and carries him to safety.

It is learned that the island mine had contained byzanium but was fully mined, and a search is on to find out what happened to the mineral. Then we learn that the byzanium was placed aboard the *Titanic,* and an intricate and expensive plan is hatched to raise the ship.

The novel features a subplot about a deteriorating

marriage along with a cast of Russian secret agents intent first on learning what the Sicilian Project is about and later attempting to stop the project by infiltrating the *Titanic,* then attempting either to take control of the ship or sink the vessel so the United States cannot recover the byzanium.

Pitt is lacking a true love interest in the story, though Clive alludes to his skill in seducing the opposite sex. It's the ending that truly captures Clive's style in convoluted plotting. After all the work to raise the *Titanic,* the millions of dollars that were spent and the lives of numerous people, we learn that the vault that should contain the byzanium is empty.

After hearing this, Pitt remembers what Bigalow had told him about the night the *Titanic* sank and about his confrontation with the madman who took him hostage. He returns to England, searches a grave in the town of Southby and finds the byzanium. At the end of the novel, Bigalow is buried at sea and the Sicilian Project is tested and proves successful.

An interesting sidelight to *Raise the* Titanic! is that in the original manuscript, the president of the United States is single, and he has an affair with Dana Seagram, the NUMA archaeologist whose marriage is deteriorating. Clive was on a talk show shortly after the book came out, and a caller asked why the president and Seagram never consummated their relationship when it appeared that was about to happen. Clive told the caller, "They did, it's on page . . . ," and reached for a copy of the book. After examining the novel, he found the scene had been edited out. Clive never really found out why the scene was cut, but it's interesting to note that Jackie Onassis was at the time an editor at the same publisher. Maybe Bantam thought the scene would offend her.

Vixen 03

For *Vixen 03,* Clive kept the plot closer to home. The novel begins at an airfield less than thirty miles from where he was living, and a large portion of the story is based in Colorado. Even though Clive had scored big on *Raise the* Titanic! he remained in his tract home in Arvada, Colorado, and wrote *Vixen 03* in his unfinished basement. Originally published in hardcover in 1978 by Viking Press, it was Viking's second and last Cussler book. The paperback was published by Bantam in 1979. The book is not as complex as later efforts, but, strangely enough, the writing has a certain undefined texture. The descriptive passages are smoothly written, and Pitt displays a humility that is not often in evidence. *Vixen 03* also introduces Pitt's love interest Loren Smith for the first time.

The story begins with a United States Air Force jet leaving Buckley Field, Colorado, with a top-secret overweight bomb load. After the jet suffers engine failure high above the Rocky Mountains, the pilot makes a landing in what he thinks is an open area but we later learn is a frozen lake that is unable to support the weight of the plane.

Pitt is introduced in the first chapter and, in a rare circumstance, is actually taking a vacation at a cabin that had been owned by Loren Smith's deceased father. Pitt finds aircraft landing gear and an oxygen bottle in Smith's garage. Intrigued, he visits the neighbors, who are named Lee and Maxine Rafferty.

The story unfolds with Pitt trying to determine where the landing gear came from. Once the serial number is traced, we learn it came from an Air Force jet on a top-secret mission.

At the same time in Africa, a former Royal Navy captain named Fawkes is recruited to lead a suicide mission to discredit the African Freedom Fighters. Clive moves between times and countries with an ease that would become more common in his future works, and the various subplots are well developed and easy to follow. In *Vixen 03,* Clive shows the seedier side of Washington, D.C., with the introduction of a corrupt politician who attempts to blackmail Pitt and Smith. The theme of governmental corruption is one Clive will continue to use in future novels.

Now the hunt is on to find out that the plane's cargo was a poisonous gas called QD. Pitt traces the flight authorization to a retired Navy admiral, and Heidi Milligan, who appears in a future novel, is introduced.

A confrontation with the Raffertys results in a shoot-out. Both Raffertys are killed, but not before Pitt is told where the warheads removed from the jet were sold. A plan is put into motion to locate the warheads. Once again, Cussler writes a story featuring high stakes. He utilizes biological weapons as a threat long before it became commonplace.

The climax is pure Cussler. The battleship *Iowa* steams upriver to Washington, D.C., with Fawkes at the helm, determined to deliver his deadly cargo and discredit the African Freedom Fighters he believes murdered his family.

The man-as-a-woman, or, more accurately here, woman-as-a-man, theme used in *Iceberg* shows up here as well. A shadowy spy we are led to believe is a man is found out after she is killed to be a woman.

In the next-to-the-last section, Pitt travels to Africa and buries Fawkes. He then explains that he knows that Operation Wild Rose was an attempt to topple the current government of South Africa so that the defense minister could take over. De Vaal, the defense minister, is then killed. The novel ends with Rongelo Island, the last location in the world with any QD, being struck by a nuclear bomb that eradicates the last trace of the deadly poison.

Night Probe!

Following the publication of *Vixen 03,* Clive started writing *Night Probe!* Unlike his normal schedule of publishing a new Pitt book every two years, *Night Probe!* didn't show up until 1981, three years after *Vixen 03* went on sale. Part of the time lag was due to a switch in publishers. Clive had been having trouble with Viking for some time. The book tour for *Vixen 03* was a farce, the promotion and marketing of the book almost nonexistent.

Clive desperately wanted to change publishers, but book contracts specify that the current publisher has an option on the next book created by the author. This practice is still widespread in the publishing business. For publishers, it protects them if a writer's works suddenly become hot. For writers, it locks them into a first right of refusal on their next work.

To fulfill his obligation, Clive submitted a book on advertising he had written, *I Went to Denver but It Was Closed.* It was promptly rejected.

Cussler was now free to change publishers. Clive is rather unique as a writer. Each of his books has outsold the one before. In addition, each has easily paid back the advance and made his publishers money. This is less frequent than one might believe. Look at the advances paid to people like Dan Quayle. Did they really sell enough copies of their books to justify the millions paid in advance money?

Landing at Bantam, a paperback house that wanted to branch out in hardcover, *Night Probe!* was published in hardcover in 1981, followed a year later by the paperback edition. For his new publisher, Clive delivered what he and others consider his best plot.

As the book begins in the past, we learn that copies of a treaty between the United States and Great Britain have been lost almost simultaneously in a pair of freak accidents. One copy is lost when a ship sinks, one when a train plunges into a river.

The book is timely. The United States is in the midst of an energy crisis, as it was in 1981, and Canada controls most of the hydroelectric power feeding the Eastern Seaboard. We learn that the treaty concerns Great Britain, in the midst of a financial crisis just before World War I, selling Canada to the United States.

Beautifully subplotted with a group of Canadian separatists, a British secret agent modeled after James Bond and a mystery train that appears like a wraith in the night, the novel moves with a smooth style. It is action-adventure at its best. Heidi Milligan, who was first introduced in *Vixen 03,* is a Pitt love interest who falls for Brian Shaw, the British secret agent. Giordino has a large part, and Sandecker, Gunn and most of the other continuing characters appear. The primary villain, Foss Gly, who appears in a later Pitt novel, is described in detail.

There are plenty of underwater scenes for the die-hard Pitt fan. And the tools NUMA uses to locate shipwrecks are beautifully detailed and explained. Pitt pursues his hobby of collecting old cars by attending an auction.

The book has a definite time line. The treaty must be recovered by Pitt before the British get their hands on it, and the president of the United States is facing national insolvency. In the end, Pitt recovers the treaty and delivers it to the president just in time. The president then announces the formation of the United States of Canada. The novel ends with Pitt delivering Milligan to Shaw, who is suspected of being James Bond.

Deep Six

Clive followed the success of *Night Probe!* with *Deep Six.* It was his first effort for his new publisher Simon & Schuster and built upon his multiple-subplot formula which he would use with increasing frequency in the years ahead. Published in hardcover in 1984 and followed the next year by the paperback edition published by Pocket Books, a division of Simon & Schuster, the book works on various levels. In addition, it begins the Cussler tradition of having maps and artwork inside the book. *Deep Six* definitely should be read by the Dirk Pitt fan if only for one reason: it features one of the single best Dirk Pitt scenes ever written.

When one of the villains of the novel, Lee Tong, makes his escape in a towboat pushing a barge, Pitt gives chase in the Mississippi paddle-wheel steamer *Stonewall Jackson.* The scene is brilliantly written.

A few years ago, Clive was asked how he developed the idea. He claimed that, as is often the case, he hadn't planned the scene. He usually has the germ of the plot—usually the beginning and often the end—but just begins writing the body of the book and unfolding the story in his head as he progresses. The *Stonewall Jackson* scene was different, however. Stuck without a climactic event near the end of the book, he was lying in bed one night when the scene unfolded in his mind in 3-D Technicolor. He raced to the computer and got the scene on paper before it faded.

Be glad he did.

The novel begins once again in the past, 1966 to be exact, when a meek bank teller named Arta Casilighio robs the bank where she is employed, then escapes on the cargo ship *San Marino*. It seems she has gotten away with the crime until she realizes that her evening drink has been drugged. Through a haze, she watches as the crew of the *San Marino* are bound and tossed overboard. Moments later, Arta joins them at the bottom of the ocean.

In Chapter One, the Coast Guard vessel *Catawaba* comes across a drifting crab boat in the Gulf of Alaska. When a boarding party, including a doctor, is sent aboard the crabber, they find the crew dead. Two of the boarding party quickly succumb, while the doctor radios back to the *Catawaba* that he, too, is being affected by whatever is on board. He orders the crabber quarantined, then, with his dying breaths, explains the symptoms he is feeling.

Next, we learn that the president will be taking a cruise on the presidential yacht *Eagle* with a congressional leader, the speaker of the House and the vice president. Later that night, the *Eagle* and all aboard disappear, setting the conflict into motion.

An evil Asian shipping magnate, Min Bougainville,

has formed a plan with the Russians to kidnap the president and implant a mind-control microchip in his brain. In researching the ship containing the nerve gas, Pitt traces it back to Bougainville.

Clive introduces the father of the bank teller as a private detective, Sal Casio, who seems written straight out of a Mickey Spillane novel. Loren Smith appears once again, and the interplay between Pitt and Giordino is further developed.

The element of time is again used to great effect, as is the idea of corrupt politicians. Pitt must rescue the vice president and have him sworn into office before the corrupt speaker of the House, Alan Moran, can be sworn in as president.

The book ends with Casio and Pitt visiting the Bougainville Maritime offices. They confront Min Bougainville, who activates a laser that cuts Casio and kills him. Pitt rolls Min in her wheelchair to an elevator and pushes her down the shaft.

Cyclops

Cyclops was Clive's second effort for Simon & Schuster, which he remains with to this day. Published in hardcover in 1986 and paperback by Pocket Books in December of the same year, *Cyclops* spent fourteen weeks on the *New York Times* best-seller list.

Here, the tradition Clive started in *Deep Six* is continued: the insertion of excellent artwork and maps designed to help the reader follow the plot. Clive also begins this novel in the past—a tradition he began with *Raise the* Titanic!—with the sinking of a United States Navy collier *Cyclops.*

The reader is then taken to the present day in Florida, where a rich industrialist, Raymond LeBaron, takes off in a blimp, never to return. Very early on, the conflict is locked in place. The president is golfing when he learns that a group of scientists have built and developed a moon colony. Pitt appears on vacation in Florida and is involved in a sailboard race when the missing blimp reappears.

A missing treasure is introduced, a theme Clive will continue to use in future novels, and a race is on to find the people who had been on the blimp when it took off from Florida. The Russians enter the picture early. They develop information about the moon colony and decide to send a manned space flight to the moon with the intent of engaging in a war to claim the moon for themselves. And an interesting subplot concerning Cuba is developed.

The trio of plot lines—the moon colony, the missing blimp and possible treasure, the Cuba angle—weave together as the novel progresses. As in *Raise the* Titanic! Clive has an older lady who helps Pitt understand the past. In *Raise the* Titanic! it was the widow of Joshua Hays Brewster; in *Cyclops,* she's the widow of Hans Kronberg, the former partner of Raymond LeBaron, who sheds light on the missing treasure, named LaDorada.

Cussler places Pitt in a variety of interesting scenes. In one, he shows his scorn for pomp and circumstance by arriving unannounced at an exclusive party. This allows one of Pitt's cars to be showcased, as well as showing that Pitt, while nice most of the time, does not suffer fools gladly.

For love interests, we have Jessie LeBaron, the wife of the missing industrialist, whom Pitt beds in a drainage pipe in Cuba, an unusual twist here, as Jessie is in her fifties and a good fifteen years older than Pitt. Foss Gly—the villain of *Night Probe!*—returns as a torturer. This, however, is his last visit. Pitt kills him with a thumb to the eye and into the brain. *Cyclops* marks the second time Hiram Yaeger appears, the first having been a brief appearance in *Deep Six* that proved successful. The tight time line again is used with the Russian cosmonauts due on the moon as well as the plot to explode a series of ship-hidden bombs in Havana Harbor.

Pitt acquires one of his strangest prizes in his collection in *Cyclops,* a cast-iron bathtub with an outboard motor aboard with which he escapes from Cuba.

When the battle on the moon is played out, another conflict is created. The Russians attempt to divert to Cuba the space shuttle that is carrying the moon colonists back to earth. They are narrowly foiled in their efforts.

Pitt, back on Cuban soil, attempts to warn Fidel Castro of the plot to explode Havana in an attempt to discredit the United States. He moves the ships carrying the explosives a distance from Havana before they explode, but it appears Pitt is lost for good. He appears, of course, battered but alive. At the end of the novel, Pitt solves the puzzle of the location of the La Dorada treasure and salvages the statues and treasure for display in a museum.

Treasure

Published in hardcover by Simon & Schuster in 1987 and in paperback the following year by Pocket Books,

Treasure is the first Pitt novel to crack the five-hundred-page barrier. From *Treasure* to the present day, no Pitt book has run shorter in length than five hundred pages. It also begins a now-defunct Cussler tradition of giving measurements in metric. Clive finally quit the tradition in *Shock Wave,* much to the delight of his U.S. readers.

Once again, we have a missing treasure—in this case, the trove of information contained in the Alexandria Library. But, unlike in *Cyclops,* here the treasure is the main plot in the story.

The prelude is a Cussler tour-de-force, imaginative, written with a detail most writers can never achieve, yet extremely interesting. We are immediately treated to a dose of archaeology as well as a subplot about a scheme to kill the secretary-general of the United Nations, Hali Kamil, a character who will reappear in future novels.

The Russians are not featured in the book. Instead, for villains we have an almost mythical messiah who wants to return Mexico to the time of the Aztecs and is named Topiltzin. Across the ocean in Egypt, his equally powerful counterpart, named Yazid, wants to develop a fundamentalist Islamic state. We learn as the novel progresses that the pair are actually brothers and part of an international crime family.

For love interests, Pitt beds both Hali Kamil and Lily Sharp, an archaeologist. For classic cars and chase scenes, Clive writes an excellent chapter featuring his L-29 Cord and a chase that culminates on a Colorado ski slope. The interplay between Pitt and Giordino is used to great effect. Their sarcastic banter in the face of grave danger is used throughout the novel.

Pitt's father, Senator George Pitt of California,

spends a fair amount of time in the story. While he appeared in previous works, *Treasure* marks Senator Pitt's longest appearance before or since. As the story unfolds, a summit of nations is convened in Uruguay, and a plot to hijack the cruise ship the world leaders are aboard is developed.

At the same time, Yaeger is hard at work attempting to find the location where the Alexandria Library was hidden. The president feels that if the library holds ancient maps of mineral and oil deposits, it might be used to locate a massive oil deposit in Israel—thus solving a multitude of the region's problems.

Once Pitt solves the riddle of what happened to the cruise ship full of politicians, named the *Lady Flamborough,* a U.S. operation is launched to recover the ship and free the hostages. Once the hostages are freed, Pitt sets off for Texas, where NUMA now believes the Alexandria Library is buried.

Before the Alexandria Library can be excavated, however, the Mexican messiah, Topiltzin, launches a wave of his Mexican followers across the Rio Grande into Texas. His goal is to steal the library and profit from the information.

With Yazid slain by the disgruntled terrorist he had hired to kill Kamil, all that is left is for Topiltzin to meet his end. He is blown to bits when one of the hills near the location of the Alexandria Library is exploded as a decoy.

In the final chapter, the president visits the site in Texas where the Alexandria Library is being excavated and catalogued. Pitt is already talking of a future adventure, the search for the golden city of El Dorado.

Dragon

In 1990, Simon & Schuster published the hardcover edition of the tenth Dirk Pitt adventure—*Dragon.* This was followed in 1991 with the paperback edition, once again published by Pocket Books. It featured the rich illustrations that were becoming a Cussler trademark. In this story, a United States Air Force cargo plane has a dangerous cargo aboard. The prelude features the flight of a plane called *Dennings' Demons* as it attempts to deliver a payload over Japan.

Dragon then concentrates on a Japanese cargo ship that explodes into pieces, a submersible containing a beautiful underwater photographer we later learn is a U.S. intelligence agent named Stacy Fox.

When the submersible is damaged by the cargo ship explosion, Pitt rescues the crew, then is forced to order the evacuation of Soggy Acres, a secret underwater installation that was built for mining which is suffering from underwater earthquakes. In the Philippines, a treasure cave from World War II thought to contain Yamashita's Gold is excavated, only to reveal the Japanese have returned and removed the treasure. At the same time, Pitt is inside a deep-sea mining vehicle named *Big John.* After being buried in the shocks from the earthquakes, he escapes and drives *Big John* toward a high point in the ocean and is rescued by Giordino in a submersible.

The reader is now introduced to the villain, Hideki Suma. Suma has devised a plan to place atomic bombs smuggled inside Japanese cars throughout the world in an effort to achieve worldwide domination. Loren Smith returns, along with a senator from New Mexico named Mike Diaz. Both favor sanctions against Japanese investment in the United States as well as embargoes on imported Japanese products, and Suma later kidnaps both. For Pitt love interests, we have both Fox and Smith.

A task force is created to find and neutralize the car bombs. Pitt attends a classic car race, where he races his creator, Clive Cussler. Clive wrote the scene as much as a farce as anything, believing that the editors would ask him to remove it. When they didn't and Clive found out the readers enjoyed seeing the author inside the novel, the scene where Pitt meets Cussler has become a staple of the series. At the race, Smith is kidnapped.

A subplot evolves when a farmer in Germany locates an underground Nazi aircraft hangar. Pitt travels to Germany and dives on the underground aircraft hangar and finds the planes and a trove of artwork stolen by the Nazis.

One of the paintings shows the island where Edo City, Suma's nuclear detonation center, is located. A plot is hatched to attack the installation, free Diaz and Smith and neutralize Suma's control center.

Next, Clive writes a scene reminiscent of *The Most Dangerous Game,* the classic story of a hunter whose prey is humans. Ingeniously, Pitt foils the hunter. With the freed hostages and a kidnapped Suma, he makes his way to a U.S. Navy ship. When the attack on Edo City is unsuccessful, Pitt volunteers for a suicide mission. Dropped from the air in a deep-sea mining vehicle, he takes the warhead from the wreck of *Dennings' Demons,* carries it to a fault line that runs to Edo City, rigs it to detonate, then tries to escape.

The book ends with an obituary for Dirk Pitt and

a tearful lunch with the two women in the book who had shared his love, Stacy Fox and Loren Smith. The final scene has Pitt in the deep-sea mining vehicle reappearing on the shores of a remote island in the South Pacific.

Sahara

Once again, Clive makes the stakes high with a tale set in Africa. In Sahara, published in 1992 in hardcover and July 1993 in paperback by Pocket Books, the menace is an environmental catastrophe that could wipe out all life in the ocean and perhaps even on land.

Clive begins the novel in the past. Near the end of the Civil War, a Confederate ironclad named the *Texas* leaves Richmond carrying part of the Confederate treasury and the kidnapped Union president, Abraham Lincoln. Next, we have a pioneer female aviator, Kitty Mannock, who crashes her plane in Africa. Her disappearance remains one of aviation's great mysteries.

Traveling to the current time, a tourist safari in Africa is attacked by villagers who we later learn have been exposed to chemicals in their water that make them mad. The entire group of tourists is killed and cannabalized. Pitt's love interest, Eva Rojas, is a scientist with the World Health Organization who is searching for the source of toxic poison in Africa. Pitt rescues her from an attempted rape and murder by killing the attackers.

Sandecker then assigns Pitt, Giordino and Gunn to find the source of the poisons. To aid them in their task, they are given the use of a high-tech boat named the *Calliope* and sent up the Niger River.

We learn that the villains of the novel, Yves Massarde, a French industrialist, and Zateb Kazim, an evil general and the true head of the country of Mali, are partners in a hazardous-waste treatment facility in the Sahara Desert. On the *Calliope,* Gunn escapes with the water samples to the airport in Mali, while Pitt and Giordino rig the *Calliope* to explode and swim to Massarde's houseboat, where they are captured.

Next, the UN World Health Organization scientists assigned to locate the poisons are captured and taken to a gold mine named Tebezza. At Tebezza, the gold is mined by convicts and slaves. Pitt and Giordino escape from Massarde's houseboat by stealing a helicopter, then ditching the helicopter in the Niger River near a town named Bourem. There they steal Kazim's classic car and take off into the desert.

Clive makes his appearance as a prospector named "The Kid," who is searching for the *Texas,* which he believes is hidden somewhere in the desert. After that, Pitt and Giordino make their way to Massarde's hazardous-waste facility, named Fort Foureau, where they are captured. After Massarde questions them, they are banished to Tebezza. They escape Tebezza, vowing to return and save the others, and set off across the desert on foot. Near death from dehydration, they stumble upon the wreckage of Mannock's plane and fashion a land yacht they ride until they are rescued by a truck driver who gives them a ride to the nearest town.

Returning with a special UN force, Pitt liberates Tebezza. Leaving Tebezza, Pitt and Giordino make their way to Fort Foureau and an old French Foreign

Legion outpost. There they fight off Massarde's security forces until Giordino returns with a U.S. Special Forces team. Kazim is killed in the fight. After Fort Foureau is secured, Massarde is staked out in the desert sun and in a fit of thirst consumes poisonous water. He later dies a horrible death. In the end, Pitt returns and leads a crash team to Mannock's plane. Then, along with Giordino and Perlmutter, Pitt locates the *Texas.* The novel ends with an explanation that the assassination of Lincoln was a hoax. Pitt travels to California to locate Eva Rojas and take her away for a romantic trip to Mexico.

Inca Gold

Another effort for Simon & Schuster, *Inca Gold* was introduced in hardcover in 1994 and paperback in March 1995. Starting with *Dragon,* the back book jackets of the hardcovers feature full-page four-color photographs of Clive with one of Pitt's cars. In the case of *Inca Gold,* the photograph is of Pitt's 1936 Pierce-Arrow with a matching Travelodge travel trailer.

Clive is still using the metric system of measurement, with most measurements converted to English in the novel.

The plot is different from most Pitt novels. Instead of an event that might affect the world, or Russian vs. American intrigue, we have a tale of artifact smuggling.

Starting with an Inca vessel burying a treasure in 1578 in an undisclosed location, Clive follows with a pirate chapter featuring Sir Francis Drake and a tsunami wave that carries a ship far inland.

Next, a university archaeological team is trapped in a limestone sinkhole. Pitt and Giordino appear to launch a rescue effort. They succeed in the rescue, but when the archaeologists, including Shannon Kelsey, one of Pitt's love interests, and Giordino are taken prisoners by rebels, Pitt is left to claw his way out.

Free from the sinkhole, Pitt finds the rotor blade of his helicopter shattered and sets off tracking the rebels and their prisoners on foot. After being taken to a stone fortress in the mountain by one of the villains, Tupac Amaru, the hostages are rescued by Pitt and escape in a helicopter owned by the rebels. Making its way out to sea with the idea of landing on a NUMA research ship offshore, Pitt's helicopter is attacked by a Peruvian military chopper which they fend off.

St. Julien Perlmutter has a large role in *Inca Gold.* He helps Pitt in his search to find Drake's vessel, as well as advising him on artifact smuggling.

The primary villains of the tale, the Zolar family, are introduced and their profiteering from stolen historical artifacts explored. Hiram Yaeger is featured, using the NUMA computer center to steer Pitt and Giordino to locating the *Conception,* the ship carried away in the tidal wave.

Using a helicopter-mounted magnetometer, Pitt is successful in finding the *Conception* and locating a box that contains the Drake Quipu, a series of ancient Inca records recorded on knotted ropes. Yaeger, using his computer, deciphers the Drake Quipu and discovers that the lost treasure of Huascar is probably buried in northern Mexico. The chase is on to locate the treasure before the Zolars.

As a cover for searching for the location of Huascar's treasure, Pitt and Loren Smith, Pitt's other love interest in the book, set off on a cross-country auto tour aboard Pitt's Pierce-Arrow. They stumble upon the Box Car Café, owned by a former prospector named Cussler. As usual, Pitt forgets the name when he tries to recall it.

Pitt and Giordino are pitted against the Zolars as they search for Huascar's treasure. They travel an underground river in a small Hovercraft to rescue Gunn and Smith. A tribe of Indians seeking the return of their ceremonial artifacts help Pitt dispatch the Zolars' men. In the end, the treasure is saved, and the river becomes a major benefit to the people living in the desert.

Inca Gold is a slight departure from the normal Cussler style. Instead of the dead-run pace of most of the Pitt novels, *Inca Gold* delves into history, and more of the book than usual is written as narrative.

Shock Wave

Shock Wave was published in hardcover by Simon & Schuster in 1996, with the Pocket Book paperback edition following in December of the same year. After the break in tension in *Inca Gold,* Clive returns with a tale of high stakes, with an evil mining family intent on destroying sea life and maybe the Hawaiian Islands.

Shock Wave begins with a ship of convicts lost in a storm. After fierce fighting and the need to abandon the ship on a small raft, few of the convicts and crew survive. The few who do set up a colony on a remote island they later find is littered with diamonds, forming the basis of a vast fortune.

In the current day, a group of tourists is visiting an island off Antarctica when a mysterious plague hits that kills land and sea animals and several of the tourists. Pitt's love interest, Maeve Fletcher, is one of the tourists' guides. Pitt arrives on the island by helicopter and helps the tourists to safety. He then saves their cruise ship from crashing into a rocky shoreline.

The evil Dorsett family is introduced—Deirdre and her rotten, evil sister Boudicca, led by their father, Arthur Dorsett. The only good person in the family is Maeve Fletcher, who uses her great-great-great-grandmother's last name. Perlmutter plays an important role, explaining the history of the Dorsett clan to Pitt.

Pitt, in an effort to trace the cause of marine-life deaths, travels to western Canada to inspect one of Dorsett's mines. He is introduced to a mining engineer named Cussler, who explains how sound waves are being used to mine diamonds. Cussler explains that the waves travel through water and converge on different locations, wreaking havoc. We now know the cause of the worldwide devastation.

Pitt, Giordino and Maeve hatch a plan to rescue her twin boys, who have been kidnapped by her father. Unfortunately, they are captured in New Zealand and taken aboard the Dorsett yacht, from which they are set adrift in a small, inflatable boat to die in the ocean. Luckily, they find the wreck of a sailboat on an island, fashion a larger wind-powered craft and make their way toward civilization.

We learn that the acoustic waves created by Dorsett's operation will converge on Hawaii and wipe it off the map if they are not stopped. Meanwhile, Arthur Dorsett is out to corner the market in colored stones. He plans to flood the market with diamonds to drive the price down to almost nothing, making colored stones more valuable.

A plan is developed to reflect Dorsett's acoustic waves. A giant parabolic dish will be lowered in the ocean from the deck of the Howard Hughes-designed ship *Glomar Explorer.* Still at sea in their fabricated craft, Pitt, Giordino and Fletcher finally reach Gladiator Island, home of the Dorsett clan.

The plan to divert the acoustic waves is successful, but the reflection sends the sound beam directly at Gladiator Island. Sandecker warns Pitt, but he doesn't have time to escape. When the wave hits, the volcanoes erupt in a firestorm of ash and lava. Pitt kills Arthur and Deirdre Dorsett, while Giordino eliminates Boudicca. In a plot twist Clive has used before, we learn Boudicca is actually a man dressed and living as a woman.

Giordino escapes by helicopter with Maeve's twin sons, but with no more room on the helicopter, Pitt and Maeve are forced to flee in the Dorsett yacht. During a shower of lava and ash, Pitt manages to steer the yacht into the ocean, but not before Maeve dies in his arms. Loren Smith shows up at Pitt's apartment after he is rescued, but Dirk asks her just to leave him alone.

Flood Tide

The fourteenth Dirk Pitt novel was published in hardcover in 1997 by Simon & Schuster and one can safely assume in paperback by Pocket Books in 1998. *Flood Tide* follows Cussler tradition and begins in the past.

A Chinese cargo ship loaded with priceless artwork sails into an intense storm that sinks her. Only two people survive, and they wash up on an unknown shore.

We next meet an Immigration and Naturalization officer, Julia Lee, who serves as Pitt's love interest. Lee is aboard a Chinese cargo ship loaded with illegal immigrants seeking a new life in the United States. Sentenced to die, she is sent to a lake in Washington State, where those too sick to become slaves are killed.

Pitt arrives on a vacation in Washington, attempting to recuperate from the thrashing he suffered in *Shock Wave.* Curious about strange affairs on the lake, he investigates the home of a rich industrialist named Qin Shang. Videotaping the bottom of the lake, he finds it littered with dead bodies and determines that Shang's lake retreat is nothing more than a human smuggling operation.

Rescuing a group of immigrants who are sentenced to die in the lake, he helps them escape in an old Cris-Craft boat while being pursued by Shang's security guards. We learn that Shang's operation is the front for a Chinese-government-approved plan to reduce population. And we learn that the S.S. *United States,* a powerful cruise ship retired in the early 1960s, is being refitted in a shipyard near Hong Kong. In addition, Shang has built a huge cargo port named Sungari in a bayou in Louisiana.

Pitt and Giordino are ordered to search the S.S. *United States,* and they enlist the help of a covert corporation manned by ex-intelligence operatives. After examining the cruise ship, they are attacked by a Chinese destroyer and manage to sink the aggressor.

Pitt returns home, and upon entering his aircraft hangar/home, he is attacked by assassins hired by Shang. He manages to kill the attackers. Later, with Lee as his escort, he attends a party hosted by Shang in Maryland. After visiting Perlmutter, Pitt and Lee are again chased by assassins, and he escapes in his 1929 Duesenberg.

Next, Pitt decides to investigate Sungari with Giordino. We learn that the S.S. *United States* will be traveling up the Mississippi River, where it will be moored at New Orleans to be used as a floating casino. NUMA now decides that Sungari is part of Shang's plan to divert the Mississippi River into the Atchafalaya River by blowing a bridge atop the Mississippi's levee and channeling the water into a canal he has built. Shang's plan is to have the S.S. *United States* bury her hull crossways in the river to form a dam.

The S.S. *United States* is attacked by National Guard forces lining the river but continues upstream. Pitt and Giordino land on the ship from hang gliders. The explosives ignite and start the flood, but Pitt manages to take control of the S.S. *United States* and drives the ship into the levee to plug the opening.

Pitt next decides to locate the Chinese cargo ship that was lost at the start of the novel. Perlmutter determines the ship sank in Lake Michigan. Finding the survivors from the wreck, Pitt pinpoints the area and then mounts a salvage operation and removes the priceless artwork. Pitt has asked Perlmutter to leak a report to Shang that the wreck has been found. When Shang finds out, he races to Lake Michigan with the hopes of recovering the already-salvaged treasures himself. In a fight on the ocean bottom, Pitt kills Shang. At the end, the treasure is displayed in a museum.

Nonfiction

The Sea Hunters

In 1996, Clive branched out in nonfiction with *The Sea Hunters.* Published by Simon & Schuster in hardcover and followed in 1997 by a Pocket Books paperback, the book was an unexpected success. It reached number five on the *New York Times* best-seller list in hardcover, and the introduction of the paperback saw the book rise to number one on the *Times* list, giving Clive his first time at the top slot.

Cowritten with Craig Dirgo, the book details the exploits of Clive's nonprofit foundation NUMA, which is named after the organization in the Pitt novels. When the idea for a book about shipwrecks was presented to Simon & Schuster, the publisher was less than enthralled. Peter Lampack, Clive's agent, distinctly remembers one editor glancing out the window during the presentation as if he was distracted—and totally disinterested.

Knowing that most historical books are about as interesting to read as the back of a cereal box, the authors set out to create a book with accurate historical facts that read like a novel. The history of the ships and their battles remained true to the facts but was enhanced with dialogue. The actual search for the vessel was written by Clive in first person to give the reader an insight into the process that goes on when a NUMA search is launched.

An excellent introduction gives the reader insight into Clive and his history as well as the formation of NUMA and its role in historic marine search and discovery.

The book features nine of the searches NUMA has undertaken. Beginning with the steamship *Lexington,* which burned and sank in Long Island Sound, the events surrounding the disaster are explored and the aftermath chronicled.

The Republic of Texas Navy ship *Zavala* is featured next, followed by a chapter about the U.S.S. *Cumberland* and the Confederate raider C.S.S. *Florida.* The fourth section details the strange life of the C.S.S. *Arkansas,* a Confederate ironclad whose career was short but exciting. Featured next is the U.S.S. *Carondelet,* a Union ironclad built for the war to control western rivers.

Section Six chronicles the interesting tale of the C.S.S. *Hunley,* the first submarine to sink a ship in battle. The chapter proved popular with readers, many of whom were unaware that submarines had even been used in the Civil War.

In a change of pace, Section Seven is about a disaster and a search that take place on land. "The Lost Locomotive of Kiowa Creek" is about a train that plunged into a river in a flood, and the search to find the truth about what happened to the locomotive took more turns than a mountain road.

For Section Eight, the book travels to Europe and chronicles wrecks from World War I in an expedition that NUMA launched in 1984. Section Nine is the tale of an event from World War II largely ignored by history. The tragedy of the sinking of the *Leopoldville* and the subsequent rescue efforts could be a book in itself.

Featuring a middle section of photographs and richly drawn maps along with a listing of ships NUMA has located over the years, *The Sea Hunters* gives the Cussler fan both insight into the man behind Dirk Pitt and a rich appreciation for the old adage that sometimes truth is stranger than fiction.

A Concordance of Dirk Pitt Novels

The Continuing Characters

Cussler, Clive. Author-adventurer who frequently turns up in the Pitt adventures. A big man with graying hair, a white beard and blue-green eyes. Races Pitt at the Richmond old car races in *Dragon.* In *Sahara,* he's a prospector searching for a Confederate shipwreck in the Sahara Desert. He stands the same height as Pitt but is more heavy than thin. In *Inca Gold,* he's the owner of the Box Car Café and described as a tall man in his early sixties, with gray hair and a white beard; he bought the café when he gave up prospecting. In *Shock Wave,* he's the mine engineer and chief foreman at the Dorsett mine on Kunghit Island who helps explain the inner workings of the mine to Pitt. In *Shock Wave,* he's the successful owner of fishing boats who loans Pitt and Giordino a houseboat.

Giordino, Albert Cassius. Attended elementary school with Dirk Pitt and has known him since kindergarten. Attended high school with Pitt and played tackle on the high school football team. Attended the United States Air Force Academy. Attended flight school with Dirk Pitt. Served two tours in Vietnam. Still holds the rank of captain in the Air Force. Joined NUMA along with Pitt at the request of Admiral James Sandecker. Lives in a recently purchased condominium in Alexandria, Virginia, where none of the furniture or decor matches. Five feet four inches in height, weight one hundred seventy-five pounds. Of Italian ancestry, he has dark curly hair, a nose that hints at his Roman heritage and dark, swarthy skin on a round face. Has a barrel chest and muscular build. Usually has a Faganlike grin on his face. His eyes are a twinkling walnut color. He is missing the little finger on his right hand after he jammed it in the barrel of a gun that was fired by Delphi Moran. He has been shot more times than an Arizona highway sign. His body shows the effects of numerous abrasions, contusions and broken bones. Assistant special projects director of the National Underwater and Marine Agency. His hobby is stealing Admiral Sandecker's custom-made cigars.

Gunn, Rudi. Childhood nickname: "Beaver Eyes." A graduate of the U.S. Naval Academy, first in his class. Formerly held the rank of commander in the United States Navy. Joined NUMA at the same time as Pitt and Giordino. Former titles include director of logistics for the National Underwater and Marine Agency and overseer of NUMA's oceanographic projects. Was skipper of the NUMA research vessel *First Attempt* in *The Mediterranean Caper.* In *Raise the* Titanic! he was captain of the submersible *Sappho I.* Current title is deputy director of the National Underwater and Marine Agency. Nominated for Nobel Peace Prize for his work in Sahara but did not win. Has a thinning hairline and wears thick horn-rimmed glasses. Has a Roman nose. Short and thin with narrow shoulders and matching hips. Wears a Timex watch. Second in command of NUMA under Sandecker.

Hunt, Leigh. Clive's friend in real life but turns up frequently in Pitt adventures in a variety of disguises. In *Treasure,* he's a reporter with the BBC. In Sahara, he's the chief pilot of the *Texas.* In *Inca Gold,* he's an engineer searching for oil who locates a vast underwater river in a cave in the Castle Dome Mountains. In *Shock Wave,* he's a colonel at Walter Reed Medical Center who performs the autopsies on people killed by the acoustic waves. In *Flood Tide,* he's the captain of the *Princess Dou Wan.*

Kamil, Hali. Secretary-general of the United Nations. Described as a tall, attractive woman with a smooth brown face and compelling coal-black eyes. Has a long-stemmed neck, delicate features and haunting looks. In *Treasure,* she is age forty-two and has a tawny complexion and long jet-black hair that falls down to her shoulders. Stands five feet eleven inches tall in heels. Never married. Her father was a filmmaker, her mother a teacher. A gourmet cook with a Ph.D. in Egyptian antiquities, she landed one of the few jobs open to Muslim women, as a researcher with the Ministry of Culture. Worked her way up to director of antiquities and later head of the Department of Information. She caught the eye of then-President

Mubarek, who asked her to serve on the Egyptian delegation to the United Nations General Assembly. Five years later, Kamil was vice chairman when Javier Perez de Cuellar stepped down. Because the men ahead of her in line refused the job, she was appointed to serve as secretary-general in the tenuous hope she might mend the widening cracks in the organization.

Mercier, Allan. U.S. national security advisor. A plump, balding character with a Falstaff face that masks a shrewd analytical mind. Wears ever-rumpled bargain-priced suits with white linen handkerchiefs sloppily stuffed in the breast pocket. Wears Ben Franklin spectacles.

Milligan, Lieutenant Commander Heidi. U.S. Navy lieutenant commander assigned to the Norfolk Navy Yard. Has eleven years to go before retirement as of *Vixen 03.* Attended Wellesley College. No children, as she had a hysterectomy. Had affairs with Admiral Bass, with Pitt and with Shaw in *Night Probe!* Described as almost as tall as Pitt when she is wearing riding boots. Looks to be in her early thirties, and her skin shows no sign of a summer tan. In *Night Probe!* she is said to have graduated fourteenth in her class at Annapolis. Described as having a svelte body measuring six feet from manicured toenails to the roots of her naturally ash-blond hair. Has Castilian brown eyes, the right eye having an imperfection at the bottom of the iris, a small pie-shaped splash of gray. Working on a doctorate at Princeton University.

Oates, Douglas. U.S. secretary of state. Has neatly trimmed slate-colored hair and brown eyes.

Perlmutter, St. Julien. Close family friend of the Pitt family. Has a fifty-million-dollar inheritance. Lives on a Street in the Georgetown section of Washington, D.C. One of the world's foremost authorities on shipwrecks and owner of one of the world's finest maritime libraries. A gourmand and bon vivant who has a four-thousand-bottle wine cellar. Weighs over four hundred pounds but is remarkably solid for a huge man. Has gray hair and gray beard, a crimson face with tulip nose and sky-blue eyes. His car is a chauffeur-driven 1955 Rolls-Royce Silver Dawn with coachwork by Hooper & Company. The automobile is painted silver and green and features a straight-six engine with overhead valves.

Pitt, Dirk Eric. Born at Hoag Hospital, Newport Beach, California, to Senator George and Barbara (Nash) Pitt. According to his family tree, his paternal ancestors were Gypsies who migrated from Spain to England in the seventeenth century. Great-grandfather was a steam locomotive engineer on the Santa Fe Railroad. Has an uncle who is one of San Francisco's leading bon vivants. Another uncle on his mother's side is Percy Nash, one of the scientists who worked on the Manhattan Project. Pitt's grandfather acquired a small fortune developing Southern California real estate. On his death, he left his grandson a considerable inheritance. After paying the estate tax, Pitt chose to invest the money in classic cars and aircraft rather than stocks and bonds. Lives at 266 Airport Place, Washington, D.C. 20001, on the grounds of Washington International Airport. Best friend is Al Giordino, whom Pitt met when the two got into a fistfight in elementary school. Was quarterback on his high school football team. Graduated thirty-fifth in his class at the U.S. Air Force Academy. While at the Air Force Academy, he was on the football team and fencing squad. Attended flight school with Al Giordino. Served ten years' active duty in the Air Force, attaining the rank of major and in the year 2000 promoted to lieutenant colonel. Served two tours in the last years of the Vietnam War. Awarded Distinguished Flying Cross with two clusters, a Silver Heart and a Purple Heart. Received a commendation for shooting down U.S. Navy Admiral James Sandecker's plane over the Sea of China to prevent him from landing at an enemy-occupied airfield. Awarded Hero of the Revolution award by Fidel Castro. Formerly surface security officer for the National Underwater and Marine Agency, he is currently the special projects director. Height six feet three inches, weight one hundred eighty-five pounds. Has black hair tending to be a bit wavy, with no indication of gray. Eyebrows dark and bushy. Straight, narrow nose, lips firm with the corners turned up in a slight but fixed grin. Skin darkened by year-round exposure to the sun. Has opaline green eyes that are set wide with a clear glimpse of the white around the iris. Far from movie-star handsome, he has a craggy face that the opposite sex finds strangely attractive. Body covered with various scars and injuries. Walks with a loose grace that is impossible for most men. Wore an Omega watch early on but now is known for wearing an orange-face Doxa dive watch. Quit smoking years ago. Changed from Cutty Sark to Bombay Gin to Sauza Commemorativo tequila over the years but also enjoys a glass of fine wine and an occasional beer. Main exercise is scuba diving. His favorite pastime is restoring and showing antique and classic cars. Astrological sign: Cancer. Chinese sign: born in the Year of the Rat.

Pitt, George. Served in World War II, then worked his way through law school selling cars. Dirk Pitt's father and senior senator from California. Elected to the Senate the same year as the president in *Deep Six.* Head of the Naval Appropriations Committee. Heads up the Senate Committee for Oil Exploration on Government Lands. Heads the Senate Foreign Relations Committee. Known as the Socrates of the Senate. In *Vixen 03,* he tells Daggat he plans to retire next year but changes his mind. Married to the former Barbara Nash, who was named Susan in *Dragon.* Lives in a colonial home on Massachusetts Avenue in Washington, D.C. Owns a ski chalet in Breckenridge, Colorado. Known for wearing expensive suits with a California golden poppy in the lapel.

Pochinsky, Zerri. Secretary to Dirk Pitt. A lively type, with a contagious smile and hazel eyes. Thirty years old at the time of *Night Probe!* she has never married. Full-bodied with long, fawn-colored hair that falls below her shoulders. Pitt has considered having an affair with her, but he doesn't believe in messing around with his staff.

Sandecker, Admiral James. Graduated U.S. Naval Academy Class of 1939. Made flag rank in the Navy before age fifty. Once served on the U.S.S. *Iowa.* Last command was the Navy guided-missile cruiser *Tucson.* In *Night Probe!* he is listed as age sixty-one. Lives in a condominium at the Watergate in Washington, D.C., six miles from the NUMA headquarters. Height is a few inches over five feet. Has a thick head of red hair that shows little indication of white. Has a precisely trimmed red Van Dyke beard. Has cold, authoritative blue eyes. Sleeps only four hours a night. Long divorced, he has a daughter and three grandchildren who live in Hong Kong. A vegetarian and health nut, he jogs and lifts weights. Takes numerous vitamins including garlic pills every day. Smokes ten custom-made cigars a day. Likes to dine at the Army and Navy Club. Also a member of the John Paul Jones Club. Has an old Navy double-ender whale boat he cruises on Sundays on the Potomac River for relaxation. After retiring from the Navy, he was made the chief director of the National Underwater and Marine Agency by then-President Ford. When he began at NUMA, it was an insignificant eighty-person agency. He built NUMA into a massive organization of five thousand scientists and employees with an annual budget that exceeds four hundred million dollars.

Smith, Loren. Congresswoman from Colorado's Seventh District, the district west of the Continental Divide. Her family has ranched the western slope of Colorado since the 1870s. Educated at the University of Colorado. Height is five feet eight inches. Age at the time of *Deep Six* is thirty-seven. She has cinnamon-colored hair cut long to frame her prominent cheekbones. Violet-colored eyes. Never married. Chest measurement is 34-B. At the time of *Inca Gold,* she is a five-term congresswoman. Lives in a townhouse in Alexandria, Virginia. Owns a cat named Ichabod. Dates Dirk Pitt, whom she met at a lawn party given by the secretary of the environment ten years ago.

Wolff, Julie. Admiral Sandecker's personal secretary in the later books.

Yaeger, Hiram. Nicknamed Pinocchio because he always sticks his nose in where it doesn't belong via his computer. Decorated three-tour Vietnam veteran who served with the U.S. Navy SEALs. Lured from California's Silicon Valley by Sandecker to head NUMA's vast computer network that includes a catalog of all known shipwrecks worldwide. Works on the tenth floor of NUMA Headquarters. Formerly lived on a farm in Sharpsburg, Maryland; he now resides in a fashionable residential section of Maryland. Has a wife who is an artist and two pretty, smart teenage daughters who attend private school. Had a 1989 Ford Taurus station wagon but now drives a nonproduction BMW. Traditionally wears Levi's and a Levi's jacket along with scruffy cowboy boots. Has graying long blond hair he wears tied back in a ponytail that frames a boyish face. Has a scraggly beard he sometimes braids. Wears granny glasses.

The World of NUMA

Andrews Air Force Base. Air Force base near Washington, D.C.

Central Intelligence Agency. U.S. intelligence agency located in Langley, Virginia, on a 219-acre site. The headquarters building is a sprawling gray marble and concrete structure. A statue of Nathan Hale stands outside the entrance.

Dulles Airport. Commercial airport in Washington, D.C.

Environmental Protection Agency. The EPA is the U.S. governmental agency that handles issues related to the environment.

Federal Bureau of Investigation. The FBI is an anticrime force that operates under the umbrella of the Department of Justice. The headquarters of the FBI are at Pennsylvania Avenue and Tenth Street in Washington, D.C.

GRU. Acronym standing for Glavnoye Razvedyvatelnoye Upravleniye. Chief intelligence directorate of the Soviet general staff. Best described as the Soviet military intelligence agency.

INTERPOL. An international police agency.

KGB. Soviet intelligence agency, also known as the Committee for State Security.

National Security Agency. U.S. intelligence agency that often works with NUMA. Based at Fort Meade, Maryland, the NSA specializes in cipher development and cracking as well as electronic eavesdropping and satellite communications and detection. Operates under the Department of Defense.

National Security Council. Advisors to the president of the United States.

NUMA Headquarters. A thirty-story tubular structure sheeted in green reflective glass that sits on an East

Washington hill above the Potomac River. Admiral Sandecker's office is on the top floor and features an immense desk made from the refinished hatch cover salvaged from a Confederate blockade runner that was sunk in Albemarle Sound. On his desk is a humidor from which Giordino allegedly steals cigars. The office is equipped with a holographic television camera so Sandecker can view the people he is talking to in 3-D splendor. The twelfth floor is an immense equipment-laden area covering fifteen thousand square feet manned by forty-five engineers and technicians who monitor the six NUMA satellites circling the globe. The tenth floor has the glass-enclosed computer center run by Hiram Yaeger. The fourth floor has the NUMA boardroom featuring a three-meter-long conference table built from a section of a wooden hull salvaged from a schooner that sank to the bottom of Lake Erie, along with thick turquoise carpeting and a fireplace with a Victorian mantelpiece. The walls are paneled in satiny teak, and there are paintings of U.S. naval actions in ornate frames. The fourth floor also has Pitt's and Giordino's offices. The lobby is an atrium surrounded by waterfalls and aquariums filled with exotic sea life. A huge globe rises from the center of the sea-green marble floor, contoured with the geological furrows and ridges of every sea, large lake and river on earth. The building has an underground parking garage.

Pitt's home. The address of Pitt's aircraft hangar/home is 266 Airport Place, Washington, D.C. 20001. The hangar is on a little-used runway at Washington International Airport and was built in 1936. Formerly housing an air carrier that was absorbed by American

Airlines, the building was scheduled for demolition in 1980. Pitt bought the building, restored the inside, then had it placed on the National Register of Historic Landmarks. From outside, the hangar appears deserted—weeds surround the building, and the corrugated walls are weathered and devoid of paint. The appearance is merely a ruse. The hangar has the latest in security measures, including an alarm system Pitt deactivates by the use of a small transmitter carried in his pocket. Outside, remote cameras film guests arriving and alert Pitt to any danger. The hangar floor is polished concrete and houses Pitt's transportation collection. Nearly fifty cars cover the ten thousand square feet, including a Hispano-Suiza, a Mercedes-Benz 540K, a Marmon town car, a beautiful blue Talbot-Lago, a Cord L-29, a Pierce-Arrow town car with matching Travelodge travel trailer, a stunning turquoise-green Stutz town car, along with a pair of Rolls-Royces, a big Daimler convertible, a Bugatti, an Isotta-Fraschini, a Delahaye, an AC Cobra, a Maybach-Zeppelin town car, a Renault Open-Drive Landaulette, a Jensen four-door convertible, an Avions-Voisin, an Allard J2X and the first car in Pitt's collection, a 1946 Ford Club Coupe. Pitt often drives his 1984 Jeep Grand Wagoneer that features a 500-horsepower Rodeck engine taken from a wrecked dragster. Other artifacts include a Ford Trimotor Tin Goose airplane, a Messerschmitt 262 Swallow, a Pullman Railroad car *The Manhattan Limited,* an old cast-iron bathtub with an outboard motor attached and a weird-looking inflatable raft with sails and a carved Haida Indian totem pole. At the far end of the garage is an ornate wrought-iron spiral staircase and a cargo elevator. The door at the top leads to a living room-study filled with shelves stacked with books about the sea along with glass-encased models of ships Pitt discovered while working with NUMA. A trophy case holds football and fencing trophies. Copper diver's helmets, mariner's compasses and wooden helm pieces share space with ships' bells and old nails and bottles from shipwrecks Pitt has excavated. A door to one side of the study leads into a large bedroom decorated like a sailing ship's captain's cabin, complete with a huge wheel as a backboard for the bed. The opposite end of the living room opens into a kitchen and dining room.

Politburo. The primary decision makers for the Soviet Communist Party.

SEALs. Elite U.S. Navy Special Forces group. The acronym stands for Sea, Air and Land.

Secret Service. Division of the U.S. Treasury Department. Handles anticounterfeiting, presidential protection and other duties.

United States Customs Service. Works to stop smuggling of illegal goods.

Washington National Airport. Location of Pitt's aircraft hangar/home.

Pacific Vortex

AC Cobra. The car Pitt drives in *Pacific Vortex.* Built in England, they featured Ford 289-cubic-inch and 427-cubic-inch engines.

Andrei Vyborg. A Russian spy ship posing as an oceanographic vessel. Follows the 101st Salvage Fleet when they attempt to locate the *Starbuck.*

Bluefin. U.S. Navy ship. Disappeared but was eventually located near seamount.

Boland, Lieutenant Commander Paul. Tall and blond. Resembles John F. Kennedy. Wounded by the men who board the *Martha Ann.*

Bounty. The ship made famous in *Mutiny on the Bounty.* The ship was later burned at Pitcairn Island. Mentioned in prologue.

Buckmaster, Lieutenant Robert M. The marine leader of the fierce attack on the radio transmitter located on Maui. The transmitter was thought to be lightly guarded, but Pisces Metal Company had sold it to the Russians.

Carter, Lieutenant. Crewman on the submarine *Starbuck.* Mentioned in Dupree's log recovered by Pitt.

Cayment Trench. Located off Cuba, site where NUMA detected a mysterious underwater object. (*See:* Kurile Trench.)

Chrysler, Dr. Elmer. Chief of research for Tripler Hospital. A short little man with a completely shaven head. Has brown eyes behind horn-rimmed glasses.

Cinana, Captain Orl. The officer in charge of Admiral Hunter's salvage fleet. Heavyset. Killed by intruders while in bed with Adrian Hunter. Was secretly cooperating with Delphi Moran.

Colt .44. Pistol used when Delphi attempts to fire at Pitt. Giordino jams his little finger into the barrel. When Delphi fires, it backfires and blows the side of his face off.

Crowhaven, Lieutenant Commander Samuel. An engineering officer on a submarine, he is drafted to lead the divers on the rescue effort. Described as blond with Scandinavian features. He brings the *Starbuck* to the surface.

Danzig, Corporal. Spad leader attacking the radio transmitter.

Denver, Commander Burdette. Described as short, almost gnomelike. Aide to Admiral Hunter.

DG-10. The poison that was in the syringe Pitt took from Summer Moran. Extremely difficult to detect, it makes a body have the appearance of a heart seizure.

Dodge truck, gray. The vehicle that was carrying the man who fired at Pitt after he left the museum. The man was later impaled on a spike on a telephone pole.

Douglas C-54. The four-engine plane flown by Pitt and Giordino to the seamount to launch the rescue effort.

Dupree, Commander Felix. Commanding officer of the U.S. nuclear submarine *Starbuck.* He has served twenty years at sea, fourteen of those in submarines.

His classmates at Annapolis nicknamed him "The Data Bank."

Explorer. Listed as the first ship lost in the Pacific Vortex. The *Explorer* was under charter to the Pisces Metal Company when Lavella and Roblemann disappeared.

F-4. A U.S. Navy submarine that sank in sixty fathoms off the entrance of Pearl Harbor. In 1915, it was successfully raised.

Farris, Seaman First Class. Crewman on the submarine *Starbuck,* mentioned in Dupree's log that was recovered by Pitt. Later discovered still alive on board the *Starbuck.*

FHX. A new long-range helicopter that Pitt is certified to fly. NUMA loans the helicopter and Pitt to the 101st Salvage Fleet.

Fujima, Henry. A fourth-generation Japanese-Hawaiian fisherman. His fishing boat is cut in half by the *Martha Ann* as it returns to base guided by control computers.

Fullerton Fracture Zone. The area where the Pacific Vortex is located.

Harper, Lieutenant. The engine-room officer on the *Martha Ann.* Weighs over two hundred fifty pounds.

Hunter, Adrian. Daughter of Admiral Hunter. Has long black hair. Her skin is the tone of polished bronze. A tramp, she is the only woman Pitt cannot satisfy.

Hunter, Admiral Leigh. Admiral in charge of the 101st Salvage Fleet. Tall and wizened. His hair is bushy and white. Has a cadaverous face.

Hyperion missiles. Nuclear missiles carried on board the *Starbuck.*

Iolani Palace. The only royal palace on American soil. Was the building that housed the Hawaii 5-O offices. Mentioned by George Papaaloa.

Ishiyo Maru. Japanese oil tanker of 8,106 tons. Reported missing in the Pacific Vortex September 14, 1964. The second sunken vessel spotted by the *Martha Ann.*

Kaena Point, Hawaii. The point in the Kauai Channel off Oahu. The spot where Pitt was sunning when he spotted the yellow communications capsule.

Kamehameha. Also known as Kamehameha the Great. King of Hawaii. Pitt is helping George Papaaloa from the museum try to locate his grave.

Kanoli. A mythical island to the north of Hawaii. Described as a barren island with few coconuts or palm trees. Also lacks streams of cold clear water. Settlers tamed the land over several generations, then proclaimed themselves gods. The natives of Kanoli then raided Kauai, Oahu, Hawaii and other islands in the Hawaiian chain.

Kurile Trench. The area off Japan where NUMA scientists detected a vessel moving underwater at very high speed and a great depth. Estimates placed the object moving one hundred ten miles an hour at nineteen thousand feet deep.

Lavella. A physicist who specialized in hydrology.

Lillie Marlene. A mysterious ship that was discovered adrift in the Pacific Vortex. A former British torpedo boat converted to luxury yacht. Owned by Herbert Verhusson, a nationally recognized film producer. On July 13, 1968, it radioed a distress call to the Coast Guard saying that it was being attacked by men who came out of the mist.

March, Lieutenant. The *Martha Ann*'s navigation officer. He served four years in nuclear submarines and is an accomplished Scuba diver. Was murdered on the *Starbuck.*

Martha Ann. The 101st Salvage Fleet's top search and salvage vessel. The ship is modern but designed to look very old. It has the superstructure of an older ship—a square boxlike shape to the superstructure and an old-fashioned vertical smokestack. Painted black with the usual red waterline; the paint used is a special compound that appears to be rusted. On the stern is painted "*Martha Ann*—SEATTLE." It sails with a small crew as the ship is completely computerized and controlled automatically.

Mauser. Model 712 Schnell Fueur Pistole serial number 47405. Fifty-round clip. Has the ability to fire single shot or automatic. Pitt's choice of protection when he goes for a drive in the AC Cobra.

Metford, Seaman. Crewman on the submarine *Starbuck*, mentioned in Dupree's log that was recovered by Pitt.

Moana Valley Lookout. A scenic lookout near the scene of the accident with the gray Dodge truck.

Monitor. The ship that launches a Hyperion missile at the seamount in the Pacific Vortex. Named after the famous Civil War ironclad.

Moran, Delphi. Described as six feet eight inches tall. Has blazing golden eyes. His face is long and gaunt and framed by a heavy layer of unkempt silver hair.

Moran, Dr. Frederick. Father of Delphi and grandfather of Summer. Called "The Oracle of Psychic Unity." Described as a giant with yellow eyes. Was one of the United States' great classical anthropologists.

Moran, Summer. The most exotic woman Pitt has ever seen. She possesses eyes so gray, they defy reality, and her hair falls in an enchanting cascade of red, presenting a vibrant contrast against the green Oriental sheath dress that adheres to her curvaceous body. Granddaughter of Frederick Moran, daughter of Delphi Moran.

New Century. A ship salvaged by the 101st Salvage Fleet off Libya.

Oceanic Star. A Liberian freighter of 5,135 tons carrying a cargo of rubber and farm machinery. Was reported missing in the Pacific Vortex June 14, 1949. The first sunken vessel that the *Martha Ann* spotted.

Pants, Avery Anson. Singer of "The Great Bikini Rip-off," number twelve on the charts. A song played by Aloha Willie on radio station POPO.

Papaaloa, George. Museum curator at the Bernice Pauahi Bishop Museum of Polynesian Ethnology and Natural History. Described as tall with white hair. Has a wide brown face, jutting chin, large lips and misty brown eyes.

Pisces Metal Company. The company that was chartering the *Explorer* when Lavella and Roblemann disappeared in the Pacific Vortex. Also the company that owned the radio-transmitting facility on a remote corner of Maui that was used to disrupt radio distress calls.

Pisces Pacific Corporation. Parent company of Pisces Metal Company.

Plumeria. A plant that grows in Hawaii with a beautiful fragrance. Pitt also notices it is the scent that Summer wears.

Riley, Lieutenant. The officer Paul Boland orders to issue the crew of the *Martha Ann* sidearms after the fog begins to cover the ship.

Roblemann. A renowned surgeon who was experimenting with a mechanical gill system so humans would be able to absorb oxygen from water.

Romando Region. A region in the Pacific southeast of Japan where ships disappear. Could be compared to the Bermuda Triangle.

San Gabriel. The first ship to appear in response to the *Lillie Marlene*'s Mayday call. After sending a boarding party to the *Lillie Marlene,* they find the crew dead and their bodies turned green, their faces melted away. When the *San Gabriel* attempts to tow the *Lillie Marlene,* the ship explodes with a huge blast and sinks.

Scopolamine. Also referred to as truth serum. The liquid that was in the syringe Summer tried to inject into Pitt.

Scorpion. U.S. Navy ship. Mysteriously disappeared but was eventually located.

Selco-Ramsey 8300. The computer system that runs the *Martha Ann.*

Selma Snoop. A small, blue, watertight, battery-operated, direction-device. It helps navigate the Douglas C-54 to the seamount for the rescue.

Southwind. A ship salvaged in the Black Sea by the 101st Salvage Fleet.

Sphyrna levini. Latin name for the hammerhead shark.

Stanley, Lieutenant. The Detection Room officer on the *Martha Ann.* Killed by the boarding party from the seamount.

Starbuck. U.S. nuclear submarine. Built in San Francisco, the vessel features a computer-designed pressure hull. Capable of cruising at one hundred twenty-five knots at two thousand feet below the surface. Total crew of sixty-three.

Tari Maru. A ship salvaged off China by the 101st Salvage Fleet.

Thresher. U.S. Navy submarine. Mysteriously disappeared but was eventually located.

Tripler Military Hospital. The location where Pitt lands the FHX helicopter with the survivors of the attack on the *Martha Ann.* Described as a great concrete edifice perched on a hill overlooking the south coast of Oahu.

Verhusson, Herbert. Nationally recognized film producer and owner of the *Lillie Marlene,* a ship discovered adrift in the Pacific Vortex.

Vortex, Pacific. An area off Hawaii similar to the Bermuda Triangle where ships disappear with regularity. Thirty-eight ships are reported missing in the area. Described as a circular area north of the Hawaiian Islands.

Waikiki Beach, Hawaii. The beach Pitt and Summer Moran walk on when they first meet. Also where Summer attacks Pitt. Pitt prevails and takes Summer hostage, holding her in his hotel room. She escapes through the window.

Willie, Aloha. Late-night disc jockey on radio station

POPO. Relays the riddle to Admiral Hunter that comes over his frequency.

Yeager, Seaman G. Admiral Hunter's aide. Thinks Pitt is crazy after he shows up at the admiral's office dressed only in a bathing suit.

York, Dr. Raymond. Head of the Marine Geology Department for the Eton School of Oceanography. Described as big, over six feet tall and wide in the shoulders. Has perfectly spaced teeth and large hands.

The Mediterranean Caper

Admiral DeFosse. French ironclad ship sunk in 1872 near Thasos.

Albatros D-3. German-made World War I biwing airplane. A single-seater with a rigid spoked-wheel landing gear, a wooden propeller and fabric-covered wings. Powered by a single in-line engine. Painted bright yellow with black Maltese crosses on the wings and fuselage. In the German Imperial Air Service from 1916 to 1918.

Allen Dive Bright. An aluminum-cased dive light waterproof to a nine-hundred-foot depth. Pitt and Giordino use it to illuminate the labyrinth so they can investigate.

Alopecia areata. A skin disease that causes complete baldness. The real Bruno von Till suffered from this disease.

Athena. The donkey Pitt rode to town after escaping the labyrinth.

Brady Air Force Base. The U.S. Air Force base in Greece where much of *The Mediterranean Caper* takes place.

Brown's Nautical Almanac. The book of charts Pitt locates in the chart room of the *Queen Artemisia.*

C-133 Cargomaster. The U.S. Air Force cargo planes stationed at Brady Field.

Clara G. British collier sunk in 1856 near Thasos.

Clisenti automatic pistol. The weapon carried by Colonel Zeno.

Coelacanth. A fish thought to be extinct over seventy million years until one was found off the coast of East Africa.

***Confident,* H.M.S.** British ship famous for keel-hulling one of its crew after he was caught stealing a cup of brandy from the captain's cabin.

Dana Gail. An old tramp steamer that Gunn remembers Pitt using to locate the mysterious seamount in *Pacific Vortex.* Interesting, because if you read *Pacific Vortex,* that is *not* the name of the ship Pitt is aboard.

Daphne. British gunboat sunk off Thasos.

Darius, Captain. Member of the Greek Gendarmerie and Colonel Zeno's partner. Described as two inches taller than Pitt and looking like a chiseled stone colossus. Pitt estimates he must weigh at least 260 pounds. His face is misproportioned and strikingly repulsive. He actually is working for Bruno von Till and shoots Pitt in the thigh in the underwater cave. Executed by Colonel Zeno.

Dragonet fish. A vivid blue and yellow scaleless fish spotted by the divers as they swim toward the underwater cave.

Ea, Delphi. Mentioned briefly on page 186. We seem to have caught Clive on this one. When *Pacific Vortex* was finally published, he had changed the name to Delphi Moran.

F-105 Starfire jet. The U.S. Air Force jets stationed at Brady Field. (The actual Air Force name for the F-105 was Thunderchief—its nickname "THUD.")

First Attempt. NUMA search vessel that was being used for the expedition to find a Teaser. Described as one hundred fifty-two feet in length and displacing eight hundred twenty tons. Has eight crew members and fourteen scientists on board.

French Sureté. The French elite police who are assisting in cracking the heroin-smuggling ring.

Ganges River. The polluted river in India that Colonel Lewis says he will settle for a drink from. Pitt offers him a Fix beer instead.

Greek National Tourist Organization. The organization that operates the tour of the ruin of the theater where Pitt ends up when he escapes from the labyrinth.

Hawk of Macedonia. Nickname for German flying ace Lieutenant Kurt Heibert. Assigned to Jagdstaffel 91, he attained thirty-two victories before attacking a weather balloon and being downed. He was reported lost in the Aegean Sea July 15, 1918.

Hersong, Gustaf. The lanky six-foot-tall marine botanist on the *First Attempt.* Dives with Pitt on the underwater cave below Bruno von Till's house.

Hypsarion. The mountain that is the highest point on the island of Thasos.

Japanese I-boat. Japanese submarine that Bruno von Till uses as the launching platform for the Albatros. Hidden inside the underwater cave, the submarine had been sunk by an American destroyer off Iwo Jima in 1945, then raised by Minerva Lines in 1951.

Knight, Dr. Ken. Described as young, blond and well tanned, he has a long, sparse yellow beard. A brilliant marine geophysicist.

Lewis, James. Air Force colonel and commanding officer at Brady Field.

Liminas, Greece. A small village six miles north, up the road from Brady Field.

Limpet mine. The type of underwater mine that Giordino wants to attach to the hull of the *Queen Artemisia.*

Macrocystis pyrifera. A brown algae of the *Phaeophyta* family. The kelp is native to the Pacific coast of the United States. Spotted by Gustaf Hersong in the underwater cave. He claims that it is fake, a plastic replica.

Mauser. The vest-pocket .25-caliber handgun that Giordino brandishes at Inspector Zacynthus when he is planning to jail Pitt and Giordino. The gun belongs to Teri von Till, and Giordino discovered it taped to her leg.

Maybach-Zeppelin. The 1936 German automobile that Bruno von Till sent to pick up Pitt to bring him to dinner at his home. A town car body style with a divider between the passenger and the chauffeur. The coachwork is painted a deep multicolored silver, and the fenders and running boards are painted black. The tires sport a distinctive diamond-shaped pattern. Pitt ends up with the automobile.

Mayday. The original name for the book *The Mediterranean Caper,* published in England as such. Also an internationally recognized distress call.

Mediterranean Tenth Fleet. The U.S. Navy battle group that Pitt recommends operate the submarine recovered from the underwater cave.

Minerva Lines. Bruno von Till's shipping company. His ships are described as decrepit rust buckets and feature a big yellow *M* painted on the smoke funnels.

Mini-Cooper. Tiny British automobile that Teri von Till drives. Her Mini-Cooper is a British racing green model with an open top. She purchased the car in London and drove it to Greece from Le Havre, France.

Moody, Airman Second Class. The air policeman at the front gate the morning Pitt awakens early and decides to go for a swim in the ocean.

Panaghia, Greece. The town near Brady Field.

PBY Catalina. A twin Pratt and Whitney–engined flying boat. The call numbers for the PBY in the book are PBY-086.

Pit of Hades. A vast underground labyrinth with a hundred different passages and only two openings, an entrance and a hidden exit which is a closely guarded secret.

Portuguese Man-of-War. Jellyfish with long purplish tentacles that the divers spot when they are swimming toward the underwater cave.

Primacord. It looks like string or rope and can be made in any thickness. It reacts like a burning fuse, only more rapidly. Pitt feels it was used to sever the cables on the *First Attempt.*

Queen Artemisia. The Minerva Lines freighter that is carrying heroin to the United States. Pitt sCUBAs out to the ship and searches it, finding no one.

Queen Jocasta. The Minerva Lines freighter that will deliver the heroin to the United States. The *Queen Artemisia* is a decoy.

Remick, Sophia. The artist who painted an amateurish painting that hangs in the captain's cabin of the *Queen Artemisia.* The inscription on the painting reads: "To the captain of my heart from his loving wife."

Scyla. Italian brig sunk in 1876 near Thasos.

Sea of Tethys. A great sea that millions of years in the past covered Tibet, India and Central Europe. All that remains of the Sea of Tethys today is the Black, Caspian and Mediterranean seas.

Spencer, Lee. The red-bearded marine biologist on the *First Attempt.* Dives with Pitt on the underwater cave below Bruno von Till's house.

Star gazer. A bottom-dwelling fish with stony eyes and grotesque fringed lips spotted by the divers as they swim toward the underwater cave.

Teaser. Fish thought to be extinct over two hundred million years until one is spotted by Pitt at the end of the book. Gunn believes it might be one of the first mammals. It might have tiny scales and a smooth porpoiselike skin or perhaps even a kind of furry hide like a sea lion.

Thasos Strait. The body of water between the island of Thasos and the Macedonian mainland.

Thasos, Greece. An island in the northern part of the Aegean Sea.

Thomas, Stan. The short runty ship's engineer on the *First Attempt.* Dives with Pitt into the underwater cave below Bruno von Till's house.

U-19. German submarine sunk in 1918 off Thasos. A model of the U-19 is in Bruno von Till's study.

Von Stroheim, Erich. Shaven-skulled German actor mentioned on page 245.

Von Till, Bruno. Described as being heavyset with a round, typically German face featuring shaved head, shifty eyes and no neck. Claims he flew with the Hawk of Macedonia, Kurt Heibert, but is actually his brother, Admiral Erich Heibert, commander of Nazi Germany's transportation fleet. Wanted for war crimes. The actual Bruno von Till was murdered in England by Erich Heibert.

Von Till, Teri. Around thirty years old. Her figure is described as a beguiling mixture of grace and firmness. Dark brown eyes and shoulder-length black hair. She has a small pockmark beside her right temple. Was married to a motorcar salesman who raced cars and was killed in the crash of his supercharged MG. Before Pitt has his way with her on the beach, she claims she was celibate for almost nine years. Half Greek and half German. Born in Greece but raised in England.

Alleged niece to Bruno von Till but actually a substitute. Real name Amy.

Whaleboat. The *First Attempt*'s shore boat was described as twenty-six feet in length and with double ends. It was powered by a single four-cylinder Buda engine.

Willie. Bruno von Till's driver and assistant. Blond-haired. Wears silver-rimmed spectacles. Wears jack-boots with hobnails. Pitt punches him in the nose, breaking it, for spying on him and Teri making love on the beach. Is killed when the weather balloon rigged with explosives blows the Albatros from the sky.

Woodson, Omar. The expedition photographer on the *First Attempt.* Dives with Pitt on the underwater cave below Bruno von Till's house.

Zacynthus, Inspector Hercules, Federal Bureau of Narcotics. Friends call him Zac. An American described as a tall, thin man with large, sad eyes. Has uncommonly even teeth and smokes a pipe. Has neatly styled hair.

Zeno, Colonel Polyclitus Anaxamander. The Greek Gendarmerie inspector who poses as a Greek National Tourist Organization tour guide and takes Pitt and Giordino into custody after they search Bruno von Till's study. Described as having a broad, white-toothed smile beneath his great moustache.

Iceberg

Andursson, Golfur. Chief gillie, or river warden, for the Rarfur River. Described as having a stern face with sea-blue eyes. Gray hair flowing around a broad forehead like a helmet on a warrior in a Flemish painting. An old man, age somewhere beyond seventy years, wearing a worn turtleneck sweater. He rescues Pitt, who has collapsed from the long walk from the staged helicopter crash. Andursson takes him in a Land Rover to his home and allows him to use his radio transmitter. Pitt radios Admiral Sandecker, who sends help by plane.

Arnarson, Sergeant. Policeman who patrols the village where Pitt is taken after the helicopter crash. Is murdered and his identity assumed by phony policeman. Described as having been five foot nine and one hundred seventy pounds. When Dr. Jonsson confirms his size, Pitt notes he is probably dead and one of the phony policemen is wearing his uniform.

B-92. USAF reconnaissance bomber that flies at twelve hundred miles an hour. The plane Pitt takes from Iceland to Disneyland.

Boyle, Jack. Australian coal tycoon. Member of Hermit Limited.

Brady. Texan and white-jacketed steward on the *Catawaba.*

Cashman, Sergeant Sam. Does freelance hydraulic work on the black Lorelei executive jet that attacks Pitt and Hunnewell. When Pitt recovers the landing gear of the crashed jet, it has the initials *S.C.* on the part, and the initials lead him to Cashman. He is assigned to Eighty-seventh Air Transport Squadron. A former crop duster in Oklahoma, he is also the pilot of the Ford Trimotor that flies the rescue team to the staged helicopter crash.

Castile, Pablo. President of the Dominican Republic who is targeted to be assassinated by Hermit Limited killers inside the Pirates of the Caribbean ride at Disneyland. Plot is foiled by Pitt and Naval Intelligence.

Catawaba. A Coast Guard supercutter. Commanded by Lieutenant Commander Lee Koski. The control room is described as science-fiction space movie. From floor to ceiling, the four steel bulkheads stand buried behind a mechanical avalanche of computers, television monitors and instrumented consoles. Endless rows of technically labeled switches and knobs, garnished by enough colored lights to fill a casino marquee in Las Vegas. Has air-search radar, surface-search radar scanners, the latest Loran-type navigational equipment of medium, high and ultra-high frequencies, not to mention computerized navigation plotting. Manned by seventeen officers and one hundred sixty enlisted men. The ship cost between twelve and thirteen million and was built at the Northgate shipyards in Wilmington, Delaware.

Chloral hydrate. Substance Pitt suspects was slipped to the passengers and crew of the *Lax* to knock them out prior to the fire. This explains why the crew was still at duty stations.

De Croix, Juan. President of French Guiana who is targeted to be assassinated by Hermit Limited killers inside the Pirates of the Caribbean ride at Disneyland. Plot is foiled by Pitt and Naval Intelligence.

Devonshire, Clarence. Master inspector at Lorelei Aircraft Limited.

Disneyland. Amusement park in Anaheim, California. The location Hermit Limited chooses to assassinate the heads of French Guiana and the Dominican Republic. Plot is foiled inside the Pirates of the Caribbean ride by Pitt and Naval Intelligence.

Dover, Lieutenant Amos. The *Catawaba*'s executive officer. Described as looking like a big bear; his voice seemed to growl from somewhere deep within his stomach.

Dupuy, Roger. French millionaire. Member of Hermit Limited.

Ford Trimotor. The famed Tin Goose. Powered by three 200-horsepower engines, with one directly in front of the cockpit and one on each wing. Described as having a corrugated aluminum skin.

Fyrie, Kirsti. Kristjan Fyrie's twin sister.

Fyrie, Kristjan. Described as a genius, adventurer, scientist, legend, the tenth-richest man in the world before age twenty-five. A kind and gentle person untouched by his fame and wealth. Wears a beautifully hand-crafted ring inlaid with eight different semiprecious stones native to Iceland, each carved in the likeness of an ancient Nordic god. At eighteen, when a seaman on a Greek freighter, he jumped on the coast of Mozambique. He caught the diamond fever and began diving in the waters offshore as all the ground leases were tied up. After five months of diving, he found diamonds and with the help of the black natives formed a company to mine them commercially. Within two years of the find, he was worth forty million dollars. After that, he mined manganese off Vancouver Island and brought in an oil field in Peru. His parents died in a fire when he was very young. Only known relative is a twin sister. After sex change, assumes Kirsti Fyrie's identity.

Grimsi. The vessel Pitt, Tidi Royal and Admiral Sandecker borrow to look for the black jet that attacked Pitt and Hunnewell. Owned by Oskar Rodheim, the old forty-foot fishing boat is not what it appears. It is powered by twin 420-horsepower Sterling gas engines and has a top-of-the-line Fleming six-ten fathometer. Described as having a square wheelhouse, perched just five feet from the stern. A very old boat—as old as the antique compass mounted beside her helm. Her mahogany deck planks are worn smooth, but she still is strong and true.

Hadley, Seaman First Class Buzz. Coast Guard radar operator who notices the iceberg on radar and notifies Lieutenant Neth and Ensign Rapp.

Hermit Limited. An evil consortium led by Oskar Rodheim that secretly merges the great mining companies from the northern border of Guatemala to the tip of Chile.

Howard, Dorothy. An attractive red-haired British actress present at the poetry reading at Oskar Rodheim's mansion.

Hull, Captain Ben. Described as a great bull of a man, tan-faced, with long blond sideburns. Head of the rescue crew on the Ford Trimotor that picks up Pitt at Golfur Andursson's house and then flies to the staged helicopter crash to aid the survivors.

Hummel, Hans Von. Small, rotund, lively, with a bald head. German millionaire. Member of Hermit Limited.

Hunnewell, Dr. Bill. Ph.D. in oceanography. Employed by NUMA and a passenger on the helicopter Pitt lands on the *Catawaba.* Tours the burned-out hulk of the *Lax* with Pitt and is flying in helicopter from the *Catawaba* to Iceland when the helicopter is attacked by a black British-made executive jet. After Pitt downs the jet by smashing it with the helicopter's rotor blade, Pitt and Hunnewell crash in the ocean. Hunnewell is badly shot in the left arm but dies on the beach in Iceland from a bad heart. A member of Hermit Limited, the consortium arranged by Oskar Rodheim to take over Central and South America.

Jonsson, Dr. Treats Pitt after helicopter crash and pronounces cause of death for Hunnewell.

Kelly, F. James Thin, distinguished, with silver hair and beard. American billionaire. Member of Hermit Limited.

Kelly, Sam. Older brother of F. James Kelly. Described as a round-shouldered heavy character in his middle seventies, with blue, knifing eyes deep set in a wizened face. Dies of an apparent heart attack at the staged helicopter crash.

Kippmann, Dean. The chief of the Naval Intelligence Agency. Described as short and almost as broad as a chair. Bald and with gray eyes. He shows up at Admiral Sandecker's office with orders signed by the secretary of defense for Pitt's reassignment. Pitt is ordered to assist Naval Intelligence by spotting the Hermit Limited killers at Disneyland.

Koski, Lieutenant Commander Lee. Forty-one years old. Has served in Coast Guard eighteen years. Described as very short with blue eyes and shaggy wheat-colored hair. Commander of the *Catawaba,* the Coast Guard's newest supercutter.

Lax. Yacht owned by Kristjan Fyrie that is discovered inside the iceberg by Pitt and Hunnewell. Supposedly had fifteen people on board including eight engineers from Fyrie Mining Limited. When it was last sighted by a Standard Oil tanker before Pitt finds it in the iceberg, its location was six hundred miles off Cape Farewell, Greenland.

Lazard, Dan. Chief of park security for Disneyland. Described as a big, tall, pipe-smoking man whose eyes stare out at Pitt from behind fashionable rimless glasses.

Lillie, Jerome P. IV. Naval Intelligence Agency officer who poses as a cab driver when he meets Pitt. Part of the Lillie beer family of St. Louis, Missouri. Is also one of the people rescued from the staged helicopter crash.

Lorelei Mark VIII-B1608. The black executive jet that attacks the helicopter Pitt and Hunnewell are flying. Built by Lorelei Aircraft Limited in Great Britain and powered by twin turbine engines.

Mahani, Iban. Iranian millionaire. Member of Hermit Limited.

Marks, Sir Eric. British millionaire. Member of Hermit Limited.

Matajic, Dr. Len. Works for NUMA studying currents below ten thousand feet. Has a camp on an ice floe in Baffin Bay with partner Jack O'Riley. Disappears after he recognizes the *Lax* under a different name.

Mundsson, Bjarni. Boy who finds Pitt and Hunnewell on the beach after the helicopter crash and goes for help. Son of Thorsteinn Mundsson, farmer.

Mundsson, Thorsteinn. Farmer and father of the boy who found Pitt on the beach when he was injured in the helicopter crash.

Nagel, Colonel. The Air Force commanding officer at

Keflavik Air Base, Iceland, and commanding officer of Sam Cashman.

Neth, Lieutenant Sam. Pilot of the huge four-engined Coast Guard patrol plane in the prologue. He is reading a paperback when told that an iceberg has been spotted.

Newporter Inn. Location in Newport Beach, California, where Pitt was with a gorgeous sex-mad redhead a week before he flew out to the *Catawaba.* Also where he tells the cab driver he wants to go in the last sentence of the book.

Novgorod. A Russian trawler crammed with the latest and most sophisticated electronic detection gear Soviet science has yet devised. It also allegedly contains the codes and data for their entire Western Hemisphere surveillance program. Supposedly crewed by thirty-five men and women, it is said to have remained off Greenland for three months. The story is a lie Pitt fabricates to explain to the captain of the *Catawaba* why he needs to land on his ship.

O'Riley, Jack. NUMA employee. Studying current flows below ten thousand feet with Dr. Len Matajic on an ice floe in Baffin Bay. Disappears after being told by Matajic that he recognized the ship they went on as the *Lax.*

Rapp, Ensign James. Copilot of the Coast Guard patrol plane in the prologue.

Rodheim, Oskar. Described as a tall, snowy-haired, distinguished-looking figure, fairly young, late thirties, with his face strong and lined by years of ocean gales and salt air. His eyes are a cool ice-blue above a strong, narrow nose and a mouth that looks good-naturedly warm. Owner of Rodheim Industries, a fishing company that uses boats painted blue and flying a red flag with an albatross. Early in *Iceberg,* he is engaged to Kirsti Fyrie and they are planning to merge their companies. Pitt warns that the combination of the two companies will give them control of the North Atlantic. Naval Intelligence file 078-34. Alias Max Rolland, alias Hugo von Klausen, alias Chatford Marazan. Real name Carzo Butera. Born in Brooklyn, New York, July 15, 1940.

Royal, Tidi. Admiral Sandecker's personal secretary. Can type one hundred twenty words a minute for eight hours without a yawn. Described as long-bodied with smiling brown eyes and fawn-colored hair. When Pitt wakes up after being wounded and brought to Reykjavik, she is wearing a red wool dress that clings to her precision-shaped hourglass figure. Described as five foot seven, one hundred thirty-five pounds, thirty-six inches around the hips, an astonishing twenty-three inches around the waist and the bust a probable thirty-six C-cup. All in all, a figure that belongs on the center spread of *Playboy.*

Sloan, Lieutenant Jonis. Chief ice observer aboard the four-engined Coast Guard patrol plane that spots the iceberg. Tosses a gallon jar of red dye on the iceberg. The stain is later chipped off, leading to false identification.

Snorri's Restaurant. Located in Reykjavik, Iceland, it is where Pitt first meets Kirsti Fyrie. Described as having a buffet table with over two hundred different native dishes. Pitt counts over twenty different salmon dishes and nearly fifteen of cod. Pitt raves about the raw cured shark meat.

Surtsey. Icelandic for *submarine.* The new name of the *Lax.*

Svendborg, Gustav. Radio operator of the burned-out hulk Pitt finds inside the iceberg. His chair was literally burned out from under him, and his corpse is described as a scorched form curled up in a fetus position, the knees drawn up to the chin and the arms pulled tightly against the sides.

Tamareztov. Russian KGB agent opposed to Hermit Limited. Described as a short, stocky man with thinning hair, brown eyes and a limping gait. Rescued from fake helicopter crash. Pitt fulfills the promise he made to him by returning and rescuing him as well as bringing him a bottle of vodka.

Thorp, Chief. Ordered by Koski to have his men ready to secure Pitt's helicopter the minute it touches down on the *Catawaba.*

Ulysses Q-55. Helicopter Pitt flies and lands on the *Catawaba.* Described as a craft capable of nearly two hundred fifty miles an hour.

Ybarra, Jesus. Doctor at the San de Sol Hospital in Veracruz, Mexico. He is the doctor who performs a sex change on Kristjan Fyrie. Member of Hermit Limited.

Zirconium. Purified zirconium is vital in the construction of nuclear reactors because it absorbs little or no radiation. Atomic number forty. Substance Fyrie allegedly found in vast quantities and was on his way to the United States to negotiate with defense contractors about when the *Lax* disappeared.

Raise the Titanic!

Alhambra. U.S. Navy vessel present at the *Titanic* recovery site.

Amanda. The hurricane that hits the *Titanic* after she is raised. Registers force fifteen on the Beaufort scale. Known as the "Great Blow of 1988," the hurricane cut a swath across three thousand miles of ocean in three and a half days before slamming into the Avalon Peninsula of Newfoundland. Estimates of damage ran as high as two hundred fifty million dollars. The death toll from the storm ran from 300 to 325 people.

Antonov, Georgi. Soviet general secretary. Smokes a pipe.

Archangel, Soviet Union. Location where the ship containing Joshua Hays Brewster was bound when he wrecks on Novaya Zemyla. Awaiting rescue, he explores the island and finds byzanium. Saving one sample, he turns the rest over to his employer, Societé des Mines de Lorraine.

Bailey, Dr. Cornelius. Doctor who performs the autopsy on Henry Munk. Described as an elephant of a man, broad-shouldered, with a thrusting square-jawed face. Sandy-colored hair falls down to his collar. His beard is cut in a Van Dyke.

Balboa Bay Club. Club in Newport Beach where Pitt first meets Gene Seagram.

Banque de Lausanne. Bank in Switzerland where Marganin claims Prevlov is stashing money. The account number is AZF 7609. The name on the account is V. Volper, an anagram of Prevlov.

Barshov, Peter. Professor from the Leningrad Institute of Geology who briefs Prevlov about the mine on Novaya Zemlya. Described as having leathery hands and graying hair and smoking a meerschaum pipe.

Bascom, Chief. U.S. Navy chief on the *Samuel R. Morse.* Described as having the face of a canvas-weary prizefighter and the body of a beer keg. Nicknamed "Bad Bascom."

Beaufort Sea Expedition. Prior NUMA expedition that Sandecker refers to when explaining how he selected the crew for the Lorelei Current Drift Expedition.

Bednaya Mountain, U.S.S.R. Mountain with the byzanium mine on Novaya Island.

Beecher's Island. U.S. Navy aircraft carrier dispatched to the *Titanic* site.

Beesley, Alexander. The scientist who discovered byzanium in 1902.

Bigalow, John L. Commodore, K.B.E., R.D., R.N.R. Was a young deck officer on the ill-fated voyage of the *Titanic.* Last surviving crew member of the *Titanic.* Described as having deep blue eyes. "The few strands of hair on his head were pure white, as was his beard, and his face showed the ruddy, weathered look of a seafaring man." Presents Pitt with the flag from the *Titanic* he had snatched as she was sinking. Pitt later hoists the pennant when the ship is raised. Dies after *Titanic* is raised and is buried at sea.

Bloeser, Ernest. Former owner of the Little Angel Mine.

Boleslavski, Issak. Great Russian chess master mentioned by Prevlov to Marganin as they try to determine what the Sicilian Project is. Boleslavski favored a chess strategy named the Sicilian Defense.

Bomberger. A new vessel constructed especially for deep-water salvage.

Boosey-Hawkes. The company that manufactured the cornet found on the ocean floor by the *Sappho I* and later identified as coming from the *Titanic.* The company is described as a very reputable and very fine British firm. The cornet was made in either October or November 1911. The cornet is a presentation model and is engraved, "Presented to Graham Farley in sincere appreciation for distinguished performance in the entertainment of our passengers by the grateful management of the White Star Line."

Borodino Restaurant. The restaurant in Moscow where Marganin is to meet the Fat Man to find out more about the Sicilian Project. He receives an envelope with information in the men's room of the restaurant.

Brewster, Joshua Hays. Respected five-foot-two-inch-tall mining engineer who led the Coloradans. Born to William Buck Brewster and Hettie Masters in Sidney, Nebraska, on April 4 or 5, 1878. Uncle of Harry Young. Graduated School of Mines, Golden, Colorado. Mined in the Klondike and Russia before returning to Leadville, Colorado, to manage the Sour Rock and Buffalo mines which were owned by French financiers. Went mad and sealed himself in the cargo hold of the *Titanic.*

Brown, "The Unsinkable Molly." Famous passenger on the *Titanic.* Wife of a Colorado silver baron. Was rescued and lived in Colorado until her death.

Burdick, John. Majority leader of the U.S. Senate. Described as a tall, thin man with a bush of black hair that seldom saw a comb.

Buski. Russian marine guard aboard the *Titanic* during Hurricane Amanda. Described as a short man with a coarse toughness. The finest marksman in his regiment. He speaks a smattering of English. Shot by U.S. Navy SEALs during Hurricane Amanda.

Butera, Lieutenant Commander Scotty. U.S. Navy lieutenant commander in command of the tugboat *Samuel R. Wallace.* Described as nearly six feet six inches tall, his chin buried in a magnificent black beard.

Byzanium. The mineral that is believed hidden in the hold of the *Titanic.* The radioactivity of byzanium is so extreme that it has disappeared in all but trace amounts. The Meta Section needs about eight ounces to fuel the Sicilian Project.

Capricorn. The support tender used on the *Titanic* project that pumps compressed air into the hull.

Cargo Hold No. 1, G Deck. Area of the *Titanic* where Joshua Hays Brewster sealed himself as she sank.

Chavez, Tom. Engineer on the *Deep Fathom.*

Collins, Marshall. Chief Kremlin security advisor to the director of the CIA.

Coloradans. Used by Koplin to describe the hard-rock miners who removed the byzanium from Novaya Zemlya. The Coloradans were said to be Cornishmen, Irishmen, Germans and Swedes. Their names were Joshua Hays Brewster, Denver; Alvin Coulter, Fairplay; Thomas Price, Leadville; Charles P. Whidney, Cripple Creek; Vernon S. Hall, Denver; John Caldwell, Central City; Walter Schmidt, Aspen; Warner E. O'Deming, Denver; Jason C. Hobart, Boulder.

Colt revolver. Serial number 204 783. The weapon Gene Seagram plans to use for his suicide on a park bench in East Potomac Park.

Curly. Bald-headed radio operator on the *Capricorn.*

Current sensor. The instrument aboard the *Sappho I* that measures the speed and direction of the Lorelei current.

D'Orsini, Claude. Fashion designer who created the dresses worn by both Dana Seagram and Ashley Fleming to a party in Chapter Six.

Deck A Stateroom 33. Stateroom where Joshua Hays Brewster tossed and turned just before the *Titanic* sank.

Deep Fathom. A submersible that belongs to the Uranus Oil Company. It is used on the *Titanic* project to install pressure-release valves.

Director of Defense Archives. Head of the division in the Department of Defense that locates the files pertaining to Secret Army Plan 371-990-R85, which pertains to the mining of byzanium.

Donner, Mel. One of the chief evaluators for the Meta Section. Described as short and almost as broad as he is tall. He has wheat-colored hair and melancholy eyes, and his face always seems to be sweating. Doctorate in physics from the University of Southern California.

Donovan, Jack. A structural engineer from Ocean Tech. He is described as a young blond fellow. He is aboard the *Sappho II* when Munk is murdered.

Doppleman Crane. Type of crane used to pull the door from the vault where the byzanium is supposedly stored.

***Dragonfish,* U.S.S.** U.S. Navy submarine that threatens to retaliate against the *Mikhail Kurkov* if she fires a Stoski missile at *Titanic.*

Drummer, Ben. NUMA marine engineer on the *Sappho I* expedition. Described as a lanky Southerner with a deep Alabama drawl. Aboard the *Sappho II* when Munk is murdered. Was actually born in Halifax, Nova Scotia, and is the Russian agent code-named Gold. His twin brother, Sam Merker, is the Russian agent code-named Silver.

Dugan, Owen. Assistant to Dr. Murray Silverstein.

Farley, Graham. Musician on the *Titanic* who owned the cornet that was found by the *Sappho I* and later restored by John Vogel. Farley was solo cornetist prior to the *Titanic* for a period of three years on the *Oceanic.*

Farquar, Joel. The weatherman on the *Capricorn.* Farquar is on loan from the Federal Meteorological Services Administration. Described as a studious little red-faced man with utterly no sense of humor and no trace of friendly warmth.

Fergus, Lieutenant. Leader of the U.S. Navy SEALs who recapture *Titanic.* The SEALs under Fergus's command board the *Titanic* from a nuclear submarine fifty feet below the surface by exiting the vessel's torpedo tubes.

First Attempt. NUMA research vessel described in *The Mediterranean Caper.*

Firth of Clyde. Navy submarine base in the British Isles where *First Attempt* docks after mission.

Fleming, Ashley. Described as Washington, D.C.'s, most elegant and sophisticated divorcee. The president's companion at the party in the East Room of the White House in Chapter Six. Wearing same exact dress as Dana Seagram.

Godhawn. Norwegian fishing trawler that tows the *First Attempt* and Koplin to within two hundred miles of Novaya Zemlya so he can test for traces of byzanium.

Gold. Code name of one of the two Russian operatives at the *Titanic* recovery site. Pitt discloses during Hurricane Amanda that Gold is actually Ben Drummer.

Gravimeter. The instrument aboard the *Sappho I* that records gravity readings.

Guggenheim, Benjamin. Millionaire passenger on *Titanic.* Stood calmly with his secretary, dressed in his finest evening clothes, as the ship sank so he could meet death as a gentleman.

Guthrie and Sons Foundry. Foundry in Pueblo, Colorado, that manufactures the ore cars used by the Coloradans on Novaya Zemlya.

Hobart, Adeline. Widow of Jake Hobart. Resides at 261-B Calle Aragon, Laguna Hills, California. Described as stout, white-haired with blue eyes and a warm, gentle look. Married Jake Hobart at age sixteen. After Seagram calls the president of the United States, who speaks to her, she discloses she saw her former husband after the Little Angel Mine disaster. She also shows Seagram postcards Jake sent from France.

Hobart, Jake. Coloradan discovered by Sid Koplin in a bunk inside the mine on Novaya Zemlya. Preserved by the cold, his corpse has red hair and a red beard. The inscription above his bed reads: "Here rests Jake Hobart. Born 1874. A damn good man who froze in a storm, February 10, 1912." The Army Records Bureau discloses his full name is Jason Cleveland Hobart, born January 23, 1874, in Vinton, Iowa. Enlisted in the U.S. Army May 1898 and served with the First Colorado Volunteer Regiment in the Philippines. Promoted to sergeant and suffered serious wounds fighting the Philippine insurrectionists. Twice decorated for meritorious conduct under fire. Hobart left the Army in October 1901. His widow stills draws an army pension of fifty dollars and forty cents a month. His cause of death in the pension records is listed as service-related, and the form awarding his widow his pension is signed by Henry L. Stimson, secretary of war under President Taft. Described by his widow, Adeline, as large, over six feet tall and barrel-chested. A blaster or explosives expert, he was considered one of the best in his field.

Hull, Peter. Reporter with the *New York Times.*

Jensen and Thor Metal Fabricators. Company that Thor Forge and Ironworks became after merger. Located in Denver, Colorado.

Jensen, Carl Jr. Runs Jensen and Thor Metal Fabricators. Described as young, no more than twenty-eight, and wears his hair long. His grandfather bought the outstanding stock of Thor Forge and Ironworks in 1942 and changed the name to Jensen and Thor Metal Fabricators. Microfilm records he shows Mel Donner disclose the drilling equipment used on Novaya Zemlya was paid for by the United States government.

Jones, Peter. Black police officer who saves Gene Seagram from suicide by telling him the *Titanic* has been raised. Described as having six children and a ninety-year-old frame house with a thirty-year mortgage.

Juneau. U.S. Navy nuclear-powered guided-missile cruiser that is patrolling near the *Titanic* recovery effort.

Kama Security Post. Security post on Novaya Island.

Keil, Joe. Engineer on the *Deep Fathom.*

Keith, Commander. Hands message to Admiral Kemper from Sandecker.

Kelly, Ensign. Ensign in the cable house of the tugboat *Wallace* who alerts Butera to a problem with the tow cable.

Kemper, Joseph. Admiral who is the U.S. Navy chief of staff. Large, with a well-fed stomach and lazy blue eyes set in a round, jovial face.

Komondor. The type of dog used by the Russian guards on Novaya Island. Stands thirty inches at the shoulders and is covered by a heavy coat of matted white hair. Dog is shot by Pitt when he rescues Koplin.

Koplin, Sid. Mineralogist rescued by Pitt on Novaya Island. Shot by Russians in left side, also suffers a hairline crack in his skull. Taken to Walter Reed Medical Center for treatment.

Laguna Star. The name of a tramp freighter of rather dubious registry that the Russian submarine uses to issue a call of distress from one hundred miles to the north of the *Titanic* to divert the *Juneau.*

Little Angel Mine. Mine near Central City, Colorado, where a fake cave-in was instituted. After the ploy the Coloradans were assumed to be dead and could continue on to Novaya Zemlya to mine the byzanium.

Lorelei Current Drift Expedition. NUMA expedition with a deep-sea submersible *Sappho I.* The Lorelei current is born off the western tip of Africa, follows the mid-Atlantic ridge north, then curves easterly between Baffin Island and Greenland, then dies in the Labrador Sea. The original plan called for the *Sappho*

I to descend in the water five hundred miles northwest of the coast of Dakar, then cruise in the current until ascending in the sea of Labrador fifty days later.

Lukas, Leon. U.S. Navy lieutenant. Salvage technician aboard the *Sappho II* when Munk is murdered.

Lusky, Herb. Mineralogist with the Meta Section. After finding that the vault in the *Titanic* is devoid of byzanium, he is bashed on the head by an insane Gene Seagram. He receives twenty stitches and a nasty concussion.

M-24. Type of automatic weapon used by Navy SEALs to recapture *Titanic.*

Magmatic Paragenesis. Term used by Koplin to describe to Mel Donner how Novaya Zemlya is now devoid of minerals.

Magnetometer. The instrument aboard the *Sappho I* that measures the ocean bottom's magnetic field including any deviations caused by localized mineral deposits.

Mahoney, Bull. Foreman of the Satan Mine in Central City, Colorado, who tries to rescue the miners allegedly trapped in the Little Angel Mine.

Marganin, Lieutenant Pavel. Underling to Andre Prevlov. Described as tall and authoritative. U.S. deep-cover intelligence agent. His real name is Harry Koskoski, and he was born in Newark, New Jersey. The real Marganin was the son of tailors from Komsomolsk-na-Amure. One of the few survivors when a Russian Kashin-class missile destroyer sank in the Indian Ocean, he was rescued but later died. Koskoski's face is surgically altered to resemble Marganin, and he assumes his identity. Raised in rank to commander and promoted to chief of the Foreign Intelligence Analysis Division after Prevlov defects.

McPatrick, Major. Major in the Army Records Bureau. Telephones Gene Seagram with the information about the Coloradans.

Merker, Sam. NUMA systems expert on *Sappho I* expedition. Described as cosmopolitan and as citified as a Wall Street broker. Later serves as engineer on the *Deep Fathom.* Was actually born in Halifax, Nova Scotia. Twin brother of Ben Drummer. Russian agent code-named Silver.

Meta Section. A government-funded think-tank that operates in total secrecy. The goal of the Meta Section is to leapfrog current technology by twenty or thirty years. The program is housed in a nondescript old cinderblock building beside the Washington Navy Yard. The building is disguised with a sign that reads "Smith Van & Storage Company." The organization is not listed in any journal of federal offices. Not even the CIA, FBI or even the NSA has any records they exist.

Mikhail Kurkov. Soviet oceanographic research vessel.

Mile-Hi Chewing Tobacco. Koplin discovers about fifty empty wrappers of this product inside the mine at Novaya Zemyla.

Modoc. Described as the finest deep-water salvage vessel the United States Navy possesses. Admiral Kemper agrees to loan the vessel to Sandecker while they are fishing on the Rappahannock River.

Moe's Pawnshop. Pawnshop where Dr. Silverstein purchases two cornets to drop in twelve thousand feet of water off Cape Hatteras, North Carolina, to simulate them being dropped from the *Titanic.*

Monterey Park. U.S. Navy ship at the *Titanic* recovery site.

Mooney, Arthur. Captain of one of the New York Harbor fireboats. Described as "A big, mischief-eyed Irishman born in the city, and a seagoing fire-eater for nineteen years." Mooney orders his crew to hit the sirens and water hoses to welcome the *Titanic* in style. All the other ships follow Mooney's lead.

Munk, Henry. NUMA instrument-component specialist on the *Sappho I* expedition. Described as a quiet and droopy-eyed wit who clearly wishes he were anywhere but on the *Sappho I.* At the start of the *Titanic* recovery effort, he is murdered while aboard the *Sappho II.*

Myers-Lentz Company. Producers of the electrolyte chemical that will be pumped into the sediment sealing the *Titanic*'s hull to the ocean floor.

Nicholson, Warren. The director of the CIA.

Novaya Island, U.S.S.R. Island due north of Zemlya Island. Novaya contains the old mine where the byzanium was originally extracted.

Parotkin, Ivan. Captain of the *Mikhail Kurkov*. Described as a slender man of medium height with a distinguished face who almost never smiles. In his late fifties; his receding hairline shows no trace of gray.

Patman or Patmore, Colonel. Army officer who arrives at Adeline Hobart's house in Boulder, Colorado, after Jake Hobart dies and swears her to secrecy. In return for her silence, he presents her with a check for ten thousand dollars.

Pelholme Aircraft Company. The company that runs the preliminary tests of the *Sappho I* prior to the Lorelei Expedition.

Phillips, John G. Radio operator on the *Titanic*. Phillips sent the first SOS in history.

Plimsoll mark. The load-line mark on a ship's hull.

Polevoi, Vladimir. Chief of the Foreign Secrets Department of the KGB.

Pratt, Lieutenant. U.S. Navy lieutenant who picked up the Coloradans from Novaya Zemyla after they double-crossed the French and stole byzanium. His vessel is attacked by a ship flying no flag off Norway. Pratt fights off the aggressor, then steers his ship to Aberdeen, Scotland.

Prescott, Dr. Ryan. Chief of the NUMA Hurricane Center in Tampa, Florida. He warns the *Titanic* recovery crew of the approaching hurricane.

Prevlov, Captain Andre. Russian intelligence officer employed by the Soviet Navy's Department of Foreign Intelligence. Described as a well-proportioned, handsome man sporting a layered hairstyle and a modishly trimmed moustache and intense gray eyes. Drives an orange Lancia and lives in an apartment above the Moscow River decorated like Peter the Great's summer home. His father is the number twelve man in the Communist Party. Drinks Bombay gin. Smokes Winston cigarettes. Wears Omega watch.

Project, Sicilian. The code name of the project that will use byzanium to create a missile defense shield over the United States. The project purchased forty-six pieces of land to house the missile defense system under the guise of the Department of Energy Studies. The majority of the sites are along the U.S.-Canadian border followed by the Atlantic seaboard. Eight sites are along the Pacific Coast, and four are along the Mexico border and the Gulf of Mexico. The sites are designed to resemble small relay power stations.

Renault Town Car. A giant brass-trimmed town car that was noticed by Bigalow blocked to the deck of the *Titanic.* Pitt later ends up with the car.

Roanoke. Ship whose keel was laid in 1728. She went onto the rocks off Nova Scotia in 1743. Model of the vessel is in one of the third-floor bedrooms in the White House and was built by the president's father.

Under the ruse of identifying the model, the president secretly meets with Dana Seagram to ask her to try to mend things with her husband, Gene.

Rocky Mountain News. Denver newspaper dated November 17, 1911, discovered inside the mine on Novaya Zemlya by Koplin. The newspaper is still in print today.

Rogovski, Dr. Chief Russian scientist aboard the *Mikhail Kurkov.*

Ross, Sandra. Great-granddaughter of Commodore Bigalow. A flight attendant with Bristol Airlines, she is described as having absorbing violet eyes framed by neatly brushed red hair. At the end of the book, Pitt tells Sandecker he will be visiting Ross if Sandecker needs to find him.

Samuel R. Wallace. One of the U.S. Navy tugboats assigned to tow the *Titanic* to New York City. A deep-sea rescue tugboat two hundred fifty feet in length with 5,000-horsepower diesel powerplants. The vessels are capable of hauling twenty thousand tons of dead weight for two thousand miles without refueling.

Sappho I. NUMA's newest and largest deep-sea research submersible. Described as appearing to look like a giant cigar on an ice skate. Built to house a seven-man crew and two tons of research equipment and instruments. The hull is made of titanium painted red, and the vessel can descend to 24,000 feet below the surface.

Sappho II. Newer and more advanced version of the *Sappho I.* It is used on the *Titanic* project to seal the smaller openings such as the air vents and portholes.

Sea Slug. U.S. Navy deep-sea submersible. Designed and constructed for deep-water salvage, she is operated from the deck of the *Modoc.* Described as twenty feet long and tubular in shape with rounded ends. Painted bright yellow, it features four large portholes on its bow. Mounted along its top, like small radar domes, are two high-intensity lights.

Seagram, Dana. Wife of Gene Seagram and NUMA marine archaeologist. Works for Admiral Sandecker. Described as having blond hair and coffee-brown eyes. Ph.D. in Marine archaeology. Ph.D. in archaeology. Thirty-one years old.

Seagram, Gene. One of the chief evaluators for the Meta Section. Described as a tall, lanky man, with a quiet voice and a courteous manner. Except for a large flattened nose, he could pass for Abraham Lincoln. Ph.D. in physics. Home is in Chevy Chase, Maryland. Nearly commits suicide on park bench but is stopped by police officer who explains that the *Titanic* has been raised. When the vault aboard the *Titanic* turns out to be devoid of byzanium, his mind snaps, and he bashes Lusky in the head with a rock, then begins smashing the remains of Joshua Hays Brewster against the walls of the vault. Diagnosed as suffering from manic-depressive psychosis.

Section R. Soviet Naval Intelligence Photograph analysis department.

Sheldon, Marie. NUMA marine geologist. When Dana Seagram leaves her husband, Gene, she moves into Sheldon's Georgetown house. Described as a small, thin, vital woman with vivid blue eyes, a pert bobbed nose and a mass of bleached blond hair shaped in a shag style. Has a square-cut chin.

Sicilian Project. Code name of the U.S. project to build a missile defense system using byzanium. Designed around a variant of the maser principle. Pushing a sound wave of a certain frequency through a medium containing excited atoms stimulates the sound to an extremely high state of emission. Described as similar to a laser beam. While a laser beam emits a narrow beam of light energy, the beam from the Sicilian Project would emit a broad fanlike field of sound energy. Any enemy missile launched against the United States would come into contact with this invisible barrier and be smashed to bits long before it entered the target area.

Silver. Code name of one of the two Russian operatives at the *Titanic* recovery site, who turns out to be Merker.

Silverstein, Dr. Murray. Professor at the Alexandria College of Oceanography who builds a small-scale model of the *Titanic* and simulates the sinking.

Sloyuk, Boris. Admiral and director of Soviet Naval Intelligence. Prevlov is Sloyuk's aide.

Smith, Edward J. Captain of the *Titanic* on her ill-fated voyage.

Smyth, Malcolm R. Fictitious author and archaeologist. Pitt uses the fake identity to check into the Pierre Hotel.

Societé des Mines de Lorraine. The group of French financiers who hired the Coloradans to fake the Little Angel Mine disaster and mine the byzanium on Novaya Zemlya.

Southby, England. A town in England with the grave containing the byzanium.

Spencer, Rick. NUMA equipment engineer on the *Sappho I* expedition. Described as a short blond-haired Californian who whistles constantly through clenched teeth.

Stannford, Dr. Amos. Inventor of the substance Wetsteel, which is used to seal the *Titanic*'s hull so she can be raised.

Stoner weapon. Type of weapon used by one of the Navy SEALs that recapture *Titanic.* Described as a wicked-looking affair with two barrels. Shoots a cloud of tiny needlelike flachettes.

Stoski. Twenty-six-foot-long Russian surface-to-surface missile that Captain Parotkin of the *Mikhail Kurkov* intends to fire at the *Titanic.*

S-T-SV-D sensor. The sensor aboard the *Sappho I* that measures outside salinity, temperature, sound velocity and depth pressure on a magnetic tape.

Stugis, Lieutenant. Helicopter pilot that lands on *Titanic.* Described as a short, thin man with sad, drooping, bedroom eyes. Uses a cigarette holder when smoking.

Sub-bottom profiler. Instrument aboard the *Sappho I* that acoustically determines the depth of the top sediments and provides indications of the underlying structure of the sea floor.

Teignmouth, Devonshire, England. Described as a small, picturesque resort town on the southeast coast of England with a population of 12,260. It is where Pitt goes to interview the dying Commodore John Bigalow.

Thomas J. Morse. One of the U.S. Navy tugboats assigned to tow the *Titanic* to New York City. A deep-sea rescue tugboat two hundred fifty feet in length with 5,000-horsepower diesel powerplants. The vessels are capable of hauling twenty thousand tons of deadweight for two thousand miles without refueling.

Thor Forge and Ironworks. Denver, Colorado, manufacturer of the drilling equipment used by the Coloradans on Novaya Zemlya.

Tilevitch, Vasily. Marshal of the Soviet Union and chief director of Soviet security.

Tin Goose. Antique Ford Trimotor airplane that Pitt buys in Keflavic, Iceland, and pilots back to his hangar at Washington's National Airport.

***Titanic*, R.M.S.** Infamous White Star line vessel that departed Southampton, England, April 10, 1912, and sank April 15, 1912, with a loss of over fifteen hundred lives. Struck iceberg and sank in North Atlantic. Last reported position 41.46'N-50.14'W. The vessel was 882 feet in length with a black hull encircled with a gold band and was built at the Belfast, Ireland, shipyard of Harland and Wolff. The yard was later leveled by German bombers during World War II. Built from 46,328 tons of steel. The vessel held 2,200 passengers and had lifeboats for only 1,180.

***Troy*, H.M.S.** British cruiser that carries the remains of Commodore Bigalow for his burial at sea.

Uphill, Lieutenant George. U.S. Navy lieutenant in command of the tugboat *Thomas J. Morse.* Described as a plump, ruddy-faced man who sports an immense Bismarck moustache.

Vampire squid. Squid Pitt and Giordino view through the porthole of the *Sea Slug* when they first reach the bottom near the *Titanic.* Described as a strange blue-black animal that looks like a cross between a squid and an octopus. Has eight tentacles linked together like the webbed foot of a duck. Two globular eyes form nearly a third of its body.

Vogel, John. Chief curator of the Washington Museum's Hall of Music. He restores the cornet found on the ocean floor by the *Sappho I.* Vogel discovers the cornet is a presentation model and was aboard the *Titanic* when she sank. Described as six feet five inches tall with a kindly face and puffs of unbrushed white hair edging a bald head. Brown Santa Claus eyes and a warm smile. Smokes a pipe.

Walter Reed Medical Center. U.S. naval hospital where Koplin is taken after being rescued by Pitt.

Woodson, Omar. NUMA photographer on the *Sappho I.* Rarely smiles. Is commander of *Sappho II* during the first phase of the *Titanic* recovery effort. Later, while aboard the *Titanic* during Hurricane Amanda, he is stabbed in the heart and killed by a Russian marine.

Young, Harry. Described as a skinny, little man. Seventy-eight years old, he has an alert, eager face. A walking encyclopedia on western mining history. Nephew of Harry Young. Explains to Donner that the Little Angel Mine disaster was a hoax.

Vixen 03

African Army of Revolution. Guerrilla army of African blacks headed by Somala that is fighting for independence from white rule.

Alabama. U.S. Navy battleship now preserved as a memorial.

Alsatian. Breed of dog used by the South African Defense Forces.

Anchorage House. Fifteen-room country inn owned and operated by Walter Bass. The inn is complete with antique plumbing and four-poster beds. The grounds are covered with pines and late-blooming wildflowers, and the inn has a duck pond out the back door. The dining room is designed in the style of an eighteenth-century country tavern, with old flintlock rifles, pewter drinking cups and weathered farm implements hanging on the walls and rafters.

Argon laser. Large-frame laser developed by the Stransky Instrument Company and used by Dr. Weir to attempt to cut through the parachute cord holding the QD shell to the skids of the NUMA Minerva helicopter. Features eighteen watts concentrated in a narrow beam that releases two kilowatts of energy.

Arizona. U.S. Navy battleship sunk at the battle of Pearl Harbor and still kept on the Navy's rolls as a commissioned ship.

Arsenal Six. Bunker at Phalanx Arms where QD warheads were stored.

Bass, Admiral Walter. U.S. Navy admiral who orders Vixen 03 to take off in spite of the weather. Described as a whiz kid who made his first star at the age of thirty-eight. Appeared to be headed for the naval chief of staff but made a mistake that resulted in being assigned to a minor boondocks fleet base in the Indian Ocean. Retired from the Navy in October 1959. Was a surface officer during thirty-year Navy career who specialized in heavy ordnance. Admiral Sandecker served under Bass in World War II. Bass operates the Anchorage House, a fifteen-room country inn located just south of Lexington, Virginia. Suffers massive heart attack when he notices that eight of the shells containing QD are missing from Vixen 03. Treated at Fitzsimmons Army Hospital in Denver but later slips into a coma and dies at Bethesda Naval Hospital.

Bethesda Naval Hospital. Military hospital near Washington, D.C., where Admiral Bass dies from effects of heart attack.

Black Angus One. Fawkes radio call sign aboard the *Iowa.*

Black Angus Two. Radio call sign for the spotter for the *Iowa.* Black Angus Two is located in a street-sweeper cruising Washington, D.C.

Boeing C-97 Stratocruiser. The type of transport plane used on Flight Vixen 03. Air-frame number 75403. The heavy transport cargo plane has four Pratt and Whitney engines driving four blades on each propeller and can carry a seventy-thousand-pound load. Described as having a two-deck fuselage and the configuration of a double-bellied whale.

British Imperial War Museum. The museum where one of the QD warheads accidentally was sent.

Buckley Field, Colorado. Naval air station outside Denver, Colorado, where Flight Vixen 03 departs. The runway is eleven thousand feet in length.

Buckner, Paul. Described as a longtime pal of Pitt's. Buckner is an agent with the Federal Bureau of Investigation.

Burgdorf, General Ernest. Chief of staff U.S. Air Force safety.

Burns, Master Sergeant Joe. U.S. Air Force master sergeant and flight engineer on Flight Vixen 03. Described as having a Buster Keaton–deadpan face.

Camp, AAR. Camp located on what formerly was a small university for the Portuguese when they ruled Mozambique. Located on Lake Malawi. Attacked by South African Defense Forces led by Zeegler. The attack causes the loss of 2,310 AAR soldiers with only four of Zeegler's troops wounded.

Carnady, Louis. A U.S. congressman described as a tall, sad-looking dude with spaniel eyes. Once double-dated with Loren Smith, Felicia Collins and Hiram Lusana. Carnady was defeated in the last elections.

Catlin M-200. Aquamarine-colored executive jet owned by NUMA that Giordino pilots to Colorado to meet Pitt. Designed to land and take off in impossible places with cargo loads twice its own weight. Type of plane Pitt pilots out to sea with Giordino, Weir and the Stransky Instrument laser to cut the parachute cord holding the QD shell to the skids of the Minerva NUMA helicopter.

Chenago. Commissioned in June 1862 in New York. The vessel was a Union ironclad that foundered in heavy seas and sank on her way to her first assignment, blockading Savannah Harbor. Her entire crew of forty-two men is entombed in her hull which is ninety feet below the surface of the water. NUMA is attempting to raise her. Designed with two circular gun turrets containing Dahlgren smooth-bore cannon that weigh several tons each.

CK-88. Type of Chinese automatic rifle carried by an observer spotted by Marcus Somala watching the Fawkes ranch. Standard issue for soldiers in the AAR.

Collins, Felicia. Described as having short Afro hair and puffy lips. Her skin is the color of cocoa, and she has conical breasts with full, dark nipples. A singer-actor with three gold records, two Emmys and an Oscar for her role as a black suffragist in the film *Road of Poppies.* She is thirty-two years old. High school classmate of Loren Smith.

Copperhead missiles. Type of missile that can be fired from F-120 jets. Missile Higgins recommends for an attack on the *Iowa.*

Cottonwood Inn. Restaurant where Steiger and Pitt eat lunch after Steiger meets with the president of the United States.

Daggat, Frederick. One of New Jersey's three black congressmen. A Democrat. Has an affair with Felicia Collins. Attempts to blackmail Loren Smith and Pitt but is rebuffed.

De Vaal, Pieter. Minister of South African Defense Forces. Speaks Afrikaans. Described as having wavy gray hair. Person behind Operation Wild Rose. Ordered the murder of Patrick Fawkes family. De Vaal also leaked the information about Operation Wild

Rose to U.S. intelligence assets, hoping to embarrass Prime Minister Koertsmann's party and later seize power himself. After his treacherous intentions are revealed by Pitt, he is killed by Machita.

Devine, Phil. Maintenance chief for United Airlines at Stapleton Field. Friend of Harvey Dolan. Said to be a "walking encyclopedia on aircraft." Described as a W. C. Fields type of character—heavy through the middle with a slow, whining voice. Smokes unfiltered cigarettes. Solves the mystery of what type of plane the landing gear Pitt finds in Loren Smith's father's garage came from.

Dolan, Harvey. Principal maintenance inspector for the Air Carrier District of the Federal Aviation Administration. Works at Stapleton Airport, Denver, Colorado.

Dollinger variable air tanks. Airlift method favored by Folsom to raise the *Chenago.*

Donegal, Brian. Helmsman on the *Molly Bender.* An Irish immigrant who is tall with shaggy hair.

Doomsday organism. One of the names for QD, or "Quick Death," the gas carried in the canisters aboard Vixen 03.

Dugan. Works at the shipyard converting the *Iowa.*

Dumbo. Nickname of the twin-rotor, turbine-engined, heavy-lift helicopter that eases Vixen 03 to shore after it is raised.

Emma. Code name of a shadowy operative. Sells Operation Wild Rose plans to Machita for two million dollars. Machita attempts to double-cross Emma and kill him but is foiled. The plans turn out to be operating procedures for military garbage removal. Sneaks aboard the *Iowa* with plans to kill Fawkes. Fawkes instead beats Emma's head to a pulp against the metal deck of the *Iowa.* After Emma is dead, Fawkes discovers that she is, in fact, a woman.

F-120. U.S. Air Force jet code-named "Specter." The fighters can be armed with Copperhead or Satan penetration missiles.

F-140. U.S. Air Force fighter jet nicknamed "Spook." Steiger pilots the F-140 to Sheppard Air Force Base in Wichita Falls, Texas, to retrieve the QD shells at the VFW post in Dayton City, Oklahoma.

Fawkes, Jenny. Daughter of Patrick Sr. and Myrna Fawkes. Nineteen years old, she is described as bigboned and large-breasted with a freckled face.

Fawkes, Myrna. Wife of Patrick Fawkes. Described as lean and tiny but possessing the toughness of two good men.

Fawkes, Patrick Jr. Son of Patrick Sr. and Myrna Fawkes. Only two months past twenty years of age, he is already three inches taller than his father.

Fawkes, Captain Patrick McKenzie. Retired British Navy captain originally from Aberdeen, Scotland. Was in the Royal Navy twenty-five years, fifteen years of those in ship's engineering. Captain of the *Audacious* for two years. Last assignment for Royal Navy was engineering director of the Grimsby Royal Naval shipyard. Described as a giant of a man, standing a shade over six feet six inches in height. His weight exceeds two hundred eighty pounds. Eyes are a somber shade of gray. Sandy-colored hair with whitening filaments in his King George V beard. Smokes a pipe. Captain of the *Iowa* in Operation Wild Rose, the attack on Washington, D.C. Is killed when the sixteen-inch gun on the *Iowa* explodes and blows him to pieces.

Felo gun. Israeli-manufactured weapon used by the South African Defense Forces in the attack on the AAR compound. The weapon shoots swarms of razor-sharp disks capable of severing an eight-inch tree trunk with one burst.

Fergus, Lieutenant Alan. Leader of the SEAL combat units that attack the *Iowa*. Has been in the U.S. Navy seven years. Wounded in the left hand while leading the assault on the *Iowa*. The bullet neatly amputated the middle finger of his left hand before biting through his palm. Also wounded in his leg.

Fisk, Donald. An inspector with the Bureau of Customs. Fisk is out jogging when the shells from the *Iowa* begin falling.

Fitzsimmons Army Hospital. Military hospital in Denver where Admiral Bass is initially treated after suffering heart attack at Table Lake.

Folsom, Jack. NUMA salvage master on the *Visalia.* Described as brawny. Chews gum.

Forbes Marine Scrap & Salvage. Salvage yard in the Chesapeake Bay where the battleship *Iowa* is refitted.

Francis, Shawn. The Irish-born constable of Ukono who convinces Patrick Fawkes over the radio that his ranch has been attacked.

Future Eyes Only. FEO is the designation of certain United States government files that can be opened only after a certain, specified date.

Gold, Lieutenant Sam. U.S. Air Force lieutenant who is Vylander's copilot on Flight Vixen 03.

Gore, Barbara. Secretary to Jarvis. Once had an affair with Jarvis, but now they are just good friends. Described as forty-three with the figure of a *Vogue* fashion model. She has remained trim with shapely legs and high-cheekboned features that have yet to flesh out with age.

Gossard, John. Head of the National Security Agency's Africa Section. Gossard came to the NSA after the Vietnam War, where he served as a specialist in guerrilla logistics. Described as a quiet man with a cynical sense of humor, he walks with a limp caused by a rifle grenade whose shrapnel severed his right foot. Known as a heavy drinker.

Grosfield, General Elmer. The chief inspector of foreign arm shipments and Mapes nemesis. Steiger poses as Grosfield over the phone to convince Mapes that he should allow Pitt to check the Phalanx Arms Corporation inventory.

Heiedriek Air Force Base. Air Force base in South Africa that De Vaal goes to for secret flight to Pembroke for his meeting with Patrick Fawkes.

Henry W. Nice Memorial Toll Bridge. Bridge over the Patuxent River the *Iowa* passes under. Location where Milkman McDonald discovers shredded plywood.

Hickham Field, Hawaii. Airfield where Vixen 03 is scheduled to make a fuel stop. The plane never makes it out of the mountains.

Higgins, General Curtis. Chairman of the Joint Chiefs of Staff.

Hocker-Rodine 27.5 automatic. Weapon used by Emma aboard the *Iowa.* The silenced handgun features a twenty-shot clip.

Hoffman, Captain George. U.S. Air Force captain who is the navigator on Flight Vixen 03.

Holland & Holland. Manufacturer of the twelve-gauge shotgun named "Lucifer" that is kept at the Fawkes ranch.

House Foreign Affairs Subcommittee. Congressional subcommittee that Lusana appeals to for aid.

Hunt, Earl. Democratic congressman from Iowa who is seated on the House Foreign Affairs Subcommittee.

Hydrogen cyanide. A blood agent that interferes with respiration, it is the poison that is falsely claimed to be dumped on Rongelo Island to keep people from visiting the island and being infected with QD.

Iowa. U.S. Navy battleship sent to Forbes Salvage for scrapping but instead converted to a shallower-draft vessel and used by Patrick Fawkes for the attack on Washington, D.C. In the conversion, two General Electric geared turbine engines are removed and half the superstructure removed and replaced with gray-painted plywood. The remaining engines feature 106,000 horsepower. The wartime operational draft was thirty-eight feet; after the conversion, the draft was a few inches less than twenty-two feet. The *Iowa* leaves Forbes Scrap and Salvage on Pearl Harbor Day, December 7. The number painted on its hull is 61. Each remaining main battery turret contains three 68-foot guns, each weighing 134 tons. The entire turret weighs seventeen hundred tons. The armor-piercing projectiles fired by the sixteen-inch guns weigh twenty-seven hundred pounds. The powder charges that propel the shells weigh six hundred pounds. The turret is protected by steel armor plating seven to seventeen inches thick.

Irvin, Colonel Michael. U.S. Air Force officer who signed the original orders for Flight Vixen 03.

Jackson, Sam. The man who takes illicit photographs of Pitt and Loren Smith making love in Felicia Collins's Alexandria love nest. Described as a tall, angular black man with braided hair, a youthful face and long, slender hands.

Jarvis, Dale. Director of the National Security Agency. Described as having a friendly, almost fatherly face. His brown hair is streaked with gray, and he wears it in a crew cut. Wears glasses.

Jones, Hiram. True name of Hiram Lusana.

Jumana, Colonel Randolph. Second-in-command to Lusana. Described as a superb leader of men and a tiger in battle but sadly lacking in administrative style. Plans a coup d'état to unseat Lusana and take over leadership of the AAR. A "favorite son" of the Srona tribe, Jumana spent eight years in a South African prison before Lusana arranged his escape.

Kemper, Admiral Joe. U.S. Navy chief of naval operations.

Kenya Education Council. Meeting in Nairobi that Daggat explains to Lusana he needs to attend.

Kiebel, Lieutenant Commander Oscar. Skipper of the Coast Guard patrol boat that delivers SEALs to the *Iowa.* Described as dour. Wounded by machine gun fire from the *Iowa* when he drops off the Navy SEALs.

Koertsmann, Prime Minister. Prime minister of South Africa.

Lincoln Memorial. Memorial in Washington, D.C., that is hit by a shell fired from the *Iowa.* Features a nineteen-foot-tall statue of a seated Abraham Lincoln.

Lo, Colonel Phon Duc. Vietnamese Army colonel and chief military advisor to the African Army of Revolution.

Lot Six. Area in Arsenal Six where the QD warheads should have been stored. They were instead placed in Lot Sixteen.

Lot Sixteen. Area in Arsenal Six at Phalanx Arms where the QD warheads were accidentally stored.

Lovell, Billy. Commander of VFW Post 9974. Described as a tall, gangly individual about fifty years old. Lovell is at least six feet five inches tall with a ruddy face and short-clipped shiny hair parted down the middle.

Lucifer. The Holland & Holland twelve-gauge shotgun kept at the Fawkes ranch.

Lusana, General Hiram. AKA Hiram Jones. Leader of the African Army of Revolution. Born in the United States of America. Using money from a lucrative armored-car robbery, he expanded his fortune through international drug smuggling. Described as a short, wiry man, medium-boned and lighter-skinned than any man in the army of Africans. The troops call his skin "American tan" behind his back. Has coffee-brown eyes. Crimes committed in the United States include everything from rape to assault, draft dodging and a plot to bomb the state capital of Alabama. Left the United States to avoid paying taxes. Was raised in one of the worst slums in the country. Lusana's father deserted his mother and her nine children when he was eight. Shot and killed by Fergus aboard the *Iowa* but manages to toss the sack containing the QD bomblets into the river.

Machias Point. Location on the Patuxent River.

Machita, Major Thomas. Chief intelligence analyst of the African Army of Revolution. American black whose aliases are Luke Sampson of Los Angeles and Charles Le Mat of Chicago. Operates out of the Mozambique consulate in Pretoria, South Africa. Cover is that he is George Yariko, diplomatic courier. Arrested and beaten by guards on Jumana's orders during coup d'état against Lusana. After almost everyone is killed by Colonel Zeegler's attack on the camp, Machita escapes from the cell. Assumes leadership of the AAR after Lusana is killed. Kills De Vaal with a knife.

Makeir, Colonel Oliver. Coordinator of the African Army of Revolution propaganda programs.

Mapes, Orville. President and chairman of the board of Phalanx Arms Corporation. Described as a screwy sort of duck looking more like a hardware peddler than a death merchant. Has gray eyes. Drives Rolls-Royce convertible. Purchased QD warheads from Rafferty's for five thousand dollars each.

March, Timothy. U.S. secretary of defense. Described as a short, dumpy man who detests any sort of physical exertion.

Massachusetts. U.S. Navy battleship now preserved as a memorial.

Mauser. A .38-caliber automatic handgun used by Machita.

Mayflower. Hotel that the U.S. Department of State rents for Lusana when he visits Washington, D.C.

McDermott. Works in Soviet analysis at the National Security Agency. He is mentioned by Gossard when discussing with Jarvis an upcoming fishing trip.

McDonald, Howard. Milkman who discovers shredded plywood on the Henry W. Nice Memorial Toll Bridge over the Patuxent River that indicates the *Iowa* has steamed past.

Metz, Lou. Superintendent of the Forbes shipyard.

Meyers, Roscoe. Republican congressman from Oregon who is seated on the House Foreign Affairs Subcommittee.

Military Air Transport Service. MATS is the division of the U.S. Air Force that the Boeing C-97 Vixen 03 was assigned. Pitt views the lettering painted on the plane's fuselage through the underwater camera and, after viewing the serial number on the vertical stabilizer, identifies the plane as Vixen 03.

Minerva M-88. Twin-turboshaft-engined NUMA helicopter that Steiger pilots with Sandecker aboard when Pitt drops on the deck of the *Iowa.* The helicopter then takes up station above the National Archives Building and snags the parachute of the shell containing the QD bomblet. Steiger and Sandecker then head out to sea on a suicide mission to dispose of the shell. Pitt chases them out to sea in the Catlin M-200 with a laser aboard. After the laser severs a few of the lines holding the QD shell to the helicopter, it overheats. Steiger then pilots the helicopter into a steep dive. When he pulls the helicopter out of the dive, the weight of the QD shell finally snaps the parachute cords, and the shell plunges into the ocean. Once the shell is free and with the Minerva nearly out of fuel, Steiger pilots the helicopter to a Norwegian cruiser and lands.

Missouri. U.S. Navy battleship maintained by the navy in Bremerton, Washington.

Molly Bender. Fishing trawler crushed by the *Iowa.*

Mount Vernon. George Washington's famous home and the site where the *Iowa* finally runs hard aground.

Mukuta, Captain John. Captain in the African Army of Revolution.

Mutaapo, Captain. Fictitious name used by a man dressed as a pilot on a BEZA-Mozambique Airlines return flight to Africa that Lusana intends to take. Described as a tall, slender man with a middle-aged black face. Wears dark green and gold braided BEZA-Mozambique Airlines uniform. Drugs Lusana's martini and has him delivered to Patrick Fawkes aboard the *Iowa.*

Natal, Africa. Borders Mozambique and is the province where the Fawkes ranch is located.

National Archives Building. Three shells are fired at the building from the *Iowa.* The first goes through the dome and plunges downward, missing the Declaration of Independence by ten feet. The second is a dud. The third, which contains the QD bomblets, is plucked from the sky by the Minerva NUMA helicopter piloted by Steiger with Sandecker aboard.

National Transportation Safety Board. Governmental agency Dolan contacts to find out if any commercial C-97 Stratocruisers were lost over the continental United States.

Neutron bomb. Type of bomb the president suggests might disable the QD warheads aboard the *Iowa.* The idea is rejected.

Nisei. Americans of Japanese descent imprisoned in internment camps during World War II. Mentioned as a model for Africans to follow by Loren Smith when talking to Congressman Daggat. After World War II, the Nisei worked in the South California fields so they could send their sons and daughters to UCLA and USC to become attorneys and doctors.

Norton Air Force Base. U.S. Air Force base in California where Colonel Abe Steiger works.

O'Keefe, General John. Aide to the Joint Chiefs of Staff.

O'Shea. Guard at the gate of Forbes Scrap and Salvage when Pitt and Jarvis first arrive.

Obasi, Daniel. Seventeen-year-old Shaba leaves in charge of the gun turret on the *Iowa* when Shaba goes below to the magazine to repair the hoist. Fires the QD shell at Washington, D.C.

Operation Wild Rose. South African plot to shell Washington, D.C., and blame the attack on the African Army of Revolution to discredit them.

Patuxent River. River that empties into the Chesapeake Bay a few miles above Forbes Scrap and Salvage. The river the *Iowa* takes toward Washington, D.C.

Pembroke, Natal. Town in Africa where Fawkes meets South African defense minister. While he is gone, his ranch is attacked and his family killed.

Phalanx Arms Corporation. Name of the company based in Newark, New Jersey, that purchased the QD warheads from the Raffertys. The company sits on five thousand acres and is rated as the sixth-largest army in terms of equipment. Phalanx Arms also ranks as the seventh-largest air force.

Pier Six. Pier in San Francisco where the QD warheads recovered from Vixen 03 in Table Lake are shipped for eventual destruction at sea.

Plum Point Marina. Location Gossard tells Jarvis they, along with Sampson and McDermott, are to leave from for the scheduled fishing trip.

Potomac River. River leading to Washington, D.C., Fawkes plans to take the *Iowa* up to shell the U.S. capital.

Quantico, Virginia. Location of a marine base Fawkes views as the *Iowa* heads past upriver.

Quick Death. The gas carried in canisters aboard Vixen 03. Biochemical name is thirty letters long and unpronounceable. Created by microbiologist John Vetterly, QD is described as an artificial form of life that in turn was capable of producing a disease strain that was and still is quite unknown. QD is a nondetectable, unidentifiable bacteriological agent able to incapacitate a living human or animal within seconds of exposure and disrupt the vital body functions, causing death three to five minutes later. Unlike other lethal agents, QD gains strength over time. If five ounces were delivered over Manhattan Island, the organism would seek out and kill ninety-eight percent of the population within four hours. Water neutralizes the organism.

Radar altimeter. Device especially designed by Admiral Bass. Has an omnidirectional indicator that signals the QD warheads' descent and releases a parachute at fifteen hundred feet elevation. At one thousand feet of elevation, the QD warhead explodes, releasing the gas.

Rafferty, Lee. Neighbor near Loren Smith's father's cabin. Retired in the summer of 1971 from the U.S. Navy as a deep-sea diver because of the bends (diving term for excess nitrogen in the bloodstream—sometimes fatal). Husband of Maxine Rafferty. Described as a string bean of a man. Likes cigars. Brews his own beer. Sold QD warheads to Phalanx Arms Corporation. After Pitt discloses he knows about the sale, he smashes Pitt in the shoulder with plumbing pipe. Pitt retrieves the pipe and swings it against Rafferty's head, breaking the bone in his temple and killing him.

Rafferty, Maxine. Neighbor near Loren Smith's father's cabin. Wife of Lee Rafferty. Described as having the look of the West about her. Heavyset, she wears rimless glasses and has bluish-silver hair. Murdered Charlie Smith with a rifle shot to the heart after he had second thoughts about selling QD warheads. Pitt hits her with a kerosene lamp, cutting her breast, then shoots her with his Colt revolver, killing her.

Ragged Point. Spot on the waterway where the *Iowa* crushes the *Molly Bender.*

Rantoul Engineering. Chicago-based firm that produces the wheels used on the Boeing C-97 that was used for Flight Vixen 03.

Ravenfoot, Commodore Jack. Head of the NSA's domestic division. Retired U.S. Navy commodore. Was executive officer aboard the battleship *New Jersey* during the Vietnam War. A full-blooded Native American from the Cheyenne tribe, Ravenfoot holds a Phi Beta Kappa key from Yale.

Red River. River that forms the border of Texas and Oklahoma. Steiger drives across the Red River on the way to the VFW post in Dayton City, Oklahoma, to retrieve QD warheads.

Remains Identity and Recovery Team. U.S. Air Force group tasked with caring for the remains of the crew of Flight Vixen 03.

Rocky Mountain Arsenal. Army installation outside Denver, Colorado, that was the primary manufacturing site for chemical weapons. Site where QD was produced.

Rocky Mountain oysters. Famous state dish of Colorado. Fried bull's testicles. Tastes like chicken.

Rongelo. Island in the South Pacific that was the intended destination of Flight Vixen 03. Located four hundred miles northeast of Bilini Island. Described as a raw, bleached knob of coral poking through the sea in the middle of nowhere. The island, actually more of an atoll, rises only six feet above the surface of the ocean. Infected with QD, the island will be uninhabitable for the next three hundred years. The island is eradicated by a nuclear missile blast fired from a U.S. Navy submarine.

Sampson. Works in Soviet analysis at the National Security Agency. He is mentioned by Gossard when discussing an upcoming fishing trip with Jarvis.

Satan penetration missiles. Type of missile carried by F-120 jets. The missiles can gouge their way through three yards of concrete.

Savannah. City on the coast of Georgia where Pitt goes to supervise raising the *Chenago,* a Union ironclad that sank off the Georgia coast during the Civil War.

Sawatch Mountain Range. Mountains in the Colorado rockies where Loren Smith's father's cabin is located.

Sawyer, Phil. Press secretary to the president of the United States. Along with Pitt, dates Loren Smith. Described as wearing white shirts and talking like a thesaurus. Smith describes Sawyer as the sort of man you marry: loyal, true blue, sets you on a gilded pedestal and wants you to be the mother of his children. Has premature gray hair; he is said to have a solid, handsome face.

Shaba, Charles. Part of the African crew Fawkes uses on the *Iowa.* Shaba is the chief engineer. After the *Iowa* grounds, he becomes gunnery officer.

Shaw, Morton. Independent Party congressman from Florida.

Sheppard Air Force Base. U.S. Air Force base in Wichita Falls, Texas, Steiger lands at when he travels to retrieve QD warheads at VFW post in Oklahoma.

Sheridan Point. Location on the Potomac River the Coast Guard patrol boat passes.

Slaughter Beach. Beach in Delaware that Steiger and Sandecker pass over in a NUMA helicopter as they head out to sea on the mission to dispose of QD warhead.

Smith, Charlie. Father of Loren Smith. Deceased. Itinerant inventor. Allegedly blown apart by dynamite, but Pitt later identifies his body as being aboard Vixen 03 in Table Lake.

Somala, Marcus. Section leader of the African Army of Revolution. Witnesses the raid on the Fawkes ranch, then is mortally wounded when shot in the back. Manages to make his way to the hospital and reports to Lusana before dying.

St. Clements Island. Island passed as the *Iowa* steams up the Patuxent River.

Stanton Probe. Name of fictitious committee Pitt cooks up to scare Mapes into allowing him to search the Phalanx Arms Corporation's inventory for the missing QD warheads.

Steiger, Colonel Abraham Levi. Works for the investigator general for safety at Norton Air Force Base in California. Dolan forwards a request to him for information about Boeing C-97 number 75403. Described as having a completely shaved head, friendly hazel eyes and an enormous Kaiser Wilhelm moustache. Wears size-twelve boots. His body is squat and barrel-chested, and Pitt estimates his weight at close to two hundred twenty pounds. Father of eight children—five boys and three girls. Pilots the NUMA helicopter that drops Pitt off on the *Iowa.* Along with Sandecker, Steiger then takes up station over the National Archives Building and snags the parachute of the shell containing QD bomblets. Then, together with Sandecker, they fly out to sea on a suicide mission to dispose of the shell.

Stransky Instrument Company. Company that employs Dr. Weir.

Swedborg, Carl. Skipper of the fishing trawler *Molly Bender.* Swedborg is seventy years old but has no wish to retire. Wife has already passed away.

Table Lake. Lake located one quarter mile over the hill behind Loren Smith's cabin. Location where Pitt finds the plane missing the canisters containing nerve gas. A man-made lake, it was formed when the State of Colorado dammed up a stream in 1945, submerging an abandoned lumber mill.

Tazareen massacre. Village in the Province of Transvaall where a senseless slaughter of at least one hundred sixty-five black villagers was instituted by the AAR.

Tiger fish. Old World relative to the South American Amazon piranha that Lusana hooks while fishing.

Tonic One. Code name for one of the groups from the South African Defense Forces that attack the AAR compound.

Tonic Two. Code name of one of the groups from the South African Defense Forces that attack the AAR compound.

Travis Air Force Base. U.S. Air Force base in California where the original orders for Flight Vixen 03 were issued.

Veterans of Foreign Wars, Dayton City Post 9974. VFW post in Oklahoma where two of the QD shells were accidentally sent. The VFW tried to fire the shells during a Veterans Day parade, but luckily they didn't explode.

Vetterly, John. Microbiologist who created Quick Death. Later dies on Rongelo Island with three of his assistants as they check the effects of QD.

Visalia. NUMA salvage ship assigned to raise the *Chenago*.

Vixen 03. Call sign of the plane that crashes into Table Lake, Colorado, carrying the QD warheads.

Vogel, Brian. Neighbor of Patrick Fawkes, who comes to the ranch after the massacre to help bury the bodies of the ranch workers.

Vylander, Major Raymond. U.S. Air Force major who is aircraft commander of Flight Vixen 03.

Walnut Point, Virginia. Location where Patrick Fawkes anchors whale boat to record the passing boat traffic in preparation for taking the *Iowa* up the Potomac River.

Walvis Bay Investment Corporation. A financial front company for the African Army of Revolution.

Weir, Dr. Paul. The head physicist of the Stransky Instrument Company. Described as a light-skinned man with Nordic features.

Wisconsin. U.S. Navy battleship scrapped in 1984. Battleship that was scheduled to lob the shells containing QD twenty miles through the air to Rongelo Island.

Yariko, George. Fictitious name that is on the Mozambique passport Machita uses when he flies to Pretoria for his meeting with Emma. Yariko's cover is that of a diplomatic courier to Mozambique.

Zeegler, Colonel Joris. Army colonel in charge of the intelligence division of the South African Defense Forces or director of Internal South African Defense. Described as a tall, slender man with compelling blue eyes.

Night Probe!

AC Cobra. One of Pitt's cars. A red 1966 model with a 427-cubic-inch engine.

Anoxia. A condition resulting from an overabundance of CO_2 in a human's system. Make the sufferer giddy and possibly hallucinatory. Klinger suffers the condition aboard the *Sappho I* when the air scrubbers don't function properly.

Argo ground-to-air missiles. Type of British hand-held missiles used for the attack on Canada One. Compact, the missiles weigh only thirty pounds.

Argus, Henry. Was due to meet Burton at the Glen Echo Racquet Club. When Argus cancels, Burton-Angus is paired with Murphy. While waiting for a racquetball court, Murphy asks Burton-Angus for information about the North American Treaty.

Arlington College of Archaeology. Where the copy of the North American treaty recovered from the *Empress of Ireland* is taken.

Army and Navy Club. Restaurant favored by Sandecker.

***Arvada*, U.S.S.** U.S. Navy amphibious landing transport vessel. Milligan is assigned as the communications officer. The ship is bound from San Diego to the Indian Ocean, but when it develops problems with the automated steering system, it is ordered to stop in Los Angeles for repairs. Clive is having some fun here. Arvada, Colorado, is the suburb in Denver where Clive was living when he wrote *Raise the* Titanic!

Asquith, Henry Herbert. British prime minister when Woodrow Wilson was president. Signed the North American treaty.

Baby. Nickname for the RSV.

Baldwin Locomotive. Atlantic type 4-4-2 owned by Ansel Magee. The locomotive rolled out of the Baldwin Works in 1906 and pulled the *Overland Limited* from Chicago to Council Bluffs, Iowa.

Beaseley, Peter. Chief librarian of the British Foreign Office in London. It is said that Beaseley knows more about the Foreign Office than any man alive. Described as white-haired. Smokes a pipe. Discovers information about the North American Treaty for the British.

Beatty, Professor Preston. Considered a leading authority on unsolved crimes. An author of numerous books on the subject. Beatty is described as having blue-green eyes over a salt-and-pepper beard. Pitt guesses his age at late forties. Has stern, craggy features and silver-edged hair. Beatty tells Pitt the history of Massey.

Bentley, Sergeant. Royal Marine commanded by Macklin.

Beretta .25-caliber. Handgun favored by Shaw.

Bond, James. Famous character created by Ian Fleming, mentioned by Pitt to Shaw after Pitt arranges for Shaw to fly on the same flight as Milligan.

Borden, Sir Robert. Canadian prime minister just prior to World War I. He was one of the signers of the North American Treaty.

Boucher, Jean. Guerrier's bodyguard/chauffeur. Finds Guerrier's corpse after he is smothered by Gly. Wife and two children. Originally hired by Guerrier in May 1962. Only witness who claims Villon was the last person to see Guerrier alive.

British Army S-66 long-range reconnaissance scope. Type of scope Shaw uses to spy on the *Ocean Venturer.* Can read a newspaper headline at five miles.

British prime minister. Described as a formidably heavy-featured man with unblinking blue eyes and a mouth that ticks up at the edges in a perpetual smile.

Brogan, Martin. U.S. director of Central Intelligence.

Brown Bess. Black-powder rifle owned by Epstein. The weapon is a flintlock seventy-five-caliber that was used by the British soldiers during the Revolutionary War.

Bryan, William Jennings. Political sage who ran for president of the United States several times. Known as "The Great Commoner." Was President Wilson's secretary of state. In the photograph Milligan secures, he looks portly and grinning.

Burton-Angus, Lieutenant Ewen. Aide to the naval attaché for the British Embassy in Washington, D.C. The last six years and four months, he has actually worked for the British Secret Intelligence Service. Owns a home in Devon, England. Present when the *Manhattan Limited* is found. Killed by fire from U.S. Marines.

Button Islands. Located in the Labrador Sea off Newfoundland. The *Doodlebug* is ten miles off the Button Islands when attacked.

Caldweiler, Eric. Former superintendent of a coal mine in Wales. Described as stockily built. Supervises the British effort to tunnel into the mountain where the *Manhattan Limited* is trapped. Smokes a pipe.

Canada One. Code name for Prime Minister Sarveux's official plane. A four-jet-engined plane that weighs two hundred tons. Forty-two men and women die when it bursts into flames when landing after being hit by an Argo missile fired by Gly's team.

Canadian prime minister's mansion. Described as having a three-story stone exterior that is cold and morbid. Has a long foyer with a high ceiling, traditional furnishings and a wide circular staircase that leads to the bedrooms.

Chase, Glen. Captain of the *De Soto.* Described as taciturn and balding. Chase refuses to use the language of the sea. Instead of *port,* he says *left;* instead of *mooring,* he says *parking.* Present when the *Manhattan Limited* is found.

Churchill, Winston. British prime minister who at the time of World War I was First Lord of the Admiralty.

Coli, Otis. Director of the Quebec Institute of Marine Engineering. Described as a gorilla of a man, barrel-chested and with a rounded, heavy-browed face. His white hair passes his collar, and his moustache, beneath a thin, sloping nose, looks as if it has been clipped with sheep shears. Smokes du Maurier cigarettes with a gold-tipped filter.

Collins. JIM suit operator who finds himself stuck in the wreckage of the *Empress of Ireland* after the explosion. Glancing around, he discovers the body of Shields, and Pitt realizes Collins is inside Shields's cabin.

Control Center. Part of the James Bay Project. Located ten floors above the generator room, it is accessed by a security card system. The room is small and spartan and contains four engineers who monitor the manual systems.

Cummings-Wray sender. Early radio device that is used by the New York & Quebec Railroad to communicate. Has a selector wheel. Harding tries to use it to call Albany, New York, to find out information about the *Manhattan Limited.*

De Soto. NUMA's new research vessel. A trim vessel sixty feet in length especially designed for cruising inland waterways.

Deauville-Hudson Bridge. Railroad bridge near the Wacketshire Station; the *Manhattan Limited* plunged off it. It is one hundred fifty feet from the bridge to the Hudson River. One section of the bridge spanned a five-hundred-foot-long truss. The bridge was the fifth longest in the world when it was constructed.

Dispatch. Code name used by Moran in the attack on Canada One.

Doodlebug. Built with six hundred eighty million dollars earmarked for the Department of Energy but diverted to NUMA. The *Doodlebug* is an underwater geology submersible. Described as "the inner half of an aircraft wing standing on end" and "the conning tower of a submarine that has lost its hull." Has an aluminum shell built around its instrument package. In briefing the president, Sandecker explains that the *Doodlebug* can see through ten miles of solid rock and identify fifty-one different minerals and metal traces. The *Doodlebug*'s instruments transmit a sharply focused, concentrated pulse of energy straight down into the earth. After escaping the attack from the U.S. submarine, the *Doodlebug* finds "the granddaddy of stratigraphic traps," or a giant oil field in the waters off Quebec. The field measures ninety-five miles by three-quarters of a mile wide and is estimated to contain as much as eight billion barrels of oil. Later used on the *Manhattan Limited* project.

Dunning, Art. NUMA team master of the dive rescue team aboard the *Ocean Venturer.* Locates the saturation chamber after the explosion on the *Empress of Ireland* and finds all the divers inside dead.

Emmett, Ray. The pilot of Canada One.

Empress of Ireland. Name of the Canadian luxury liner bound for England that sinks after being rammed by a Norwegian coal collier named *Storstad* in the St. Lawrence River. A copy of the North American Treaty is aboard. Owned by the Canadian Pacific Railway, the vessel and her sister ship, the *Empress of Britain,* displaced fourteen thousand tons and were five hundred fifty feet long. Twin-screw vessels. One of the twenty-foot diameter, thirty-ton, four-bladed bronze propellers was salvaged in 1968.

Epstein, Joe. A columnist for the *Baltimore Sun.* Epstein is an avid black-powder marksman on weekends. Described as bald-headed.

Ericsson, Dr. Medical chief of staff at the hospital James Sarveux is taken to after the attack on Canada One.

Esbenson, Robert. Buyer of the Mercedes-Benz 540K at the Richmond Auction Pitt attends. In real life, Esbenson was Clive's partner in the classic car business.

Essex, John. Grandson of Richard Essex. Seventy-five years old. Operates a sophisticated oyster farming operation in ponds along the Potomac River near Coles Point, Virginia. Described as having twinkling blue eyes and prominent high cheekbones. Has a white beard and moustache. His body shows no fat. Was once assigned to the American Embassy in London. His wife died ten years ago. Has three children. Inside an ornately carved antique credenza with a secret compartment in his office, he holds information about the North American Treaty. His decomposing body is discovered by Pitt after he dies from a clot in his coronary artery.

Essex, Richard. The person in charge of transporting the copy of the North American Treaty on the *Manhattan Limited.* Was President Wilson's undersecretary of state. In the photograph Milligan secures, he is said to appear dapper and refined and to be wearing a broad smile. Died in 1914 at age forty-two.

Field Foreman. Code name used by Gly in the attack on Canada One.

Finn, Commissioner Harold. Commissioner of the Canadian Mounties. Described as an unimpressive little man in rumpled clothes, the sort who is lost in a crowd or melts in with the furniture during a party. His charcoal hair is parted down the middle and contrasts with his bushy white eyebrows. Solves the mystery of Gly impersonating Villon. Is present at the payoff to Gly, and supervises the work on the jet's autopilot so Gly and his plane crash into the ocean.

Forbes Excavation Company. Company that operated the quarry from 1882 to 1910, where limestone was mined and sent along the spur at Mondragon Hook Junction.

Foreign Office. The branch of the British government office of internal affairs. Where the North American Treaty was headed aboard the *Empress of Ireland.*

Free Quebec Society. Known by the acronym FQS, an underground terrorist movement. Tied to Moscow, the FQS has assassinated several Canadian officials.

Galasso, Dr. Melvin. Person at the Arlington College of Archaeology who attempts to remove the North American Treaty from the leather bag found aboard the wreck of the *Empress of Ireland.* Described as sixtyish, walking with a slight stoop and possessing a face like Dr. Jekyll after he becomes Mr. Hyde. After carefully removing the treaty from the leather bag, he finds it is an unreadable mush.

Gallopin' Lena. Nickname of the 2-8-0 Constellation-type locomotive that pulls the *Manhattan Limited.* Built by Alco's Schenectady Works in 1911 out of 236,000 pounds of iron and steel, she is finished in gloss black with a red stripe. Her number is 88, and it is neatly hand-painted in gold.

Gardner, Mildred. Head archivist of Princeton University. Has a nineteen-fortyish pageboy haircut.

Generator room. Part of the James Bay Project, the generator room spans twelve acres of space carved out of solid granite four hundred feet underground. Three rows of huge generators, five stories high and driven by water turbines, fill the space. Each generator produces five hundred thousand kilowatts of electrical energy.

George V. King of England just prior to World War I.

Gilmore. NUMA worker in the engine room of the *Ocean Venturer.* Survives the explosion with a skull fracture.

Gly, Foss. Person who tries to assassinate Sarveux. Described as having a great mass of sandy-colored hair and a square, ruddy face. Has congenial brown eyes and a firm-cut chin. His nose is large and misshapen from numerous breaks suffered in back-alley brawls. Occasionally smokes cigarettes. Born in Flagstaff, Arizona, as a result of a drunken coupling between a professional wrestler and a county sheriff's daughter. His childhood was a nightmare of suffering and whippings from his grandfather. When older, he beat the sheriff to death and fled the state. Later, he rolled drunks in Denver, led a string of auto thieves in Los Angeles and hijacked gasoline trucks in Texas. Professional assassin who prefers to think of himself as a coordinator. Where most murders follow a pattern, Gly's is that he does not have one. Disguised as Henri Villon, Gly goes to murder Guerrier with the intent of using an exotic poison, then decides instead to smother him with a pillow.

Gosset, Miss. Secretary to Beaseley. Helps Beaseley in the search at the Sanctuary Building for records pertaining to the North American Treaty.

Grey, Sir Edward. British foreign secretary during the time of Woodrow Wilson's presidency.

Guerrier. Premier of Quebec and the Parti Quebecois. Described as in his late seventies, tall and slender with unkempt silver hair and thick, tangled beard. Has false teeth. Smothered with a pillow by Foss Gly disguised as Henri Villon.

Harding, Sam. Ticket agent at the Wacketshire office of the New York & Quebec Railroad. After the Wacketshire Station is robbed by Massey, Harding runs down the tracks looking for the *Manhattan Limited;* falling, he gashes his leg on a railroad spike.

Heiser Foundation. An analytical laboratory in Brooklyn, New York, to which Pitt takes pieces of the Deauville-Hudson Bridge. The laboratory quickly determines the bridge was cleverly and systematically blown up.

Hoker, Doug. NUMA operator of the RSV controlled from aboard the *Ocean Venturer.* Described as a cheerful fat man with curly strawberry hair and freckles. Has a great flash of teeth.

Holographic Communications System. A three-dimensional telephone-television system installed in the White House.

Honjo Maru. Japanese container ship six hundred sixty-five feet in length. After delivering four hundred new electric cars from Kobe, Japan, the vessel is making a return trip loaded with a cargo of newsprint paper. Gly rams this vessel with the hydroplane.

Hooper, Sergeant. U.S. Marine Force reconnaissance sergeant present at the flooded mountain that contains the *Manhattan Limited.* Chews tobacco.

Humberly, Graham. A well-heeled Los Angeles Rolls-Royce dealer. Humberly is a former British subject who cultivates an enormous channel of important contacts, particularly in the United States Navy. Described as a small man with a head too large for his shoulders. Lives in a posh house in Palos Verde, a bedroom community of Los Angeles. The house is a blend of contemporary and California Spanish, with rough-coated plaster walls and ceilings, laced with massive weathered beams covered by a roof of curved red tile. A large fountain splashes on the main terrace and spills into the swimming pool. The house has a view of the Pacific Ocean and Catalina Island. At a party at his home, Humberly introduces Shaw to Milligan.

Hunt, Malcom. Deputy prime minister of Canada. Smokes a pipe. Hunt is of British descent and a graduate of Oxford University.

***Huron*, H.M.C.S.** Canadian destroyer ordered to chase the *Ocean Venturer* away from the wreck of the *Empress of Ireland.*

Huston, Mrs. Formerly the secretary to the head of the British Secret Intelligence Service. A year after Shaw retired, she married Graham Huston, who then worked at the British Secret Intelligence Service in the cryptographic analysis section. Both she and her husband are now retired and pensioned and operate an antique shop in London.

Jackson. NUMA worker in the engine room of the *Ocean Venturer.* Survives the explosion with a broken knee.

James Bay. Canadian hydroelectric project. James Bay has eighteen dams, twelve powerhouses and a work force of nearly ninety thousand people. The project involved the rechanneling of two rivers the size of the Colorado River. James Bay is the largest and most expensive hydroelectric project in history, built at a cost of twenty-six billion dollars. The project was begun in 1974 and generates over one hundred million kilowatts of electricity which will double in the next twenty years. The amount of electricity that flows to the United States is enough to light fifteen states. The project is guarded by a five-hundred-man security force.

Jeffrey, Ian. Sarveux's principal secretary. Described as a serious-faced man in his late twenties.

Jensen Convertible, 1950. A four-door, two-tone straw and beige 130-horsepower automobile at the auction in Richmond that Pitt attends. He buys the Jensen and drives it home to his garage with Moon as passenger.

JIM suit. An articulated deep-water atmospheric diving system. It is constructed of magnesium and fiberglass. In air, the suit weighs eleven hundred pounds; underwater, it weighs only about sixty.

Kemper, Admiral Joe. Chief of U.S. naval operations. Sandecker calls Kemper to halt the attack on the *Doodlebug.*

Kendall, Captain. Captain of the *Empress of Ireland* the night she sank.

King, Dr. Ramon. The creative genius behind the *Doodlebug.* Described as having a light-skinned, narrow, gloomy face, with a jutting jaw and barbed-wire eyebrows—the kind of face that mirrors nothing and barely displays a change of expressions.

Kitchner, Lord, Field Marshal. British secretary of war during World War I.

Klein, Dr. Ronald. The secretary of energy. Described as a scholarly-looking man with long white hair and a large condor nose. He is six feet five inches tall.

Klinger, Sid. One of the NUMA operators of the *Sappho I.* Loses a tooth when the explosives are ignited on the *Empress of Ireland.*

Labrador Sea. Where the *Doodlebug* is operating when it is attacked by U.S. Navy Amberjack-class submarine.

Lac St. Joseph. Location of the airfield near Quebec City that belongs to the Royal Canadian Air Force. Site of the payoff from Sarveux to Gly.

Lasky, Bill. Electronic panel operator on the *Doodlebug* when it is attacked by Navy Amberjack-class submarine.

Le Mat, Jules. Captain of the work ship that first delivers Pitt to the site on the St. Lawrence River the *Empress of Ireland* is under.

Library of Congress. Famous library in Washington, D.C., where John Essex tells Milligan his grandfather's personal papers are stored.

Lubin, Jerry. A mining consultant with the Federal Resources Agency. Described as a small, humorless man with a pawnbroker nose and bloodhound eyes. Lubin supervises the NUMA team locating the *Manhattan Limited.*

Macklin, Lieutenant Digby. Leader of the fourteen British Royal Marine paratroopers who parachute onto the hill where the *Manhattan Limited* is hidden.

Wounded in arm and foot by fire from U.S. Marines. Surrenders to Sanchez.

Magee, Annie. Wife of Ansel Magee. Described as carrying herself languidly and standing tall. Her shape is pencil thin, and Pitt guesses she was once a fashion model. Her hair is salt-and-pepper and gracefully styled.

Magee, Ansel. Famous sculptor who owns a home near the Deauville-Hudson Bridge. Described as having a kindly, elflike face. Has suffered several heart attacks. Has the Wacketshire station restored and attached to his house.

Maggie. Secretary to the president of the United States.

Magnificent Pitt, the Illusionist. What Pitt calls himself to Milligan when he produces Shaw at Kennedy Airport and disappears.

Manhattan Limited. The train taken by Richard Essex. The train carries ninety passengers, not including the crew and the special government car Essex is aboard. Essex has a copy of the North American Treaty. The copy is lost when the train disappears. Pitt discovers that the train was also carrying St. Gauden's twenty-dollar gold pieces struck in 1914 at the Philadelphia mint, worth two million dollars. Gold is now worth over three hundred million dollars.

Manuden, England. A village outside London where Shaw attends the funeral for the former chief of the British Secret Intelligence Service.

Martha. The young girl who dies in the collision of the *Empress of Ireland.* Described as having golden hair nearly three feet long. Her father finds her body with the help of Shields and chooses to stay with her as the ship sinks.

Masey, Clement. Alias Dapper Doyle. Man who robs the Wacketshire station of the New York & Quebec Railroad. Described as being built like a jockey, rail-thin and short. His moustache is as blond as his hair, which is tucked under a Panama straw hat. A fastidious dresser, he wears a Weber and Heilbroner English-cut suit with silk stitching. The razor-creased pants stop evenly above a pair of two-tone brown suede and leather shoes. Comes from a wealthy Boston family. Graduated Harvard summa cum laude. Established a thriving law practice that catered to the social elite of Providence, Massachusetts. Married a prominent socialite. Father to five children. Twice elected to the Massachusetts Senate. Turned over the money from the robberies he masterminded to the poor.

Mauser Automatic Pistol 7.63 Caliber. Weapon used by Massey when he robs the Wacketshire station. Pitt uses the handgun to wound Shaw.

May, Jack. Copilot of Canada One.

McComb, Superintendent. Officer in charge of records for the Canadian Mounted Police. McComb calls Villon with information about Roubaix.

McComb, Dr. Walter. Chief chemist at the Heiser Foundation. Described as fifteen years older than Pitt and seventy pounds heavier.

McGovern, Dr. Abner. Doctor who performs the second autopsy on Guerrier. Has been with the Canadian Mounties forensic pathology staff for forty years. Discovers Guerrier was murdered.

Meechum, Hiram. The Western Union night man at the Wacketshire station of the New York & Quebec Railroad. When Meechum attempts to signal the *Manhattan Limited,* Massey shoots him in the hip, then smashes his Mauser pistol against his head.

Mercedes-Benz 540K, 1939. Pearl-white automobile with custom Freestone & Webb bodywork, purchased at the Richmond car auction by Esbenson.

Metz. NUMA chief engineer aboard the *Ocean Venturer.*

Model T. Famous Ford automobile. The Wacketshire station of the New York & Quebec Railroad uses one as the depot hack. The hack has leatherette side curtains over oak side panels that are attached with Murphy fasteners.

Moffat, Alexander. Described as looking and acting like the archetype of a government official. His hair is trimmed short with an immaculately creased left-hand part. He exhibits a ramrod spine and precise correctness in speech and mannerism. Burton-Angus asks Moffat about the North American Treaty after talking to Murphy.

Mondragon Hook Junction. Place where rail spur leaves the main line used by the *Manhattan Limited.*

Montserrat. Island in the Lesser Antilles southeast of Puerto Rico. Intended destination of Gly after he receives thirty-million-dollar payoff and jet from Sarveux.

Moon, Harrison IV. The chief of staff for the president of the United States. Described as being in his late twenties. Asks Pitt to search for the North American Treaty. Is present when Pitt delivers the treaty to the president in Canada.

Moran, Claude. Described as a reed-thin, pockmarked Marxist who works for the governor general of Quebec. In the missile attack on Sarveux, he is code-named Dispatch.

Munson, Dr. Doctor at the hospital Sarveux is taken to after the attack on Canada One. Administers a narcotic to Sarveux after his wife leaves.

Murphy, Jack. The Senate historian.

National Archives. Located in Washington, D.C., the archives contain important papers pertaining to the United States.

New York & Quebec Northern Railroad. Company that operated the *Manhattan Limited,* later absorbed by the New York Central Railroad.

Night probe. Old divers' term for exploring the dark of underwater caves.

North American Treaty. Treaty signed by the United States and Britain that sells Canada to the United States. The deal was arranged because Britain was short of funds just prior to the outbreak of World War I. The price was one billion dollars, and one hundred fifty million was the down payment which, after the loss of the treaty copies, was converted to a loan.

O'Leery, Ms. Self-made woman with vast cosmetics fortune. Bids against Pitt for the Jensen Convertible but backs down. Pitt had a fling with her in the past.

Ocean Venturer. NUMA research vessel. Designed with a rounded bow and oval fantail, the egg-shaped bridge rests on an arched spire. Amidships is a derrick like those at an oil field. Hull is white-colored and double-hulled for breaking through ice. The vessel is heavily damaged by an explosion from the *Empress of Ireland* detonated by Gly. Total deaths from the explosion total twelve.

Official Secrets Vault. Section in the basement of the Sanctuary Building where Beaseley discovers the meaning of the North American Treaty.

Parkenham, Sir Edward. Led the last British force before the Royal Marines in *Night Probe!* to invade the United States. Parkenham and his group invaded New Orleans in 1814.

Parti Quebecois. Canadian political party that advocates a free Quebec.

Peace Tower. The tower, two hundred ninety-one feet tall, that forms the center block of the Canadian Parliament. Pitt orders Westler piloting the Scinletti to land in front of the tower.

***Phoenix*, U.S.S.** U.S. Navy guided missile cruiser that is ordered to protect the *Ocean Venturer* from the *Huron.*

Pilcher, Nathan. With wife, Hattie, was owner of the Pilcher Inn in Poughkeepsie, New York. Murdered, then cooked and served between fifteen and twenty people.

Pointe au Pere. Also known as "Father's Point" in English. Location of the cemetery maintained by the Canadian Pacific Railway that holds the graves of the eighty-eight, mostly third-class passengers that were unidentified victims of the sinking of the *Empress of Ireland.*

Powers, Marv. One of the NUMA operators of the *Sappho I* on the *Empress of Ireland* project. Breaks both arms and suffers a concussion when the explosives explode on the *Empress of Ireland.*

President of the United States. Described as looking tired and worn. The president is small in stature, with brown hair streaked with white and thinning; his features, once cheerful and crinkling, are now set and solemn. A native of New Mexico, he was inaugurated only a few weeks prior after serving twenty years in the Senate. By education and occupation, he is an attorney.

Pullman car. Famous maker of railroad cars. The one Essex rides in is seventy feet long and finished in elaborately carved Circassian walnut. Brass electrical lights adorn the walls, and it features red velvet revolving chairs and potted palms. The sleeping compartment features beveled mirrors and ceramic tiled floors in the lavatories.

Pyroxone. A pliable incendiary substance that can burn underwater at incredibly high temperatures. Once molded to the surface to be burned, it is ignited by an electronic signal. Burns at three thousand degrees Celsius, so pyroxone can even burn through rock.

Quayle, Sam. Electronics wizard on the *Doodlebug* when it is attacked by U.S. Navy Amberjack-class submarine.

Quebec, Canada. French-Canadian providence in Canada that votes to become an independent country detached from the rest of Canada.

Quebec Hydro Power. The Canadian power company responsible for building and operating the James Bay Project.

Remote Search Vehicle. NUMA underwater propulsion vehicle used on the *Empress of Ireland* project. Described as shaped like an elongated teardrop, only three feet long and ten inches in diameter, it showed no protrusions on its smooth titanium skin. Steering and propulsion are provided by a small hydrojet pump with variable thrusters. Remotely controlled from aboard the *Ocean Venturer.* Nicknamed "Baby." The RSV is taken from the *Empress of Ireland* to a nearby trawler Shaw is aboard. Before the cameras are damaged, it records a picture of Shaw that Milligan identifies.

Rheingold, Mr. Curator of the Long Island Railroad Museum. Rheingold is an elderly, retired accountant with a lifelong passion for railroads.

Riley, Nicholas. NUMA chief diver on the *Manhattan Limited* project. Pitt's dive partner on the night probe. Smashes his face mask against a stalactite and loses his left eye. Pitt places his hand on the safety line and orders Riley to follow it back to the entrance while he continues on toward the *Manhattan Limited.*

Rimouski, Quebec. Town in Quebec where Pitt meets Jules Le Mat and leaves aboard Le Mat's boat for the trip out to where the *Empress of Ireland* sank.

River Blackwater. River near Seward's End, Essex, England, where Morris meets with the British prime minister.

Roubaix, Max. Canadian mass-murderer later hung for his crimes. His early life is sketchy, no date of birth. An orphan. First official records begin at age twelve, when he was charged with killing chickens. Graduated to killing horses and was sentenced to two years in jail at age fourteen. After his release, bodies of tramps and drunks began turning up around Moose Jaw, Saskatchewan, where he resided. When evidence linked Roubaix to the killings, he disappeared into the Northwest Territories. Resurfaced six years later during Reil's Rebellion in 1885. Credited with killing thirteen Mounties during the rebellion. His favored method of killing was a garrote using a rawhide cord attached to wooden hand grips intricately carved into timber wolves to strangle the victims in their sleep. Described as frail of build and rather sickly, he suffered from consumption or what now is called tuberculosis. When Villon asks McComb to describe Roubaix, he replies: "I guess you could call him a homicidal maniac with a fetish for the stranglehold."

RSV. Acronym for *remote search vehicle.*

Ryan, Sergeant. U.S. Marine Force reconnaissance sergeant.

Saban, Mrs. Molly. Guerrier's secretary. Delivers a bowl of chicken soup to Boucher at eight-thirty the night Guerrier is murdered.

Sakai, First Officer Shigaharu. First officer of the *Honjo Maru.*

Sanchez, Lieutenant. Leader of the three-squad, forty-man, United States Marine force reconnaissance team that arrives in armored cars when the *Manhattan Limited* is found to support NUMA. Wounded in thigh.

Sanctuary Building. One of the five buildings scattered about London that hold records from the Foreign Office. The Sanctuary Building is located on Great Smith Street. The records of dealing with the United States during 1914 are on the second floor of the east wing.

Sappho I. NUMA deepwater recovery vessel. Also used on *Titanic* project.

Sarveux, Danielle. Wife of James Sarveux for the last ten years. Described as having delicate features and raven hair that sweeps down in a cascade onto her right shoulder. Dresses in a fashion described as showy elegance. Is a secret supporter of the FQS. Had a long-running affair with Villon. Sleeps with a disguised Gly posing as Villon. Buried alive along with Villon in his automobile by Gly under orders from Charles Sarveux.

Sarveux, James. Prime minister of Canada. Described as a handsome man, his light blue eyes possess a mesmeric quality. His sharp-cut facial features are enhanced by a thick mass of gray hair loosely styled in a fashionable but casual look. Has a trim, medium height body. Purchases his suits off the racks of department stores. In the attack on Canada One, he suffers abrasions on over fifty percent of his body, heavy tissue loss on his hands and multiple fractures that may require him to use a cane. Many years ago, he was involved in an automobile accident that killed his mother. Discovers wife having affair with Villon. Orders Gly to kill the pair by burying them alive. Along with Finn, orders a thirty-million-dollar payoff to Gly to leave Canada. Secretly orders the plane rigged so it crashes into the ocean. Orders a press release that states that his wife, Danielle, and Villon were aboard the Gly plane. Has conducted secret talks with the president of the United States for years on the subject of United States and Canada uniting as a single country.

Saturation tank. A pressurized chamber divers live inside breathing a mixture of helium and oxygen. This mixture helps prevent the negative of nitrogen building up in the divers' bodies and creating a condition known as the bends.

Scinletti 440. Italian-made, vertical takeoff and landing two-engined jet. Pitt charters the jet to fly over the railroad tracks near the Deauville-Hudson Bridge.

Semaphore Lantern. Type of lantern used to signal trains.

Shaw, Brian. Former British secret agent who appears to be remarkably like Ian Fleming's James Bond. After twenty-five years of retirement, is pressed back into service for M16. Sixty-six years old, he is described as having black, carefully brushed hair, receding and sprinkled with gray. His face is handsome, and the ruthless look has softened. Smokes specially ordered cigarettes. Wears reading glasses. Practices judo. Was married for a brief time, but his wife was killed. After retirement, he lived for a time in the West Indies but now owns a small working farm on the Isle of Wight. Has killed more than twenty men but has not fired a handgun in more than twenty years. When Pitt saves him from a certain death at the hands of Gly, he recites Shaw's statistics from his file: sixty-six years old, weight one hundred seventy pounds, height six feet one inch, right-handed, numerous scars. Twice seduces Milligan in an attempt to gain information about the North American Treaty. Is it possible Shaw might really be Bond?

Shields, Harvey. The person responsible for transporting the copy of the North American Treaty aboard the *Empress of Ireland.* A representative of Her Majesty's government. In the photograph Milligan secures, he is said to have his head tilted back in a belly laugh, displaying two large, protruding upper teeth surrounded by a sea of gold inlays.

Simms, Brigadier General Morris V. Head of the British Secret Intelligence Service. Described as having peacock-blue eyes. Recruits Shaw back into service.

Sky Hook. A special heavy-lift helicopter used on the *Manhattan Limited* project. One hundred five feet long, the aircraft looks like a praying mantis.

SMERSH. Russian Spy Agency mentioned by Mrs. Huston to Shaw at the funeral of the former head of the British Secret Intelligence Service.

Soult, Nanci. Best-selling Canadian novelist who now resides in Ireland to beat taxes. Occasionally visits family and friends in Vancouver but has not been in Quebec in more than twenty years. Without her knowledge, she has a town house in her name in Quebec. The town house is the site of secret liaisons between Danielle Sarveux and Villon.

Standish. Ticket agent for the New York & Quebec Railroad at the Germantown station. Plays chess with Harding over telegraph lines.

Storstad. Norwegian collier that rammed and sank the *Empress of Ireland.* A six-thousand-ton vessel, the *Storstad* was loaded with eleven thousand tons of coal.

Stuckey, Percival. The chief director of the James Bay Project.

Trisynol. An explosive used underwater that is three times as powerful as TNT. Twenty-four hundred pounds stored in two-hundred-pound containers are stashed aboard the forecastle of the wreck of the *Empress of Ireland* by Gly and an accomplice. What no one but Gly knows is that he stored a radio detonator aboard one of the containers.

Ungava Bay. Location of the massive Canadian oil field discovered by the *Doodlebug.*

United States of Canada. New country proposed by the president of the United States with the consent of Charles Sarveux, president of Canada.

Upper Deck D Cabin Forty-six. Location aboard the *Empress of Ireland* for Shields's cabin.

Val Jalbert. Location of the Canadian Army arsenal where the Argo missiles are stolen.

Villon's wife. Described as a pretty woman with dark brown hair and blue eyes.

Villon, Henri. A respected member of the Canadian Parliament who is in the Liberal Party. Minister of internal affairs. Villon is also secretly the head of the

FQS. An old family friend of the Sarveuxs, he is also Danielle Sarveux's secret lover. Described as having the body of a muscleman, he keeps his entire body clean-shaven. Wears a wig. Has a chiseled face with a Roman nose and indifferent gray eyes. Married, he has a daughter. Villon orders the five-minute blackout of the James Bay Project. Intends to run for president of the independent country of Quebec. Instead, he is shot and then buried alive in his automobile by Gly, who intends to impersonate Villon and run for president himself.

Wacketshire. A small farming community along the tracks of the New York & Quebec railroad and location of the railroad station of the New York & Quebec railroad. Wacketshire Station is where the *Manhattan Limited* disappears.

Watergate. Famous Washington, D.C., apartment-hotel complex where Sandecker has an apartment. Also site of the Watergate breakin that brought down the presidency of Richard Nixon.

Weeks, Lieutenant Commander Raymond. Canadian officer in command of the *Huron.* Described as a jolly-looking man with laughing gray-blue eyes and a warm face. He has a pleasant, ringing voice that comes out of a short body with a noticeable paunch.

Westler, Jack. Pilot of the Scinletti 400 Pitt hires to fly over the railroad tracks near the Deauville-Hudson Bridge. Described as having a boyish face, with freckles and red hair and a boyish grin.

Willapa, Corporal Richard. U.S. Marine Force reconnaissance corporal. Direct descendant of Chinook Indians in the Pacific Northwest. Killed by fire from the British Royal Marine Bentley.

Yubari, Captain Toshio. Captain of the Japanese container ship *Honjo Maru.* described as a solid, weatherworn man in the prime of his early forties.

Deep Six

Aiken, John. Secret Service agent on the *Eagle* detail.

Air Force Weather Recon 040. Call sign for the plane flown by Grant. We caught Clive on this one. Grant is a United States Navy pilot who *was* flying a Navy plane.

Alhambra Iron and Boiler Company. The Charleston, South Carolina, company that manufactured the boilers on the *Pilottown.* Located on Spruill Avenue near the naval base. The building housing the company was built in 1861. The company quit building boilers in 1951 and now produces metal lawn furniture. Clive is having some fun here. Alhambra is the town in Southern California where he lived as a child. You will see Alhambra as the name of ships, on boilers and other oddities in several of the Dirk Pitt books.

Amie Marie. The vessel the *Catawaba* rushes to rescue. A crab boat one hundred ten feet in length with a steel hull probably built in New Orleans. The *Amie*

I couldn't sit still even when I was a baby. Notice how my mother is clutching me.

A love for the sea came early.

As an Eagle Scout (rear row, left).

High school graduation picture with pompadour front curl and hair swept on the sides into a ducktail, 1949.

Air Force basic training. We lived in tar-paper shacks.

Golf on dead grass in Wichita Falls, Texas, 1951. Can you tell I'd been drinking?

It takes an XK-120 Jaguar to get the beautiful girls.

Marriage to Barbara Knight, 1955.

With my partner, Dick Klein, in our "Petrol Emporium," 1957.

The family man. From left: Dirk, Barbara, Dana, Clive, and Teri, 1966.

Story time while shooting a TV commercial with Margaret Hamilton, the beloved Wicked Witch in *The Wizard of Oz.*

Doing overlays of Galveston Harbor before discovering the Republic of Texas Navy ship *Zavala* under a parking lot.

A winner at the Pebble Beach Concours d'Elegance with the 1930 Cord L-29 town car that Dirk Pitt drove down a ski slope in the book *Treasure*.

From left: Barbara, Teri, Clive, Dana, and Dirk. The old man receives his doctorate in marine history from the New York State Maritime College.

Clive and Barbara Cussler.

Marie's owner and captain is Carl Keating, and the vessel's home port is Kodiak.

Amytal. Drug that Lugovoy orders injected in the president's carotid artery. Amytal puts the left and right hemispheres of the brain in a drowsy state.

Anacostia River. The river in Washington, D.C., that empties into the Potomac. The route taken by *Eagle* on the way to Mount Vernon.

Antonov, President Georgi. President of Russia. Is on a state visit to Paris when the president of the United States disappears. Age sixty-two.

Augustine Volcano. Named by Captain Cook in 1778, she's the most active volcano in Alaska, erupting six times in the last century. Her last eruption was in 1987 and surpassed the power of the Mount St. Helens eruption in Washington State. The volcano erupts when Pitt and crew are aboard the *Pilottown.*

Bag Man. Nickname of the field grade officer who is always near the president. The Bag Man is in charge of the briefcase containing the codes for nuclear launch.

Belcheron, Melvin. Sixty-two years old, Belcheron has been captain of the *Stonewall Jackson* for the last thirty years. Described as a wiry-built little man with a big white-bearded head. Chews tobacco.

Belkaya, Oskar. A Soviet painter who was taken from his home and reprogrammed by the KGB in a sanatorium near Kiev, Russia. His RNA is implanted into the brain of the president.

Belle Chase. A Korean registered vessel owned by the Sosan Trading Company. *Belle Chase* is actually the *San Marino.* Allegedly scrapped in Pusan, Korea, two years after being spotted by Dewhurst in Singapore.

Blackowl, George. Secret Service advance agent and acting supervisor. Described as a dark-skinned man with stony facial features. One-half Sioux Indian. Chews gum constantly.

Blair, Megan. Secretary to the president of the United States. Described as a handsome, perky woman in her early forties. Wears her black hair cropped short and is ten pounds on the skinny side. Has a small-town friendliness. Unmarried.

Boiler 38874. Boiler found aboard the *Pilottown.* Pitt traces it back to the manufacturer and finds it was installed in the *San Marino.*

Borchavski, Admiral. Russian navy officer tasked with recovering the gold from the sunken *Venice.*

Boss. Code name the Secret Service uses for the president of the United States.

Bougainville Maritime Lines Incorporated. Korean shipping dynasty located on the one-hundredth floor of the World Trade Center in New York City. The offices cover the entire floor and are decorated in expensive furnishings and Oriental antiques. Their legitimate ships fly the flag of the Somalia Republic.

Bougainville, Min Koryo. Chairman of Bougainville Maritime. Described as eighty-nine years old and weighing the same. Her gray hair is worn pulled back from her head in a bun. Her face is strangely unlined, yet her body looks ancient and frail. She has intense blue eyes. When she was age twelve, her father sold her to a Frenchman who operated a small shipping line between Pusan, Korea, and Hong Kong. Bore Rene three sons who were drafted into the Imperial Japanese Army. All three later died. Grandmother to Lee Tong. Built Bougainville shipping into huge shipping conglomerate.

Bougainville, Rene. Frenchman who bought Min Koryo. Father to their three sons. Killed in bombing raid in World War II. Grandfather to Lee Tong.

Brock, Lyle. Secret Service agent who was guarding the *Eagle.* His corpse is later found by Pitt inside the cargo hold of the sunken *Eagle.*

Brogan, Martin. Head of the Central Intelligence Agency. Described as urbane and intellectual. An ex-college professor. Tall.

Buras. Bougainville towboat. Powered by four engines generating 12,000 horsepower, the towboat has four forward rudders and six backing rudders. The vessel's top speed is sixteen miles an hour.

Casilighio, Arta. Employed as a teller at the Beverly-Wilshire Bank in California. Daughter of Sal Casio.

Robs the bank she works at and, after changing identity to Estelle Wallace, flies to San Francisco aboard the *San Marino.* Later drugged and dropped overboard from the *San Marino* under the orders of Lee Tong.

Casio, Sal. Private detective. Father of Arta Casilighio. Described as having hard, stark eyes still clear and undimmed after sixty years. Wide and stocky. Favors a .45-caliber automatic he wears in a leather holster on his left shoulder. Is killed by a laser beam slicing open his stomach when he goes with Pitt to Min Koryo Bougainville's office to avenge his daughter's death.

Catawaba. U.S. Coast Guard cutter. Pitt first saw the *Catawaba* in the North Atlantic when he landed a helicopter on her deck. Now assigned to Alaska.

Ch'in Shin Huang Ti. Early Chinese emperor. Lugovoy recognizes the life-size terra-cotta warriors in the Bougainville. Maritime offices as Ch'in Shih Ti's tomb guardians.

Chalmette. The Bougainville-owned containership that rescues select survivors from the *Leonid Andreyev.*

Chao, Kim. First officer of the *Venice.*

CIA Phantom Navy. Fleet of ships owned by the CIA for covert operations.

Clarke, Colonel Ward. U.S. Marine colonel and Vietnam Medal of Honor winner leading troops who bar the congressmen from Lisner Auditorium.

Collins, Commandant. Head of the U.S. Coast Guard.

Colt Thompson submachine gun. Pitt's personal weapon. Serial number 8545. Uses circular drums loaded with .45-caliber ammunition. Pitt uses the weapon to shoot up the *Buras.*

Colt Woodsman. Brand of pistol Suvorov uses in the laboratory. His is a .22-caliber automatic with a four-inch noise suppressor.

Conium maculatum. Technical name for hemlock, the poison given to Socrates. Found in high concentrations in the bodies retrieved from the *Eagle.*

Cowan, Bonnie. An attorney in Washington, D.C., who dates Sandecker. Described as not yet thirty-five years of age and unusually attractive and petite. Her hair is long and silken and falls beyond her shoulders. Her breasts are small but nicely proportioned, as are her legs.

Critical Operations Force. U.S. Marine special operations force the mind-controlled president orders into Washington, D.C.

Crown. Code name for the Secret Service command post inside the White House.

Cumberland. Famous Union Civil War vessel. Battled the *Merrimac.* For a more detailed description of the battle, read *The Sea Hunters* by Clive Cussler and this author.

Cutty Sark. Code name for Ed McGrath.

Delta Oil Limited. Name of FBI front company painted on helicopter Pitt and Giordino fly aboard to seek the floating laboratory.

Department of the Interior. U.S. government organization. Pitt has a friend who works for the department and receives a satellite photograph from the friend that helps him set the search grid to locate the wreck of the *Eagle.*

Devil's Fork. The bar on Rhode Island Avenue in Washington, D.C., that Pitt and Giordino retire to after Pitt's Talbot-Lago explodes.

Dewhurst, Rodney. Lloyd's of London marine insurance underwriter for the Lloyd's office in Singapore. Suspects that the *Belle Chase* is *San Marino.*

Dodds, Lieutenant Homer. Leader of the U.S. Navy SEALs that approach the *Buras* in a transport helicopter.

Dodge Island. Location of the docking terminal for the Port of Miami.

Dover, Lieutenant Commander Amos. Commander of the *Catawaba.* Described as a great bear of a man, tough and wind-worn. Is ambling in physical movement but possesses a calculatorlike mind that never fails to awe his crew.

Eagle. U.S. presidential yacht. Built in 1919 for a wealthy Philadelphia businessman, the *Eagle* was purchased by the Department of Commerce in 1921 for presidential use. Designed with the old straight-up-and-down bow, the mahogany-trimmed yacht displaces one hundred tons and measures one hundred ten feet in length with a beam of twenty feet. Her draft is five feet, and her top speed is fourteen knots. The vessel has five staterooms, four heads and a glass-enclosed salon for entertaining. Crewed by thirteen Coast Guardsmen, the crew cabins and galley are forward near the bow.

Edgely, Dr. Raymond. Director of *Fathom,* the CIA special study into mind control that is operated at Raton University in Colorado. A professor, Edgely is described as having an old-fashioned crew cut and wearing a bow tie. He is slender and has a barbed-wire beard and bristly dark eyebrows.

Emmet, Sam. Director of the FBI. Described as gruff-spoken.

F-20 Fighter. U.S. Navy jet that Sutton is flown to Washington, D.C., aboard so he can impersonate the president.

F/A 21. U.S. Navy strike aircraft. Drops two laser-guided antimissiles that destroy the *Pathfinder.*

Fawcett, Daniel. Chief of staff to the president of the United States.

Federal Reserve Bank. U.S. central bank. Supplies currency to the member banks. Federal Reserve wrappers are around the bills. Casilighio examines one of the wrappers just before being killed.

Fifth Marine Regiment. Fawcett served with this group in Korea.

Finkel, Bob. Reporter with the *Baltimore Sun.* Claims in jest that Thompson graduated from the Joseph Goebbels School of Propaganda.

Florida Cross State Canal. A canal for ship traffic that runs from Jacksonville, Florida, on the Atlantic Ocean to Crystal River in the Gulf of Mexico.

Foggers. U.S. Navy fog generators mounted on destroyers during World War II to create smokescreens. Used to shield the movements of the kidnappers who attacked *Eagle.*

Fort Jackson. Civil War fort in Plaquemines Parish.

Fort St. Phillip. Civil War fort in Plaquemines Parish.

French Transatlantic Steamship Company. Owners of the *Normandy,* the famous French passenger liner that burned and sank in New York Harbor. Perlmutter used china from the ship to serve Pitt and Smith breakfast.

Gaddafi, Colonel Muammar. Leader of Libya. Mentioned by Metcalf in conjunction with the disappearance of the president.

Georgia Shipbuilding Corporation. Savannah, Georgia, shipyard where Boiler 38874 was shipped. Boiler was installed in the *San Marino.*

Glover Culpepper Gas & Groceries. The abandoned business whose sign Suvorov notices soon after leaving the laboratory in the Cadillac. The clue that helps him return to the general area when he is in the helicopter.

Goodman. FBI agent who works in communications. Goodman links Griffin to Emmett, who is in Washington, D.C.

Goose Lake. A private fishing reserve a few miles below the Quantico Marine Corps Reservation. Moran and Larimer are allegedly fishing at the lake when they are in fact on the *Leonid Andreyev.* Lindemann discovers this and alerts Smith before the telephone line is disconnected.

Grand Island. Island off Louisiana not far from where the Mississippi River empties into the Gulf of Mexico.

Grant, Ulysses S. U.S. Navy pilot named after the eighteenth president of the United States. His father was a famous third-baseman. Pilots a Navy four-engined reconnaissance plane that is the first airplane to arrive over the *Buras.* Described as a boyish-faced young man in his middle twenties.

Greenberg, Dr. Harry. A pipe-smoking, respected psychiatric researcher who consults with Edgely. Greenberg gathers the data from the president's brain waves so he can fool Lugovoy.

Greenwald, Ben. Director of the Secret Service. Immediately after being notified of the abduction of the president, he's on his way to the observatory for a crisis meeting when his automobile is struck by a street sweeper. Greenwald is killed.

Griffin, Clyde. FBI special agent in charge of the Louisiana field office.

Gromyko, Foreign Minister. Russian foreign minister whom Margolin has met with to discuss aid.

Gruber, Charlie. Identity Pitt assumes to board the *Leonid Andreyev* undetected. Claims to be married to Zelda and from Sioux Falls, Iowa.

Gruber, Zelda. Wife of the fictitious Charlie Gruber. Zelda is actually Giordino dressed in drag. Charlie claims Zelda turns on to Greeks.

Guantanamo Bay, Cuba. U.S. Marine base inside Cuba.

Gwynne, Dr. Harold. The personal physician for the president of the United States. Described as a cherubic little man with a balding head and friendly blue eyes.

Hero of the Soviet Union. Award similar to the Congressional Medal of Freedom. Lugovoy daydreams that he will be awarded the medal.

Hippocampus. The seahorse-shaped ridge running under the horns of the lateral ventricles, a vital section of the brain's limbic system.

Hobson. Part of the CIA's phantom fleet, the vessel is a common cargo carrier extensively modified. The vessel disappeared with all hands off the Pacific coast of Mexico. The vessel later turns up in Sydney, Australia. Her name changed to *Buras,* the vessel is registered to a Philippines company called Samar Exporters.

Hogan, Slats. FBI agent and helicopter pilot who operates the Delta Oil helicopter. Described as a thin, blond, dreamy-eyed woman who speaks in a slow, deep drawl.

Hoki Jamoki. Described as a tired old Chesapeake Bay clamming boat. The hull is worn from hard use, and most of her paint is gone. Powered by a diesel engine. Pitt uses the boat to locate the wreck of the *Eagle.*

Hong, Mr. Japanese chemist tasked with checking the Russian gold aboard the *Venice* for purity. Described as a small, moon-faced man with thick-lensed spectacles.

Huckleberry Finn. Code name used by Antonov in referring to the Bougainville/Russian project to alter the president's thoughts.

Hudson Street. Location of building where, on the tenth floor, Casio monitors the conversations of Tong and Bougainville.

Iranov, Sergei. Deputy director of the KGB.

Isotta-Fraschini. One of the cars in Pitt's aircraft hangar/home. The automobile is a 1925 model with a torpedo body by Cesare Sala. The vehicle has a disappearing top and a coiled cobra on the radiator cap.

James River. River in Virginia that empties near Newport News. Location where Pitt and Giordino are leading a NUMA expedition to find the ram off the famous Civil War ironclad, *Merrimac.*

Jones, John Paul. American Revolutionary War captain of the *Bonhomme Richard.* Famous for: "I've not yet begun to fight." What Cowan calls Sandecker.

Kazinkin, Erik. Chief engineer on the *Leonid Andreyev.*

Keating, Carl. Owner and captain of the *Amie Marie.*

Kiev, Russia. City the president dreams about after the microchip is implanted in his brain.

Klein Hydroscan Sonar. The brand of sonar Pitt operates off the *Catawaba.*

Klosner, Jack. The regular Coast Guard steward aboard the *Eagle.* Not working the night of the presidential abduction.

Kobylin, Basil. Head of KGB undercover operations in New York City.

Kolodono, Peter. Russian purser on the *Leonid Andreyev.*

L'Estrange, President. President of France.

Larimer, Marcus. U.S. Senator. Described as big and rough-cut, he habitually wears brown suits. His hair is sandy-colored and styled dry. Is invited by the president for an overnight trip on the *Eagle.* Opposes the president's Eastern Europe aid program. Kidnapped from the *Eagle* along with the president and others, then rescued from the laboratory by Suvorov. Later, he dies from a failed heart off Cuba.

Laroche, Leroy. Commander of the 6th Louisiana Regiment. Operates a travel agency. Husband and father. Described as an enormous man with the stout build of an Oliver Hardy. Wears the uniform of a Confederate major.

Lawrence, Lieutenant Marty. Coast Guard Lieutenant and one of the boarding party sent from the *Catawaba* to the *Amie Marie.* Dies from exposure to the nerve agent.

Le Mat revolver. Handgun loaned to Pitt by Laroche. Shoots 9.42-caliber shells through a rifled barrel and a smoothbore barrel that fires a load of buckshot. Laroche's grandfather used it from Bull Run to Appomattox in the Civil War.

Leonid Andreyev. Russian cruise ship whose passengers are non-Russians. Part of the Soviet-subsidized passenger line whose purpose is to generate hard Western currency for the Soviet Union. A fourteen thousand–ton vessel, the *Leonid Andreyev* was built in Finland. It has a capacity of four hundred seventy-eight passengers and three hundred–plus crew. The vessel features indoor and outdoor pools, five cocktail bars, two nightclubs, ten shops featuring Russian merchandise and liquor, a movie and stage theater, and a well-stocked library. There are more than three hundred staterooms and eleven decks, and the overall length is more than five hundred feet. Home port is Sevastopol in the Black Sea. A twin-screw vessel, she is powered by 27,000-horsepower turbine engines.

Liftonic Elevator QW-607. Brand of elevator that leads to the Bougainville offices. Pitt pushes Min Koryo Bougainville in her wheelchair down the empty shaft.

Lindemann, Sally. Loren Smith's secretary.

Lisner Auditorium. Located at George Washington University, it is the site where the members of Congress decide to meet to proceed with impeachment proceedings against the president.

Love Boat. Secret Service code name for *Eagle.*

Lucas, Carolyn. Wife of Oscar Lucas. Has a cascade of blond hair.

Lucas, Oscar. U.S. Secret Service special agent in charge of the Presidential Protection Division. Described as lanky, over six feet tall. His head is bald except for a few graying strands around the temples. Has bushy eyebrows that hover over oak brown eyes. Lucas is in his early forties, is married to Carolyn, and has two daughters. Was a rookie agent in Denver. After Greenwald is killed in an automobile accident,

Oates promotes Lucas to director of the Secret Service.

Lugovoy, Aleksei. Soviet representative to the World Health Organization. A respected psychologist, he is admired for his work in mental health among developing countries.

M-20 automatic rifles. Type of weapon carried by U.S. soldiers that are ordered by the mind-controlled president to shut down the American government.

Mangyai, James. Captain of the *Venice.* Has worked for Bougainville Maritime for over twenty years.

Margolin, Beth. Wife of Vince Margolin.

Margolin, Vincent (Vince). Vice president of the United States. Married, his wife's name is Beth. Described as tall, nicely proportioned, not a bit of fat, with a handsome face and bright eyes and warm outgoing personality. Was first a state senator then governor and senator before becoming vice president.

Marmot Island. Island in Alaska where the car ferry with three hundred twelve aboard runs aground.

Marsh, Ray. Reporter with the *New York Times.* Questions Moran after he makes his way back to Washington, D.C., and attempts to assume the presidency.

Masters, Captain Irwin. Captain of the *San Marino.* Described as a tall man with graying hair and merry blue eyes.

Mathias Point. On the Potomac River, where Pitt locates the wreck of the *Eagle.*

Mauritania, Atar. Location where the president, while under Soviet mind control, claims he was while he was gone. Mauritania is a country that borders Morocco in Western Africa.

Mauser. Handgun Casio finds taped behind a half-gallon bottle of gin in Pitt's refrigerator. The Mauser is a 32-caliber whose serial number is 922374.

Mayo, Curtis. Television newscaster with the CNB network.

McGeen. The chief engineer on the *Stonewall Jackson.* Described as a crusty old Scot.

McGrath, Ed. Secret Service agent on the *Eagle* detail. McGrath has fifteen years' experience. Discovers the president, guests and crew are missing from the *Eagle.*

Medoza, Julie. Chairman of the Regional Emergency Response Team for the Environmental Protection Agency. Described as in her mid-forties with a suave and slim body. Medoza is about five feet seven, her hair is the color of aspen gold and her skin is a copper tan. She dies after being exposed to Nerve Agent S aboard the *Pilottown.*

Merchant Marine Transport Committee. U.S. government committee chaired by Loren Smith. The committee is involved in efforts to support the idea of an American-flagged cruise ship.

Metcalf, General Clayton. U.S. Army general and chairman of the Joint Chiefs of Staff. Smokes a pipe.

Mexican Zapata Brigade. Mexican terrorist organization mentioned by Miller in discussions with Emmett.

Microminiaturized implant. The microchip that is implanted in the cerebral cortex of the president's brain.

Miller, Don. Deputy director of the FBI.

Mitchell, Norm. Cameraman who works with Mayo. Described as a loose, ambling scarecrow character.

Montrose, Rocky. Sound man who works with Mayo. Described as beefy.

Moran, Alan. Ferret-faced speaker of the U.S. House of Representatives. Invited by the president to go for an overnight trip aboard the *Eagle.* Moran opposes the president's proposed Eastern Europe aid program. He is kidnapped along with the president from the yacht. Rescued from the laboratory by Suvorov. Escapes from the *Leonid Andreyev* and weasels his way aboard a rescue helicopter. Quickly makes his way to Washington, D.C., demands to be sworn in as president. Described as a closet atheist who has never married and has no close friends. He lives frugally, like a penitent monk in a small, rented apartment. Is foiled in his plan to become president when Margolin is rescued by Pitt and reappears.

Motorola HT-220 radio receiver. Small receiver used by the Secret Service agents to communicate with one another.

Mount Fuji. Famous Japanese mountain. The profile of the Augustine Volcano is very similar.

Mount Vernon. Former home to George Washington. Location where the presidential yacht *Eagle* is moored when the abductions occur.

Murphy, Ensign Pat. Coast Guard ensign and one of the boarding party sent from the *Catawaba* to the *Amie Marie.* Dies from exposure to the nerve agent.

Nashville Bridge Company. Name of the Nashville, Tennessee, company that manufactured the dry cargo barge that houses the Bougainville laboratory. Yaeger finds the information from his computers.

Nerve Agent S. A chemical warfare agent developed by scientists working for the United States government at Rocky Mountain Arsenal just north of Denver, Colorado. Nerve Agent S can kill within a few seconds of touching the skin. It clings to everything it touches. Nerve Agent S proved too unstable and was ordered destroyed. The United States Army decided to bury it in the Nevada desert, but while en route a boxcar containing nearly one thousand gallons vanished. A person who comes in contact with Nerve Agent S literally drowns in his or her own blood as internal membranes burst. Every body orifice bleeds like a river, then the corpse turns black.

Nerve Agent S drums. One-ton standard shipping containers. Department of Transportation approved. They measure eighty-one and a half inches in length by thirty and a half inches in diameter with concave ends.

They are silver-colored. There are twenty drums of Nerve Agent S aboard the *Pilottown.*

Oakes, Charlie. President of Alhambra Iron and Boiler Company. Described as a rotund, smiling, unedged little man.

O'Brien, Nelson. Chief justice of the U.S. Supreme Court. Slated to swear in Moran. Begins the ceremony but stops when Margolin appears.

Observatory. The name of the residence occupied by the vice president of the United States while in office.

Oerlikon Machine Gun. Brand of twenty-millimeter machine gun mounted on Bougainville barge that fires on the Delta Oil helicopter and shoots it down.

Ombrikov, Geidar. Chief of the KGB residency in Havana, Cuba. Described as having a squat body and the skin tone of an old wallet. Boards the *Leonid Andreyev* from the *Pilar* to remove Larimer and Moran but finds they have disappeared.

One Army Special Counter Terrorist Detachment. Special U.S. Army soldiers stationed at Fort Belvoir. The mind-controlled president orders them into Washington, D.C.

Pathfinder. Bougainville-owned ship disguised as a oceanographic research vessel. Formerly a Norwegian merchantman, the ship was bought by Bougainville Maritime seven years ago and refitted to fool customs inspectors.

PBY Catalina Flying Boat. Older propeller-driven plane designed to take off and land on water. Owned by NUMA, the plane has an aluminum hull covered in aquamarine paint.

Persimmon Point. Location on the Potomac River near where Pitt locates the wreck of the *Eagle.*

Perth, Dr. Grace. Professor of anthropology at the University of Pennsylvania. Pitt calls Perth on the telephone to inquire about physical differences in Asian males.

Petrel. Type of sea bird that soars over the *San Marino.* Petrels usually have a small body and long wings and can be found far out to sea.

Pilar. Described as a small mahogany powerboat with a straight-up-and-down bow. Formerly owned by author Ernest Hemingway but now belongs to Fidel Castro.

Pilottown. First named the *Bart Pulver,* later the *Rosthena.* Built by Astoria Iron & Steel Company in Portland, Oregon, and launched in November 1942. Hull number 793. After World War II, the vessel was sold to Kassandra Phosphate Company Limited of Athens, Greece. Greek registry. Ran aground off Jamaica, June 1954. Refloated. Sold to Sosan Trading Company, Ichon, Korea. Vessel the *San Marino* became. The legend of the *Pilottown* was that after tramping back and forth between Tokyo and the West Coast of the United States, she was reported sinking about ten years ago. The vessel then became a drifting derelict and was trapped in an ice floe above Nome, Alaska. She continued to drift, crewless. Nicknamed the "Magic Ship."

Pokofsky, Yakov. Russian captain of the *Leonid Andreyev.* Described as a charming man with thick silver hair and eyes as round and black as caviar. Smokes cigarettes. Joined the Russian navy at seventeen. After twenty years in the navy, transferred to the Soviet-subsidized passenger service. Is rescued after the explosion aboard the *Leonid Andreyev* by Ombrikov but commits suicide by jumping in the water.

Polaski, Carl. Secret Service agent who was guarding the pier leading to the *Eagle.* Has a Bismarck moustache.

Polevoi, Vladamir. Director of the KGB.

Potter, Kenneth. Postmaster general whose son was sniping at U.S. troops occupying Washington, D.C.

President of the United States. Described as carrying himself like a tall man but is only two inches taller than Sandecker. His hairline is recessed and graying, and his narrow face wears a perpetually solemn expression. Has a ranch in New Mexico thirty miles south of Raton. Usually wears a Timex watch with an Indian silver band inlaid with turquoise.

Princeton University. University in New Jersey. Lucas gives a speech there.

Pujon, Kim. Bougainville Mississippi River pilot who operates the towboat *Buras.* Pujon is killed when his head is blown off by shots fired from the *Stonewall Jackson.*

Purdey Shotgun. Over and under brand of shotgun used by Antonov when he is on bird hunt with L'Estrange.

Rhinemann, Hank. Secret Service supervisor in charge of vice presidential security.

River Watch. Code name of the Coast Guard cutter patrolling the Potomac River near where the *Eagle* is docked.

RNA. Acronym for *ribonucleic acid.* The RNA of a Soviet dissident named Oskar Belkaya is injected into the hippocampus of the president.

Rolls-Royce Silver Ghost. One of the cars in Pitt's aircraft hangar/home. The automobile is a 1921 model with a Park-Ward body.

Russell Building. Washington, D.C., building where the vice president has an office.

Samantha. Sister ship to the *Eagle.* The last registered owner of the *Samantha* was a stockbroker in Baltimore. He sold it to someone who went by the name of Dunn. Under the cover of fog, the *Samantha* was switched for the *Eagle.*

Samar Exporters. Philippine front company for Bougainville Maritime. Registered as owners of the *Buras,* formerly the CIA vessel *Hobson.*

San Marino. Cargo vessel Casilighio escapes aboard. At the time of her journey under the identity of Estelle Wallace, the *San Marino* is bound for Auckland, New Zealand. Built during 1943 at Georgia Shipbuilding Company to standard Liberty design. Hull number 2356. The *San Marino* carried military supplies across the Atlantic to England. Struck once by torpedo fired from German U-Boat U-573 but made it to port in Liverpool under her own power. After World War II, she was sold to Bristol Steamship Company, Bristol, England, then sold in 1956 to the Manx Steamship Company of New York. Registered in Panama. The *San Marino* features a three-deck-high midships superstructure. Measuring four hundred forty-one feet in length, the vessel has a raked stem and cruiser stern. Just before leaving port with Wallace, ten crew members mysteriously disappear. They are replaced by Tong and nine other Koreans who hijack ships. Later, the *San Marino* was converted into the ore carrier *Belle Chase.*

San Salvador. City in El Salvador where Charlie and Zelda Gruber board the *Leonid Andreyev*.

Satellite Survey Number 2430A. Chart or marine map that shows the south shore of Augustine Island. It is on this grid that Pitt locates the wreck of the *Pilottown.*

SDECE. Initials for French Internal Security Agency.

Secretariat Building of the United Nations. One of the buildings at the United Nations. Location of the office of the Soviet representative to the World Health Organization.

Semper paratus. Latin for: "Always ready." *Semper paratus* is the motto of the U.S. Coast Guard.

Shakespeare. Secret Service code name for Margolin.

Shaw, Hampshire and Farquar. The Chicago stock-brokerage firm that is a front for Moran's bribery and payoffs. The name of the company is bogus. The names came from tombstones in Fargo, North Dakota.

Simmons, Jesse. U.S. secretary of defense. Described as a taciturn man. Has a leathery face from his hobby of water skiing.

Sixth Louisiana Regiment. Civil War reenactors who board the *Stonewall Jackson* and attack the *Buras.* In the attack, eighteen are wounded, two seriously.

Smith-Wesson Model 19. Handgun with a two-and-a-half-inch barrel and .357 caliber favored by Lucas. Standard U.S. Secret Service issue.

Sosan Trading Company. Shipping company based in Inchon, Korea. Owned by the Bougainvilles. Company that owned the *Pilottown.*

Spatial Analyzer Probe. Also known as SAP. The machine takes a series of high-speed X-rays that reveal the precise moving pictures of every millimeter of tissue and bones.

Springfield Rifles. Weapon used by the 6th Louisiana Regiment. Fifty-eight-caliber, the rifle shoots a Minie ball five hundred yards.

SS-30 Multiple Warhead Missiles. Soviet nuclear missiles arranged along the northeast coast of Siberia and targeted at the United States. When Brogan mentions that the Russians have the missiles, the president, under Soviet mind control, claims they will be dismantled under the disarmament plan he was reached with the Russians.

Stark, Joe. Reporter from the *United Press.* Questions Moran after he returns from being held captive.

Steyr-Mannlicher AUG Assault Carbines. Brand of .223-caliber automatic weapons the Koreans aboard the *Buras* use to attack the Navy SEALs helicopter.

Stonewall Jackson. Paddle-wheel steamship built in 1915 at Columbus, Ohio. Her hull measures two hundred seventy feet by forty-four. Powered by two horizontal noncondensing engines. Has four high-pressure boilers. Rated at slightly more than one thousand tons, she draws just over twenty-two inches. Has twin smokestacks. The Confederate flag flies from her mast. Her top speed is rated at fifteen miles an hour, but she can do twenty.

Strategic Rocket Forces. The Russian military division tasked with launching a nuclear strike on the United States.

Sumpter Airborne Ambulance. The ambulance service that owns the helicopter Suvorov, Larimer and Moran board and fly to Savannah, Georgia.

Sutton, Jack. An actor who looks exactly like the missing president.

Suvorov, Viktor. Father of Yuri (Paul) Suvorov. Russian agriculture specialist.

Suvorov, Yuri (Paul). Member of the KGB. Described as a stocky man with Slavic features and shaggy black hair. Travels along with Lugovoy to the Bougainvilles' secret laboratory. Escapes the laboratory with Moran and Larimer.

Suzaka Chemical Company Limited. Name stenciled on the boxes containing the gold aboard the *Venice.*

Sylvia. Sandecker's secretary.

Talbot-Lago. Beautiful 1948 Saoutchik-bodied automobile. Pitt's is valued at more than two hundred thousand dollars. Smith drives the automobile to the airport to pick up Pitt.

Thayer, Lieutenant Commander Isaac. Known as Doc Thayer, he's the most popular man aboard the *Catawaba.* Pilots a second Zodiac to the *Amie Marie* when Lawrence and Murphy report everyone aboard dead. Dies from exposure to the nerve agent after reporting the symptoms as they occur.

Thompson, Jacob (Sonny). White House press secretary. Described as having bright white teeth capped with precision, long sleek black hair, tinted gray at the temples, and dark eyes with the tightened look of cosmetic surgery. Thompson has no second chin and no visible sign of a potbelly. He's a classy, breezy guy.

Thornburg, Colonel Thomas. U.S. Army colonel whose title is director of comparative forensics and clinical pathology. Thornburg performs the autopsies on the bodies retrieved from the *Eagle.*

Titanium ingots. Cargo of the *San Marino* prior to her disappearance. The value of the cargo of ingots is eight million dollars. Titanium is a silver-gray metallic mineral that is light and strong. More expensive than most metals, it is used in applications where weight is a concern, such as space stations, advanced aircraft, etc.

Tong, Lee (Bougainville). Gap-toothed messboy on the *San Marino,* he masterminds the murders of the passenger and crew and theft of the vessel. Grandson of Min Koryo Bougainville. Graduate of Wharton School of Business with a master's degree. Described as having a round, brown face split in a perpetual grin. Smokes cigarettes through a long silver holder. Kidnapped the president along with a team of seven men whom he later murdered. Killed by Pitt aboard the *Buras* when he is shot in the throat with a load of buckshot fired from the Le Mat revolver.

Tournier, Marvin. Reporter with the Associated Press Radio Network. Questions Moran when he returns from being held captive.

Treasury Building. U.S. Treasury Department building. Across the street from the White House. From the Treasury Building there is a secret tunnel to the White House.

United Emergency Response Team. U.S. Marine task force from Camp Lejeune, North Carolina. Two thousand marines on twenty-four-hour alert who are ferried aboard tilt-rotored assault transports.

***United States,* S.S.** Famous passenger liner that was the fastest in her day. Laid up in drydock in Norfolk for the last twenty years. The Merchant Marine Transport Committee wants to refurbish the vessel and put her back in service.

Venice. Bougainville-owned ship 540 feet in length. It is loaded with Russian gold payment to Min Koryo Bougainville in the Black Sea port of Odessa. The vessel is bound for Genoa, Italy, where the gold will be off-loaded for transport to Lucerne, Switzerland. The *Venice* is torpedoed and sunk by a Russian submarine near the Tzonston Bank in the Aegean Sea so the Russians can retrieve the gold.

Wallace, Estelle. False identity used by Arta Casilighio. Arta finds a passport with Wallace's name on it wedged in the seat of a cab.

Whitman, Jacob. Congressman from South Dakota whose son was sniping at the U.S. troops that were occupying Washington, D.C.

World Health Assembly. United Nations organization.

"Yellow Rose of Texas." Song being played on the steam calliope when the *Stonewall Jackson* attacks the *Buras.*

Zodiac. Brand of inflatable boat that the boarding party drives from the *Catawaba* to the *Amie Marie.*

Cyclops

Alice. The CIA nursemaid assigned to Pitt when he is at the CIA headquarters. Described as a tall, high-cheekboned woman with braided hair.

Alpha Two Clearance. Level of clearance the president gives to Hagen so he can investigate the Inner Core. Vice president of the United States has a Level Three clearance.

Amy Bigalow. Registered in Panama and allegedly owned by Cuban anti-Castro exiles, the vessel is, in fact, owned by the KGB. The anti-Castro front is designed to lay the blame for the explosion in Havana on the United States of America. The *Amy Bigalow* is a bulk carrier with a cargo of twenty-five thousand tons of ammonium nitrate. Has a sixty-foot-high stem. Piloted by Pitt with Manny in the engine room, the vessel is in the center when the *Pisto* tows the three ships out to sea.

***Amy Bigalow's* launch**. After Pitt, Manny and the rest of the crew leave the *Amy Bigalow* running at full steam and take to the launch, they are swept up in the tidal wave caused by the explosion triggered by Velikov. The launch itself smashes into the second story of an apartment building used to house Soviet technicians. The four-cylinder diesel engine is tossed through a broken window and ends up in the stairwell.

Angelo. Chauffeur of the stretch Cadillac limousine that delivers the LeBarons to the *Prosperteer*'s base. Described as a somber Cuban with the etched face of a postage stamp engraving.

Antonov, Georgi. President of the Soviet Union. Said to have a ruddy face.

Beagle, Dean. *See* Dean Porter.

Beretta .38-caliber. Handgun Hagen disarms from fake gas station attendant.

Booth, Clyde. Member of the Inner Core. Was an all-American football star at Arizona State. Owns a company called QB-Tech. *QB* stands for *quarterback.*

Borchev. Soviet officer who calls Velikov and explains that the security detail guarding the ships that are to be used in Operation Rum & Cola have been replaced. Velikov orders him to form a detachment and proceed to the wharves. In the fighting at the wharves, Clark grabs him and tosses him into the harbor.

Borscht paste. A food supplement given to Russian cosmonauts. The stomachs of the bodies found on the *Prosperteer* when it reappears are filled with the paste.

Brandeis University. University in Waltham, Massachusetts. Hagen calls there when he is examining Mooney's telephone logs.

Brogan, Martin. Director of the Central Intelligence Agency.

Burkhart, Carl. Copilot of the *Gettysburg*. A twenty-year veteran of the space program.

Busche, Steve. Member of the Inner Core. Director of NASA's Flight Research Center in California.

Butterfly Catcher. Nickname for the *Prosperteer* ground crewman who holds a wind sock on a pole so the pilot can note the exact direction of the wind on takeoff.

Cabot, Sandra. Jessie LeBaron's personal secretary. Described as a prim woman who wears large-lensed glasses.

Caesar, Buck. Treasure hunter who owns Exotic Artifact Ventures Inc. Described as wearing a constant smile on a gentle middle-aged face that has the texture of cowhide. His gaze is shrewd, and his body has the firmness of a boxer. After being captured and taken to Cayo Santa Maria, he eludes his guards during an exercise period outside the compound. Using the trunk of a fallen palm tree as a raft, he attempts to swim to freedom. Instead, he is eaten by sharks, and the remains of his body wash up on the island three days later.

Cardenas, Cuba. City in Cuba. When Raul Castro is on an inspection tour of an island defense system outside Havana, Raymond LeBaron and crew on the *Prosperteer* are detected. The blimp is ordered to land in Cardenas.

Cartier. Jeweler. Raymond LeBaron owns a gold Cartier watch with matching band. The Roman numerals on the face are marked by black diamonds, his birthstone.

Castro's hunting lodge. Located in the hills southeast of Havana. Set behind an electronically controlled gate that shields a road that curves two miles into the hills. The lodge itself is a large, Spanish-style villa that overlooks a panorama of dark hills dotted by distant lights. Where Hagen and Jessie LeBaron contact the Castro brothers.

Castro, Fidel. Leader of Cuba. Described as having a muscular body that once earned him the title of Cuba's best high school athlete. Now has softened and expanded with age. Gray curly hair and barbed-wire beard. His dark eyes still burn with a revolutionary fire he brought down from the Sierra Maestra Mountains. Smokes cigars.

Castro, Raul. Younger brother of Fidel Castro and second-in-command of Cuba. President of the Council of Ministers. Described as witty and congenial in private. His hair is black, slick and closely trimmed above the ears. Has a pixie face and dark, beady eyes. Has a narrow moustache on his upper lip; the pointed ends stop precisely above the corners of his mouth.

Cathedral Square. Location in old Havana near where Sloppy Joe's is located. After the explosion, the clock on top of a building there is stopped at 6:21.

Cavilla, Joe. Copilot with Raymond LeBaron of the *Prosperteer*. Described as a sixty-year-old, sad-eyed, dour individual. His family immigrated from Brazil, and at age sixteen Cavilla joined the U.S. Navy, flying blimps until the last airship unit was formally disbanded in 1964. After being captured and taken to Cayo Santa Maria, he is tortured in Room Six by Gly, later goes into a coma and then dies.

Cayo Santa Maria. Island off Cuba near where the *Cyclops* sank. Island where Pitt runs the inflatable boat ashore during hurricane Little Eva after investigating the wreck of the *Cyclops*. The Russians ordered the native islanders off the island, then built a vast communications center. When Pitt and his group first stumble upon the outside of the structure, it is described as having a massive iron gate whose bars are welded in the shape of dolphins. A wall topped by broken glass stretches into the darkness and stands astride a guardhouse that is deserted because of Little Eva. Following the road leading from the guardhouse, the group finds it ends in a circular drive in front of a castlelike structure whose roof and three sides are covered with sandy soil planted with palmetto trees and native scrub, thus hiding the structure. The compound houses an electronically advanced and powerful facility capable of intercepting radio or telephone communications and then uses time-lag technology to allow a new-generation computerized synthesizer to imitate the callers' voices and alter the conversation.

Celestial Mechanics in True Perspective. Book by Horace DeLiso located in Mooney's office. Hagen finds Mooney's private notebook hidden inside the book.

Centennial Supply. A company that supplies specialized parts and electronics for recording systems. Hagen calls the company after examining Mooney's telephone logs.

Charlie. CIA analyst Brogan defers to after Pitt describes the compound on Cayo Santa Maria. Described as a studious-looking man.

Chekoldin, Admiral. Velikov orders Borchev to find Admiral Chekoldin and return the ships to be used in Operation Rum & Cola to port.

Chevrolet, 1957. Automobile owned by Figueroa and later stolen by Pitt. Has a 283-cubic-inch V-8 motor. The car has more than six hundred eighty thousand kilometers on the odometer.

Church, Lieutenant John. Described as a thin, prematurely gray-haired man a few months shy of thirty years of age. Has been in the Navy twelve years and worked his way up to commissioned officer. Dies in the cargo hold of the *Cyclops*.

Clark, Tom. Chief of the Special Interests Section. Described as an athletic thirty-five or so, with a tan face, Errol Flynn moustache, thinning red hair neatly combed forward to hide the spreading front, blue eyes and a nose that has been broken more than once. Cover is that he works for the State Department, but he actually works for the CIA. Organizes the movement of the ships that are to be used in Operation Rum & Cola. Later killed in the fighting between the Russian Marines under Borchev and his own troops. His body is fished out of the channel by a fishing boat and returned to the United States for burial.

Clinometer. Instrument used by Gunn aboard the *Prosperteer* to approximate the length of the object he detects with the Schonstedt Gradiometer.

Coker, Fireman First Class James. Formerly stationed on the cruiser *Pittsburgh*. Described as tall and rangy with heavily muscled arms. Sentenced in the murder of Stewart to death by hanging which was carried out in Brazil. Held along with DeVoe and four other prisoners in the *Cyclops*'s brig when she sank.

Columbus. The U.S. space station. The experiments performed aboard the station include the manufacture of exotic medicines, the growth of pure crystals for computer semiconductor chips and gamma-ray observation.

Combat Magnum .357-caliber. Two-and-a-half-inch-barreled handgun Hagen uses to threaten the fake gas station attendant into revealing the identity of Clyde Ward. The weapon is loaded with wad-cutter bullets.

Conde, Bob. Executive chairman of the board of Weehawken Marine Products.

Congressional Country Club. Country Club in Potomac, Maryland, where the president first hears about the Jersey Colony.

Cooper. One of the Jersey Colonists.

Cordero, Alicia. Cuban woman politician tapped by the Soviets to be the next leader of Cuba after they assassinate Fidel and Raul Castro. Currently secretary of the Central Committee and secretary of the Council of State. Said to be idolized by the people of Cuba for the success of her family economic programs and fiery oratory.

Cosmos 1400 killer satellites. Type of Soviet killer satellite that poses a threat to *Columbus* and *Gettysburg*.

Crate. Loaded aboard the *Cyclops* in Rio de Janeiro, the wooden crate is described as measuring nine feet long by three feet high by four feet wide. When Church inquires about the contents, Gottschalk explains it contains archaeological artifacts.

Crogan Castle. Vessel that radios the *Cyclops* a distress call. She reports her prow stove in, her superstructure heavily damaged and that she is taking on water.

Cuban Special Security Forces. The Cuban equivalent to U.S. Navy SEALs. The attack on Cayo Santa Maria was done by Cuban exiles posing as Cuban Special Security Forces.

Cyclops. The vessel that sinks at the start of the novel. Built in Philadelphia by William Cramp & Sons and launched May 7, 1910, the *Cyclops* is assigned to the Naval Auxiliary Service, Atlantic Fleet. A collier, she is five hundred forty-two feet in length with a sixty-five-foot beam. Draft is twenty-seven feet eight inches. Tonnage 19,360 displaced. Speed fifteen knots. Armament is four four-inch guns. Set out from Rio de Janeiro on February 16, 1918, bound for Baltimore, Maryland. On March 4, 1918, on the same voyage, she made an unscheduled stop at Carlisle Bay on the island of Barbados. Her seven holds can carry 10,500 tons of coal. On her final voyage, the vessel has three hundred nine passengers and crew and is operating on only her port engine. Loaded with 11,000 pounds of manganese ore, she is riding a good foot lower than her Plimsoll mark on her last voyage. When the *Prosperteer* crashes off Cuba, the *Cyclops* is found by Pitt.

Daimler. One of Pitt's cars. His example is a 1951 powered by a 5.4-liter straight-eight engine with Hooper coachwork. Described as a veritable monster, measuring nearly twenty-two feet from bumper to bumper and weighing more than three tons. The hood and doors are silver-gray and the fenders a metallic maroon. A convertible, its top is completely hidden from view when folded down.

Dashers. Small water-propulsion vehicles made in France for seaside recreation. Has the look of two torpedoes attached side by side. Controlled by an automobile-type steering wheel. High-performance batteries power the craft through the means of water jets on smooth seas at speeds of up to twenty knots for three hours before recharging.

Dawson. One of the Jersey Colonists.

Deep-sea diving suit. Old-style diving suit worn by salvors. They feature a brass diving helmet and

Frankenstein-style weighted boots. The suits use surface-supplied air. Pitt finds a suit with a severed air hose and the body of a diver in the *Cyclops.* That makes him believe the statue of La Dorada has already been salvaged.

Denver. U.S. Navy attack submarine that rescues Pitt when he runs out of gas in the Bahama Channel in his cast-iron bathtub.

DeVoe, Fireman Second Class Barney. Formerly stationed on the cruiser *Pittsburgh.* Described as having the size and shape of a grizzly bear. Sentenced in the murder of Stewart to fifty to ninety-nine years in Portsmouth Naval Prison. Held along with Coker and four other prisoners in the *Cyclops*'s brig when she sank.

Don. Name Soviet ground controller mistakenly calls Jurgens on first radio transmission.

Dupuy, Irwin. *See* Irwin Mitchell.

Eileen. Henry's secretary at the CIA. Thornburg calls Henry to explain Operation Rum & Cola.

El Dorado. Famous treasure Raymond LeBaron believed was aboard the *Cyclops.* Also known as El Hombre Dorado, which is Spanish for *the golden man* or *gilded one.* First heard of by the Spanish conquistadores, the legend tells of a gilded man who ruled an incredibly wealthy kingdom somewhere in the mountainous jungles east of the Andes. Rumors had him living in a secluded city built of gold with streets paved in emeralds and guarded by a fierce army of beautiful Amazons.

Emmett, Sam. Director of the FBI. Described as outspoken.

Entrada Channel. Channel leading out of Havana Harbor.

Eriksen, Dr. Gunnar. Member of the Inner Core. Allegedly died in the light-plane crash with Hudson. Described as a brilliant astrophysicist. His specialty was geolunar synoptic morphology for industrialized peoplement, or the idea of building a colony on the moon. Listed in the notebook Hagen steals from Fisher as Gunnar Monroe. Described as having a round, unlined face. Smokes a pipe.

Farmer, Jack. Alias Pitt uses when calling Weehawken Marine Products.

Fawcett, Daniel. Member of the Inner Core. Advisor to the president of the United States. Described as an intense-looking man with a square red face and a condor nose.

Fernandez, Juan. Chief of Fidel Castro's security.

Figueroa, Herberto. Cab driver who takes Pitt and Jessie LeBaron across Cuba. He is away from Havana to attend his brother-in-law's funeral in Nuevitas. After Pitt takes Velikov prisoner at a roadblock, Figueroa is ordered from his car, and Pitt takes over the wheel. When Pitt meets Fidel Castro, he receives permission to ship Figueroa a restored 1957 Chevrolet to replace the one he ruined in the chase.

First Chief Directorate. The foreign operations arm of the KGB.

Fisher, General Clark. Member of the Inner Core. Head of the Joint Military Space Command and commanding officer at the Unified Space Operations Center. A four-star general. Described as tall, athletically built and quite handsome in a Gregory Peck way.

Foley, Merv. Flight director at the Houston Space Control Center.

Forbes, Lieutenant David. Executive officer of the *Cyclops.* The photograph Hope displays for Pitt shows a man with the face of a greyhound, long, narrow nose, pale eyes whose color cannot be determined from the photograph. His face is clean-shaven, and he has arched eyebrows and slightly protruding teeth. Confined to quarters by Worley on the last voyage of the *Cyclops.*

Fremont, Dr. Donald. A professor at Stanford, now retired. Formerly taught at the University of Southern California. Mooney was a student of Fremont. Hagen calls him when he is examining Mooney's telephone logs.

French Bay. Location of the CIA staging area for the attack on Cayo Santa Maria. A remote beach on the southern tip of San Salvador.

Fulton, Commander Kermit. Commanding officer of the U.S. Navy attack submarine *Denver*.

Gallager. One of the Jersey Colonists.

Gettysburg. A U.S. space shuttle that is launched from Vandenberg Air Force Base.

Gly, Foss. Pitt describes Gly as having chest and shoulders so ponderous they seem deformed. His head is smooth-shaven, and his face could have been described as handsome but for his large misshapen nose. Pitt breaks his nose again when he is torturing Pitt in Room Six. An American mercenary born in Arizona. Said to have thick, protruding lips, and the pupils of his eyes are deep, dark and empty. In the attack on Cayo Santa Maria, Pitt fights with Gly. Pitt jams his thumb into Gly's eye socket and into his brain. Then Jessie LeBaron shoots him three times in the groin with a pistol.

Goodfly, George. One of the aliases used by Hagen when he is in New Mexico. Goodfly is said to be from New Orleans.

Gorman, Adrian. Senator who is having a breakfast meeting with Oates when the president is returning from Rock Creek Park along with Hudson. Hudson claims that attached to their table is a bomb.

Gottschalk, Alfred L. Morean. The American consul general to Brazil. He is aboard the *Cyclops* when she sinks. Described as having a short, round, almost comical frame. He wears his silver-yellow hair cropped excessively short in a Prussian style. He has narrow eyebrows that very nearly match his clipped moustache.

Guinchos Cay. Location on the Bahama Bank. The *Prosperteer* is five miles due south of the cay when the ground crew receives its last radio message.

Hagen, Ira. Described as a thick-bodied man with a round head covered with ivory hair. His stomach is immense and hairy, and his arms and legs protrude like tree trunks. Formerly an undercover operative for the Justice Department. Former wife's name was Martha; when she died, Hagen retired. Has three daughters and five grandchildren. Brother of the president of the United States. Resides in Denver, Colorado. Solves the riddle of the identity of the inner core for the president. After the attack on Cayo Santa Maria, is ordered by the president to Havana, Cuba.

Harris, Jack. Works for NUMA. Sandecker assigns him to replace Pitt on the Bering Sea Survey after he orders Pitt to search for Raymond LeBaron.

Harvey Pattenden National Physics Laboratory. Located in Bend, Oregon. The building is described as typical of the tech centers that have sprung up around the United States. Featuring contemporary architecture with heavy use of bronze glass and curving brick walls. The grounds are landscaped with pine trees and moss rock amid rolling mounds of grass. Mooney describes the laboratory as a research facility. Judge corrects him and explains that the laboratory works on the design of nuclear rocketry and third-generation nuclear weapons whose power is focused into narrow radiation beams that travel at the speed of light and can destroy targets deep in space.

Hero of the Revolution. Honorary title bestowed on Pitt by Fidel Castro.

Herras, Captain Roberto. Cuban captain Clark tricks into withdrawing the Cuban troops guarding the ships that are to be used in Operation Rum & Cola.

Hollyman, Major Gus. U.S. Air Force pilot of F-15E night attack fighter. Has almost one thousand hours of flight time. Hollyman is ordered to shoot down the *Gettysburg* so it can't land in Cuba. Called off at the last second, he instead leads the *Gettysburg* to a safe landing at Key West Naval Air Station.

Hope. The synthesized-voice computer in the NUMA computer room.

Horizon Communications System. Type of telephone system Pitt tells Victor most police departments utilize.

Horse and Artillery Inn. The inn overlooks Valley Forge State Park. Built in 1790 as a stagecoach stop and tavern for colonial travelers, it sits among sweeping lawns and a grove of shade trees. A picturesque three-story building with blue shutters, it has a stately front porch. An example of early limestone farm architecture, it bears a plaque designating it as listed on the National Register of Historic Places.

Hoskins, Elmer. Secret Service advance man when the president visits the Congressional Country Club and first learns of the Jersey Colony.

Hudson, Leonard. Member of the Inner Core. Nicknamed Leo when he was a child. Played catcher on the president's baseball team. Was fat as a child but became a health nut and lost sixty pounds. Graduated with honors from Stanford University and later became director of the Harvey Pattenden National Physics Laboratory in Oregon. Faked his death in a light-plane crash in the Columbia River in 1965. Eriksen was also allegedly aboard the plane when it exploded while the two men were flying to a seminar in Seattle. Listed in the notebook Hagen steals from Fisher as Leonard Murphy. Described as having thick gray hair and a Satan-style beard.

Hydrogen. Gas that the *Prosperteer* was filled with when she reappeared. Hydrogen is not used in blimps since the *Hindenburg* disaster. Helium is used instead.

Inner Core. Group of nine men who originally conceived and implemented the Jersey Colony.

Jack. Alias for CIA operative in Cuba. Described as the stereotypical Latin out of a 1930s movie—flashing eyes, compact build, fireworks teeth, triangular moustache. Is ordered to operate the tugboat that will help move the ship out of Havana Harbor. Killed in the explosion, his remains are never recovered.

Jersey Colony. Conceived two months before President Kennedy's death, the Jersey Colony was designed to be a highly secret leapfrog project to place a United States colony on the moon. The Jersey Colony is located in a large cavern on the southern hemisphere of the moon's far side. Named for the nursery rhyme "Hey diddle diddle, the cat and the fiddle, the cow jumped over the moon." Jersey is a breed of cow.

Joe. One of the Inner Core and the person who first briefs the president on the Jersey Colony. Described as having a slender, almost frail body with slim hips. Has indigo-blue eyes and gray hair. His facial features are described as narrow and vaguely Scandinavian. *See* Leonard Hudson.

Jones, Anson. Called by Hagen when he is examining Mooney's telephone logs. Member of the Inner Core. *See* General Clark Fisher.

Judge, Thomas. Alias used by Hagen in the investigation at the Harvey Pattenden Laboratory. Claims to be with the General Accounting Office.

Jurgens, Dave. Flight Commander of the *Gettysburg*.

Kaltenbach, Senator Henry. Senator famous for finding government fraud. Hagen claims to Mooney that it is he who ordered a probe of the Pattenden Laboratory.

Kazakhstan. Soviet province on the border with China where Soviet spacecraft usually touch down after reentry. Also the location Selenos 8 is launched from.

Kennedy Spaceport. Location on Cape Canaveral where the *Gettysburg* is due to land. Also location of the medical facilities where the Jersey Colonists are transferred after they land aboard the *Gettysburg* at Key West Naval Air Station.

Key West Naval Air Station. U.S. Navy base that lies at the end of the Florida Keys. The runway is one and a half miles long and two hundred feet wide. The base power is out when the *Gettysburg* lands there.

Kleist, Colonel Ramon. U.S. Marine Corps colonel. Congressional Medal of Honor winner. Pitt guesses his age as late fifties. He is a medium-skinned black, born in Argentina, the only child of a former SS officer who fled Germany after the war and married the daughter of a Liberian diplomat. Sent to a private school in New York, he decided to drop out and make a career in the Marines.

Kolchak, Colonel General Viktor. Soviet officer in charge of the fifteen thousand Soviet military forces and advisors based in Cuba. Soviet in charge of the fifteen hundred troops awaiting the *Gettysburg*'s arrival at Santa Clara.

Kornilov, Sergei. Chief of the Soviet space program.

Kronberg, Hans. Partner of Raymond LeBaron. Found by Pitt in the wreck of the *Cyclops* with his air hose cut. Crippled from the bends, he continues to dive.

Kronberg, Hilda. Wife of Hans Kronberg and first wife of Raymond LeBaron. Known as Hillary when married to LeBaron. Now in a senior citizen rest home near Leesburg, Virginia. Described as sickly thin with skin as transparent as tissue paper. Her face is heavily made up and her hair skillfully dyed. Her diamond rings would buy a small fleet of Rolls-Royces. Pitt guesses her age as a good fifteen years younger than the seventy-five she appears. Seventeen years younger than Hans Kronberg, she had been married for three years before Hans brought Raymond LeBaron to their home for dinner, and soon after they entered into an extramarital affair.

La Dorada. Also known as La Mujer Dorada, *the golden woman.* Mentioned by O'Meara as the true sex of the famous golden statue that is the most sought-after piece of the El Dorado treasure. Ordered constructed by a South American king in honor of his most beloved concubine, whom priests ordered to be sacrificed. Described as standing nearly six feet tall, on a pedestal of rose quartz. Her body is solid gold, and O'Meara estimates the statue must weigh nearly one ton. Embedded in her chest where the heart should be is a great ruby, judged to be in the neighborhood of twelve hundred carats. The entire head of the statue is rumored to be one giant carved emerald, deep blue-green and flawless, which O'Meara guesses must weigh in the neighborhood of thirty pounds. When it is found by Hans Kronberg and Raymond LeBaron on the *Cyclops,* LeBaron kills Kronberg, pries the ruby from the heart and breaks it up, forming the nucleus of financing for his financial empire. Because of the revolution, he hides the body of La Dorada on top of the site where the *Maine* sank. Later recovered by Pitt, the statue is put on display at Washington's National Gallery.

Lake Guatavita, Colombia. Possible location of the El Dorado treasure. In 1965, the government of Colombia declared Lake Guatavita an area of cultural interest and banned all salvage operations.

Lariat Type 40. American-made hand-held surface-to-air missile. The weapon homes in on its target with a guidance beam. The range is ten miles on earth but probably longer in the moon's rarefied atmosphere.

Larson, Steve. *See* Steve Busche.

LeBaron's house. Located on Beacon Drive in Great Falls Estate. The house is described sitting on a low hill above a tennis court and a swimming pool. A three-story brick colonial with a series of white columns holding up the roof over a long front porch, the wings extending to each side.

LeBaron, Jessie. Described as vibrant and bouncy with a repertory of a dozen different smiles, she is six months past fifty but looks closer to thirty-seven. She is slightly heavy-bodied but firm, and her facial skin is creamy-smooth. Her hair is a natural salt-and-pepper. Her eyes are large and dark. She is both scuba and sky-diving certified. Sent by the president to meet with Fidel Castro to discuss a treaty with Cuba. Met Raymond LeBaron when she was a senior editor at *Prosperteer* magazine. Carried on an affair with Raymond LeBaron for years, then married him even though he never divorced Hilda Kronberg. Was third in an all-state high school swim meet in Wyoming. Speaks Spanish, Russian, French and German.

LeBaron, Raymond. Member of the Inner Core. Publisher and owner of *Prosperteer* magazine. Graduate of Stanford University. Described as a very trim and healthy sixty-five-year-old who stands six feet seven inches tall. His eyes are the color of light oak, and he has meticulously combed graying hair. Came from a fairly affluent family. His father owned a chain of hardware stores. In the middle 1950s, he and a partner named Kronberg owned a marine salvage firm. The salvage company went broke, and two years later LeBaron launched his magazine, the *Prosperteer.* His first wife was named Hillary; his second wife is Jessie. Hillary is actually Hilda Kronberg, widow of Hans Kronberg. LeBaron was married to Hilda for thirty-three years. He told everyone Hilda was dead because divorcing an invalid was abhorrent to him. Listed in the notebook Hagen steals from Fisher as Ray Sampson. After the *Prosperteer* is captured and forced to land in Cuba, Raymond is taken prisoner and held on Cayo Santa Maria. Later dies on Cayo Santa Maria when a bullet meant for Pitt strikes him instead. His last words sound like "Look on the main sight."

Leopoldville. World War II troop transport ship torpedoed in the English Channel on Christmas Eve, 1944. The book *Cyclops* is dedicated to the men who lost their lives. For more detail on the *Leopoldville,* see the book *The Sea Hunters.*

Leuchenko, Major Grigory. A Russian specialist in guerrilla warfare who won many victories against the Afghanistan Freedom Fighters.

Little Eva. Late-season hurricane that is moving past Florida when Pitt takes off in the *Prosperteer.* At first, the hurricane appears to pose no problem for Pitt aboard the *Prosperteer,* but it grows to Force 6.

Lopez, Corporal Maria. Alias used by Jessie LeBaron as she and Pitt travel across Cuba with Figueroa.

Lopez, Sergeant. One of the American attack force that storms Cayo Santa Maria. Doesn't speak English.

M-14 national match rifle. Type of rifle the Jersey Colonists have.

M-72 missile launcher. Weapon that fires a sixty-six-millimeter rocket. Giordino uses it to shoot down the Cuban helicopter that threatens the *Prosperteer.*

Mack truck. Brand of truck that delivers the mysterious crate to the *Cyclops.* The Mack truck is a chain-drive.

Maine. Famous ship that was blown up in Havana Harbor. The attack on the *Maine* led to the start of the Spanish-American War. Her hulk was raised and towed out to sea in 1912, where she was sunk with her flag flying.

Maisky, Lyev. Deputy head of the First Chief Directorate, the foreign operations arm of the KGB. Described as having a common, blank face as one-dimensional as his personality. Has a platinum cigarette holder and smokes long, unfiltered cigarettes.

Makarov 9-millimeter pistol. Automatic pistol Jessie LeBaron uses to force Pitt to the Cuban mainland when the attack on Cayo Santa Maria is completed.

Manny. Alias for CIA operative in Cuba. Described as a huge black with a deeply trenched face, wearing an old faded green shirt and khaki trousers. Described as looking like a man who had experienced the worst of life and had no illusions left. Smokes cigarettes. Is ordered to get the *Amy Bigalow* out of the Havana Harbor. Is aboard the *Amy Bigalow*'s launch with Pitt when the explosion occurs. Killed, his body is later identified and shipped back to the United States for burial.

Metcalf, General Clayton. Chairman of the Joint Chiefs of Staff. Ordered by the president to coordinate relief efforts to Cuba after the explosion.

Mikoyan, Colonel. Soviet colonel Velikov orders to inspect the security measures around the ships that are to be used in Operation Rum & Cola after Clark switches guards. Mikoyan cannot be reached by radio because he and his driver are killed by Clark and their car pushed into the water.

Miniature electrical impulse jammer. Device contained in a fake cigarette lighter that Hagen/Judge uses to jam the observation cameras at the Pattenden Laboratory so he can search Mooney's office.

Mitchell, Irwin. Member of the Inner Core. Director of NASA's Flight Operations Center.

Modoc missile. Type of radar-guided missile Hollyman is ordered to use to shoot down the *Gettysburg*.

Moe. Alias for CIA operative in Cuba. Described as wearing the image of an academic—lost expression, unruly hair, neatly sculpted beard. Wears glasses. Is ordered to get the *Ozero Zaysan* out of Havana Harbor. Killed in the explosion, his remains are never recovered.

Monfort, Admiral Clyde. Head of the Caribbean Task Force. The president claims Monfort has the Navy searching for Pitt. When Sandecker calls Monfort to confirm, he finds it is false. The Navy is in fact conducting an amphibious landing exercise off Jamaica.

Monterey. Steamship Hans Kronberg sailed to Havana on December 10, 1958, to search for the *Cyclops.* It was the last time Hilda Kronberg saw her first husband.

Mooney, Dr. Earl J. Described as thirty-six years old with pine green eyes under thunderous eyebrows. Has a Pancho Villa moustache. A fat kid who went thin, he shares a similar academic record to Hudson's.

Morro Castle. Famous Cuban landmark that is described as a grim fortress guarding the entrance to Havana Harbor.

Murphy, Lieutenant Regis. Radar observer on Hollyman's F-15E. Chews gum.

National Science Foundation. Located in Washington, D.C. Hagen calls the foundation when he is examining Mooney's telephone logs.

Nitrogen narcosis. Malady that affects divers with too much nitrogen in their blood. Makes a diver light-headed and can lead to feelings of euphoria. Jessie LeBaron begins to suffer from it after the *Prosperteer* crashes.

O'Hara, Major Paddy. Alias Pitt uses in Cuba with Figueroa. Said to be in the Irish Republican Army on assignment as an advisor to the Cuban militia.

O'Meara, Dr. Ralph. Archaeologist. Described as having a thick Gabby Hayes beard that hides his face from the nose down.

Old cast-iron bathtub. Pitt finds the bathtub outside an abandoned shed on Cayo Santa Maria. He later uses it to escape from the island. Later in Pitt's garage.

Order of Lenin. Soviet medal that Maisky tells Velikov he will receive after recovering the *Gettysburg*.

Orinoco River. River in South America mentioned by O'Meara when speaking with Pitt at the Old Angler's Inn.

Ostrovski, Sergeant Ivan. Part of the Soviet attack force from Selenos 8. Described as a hardened veteran of the Afghanistan fighting.

Ozero Baykai. Soviet two hundred thousand–ton oil tanker. Docked near Antares Inlet. Described as eleven hundred feet in length with a one hundred sixty–foot beam. On the starboard side when the *Pisto* tows the three vessels out to sea. Cast off when she is a good mile from the center of town and away from the oil refinery.

Ozero Zaysan. Soviet cargo ship carrying military supplies and cargo. Docked in Havana Harbor to be used in Operation Rum & Cola. Has a cream-colored hull. Described as twenty thousand tons. When Moe boards the ship, he finds the Soviet crew has taken sledgehammers to every valve in the engine room.

Pattenden, Dr. Harvey. Founder of the laboratory that bears his name.

Perez, Colonel Ernesto. Alias used by Clark in tricking Herras into withdrawing his troops from the ships that are to be used in Operation Rum & Cola.

Perry, Kurt. One of the Jersey Colonists. A brilliant biochemist, he is the single fatality in the attack on the Soviets from Selenos 8.

Petrov, Lieutenant Dmitri. Part of the Soviet attack force from Selenos 8.

Pinon, Captain Manuel. Captain of the Russian-built Riga-class patrol frigate that is guarding the entrance to Havana Harbor. Described as a thirty-year-old ship retired by the Russian Navy. Has four-inch guns it fires at the *Pisto, Amy Bigalow* and *Ozero Zaysan.* Crushed in half by the *Amy Bigalow.*

Pisto. Tugboat piloted by Jack. Used to move the ships that are to be used in Operation Rum & Cola out of Havana Harbor. Named after a Spanish dish of stewed red peppers, zucchini and tomatoes. The sides of the tugboat are streaked with rust, and her brass is covered with verdigris. Powered by a big, 3,000-horsepower diesel engine. Single propeller. First attaches lines to the *Ozero Baykai* and begins to push her out to sea. Returns next and moves the *Ozero Zaysan*. Later casts off the *Ozero Baykai* and tows the *Amy Bigalow* and the *Ozero Zaysan* out to sea. Blown two hundred feet high when Velikov activates the pocket transmitter.

Polevoi, Vladimir. Chief of KGB. His office is in Dzerzhinski Square.

Porter, Senator Dean. Member of the Inner Core. Joined the Inner Core in 1964 and helped set up the undercover financing. Once chaired the Foreign Relations Committee and narrowly lost a presidential primary race to George McGovern. Described as a bald-headed man in his late seventies, he has an unimpressive figure with a grandfatherly face.

Porterhouse. Code name for the helicopter pilot Hagen has trailing Hudson after he meets with the president.

Portsmouth, New Hampshire. Site of the U.S. Navy prison where one of the prisoners aboard the *Cyclops* is bound.

Post, Allan. Air Force general who heads up the military space program.

President of the United States. Formerly vice president, he was sworn into office after the former president lost his mind in *Deep Six*. Described as an energetic man who stands more than six feet tall and weighs a solid two hundred pounds. His face is square-jawed with firm features and a brow usually furrowed in a thoughtful frown. His intense gray eyes can be deceptively limpid. His silver hair is always neatly trimmed and parted on the right. A lieutenant in the Marine Corps, he served with an artillery company during the Korean War. Likes to drink guava juice. Secretly smokes Cuban Montecristo cigars. An old trusted school chum smuggles in a box from Canada every two months. Favorite sandwich is tuna with bacon.

Prosperteer. Blimp owned by Raymond LeBaron. Described as a tired-looking old airship with an aluminum skin that was once silver but is now white and spotted by several patches. Originally designated ZMC-2, Zeppelin Metal Clad Number Two. Constructed in Detroit and turned over to the U.S. Navy in 1929. Powered by two Wright Whirlwind engines each with 200 horsepower, she features eight stabilizing fins on her tail instead of the usual four. Measures one hundred forty-nine feet in length, and the aluminum gas envelope contains two hundred thousand cubic feet of helium. In service until 1942, the *Prosperteer* then languished in a deserted hangar in Key West, Florida, until 1988, when LeBaron bought the property and restored her.

QB-Tech. Company owned by Booth. Invents and manufactures scientific gadgets used in space. The plant is located ten miles west of Santa Fe, New Mexico.

Quintana, Major Angelo. Marine major who will lead the attack on Cayo Santa Maria. Described as a dark-skinned man with slick, night-black hair and an enormous moustache. Sad eyes stare from a face wrinkled by long exposure to the wind and sun, and his lips barely move when he smiles.

Raleigh. Cruiser that collides with the *Cyclops*.

Raleigh, Sir Walter. Famous British explorer and treasure hunter mentioned by O'Meara as having searched for the El Dorado treasure. After his second unsuccessful attempt, King James had him beheaded.

Redfern, Lieutenant Commander. Commanding officer of the Key West Naval Air Station. Informs Mitchell that the runway lights are not functioning because a fuel tanker crashed into the power lines and the backup diesel generators failed from a mechanical malfunction. Mitchell orders Redfern to line the runway with cars and trucks with their headlights turned on.

Rock Creek Park. Park where the president holds a speech to commemorate the American servicemen who died in the sinking of the *Leopoldville* on Christmas Eve, 1944.

Roger. The Secret Service chauffeur who drives the president and Hudson from Rock Creek Park.

Ronsky, Ivan. One of the three Russian cosmonauts whose frozen corpses were placed aboard the *Prosperteer* before it reappeared. A veteran cosmonaut.

Room Six. Location on Cayo Santa Maria where Gly tortures the captives.

Rooney, Dr. Calvin. Coroner for Dade County, Florida. A native of Florida, Rooney is a U.S. Army veteran and Harvard Medical School graduate.

Rum & Cola. Code name for the Russian plan to eliminate Fidel and Raul Castro and take control of Cuba. The plan is designed to be blamed on the CIA.

Russell. One of the Jersey Colonists.

Russian frigate. Riga-class patrol frigate that fires on the *Amy Bigalow* and the other ships heading to sea. Run down and sliced in half by the *Amy Bigalow*.

Rykov, Anastas. Soviet geophysicist working on the Cosmos Lunar Project that discovers proof of the Jersey Colony from lunar photographs taken by Selenos 4. Works at the Geophysical Space Center.

Salazar, Reggie. The president's golf caddie. Described as a short, wiry Hispanic. A wit and philosopher, Salazar always dresses for caddie duties like a field laborer—denim jeans, western shirt, GI boots and a rancher's wide-brimmed straw hat. Captured by Joe and drugged after the president plays the front nine holes of golf.

SALT IV. Nuclear reduction treaty the president and Antonov are negotiating.

Salyut 9. Soviet space station that is circling the earth. Carries four cosmonauts.

Salyut 10. New Soviet space station.

Sam. Alias for Pitt that Clark gives Manny, Moe and Jack.

San Salvador. The smallest island of the Bahamas and staging area for the troops who will attack Cayo Santa Maria. Known by the old mariners as Watling Island after a zealous buccaneer who flogged the members of his crew who did not observe the Sabbath. Also believed to be the island where Columbus first stepped ashore in the New World. Has a picturesque harbor and a lush interior blued by freshwater lakes.

Santa Clara. Location in Cuba where the Soviets want to attempt to force the *Gettysburg* to land.

Santa Clara Convent. Dating from 1643, the Havana convent is taken over and used as a temporary hospital after the explosion.

Schonstedt Gradiometer. An instrument used by NUMA to detect iron by measuring magnetic intensity. Gunn is operating one aboard the *Prosperteer* when Pitt sets out to find the *Cyclops.*

Selenos 4. Russian lunar probe that, instead of landing in Siberia, landed in the Caribbean Sea. Allegedly unmanned but instead carrying three cosmonauts. Raymond LeBaron was searching for the probe when he disappeared.

Selenos 8. The Soviets' first manned lunar landing mission. It is scheduled for launch in seven days from the time the Soviets first learn of the Jersey Colony. Described as a super rocket with four strap-on boosters generating fourteen million pounds of thrust. The rocket throws out a tail of orange-yellow flame one thousand feet long and three hundred feet wide. It carries a one hundred ten–ton manned lunar station.

Shea, Willie. The Jersey Colony's geophysicist. Has a hint of a Boston twang.

Sherman, Jack. Commander of the *Columbus.*

Sigler, Colonel Ralph Moorhouse. Described by O'Meara as a real character from the old explorer school. Arrived in the summer of 1916 in Georgetown in what was then British Guiana. With a party of twenty men, he set out into the wilds, then was not heard from until two years later, when he was found five hundred miles northeast of Rio de Janeiro by an American expedition surveying for a railroad. More dead than alive, he described stealing the La Dorada statue, then fighting off the Zanona Indians, dragging it to a river and floating it by raft downstream. O'Meara and Pitt believe Gottschalk found out about Sigler and the statue and recovered it himself.

Simmons, Jess. U.S. secretary of defense.

Sirloin. Code name for Hudson when Hagen is trailing him.

Sloppy Joe's. A onetime watering hole in old Havana patronized by wealthy American celebrities. Now a dingy hole in the wall, long forgotten except by an elderly few. Location where Castro questions Velikov and where Velikov triggers the explosion with his pocket transmitter.

Snodgrass, Elmer. Alias Pitt uses when he is first questioned by Velikov. Said to be from Moline, Illinois. Velikov is not taken in by the ruse and produces a dossier on Pitt.

Socotra. Island near Yemen where the Soviets have a ground tracking station. Space signals from Selenos 4 were transmitted there, and that is where the Soviets got proof of the existence of the Jersey Colony.

Southern Comfort. Thirty-five-foot white fishing boat that is used by Sweat as his second office. Powered by a single 260-horsepower turbocharged diesel, the vessel cruises at fifteen knots. Built in Australia by a company called Steber-craft.

Sparks. Nickname of the wireless operator aboard the *Cyclops.* Is ordered by Worley not to transmit any messages until the *Cyclops* reaches Baltimore.

Special Interests Section. Group that is based in the American Mission at the Swiss Embassy. Located on the Malecon facing the water in Havana, Cuba.

SPUT. Acronym for *Special-Purpose Undersea Transport.* Submarine used to transport the troops who will attack Cayo Santa Maria close to the shoreline. Pitt describes it as slightly more than three hundred feet long and shaped like a chisel turned sideways. The horizontal wedgelike bow tapers quickly to an almost square hull that ends in a boxed-off stern. The upper deck is almost completely smooth without any projections. The vessel is totally automated with a nuclear powerplant that turns twin propellers or, when required, soundless pumps that take in water from the forward momentum and thrust it silently through vents along the sides. Specially designed to support covert operations, she can run as deep as eight hundred feet at fifty knots. She is also capable of running onto the beach, spreading her bows and disgorging a two-hundred-member landing force along with several vehicles.

Steinmetz, Eli. In charge of the Jersey Colony on the moon. Graduated from Caltech, then received a master's degree from MIT. Described as the kind of engineer who overcomes obstacles by designing a mechanical solution and then building it with his own hands. Prior to joining the Jersey Colony Project, he supervised construction projects in half the countries of the world, including Russia. First stepped on the moon at age fifty-three; he is now fifty-nine. His head is shaven, and he has no beard. His skin has a dusky tint, and his eyes are slate black. Described as a fifth-generation American Jew who could walk into a Muslim mosque unnoticed. His father was killed at Wake Island in World War II.

Stewart, Fireman Third Class Oscar. Formerly stationed on the cruiser *Pittsburgh*. Murdered by Coker and DeVoe.

Sweat, Sheriff Tyler. Dade County, Florida, sheriff. Described as a medium-built, brooding man with slightly rounded shoulders.

Swiss Embassy. Location of the American Mission, a sort of quasi official U.S. embassy. The building used by the Swiss was formerly the U.S. embassy.

TAEM. Terminal-area energy management. A process used on the *Gettysburg* for conserving speed and altitude.

Tass. Soviet news organization mentioned by the president.

T-Bone. Code name Hagen uses when trailing Hudson after he meets with the president.

Thornburg, Bob. Chief document analyst for the CIA at the headquarters in Langley, Virginia.

Unified Space Operations Center. U.S. military space organization near Colorado Springs, Colorado. Described as nineteen miles east of Colorado Springs down Highway 94 and Enoch Road. A two-billion-dollar project, the center was constructed on six hundred forty acres of land and is manned by five thousand uniformed and civilian personnel. The center controls all military space vehicle and shuttle flights as well as satellite monitoring programs. Nicknamed the Space Capital of the World.

Velikov, General Peter. Mastermind behind Rum & Cola. Described as a short, trim man. Pitt judges him to be no more than five foot seven, weighing about one hundred thirty pounds, somewhere in his late forties. His hair is short and black with a touch of gray at the side-burns and receding around a peak above the forehead. His eyes are as blue as an alpine lake, and his light-skinned face seems sculpted more by classic Roman influence than Slavic. With the GRU, Velikov is considered a wizard at Third World government infiltration and manipulation. His American-accented English is letter-perfect. When captured by the Castros and taken to Sloppy Joe's for questioning, he activates the pocket transmitter early and unleashes the explosion.

Victor, Detective Lieutenant Harry. A lead investigator for the Dade County Police Department. Wears rimless glasses and a blond hairpiece. Described as a tidy man who enjoys making out reports.

VIKOR. Navigational system that utilizes satellites. Aboard the *Prosperteer* when Pitt takes off. Pitt radios his last VIKOR reading as H3608 by T8090, which places the blimp five miles due south of Guinchos Cay.

Walter Reed Army Hospital. Hospital near Washington, D.C., where the remains of the three men found aboard the *Prosperteer* are taken.

Ward, Clyde. Alias for Clyde Booth.

Weehawken Marine Products. Company in Baltimore that manufactured the diving helmet worn by Kronberg aboard the *Cyclops*. The helmet reads: "Weehawken Products Inc., Mark V, Serial Number 58-67-C." Weehawken has been making the helmet since 1916. It is constructed of spun copper with bronze fittings and has four sealed-glass viewports. The helmet is still popular for certain types of surface-supplied diving operations. Farmer explains the serial number: 58 is the year it was made, 67 is the production number, C stands for *commercial.*

Wintrop Manor Nursing Home. Nursing home near Leesburg, Virginia, where Hilda Kronberg resides. Described as an idyllic setting, with a nine-hole golf course, tropical indoor pool, an elegant dining room and lush landscaped gardens.

Worley, Lieutenant Commander George. Described as a bull of a man. His neck is almost nonexistent, with a massive head that seems to erupt from his shoulders. His hands are long and as thick as an encyclopedia. Never a stickler for Navy regulations; his uniform aboard ship usually consists of bedroom slippers, derby hat and long-john underwear. Speaks with a slight German accent. His real name is Johann Wichman. Born in Germany, he illegally entered the United States when he jumped a merchant ship in San Francisco during 1878. While commanding the *Cyclops,* he lived in Norfolk, Virginia.

Wykoff, Victor. Deputy secretary of state. Works under Oates.

X-ray laser defense system. Space weapons system mentioned by Post to the president. The system won't be operational for another fourteen months.

Yasenin, General Maxim. Head of the Soviet Military Space Command. Described as a big, beefy man with a red face. His hair is smoke-gray and his eyes steady and hard. Smokes cigarettes that he stores in a thin gold case.

Yudenich, Alexander. One of the three Russian cosmonauts whose frozen corpses were placed aboard the *Prosperteer* before it reappeared. A rookie cosmonaut.

Yushchuk, Corporal Mikhail. Part of the Soviet attack force from *Selenos 8.*

Zanona. Word uttered by Gottschalk just before a South American Indian assassin stabs him with the spear in the cargo hold of the *Cyclops.* A tribe of cannibalistic Amazon Indians who allegedly guard the treasure of El Dorado.

Zil limousine. Soviet-made seven-seater limousine used by high-ranking government and military officials. Powered by a seven-liter 425-horsepower engine. Velikov is aboard a Zil when Pitt is stopped at a roadblock.

Zochenko, Sergei. One of the three Russian cosmonauts whose frozen corpses were placed aboard the *Prosperteer* before it reappeared. A veteran cosmonaut.

Treasure

AK-74. Soviet-made automatic weapon used by Ammar's terrorists as they storm the crushing mill on Santa Inez Island.

Al-Hakim Mohammed. A scholarly mullah who is Yazid's shadow. Present at the meeting with Yazid where the hijacking of the *Lady Flamborough* is planned. Described as having the face of a man who spent half his life in a dungeon. His pale skin seems almost transparent.

Alexander the Great. King of Macedonia. Died in 323 B.C. in Babylon. His gold-and-crystal coffin was removed from Alexandria and packed around the sides with three hundred twenty copper tubes that read: "Geologic Charts." This, along with sixty-three tapestries, was buried by Venator's men near the Hills of Rome.

Alexandria Library. Vast information source that contained knowledge of the Egyptian, Greek and Roman empires along with little-known civilizations outside the Mediterranean. In A.D. 391, Christian Emperor Theodosius ordered all books and art depicting anything remotely pagan, which included the teachings of the immortal Greek philosophers, burned and destroyed. Much of the collection was thought to have been secretly saved and spirited away. What became of it, or where it was hidden, remains a mystery sixteen centuries later. A group led by Venator buries it in an unknown land. The entire party, minus four sailors who escape on a small merchant ship named the *Serapis,* are slaughtered by the barbarians in retaliation for an attack on their village. Rothberg describes the library as a library/museum/university, an immense structure of white marble that contained picture galleries, statuary halls and theaters for poetry readings and lectures. There were also dormitories, a dining hall and animal and botanical parks. The contents of the library are later found by Pitt in Roma, Texas, under No Name Hill. After Sharp catalogs them, the contents are transported to a secure building complex in Maryland for restoration and preservation. A replica of the Alexandria Library is scheduled to be built on the Washington Mall.

Antonov, Georgi. President of the Soviet Union. Likes to ball his mistress in the backseat of his limousine on the way to the Kremlin.

Ardencaple Fjord. Fjord on the northeast coast of Greenland. Site near the University of Colorado archaeological dig, where Pitt is searching for missing Soviet submarine. Location where Nebula Flight 106 crashes.

Aristophanes. Was head of the Alexandria Library two hundred years before Christ. The father of the dictionary.

Arnold, Joe. Person in the Treasury Department who goes with Nichols to Kingston to meet with debtor nations that want to forget debts.

Aziz Ammar, Suleiman. Terrorist who kills Lemke and replaces him on Nebula Flight 106. Described as having olive-brown eyes with a Gypsylike piercing quality. His nose has been broken more than once, and a long scar runs down the base of his left jaw. Has close-cropped gray hair and a lined face that suggests an age somewhere in his late fifties. Has a receding hairline and a large black moustache. A good practicing Muslim who has little interest in politics, a mercenary with no known association with fanatical

Islamic die-hards. Does contract work for Yazid. His wealth is estimated at more than sixty million dollars. Plans and executes the hijacking of the *Lady Flamborough* by impersonating Captain Collins. Smokes Dunhill cigarettes. After he meets Pitt under a white flag of truce at the crushing mill on Santa Inez Island, he attempts to shoot Pitt in the back. Pitt, wearing a bulletproof vest, returns fire, striking Ammar in the right shoulder, chin, lower jaw and wrist, and the fourth round passes through his face from side to side, removing his eyes. Now blind. Telmuk hides him from the Special Operations Force and then fashions a crude raft and floats with the current until picked up by a Chilean fishing boat. After stealing an airplane in Puerto Williams, they fly to Buenos Aires, where they charter a plane to Egypt. Goes to Yazid's home to seek revenge. With a knife, he stabs Yazid and kills him.

Aztec. Nahuatl-speaking civilization that was conquered by Cortez.

Baker, Sergeant. Special Operations Force sergeant who finds the hostages on Santa Inez Island.

Barnegat Bay, New Jersey. Location where Yaeger first believes the Alexandria Library was buried. Near the Pine Barrens, an area with dwarf pines similar to what Ruffinus described. It also is near a quarry where the crew of the *Serapis* could have found the ballast stones they mentioned loading aboard. Turns out to be wrong.

Bashir, Colonel Naguib. Leader of a clandestine group of Egyptian military officers who support Yazid. Is present at the meeting with Yazid where the hijacking of the *Lady Flamborough* is planned.

Benelli Super Ninety. Type of semiautomatic shotgun Pitt gives Findley when they arrive at Santa Inez Island.

Benning, Richard. Special Operations Force dive team leader.

British Westland Commando. Ammar's intended escape helicopter. An older but reliable craft designed for troop transport and logistic support. It can carry thirty or more passengers if they're crammed inside.

Brogan, Martin. Director of the CIA. Described as slim and urbane, he has long-fingered violinist's hands. Drinks his coffee with a teaspoon of sugar.

Bucinator. Roman bugler who sounds the call to battle assembly.

Buckley Field. Air National Guard base near Denver, Colorado, where government jets, including the one that removes Kamil from Colorado, land.

Byzantium. Civilization whose capital was Bosporus (formerly Byzantium). Bosporus became Constantinople, which became Istanbul.

C-6 nitroglycerine gel. Type of explosive, two hundred kilograms, Pitt asks Hollis to secure. Ten kilograms of C-6 can take out a battleship. Nitrogel is shock-hazardous. The charge blows the top of Gongora Hill ten meters in the air.

C-140. Military cargo and troop transport plane. A C-140 transports the Demon Stalkers to South America.

Cabo Gallegos. A Chilean ore carrier bound from Punta Arenas to Dakar with a load of coal. Turns up in the Landsat picture.

Callimachus. A famous writer and authority on Greek tragedy. While at the Alexandria Library, he compiled the world's first *Who's Who.*

Campos, Harry. Harbor pilot for Punta del Este. Described as having tobacco-stained teeth, with an accent more Irish than Spanish. Smokes cigars. Has known Collins for almost twenty years.

Cannonball Express. What Pitt nicknames the narrow-gauge locomotive he commandeers on Santa Inez Island.

Cantegril Country Club. Exclusive country club in Punta del Este where some of the heads of state stay during the economic summit.

Capesterre family. A family crime dynasty that started after World War II. A billion-dollar empire run by the father, mother, three brothers and a sister along with various uncles, aunts and cousins. Roland and Josephine are the father and mother. The oldest son is Robert (Topiltzin), the next brother in line is Paul

(Yazid), Karl and Marie are the younger brother and sister. The grandfather launched the criminal family by immigrating from France to the Caribbean and smuggling stolen goods and booze during Prohibition. The enterprise is now said to be worth twelve billion dollars.

Carrier Pigeons. Small, silent Special Operations Force helicopters. They carry a pilot in the enclosed cockpit and two men on the outside. Come equipped with an infrared red dome and silenced tail rotors. They can be broken down or assembled in fifteen minutes, and six of the Carrier Pigeons can fit into each C-140.

Chandler, Brigadier General Curtis. U.S. Army general. Served three tours in Vietnam. Nicknamed Steeltrap Chandler. Hollis served under Chandler in NATO. His wife died a year ago. He has no children. Served with the president when they were both lieutenants of artillery in Korea. After defying a direct order to fire on the Mexican women and children storming across the border, he is promoted to two-star general by the president.

Chavez, Carlos. Son of Luiz Chavez. Helps to find the wreckage of the *Lola.*

Chavez, Luiz. The old fisherman who found the wreckage of the *Lola.* Described as having a grizzled beard. His boat crew consists of his son Carlos, along with Raul, Justino and Manuel.

Collins, Captain Oliver. Captain of the *Lady Flambor-*

ough. Described as a slim man who stands straight as a plumb line. Never refers to anyone by his or her Christian name. Kidnapped with the rest of his crew by Yazid.

Cord L-29. A 1930-model American car that features front-wheel drive. Pitt's example is a town car with an open front for the driver. The body is painted burgundy, while the fenders are a buff color that matches the leather-trimmed roof over the passenger compartment. The Cord factory had stretched the chassis until it measures five and a half meters from front to rear bumper. Almost half the length is hood, beginning with a race-car-type grill and ending with a sharply raked windshield. Best speed recorded for an L-29 was seventy-seven miles an hour. Powered by a straight-eight engine with 115 horsepower. Weighs 2,120 kilometers. Pitt attempts to escape Ismail and his men by driving the Cord up a ski area access road. When that doesn't work, he turns the Cord down a ski slope. The two Mercedes are wrecked. At the end of the run, the Cord crashes into the base lodge.

Corpus Christi Naval Air Station. Where the NUMA jet carrying Pitt, Sandecker and Sharp lands as they begin the search for the Alexandria Library. Located along the Gulf of Mexico in Texas.

Cranston, Captain Louis. U.S. Army captain with the 486th Engineering Battalion. Orders Hollis and Pitt from Gongora Hill. Hollis refuses.

Daneborg. Village in Greenland with a weather station that Gronquist orders Graham to contact after Nebula Flight 106 crashes.

De Pineda, Alonzo. First European explorer to sail up the Rio Grande.

Deep Rover. The submersible aboard the *Sounder. Deep Rover* is a two hundred forty–centimeter sphere divided by large O-rings and sits on a rectangular pod that holds 120-volt batteries. All sorts of strange appendages sprout from the sphere: thrusters and motors, oxygen cylinders, carbon dioxide removal canisters, docking mechanisms, camera systems and a scanning sonar unit. Has manipulators that extend in the front that are best described as mechanical hands and arms. Used by Pitt and Giordino to find the wreck of the *General Bravo.*

Delgado, Jorge. Radio operator Machado sends for after Ammar and his crew disappear.

DeLorenzo, President. President of Mexico. Is aboard the *Lady Flamborough* when the ship is hijacked. Described as a short man in his early sixties, physically robust with wind-blown gray hair, mournful dark eyes and the suffering look of an intellectual confined to a mental institution.

Demon Stalkers. The eighty-man group of Special Operations Force commandos under Hollis's command.

Dillinger, Major John. Second-in-command of the Demon Stalkers. A lean, stringy man with a pinched face. Has a Texas twang to his voice. Rescues the hostages from Santa Inez Island. Later is assigned to assist Pitt in Roma.

Dionysius. Organized grammar into a coherent system while at the Alexandria Library and wrote the *Art of Grammar,* which became the model text for all languages written or spoken.

Dodge, Major General Frank. Commander of the Special Operations Force.

Dragonfish. Ugly deep-sea fish encountered by Pitt and Giordino aboard the *Deep Rover.* Has a long eel-shaped body, outlined by luminescence like a neon sign. Has frozen, gaping jaws that are never fully closed, kept apart by long, jagged teeth that are used more for trapping prey than for chewing. One eye gleams nastily, while a tube that was attached to a luminated beard dangles from its lower jaw to lure the next meal.

Drake Passage. The strip of water between South America and Antarctica.

Earth Resources Tech Satellite. Also known as Landsat. Photographic images from the Landsat are used by the Uruguayans and NUMA to try to locate the *Lady Flamborough.*

Esbenson, Robert. A tall man with a pixie face and limpid blue eyes. He found Pitt's Cord stored in an old garage under forty years of trash and restored it.

Euclid. Great mathematician who wrote the first textbook on geometry while at the Alexandria Library.

Executive Office Building. Located on Seventeenth and Pennsylvania Avenue in Washington, D.C. Where packages are searched before being forwarded to the president.

Falcon. Code name for Dillinger in the assault on the *Lady Flamborough.*

Farquar, Keith. A CIA agent. Described as having a bushy moustache, thick brown hair and horn-rimmed glasses. A large, no-nonsense type of man with contemplative eyes. Briefs Nichols about Yazid.

Fawzy, Khaled. Ramrod of Yazid's revolutionary council. Described as young and arrogant and tactless. Has dark eyes. Is present at the meeting with Yazid where the hijacking of the *Lady Flamborough* is planned. Later is stabbed in the heart and dies when Ammar attacks Yazid and Fawzy with a carbon-composite knife.

Findley, Clayton. NUMA scientist aboard the *Sounder.* Black, medium height. Wears a stern expression and has a deep, rich baritone voice. Before NUMA, he was the chief geologist for an Arizona mining company who thought it could make a zinc mine on Santa Inez Island pay off. Pitt recruits him to go to the island because of his unique knowledge of the area. Seriously wounded in the gunfight in the ore-crushing building on Santa Inez Island. Bullets enter his right side and lodge in a lung and kidney. He is airlifted off the island and taken to Walter Reed Medical Center.

Finney, Michael. First officer of the *Lady Flambor-*

ough. Hates the fact that one of his duties is to entertain passengers on cruises. Described as big, with a barrel chest. His father was a sales rep for a Belfast machinery company, and he was born in Montevideo, Uruguay. Signed on with a Panamanian ore carrier when he was sixteen.

Flores, Captain Ignacio. Captain in Uruguayan Naval Affairs who coordinates the Uruguayan air/sea hunt for the *Lady Flamborough.*

"Fly Me to the Moon." Song Pitt requests from the piano player after the Cord crashes into the Base Lodge at the ski area.

Fort Hood. U.S. Army base in Texas. The Army engineers are dispatched from here to take over the excavation for the Alexandria Library.

Foster, Sergeant Jack. Dillinger's sergeant. When parachuting onto the glacier, he suffers a possible broken wrist.

Gale, Dr. Jack. Doctor on the *Polar Explorer* who helps find survivors from Nebula Flight 106.

Garza, Dr. Herb. NUMA's chief geologist. Described as short, plump, brown-skinned, with a few pockmarks on his cheeks. Has gleaming black hair. Born and raised in Laredo, Texas, he took his undergraduate work at Texas Southernmost College in Brownsville.

General Bravo. A Mexican-registered container ship carrying supplies and oil-drilling equipment to San

Pablo, a small port on the tip of Argentina. Turns up in the Landsat picture. Has a red hull with white superstructure. Sunk under orders of Ammar. The *Lady Flamborough* was then disguised to look like the *General Bravo.*

Georadar One. An electromagnetic reflection profiling system for subsurface exploration. A ground-probing radar unit. Manufactured by the Oyo Corporation. Used by Pitt to search Gongora Hill for the Alexandria Library.

Gerhart, Jim. Special agent in charge of physical security for the White House.

Gibraltar Straits. Exit from the Mediterranean Sea leading into the Atlantic Ocean. Pitt thinks Venator sailed his fleet through the straits and on to America to hide the Alexandria Library.

Gladius. A double-edged pointed sword eighty-two centimeters long. One of the weapons used by the centurions.

Glomar Explorer. Famous deep-sea research and salvage vessel built by Howard Hughes for the CIA. Used in recovering a Soviet Golf-class submarine near Hawaii in 1975.

Gold Miliarensia. Type of coin Sharp finds at the Greenland site, thirteen and a half grams in weight. Graham values the coin at between six and eight thousand dollars. On the face is a likeness of Theodosius the Great, emperor of the Roman and Byzantine empires. The image of Theodosius shows captives at his feet, while his hands hold a globe and a labarum. The banner bears the Greek letters *XP* and forms a kind of monogram meaning *in the name of Christ.* Coined during the rein of Theodosius, which was A.D. 379 to 395.

Graham, Mike. One of the leading field archaeologists in the world. An expert on old coins. Described as being as laidback as a mortician. A light-skinned man with thinning sandy hair, Graham enjoys reading paperback adventure novels. Thrown from one of the rescue snowmobiles when they are driving out to the wreckage of Nebula Flight 106.

Greave. A guard worn over the shins by the centurions. A sort of body armor.

Green, Sid. A photo-intelligence specialist with the National Security Agency.

Gronquist Bay Village. The ancient Eskimo village on Greenland inhabited one to five hundred years after Christ. Named after Hiram Gronquist, the University of Colorado professor who discovered the village five years ago.

Gronquist, Hiram. The chief archaeologist for the four-person dig near Ardencaple Fjord. A large-bellied man with a black-whiskered, kindly-looking face. Is injured with a nasty contusion to the head when he crashes one of the rescue snowmobiles into a shattered wing from Nebula Flight 106. Saved by Pitt.

Gulfstream IV. Type of plane that takes Pitt, Giordino and Sharp from Thule to Washington, D.C. Designed to carry up to nineteen passengers.

Gyrfalcons. White arctic birds that are of a select few species that remain in the north during the winter.

Hamid, Abu. Defense minister of Egypt. Demands that if he supports Yazid's takeover of the Egyptian government, Kamil would remain as secretary-general of the United Nations.

Hartley, Frank. Flight engineer on Nebula Flight 106. Described as a freckle-faced man with sandy hair. We caught Clive here. On page 26, he describes Hartley as above, but on page 28, Hartley has transformed: "wore a bushy moustache, had thin gray hair and a long, handsome face." It really doesn't matter—he is quickly killed by Ammar with an injection of the nerve agent sarin.

Hasan, Nadav. Recently installed president of Egypt. Just past his fifty-fourth birthday, with thinning black hair. He stands slim and tall but moves with the halting movements of a man who is physically ill. His dusky eyes are watery and seem to stare through a filter of suspicion. Is on board when the *Lady Flamborough* is hijacked by Ammar.

Heckler & Koch MP5. Submachine gun used by Ismail in the attack on Senator Pitt's ski chalet. Silenced machine guns borrowed from the Special Operations Force weapons locker by Giordino. Weapon carried by Giordino on Santa Inez Island.

Hell hole. A small electronics bay below the cockpit of commercial airliners accessed through a trapdoor.

The Hills of Rome. Site where Venator ordered the Alexandria Library buried.

Hipparchus the Greek. Man who determined the position of earth landmarks by figuring their longitude and latitude one hundred thirty years before Christ.

Hollis, Colonel Morton. Field leader of the Special Operations Force that is ordered to capture the *Lady Flamborough.* Described as short and almost as wide as he is tall. Forty years old. Has close-cropped, thin brown hair that is graying early. His eyes are blue-green with the whites slightly yellowed from too much time in the sun without proper glasses. Leads the attack on the *Lady Flamborough* and later rescues the hostages from Santa Inez Island. Assigned to assist Pitt in Roma.

Hoskins, Sam. A New York architect with a love for archaeology, Hoskins allows two months a year out of his busy schedule for digs around the world. Described as having neck-length blond hair and an enormous handlebar moustache. Thrown from one of the rescue snowmobiles when they are driving out to the wreckage of Nebula Flight 106.

Hoyo de Monterrey Excaliburs. Type of cigar favored by Sandecker and routinely stolen—two per week—by Giordino.

Huitzilopochtli. One of the Aztecs' revered gods.

Husayn, Saddam (Hussein). Clive rarely is wrong about the future in his books, but he calls this one wrong. On page 92, Korolenko mentions that Iran defeated Iraq and Husayn (Hussein) was assassinated.

Inter-American Economic and Social Council. Meeting held in Punta del Este at which was proclaimed the Alliance for Progress in which the debtor nations except Egypt repudiated their loans and erased foreign debt. That would lead to a worldwide banking collapse.

Ismail, Muhammad. An Egyptian with a round face that is a curious blend of malevolence and childish innocence. His black beady eyes gaze with evil intensity over a heavy moustache, but they lack the power of penetration. He is bravado without substance. An obscure village mullah, he is present when Ammar parachutes from Nebula Flight 106. Later ordered to kill Kamil in Colorado. Is killed himself when his Mercedes goes over a ski jump and lands on its roof, crushing everyone inside.

Jones, Isaac. The third officer on the *Lady Flamborough.* Described as a Scotsman with red hair.

Jones, Lieutenant Samuel T. Works for Dodge in the Special Operations Forces Readiness Command.

Keith, General. General at the Pentagon who informs Nichols that an elite Special Operations Force has left an hour ago for Tierra del Fuego. Nichols informs the president.

KH-15. Type of U.S. spy satellite.

Khomeini, Ayatollah. Mullah who rose to power in Iran after the departure of the Shah. A fanatical Muslim.

Klein Sidescan Sonar. Brand of sonar being used aboard the *Polar Explorer*.

Knight, Commander Byron. U.S. Navy commander. Skipper of the *Polar Explorer*.

Kornilov, Sergei. Head of the Soviet space program. Has a son who works at the Soviet embassy in Mexico City.

Korolenko, Aleksey. Soviet deputy chief in Washington, D.C. Described as heavy-bodied; his face wears a fixed jovial expression.

Labarum. What a banner was called in Roman times.

Lady Flamborough. British cruise liner that Ammar hijacks from Punta del Este. Beautiful, with a streamlined superstructure. Instead of the traditional British black hull and white on the upper works, the ship is painted entirely in a soft slate blue with a sharply raked funnel banded in royal purple and burgundy. She is one hundred one meters in length and features only fifty large suites catered to by an equal number of staff. Home port is San Juan, Puerto Rico. Diesel-powered with big bronze screws (propellers). After Ammar sails the ship and the hijacked passengers into the ocean, the *Lady Flamborough* is disguised with the clever use of fiber-board panels and paint to appear as the *General Bravo.* Forty kilometers off the starboard bow from the *General Bravo*'s scheduled destination of San Pablo, Argentina, the ship veers and continues south. Hidden by Ammar alongside a glacier on Santa Inez Island, the ship is later liberated by the Special Operations Force and towed back to Punta Arenas by the *Sounder.*

Lake of the Ozarks. Chain of lakes in Missouri that is the location of the president's hideaway cottage. The president meets here with Nichols, Schiller, Senator Pitt and Sandecker. The president, on Wismer's advice, wants to turn the excavation of the Alexandria Library over to the military. Luckily for NUMA, the story about the possible find has already broken in the newspapers.

Landsat. *See* Earth Resources Tech Satellite.

Laser parabolic. A sensitive microphone that receives sounds from inside a room by vibrations on a windowpane, then magnifies them through fiber optics onto a sound channel. Used by the mercenaries hired by Yazid to record the conversation that explains Kamil has been taken to Breckenridge.

Lemke, Captain Dale. Commercial airline pilot due to fly Nebula Flight 106. Murdered and replaced by Ammar. His body is later found in the trunk of a car parked at Heathrow.

Lola. Large custom-designed motor yacht owned by Rivera. Forty meters in length with a beam of eight meters.

Rivera was hosting a party for Argentinian and Brazilian diplomats when the *Lady Flamborough* rammed the *Lola* and broke the vessel in two. Rivera and his wife plus twenty-three guests and five crew members were aboard.

Lopez, Armando. The president's senior director of Latin American affairs.

Luger. German 9-millimeter handgun carried by Fawzy. He uses it to shoot Ammar after he stabs Yazid to death.

Macer, Latinius. A Gaul who is chief overseer of the slaves. Described as a huge, hard-bitten character. A giant, he stands a good full head above everyone else. Has great hips and shoulders joined nearly as one and a pair of oak-beam arms ending in hands that drop almost to his knees. Killed by the barbarians.

Machado, Juan. Captain of the *General Bravo.* He and his crew of eighteen are transferred to the *Lady Flamborough* after the *General Bravo* is scuttled. Works for Topiltzin. Has oily hair and dirty fingernails. One whiff is enough to realize he seldom bathes. Ammar concludes that Topiltzin intends to have Machado murder him and his crew. Killed by the Special Operations Force when they storm the *Lady Flamborough.*

Machineel. Also called poison guava, it is native to the Caribbean and the Gulf Coast of Mexico. It comes from a tree that bears a deadly, sweet-tasting, apple-shaped fruit. Poison that was placed in the passengers' meal on Nebula Flight 106.

Magellan Islands. String of islands around the Straits of Magellan. Landmarks include Break Point Peninsula, Deceit Island, Calamity Bay, Desolation Isle and Port Famine.

Mahfouz, Mustapha. Identity Ammar uses to gain access to Yazid's home to murder him. The real Mahfouz is allegedly an uncle of Yazid.

Mercedes-Benz 300 SDL. Car driven by Ismail when he chases Pitt in the Cord. Powered by turbocharged diesel engine, it is capable of two hundred twenty kilometers an hour. Ismail's two cars were driven across the Mexican border to Colorado and are registered to a nonexistent textile company in Matamoros, Mexico. Giordino tosses a socket wrench through the windshield of one of two Mercedes following the Cord and smashes its windshield, causing a wreck with the 300 SDL behind it. When Pitt takes the Cord down the ski slope, the first car is smashed in the mogul field. Pitt tricks Ismail's driver into going off a ski jump.

Metcalf, General Clayton. Chairman of the Joint Chiefs of Staff.

Mifflin, Jack. Pilot of the helicopter that takes Pitt, Sandecker, Sharp and Garza from Corpus Christi to Roma.

Miguel Aleman. Town on the Mexican side of the border across from Roma.

Military Command Center. Area in the Pentagon where planning for the recovery of the *Lady Flamborough* takes place.

Millhiser, Marlys. Author of *The Threshold,* a book Sharp is reading.

Minerva. Brand of vertical-lift aircraft that resupplies Gronquist Bay Village every two weeks.

Moheidin, Mussa. A famous Egyptian writer. In his mid-sixties, he is described as a witty, urbane and articulate man with a slow and gracious manner. A journalist who is Yazid's chief propagandist. Is present at the meeting with Yazid where the hijacking of the *Lady Flamborough* is planned.

Monte Alban. Site of ancient pyramids, where Topiltzin preaches.

Mount Italia. Mountain on Tierra del Fuego where a glacier flows down to the ocean.

Mount Sarmiento. Tierra del Fuego mountain where a glacier flows down to the ocean.

Mullah. Islamic religious leader.

Narrow-gauge locomotive. Found by Pitt at the zinc mine on Santa Inez Island, the locomotive is a 0-4-0 wheel arrangement. Commandeered by Pitt and his crew.

Nebula Air. A plush airline that caters to VIPs. Operates on charter only. The airline's colors are three stripes running down the hull, light blue and purple separated by a band of gold.

Nebula Flight 106. United States chartered flight that is carrying Kamil. A Boeing 720-B. After Ammar kills the crew and steers the plane north, he bails out over Iceland. The plane continues on to Greenland, where it crashes in Ardencaple Fjord.

Nichols, Dale. Special assistant to the president of the United States. Gives off the image of a college professor, which he had been at Stanford before the president persuaded him to switch jobs. Has a thicket of coffee-brown hair, neatly parted down the middle, and old-style spectacles, with small round lenses and thin wire frames. Wears a bow tie and smokes a pipe. Learned Spanish during a two-year stint in the Peace Corps.

No Name Hill. True location of the Alexandria Library.

Noricus, Artorius. A young legionnaire under the command of Severus. First to alert Severus and Venator the barbarians are attacking.

NUMA Seasat. NUMA-operated satellite mentioned by Dodge on page 333.

O'Hara, Sergeant. U.S. Army sergeant whom Cranston orders to clear Gongora Hill.

Obsidian knife. Weapon used to remove Rivas's heart. Obsidian is stone, and the knife is razor-sharp.

Operation Stogie. Code name for the theft of Sandecker's cigars. Launched by Giordino and an old Air

Force buddy who is now a professional burglar for an intelligence agency.

Orinoco River. River in Venezuela. Pitt wonders if it is where Venator might have buried the Alexandria Library.

Osman, Mustapha. Arab who reports that Pitt's group has taken over the crushing mill and has possession of the escape helicopter.

Osprey assault aircraft. Vertical takeoff and landing aircraft that the Special Forces unit takes to Argentina. Has a tilt rotor. The bullet-shaped aircraft takes off like a helicopter but flies like a plane in excess of six hundred kilometers an hour. Has a terrain-following computer that controls most flight operations.

Oswald, Jerry. Copilot on Nebula Flight 106. Described as a big man with the pinched features of a desert prospector. After being injected with the hypodermic containing the nerve agent sarin, he fights with Ammar and almost succeeds in strangling him before the poison ends his life.

Papyrus. A tropical plant. The Egyptians made a paperlike writing material out of Papyrus stems.

Parchment. Also called vellum. It is produced from the skin of animals, especially young calves, kids or lambs. Used as a writing material.

Parker, Herbert. Second officer on the *Lady Flamborough.* Described as physically fit, suntanned, with a smooth boyish face that seems as if it only needs a razor on Saturday night. Ammar, disguised as Collins, slips up and calls Parker by his first name, something the real Collins would never do.

Partido Revolucionario Institucional. Also known as PRI, the political party that dominates Mexican politics.

Patton, Vic. Green's supervisor at the National Security Agency.

Pharos of Alexandria. One of the Seven Wonders of the Ancient World. A famed lighthouse that once stood a towering 135 meters. Near where Topiltzin meets Yazid.

Pilum. A two-meter throwing and thrusting sword. Weapon used by the centurions.

Pliny. A celebrated Roman of the first century A.D. who wrote the world's first encyclopedia while with the Alexandria Library.

Polar Explorer. A sturdy new vessel especially designed for sailing through ice-covered waters. The massive boxlike superstructure towering above the hull resembles a five-story office building, and her great bow, pushed by her 80,000-horsepower engines, can pound a path through ice up to one and a half meters thick. Based in Portsmouth, New Hampshire.

President of the United States. Described as having silver hair and limpid gray eyes. He is tall, weighs two hundred pounds and has a bone-crushing grip.

Ptolemy. One of Alexander the Great's generals. After Alexander's death, his empire was divided by his generals. Ptolemy took Egypt and became a king. He also managed to get Alexander's corpse and encase it in a gold-and-crystal coffin which he enshrined in a mausoleum. Around the mausoleum, he built a city which became Alexandria. Ptolemy started the Alexandria Library.

Punta Arenas. The southernmost large city in the world, on the Brunswick Peninsula in Chile. The Special Operations Force bases its operations there.

Punta del Este. Coastal city in Uruguay. Location of an international economic summit meeting.

Pytheas. Famous Greek navigator who made an epic voyage in 350 B.C. The legends say he sailed north and eventually reached Iceland.

Qaddafi, President Muammar. President of Libya. Mentioned by Brogan when talking to the president. Here we catch Clive predicting the future incorrectly: the president mentions to Brogan that Qaddafi died of cancer. As of this writing, he's still alive.

Quetzalcoatl. Five-step pyramid in the Toltec city of Tula. Site where Rivas is sacrificed. Named for one of the Aztecs' revered gods.

Redfern, Dr. Mel. A tall man with blond hair that has receded into a widow's peak. Wears designer glasses. Has blue-gray eyes. Still reasonably trim for a man of forty but has a slight paunch. A former college basketball star who passed on playing in the pros to earn his doctorate in anthropology. One of the world's leading experts in classical marine archaeology. While analyzing the tablets Pitt had removed from the *Serapis,* Redfern finds the reason for the voyage: to hide the Library of Alexandria.

Rio Grande. The river that divides Mexico and the United States and forms the Texas-Mexico border. Known as Rio Bravo in Spanish.

Rivas, Guy. Special representative for the president of the United States. Picked because he speaks Nahuatl, the language of the Aztecs. His family immigrated to America from the Mexican town of Escampo, where he was taught Nahuatl at a very early age. Married, he has four children. After being sent to meet with Topiltzin, his heart is removed with an obsidian knife, and he is skinned.

Rivera, Victor. Speaker of the Chamber of Deputies in Uruguay. Owned the *Lola,* named for his wife, which the *Lady Flamborough* rammed and sank.

Rojas, Colonel Jose. Uraguayan chief coordinator for special security. Trained with the British Grenadier Guards.

Roma, Texas. Town near the site where the Alexandria Library was buried. On seven hills like its namesake in Italy. *Viva Zapata,* a Marlon Brando movie, was filmed in Roma.

Rooney, Teri. An actress who is asked to be a double for Kamil.

Rothberg, Dr. Bertram. A professor of classical history at the University of Colorado. Rothberg has made the study of the Alexandria Library his life's work. Described as having a jolly smile beneath a splendid gray beard. Has sparkling blue eyes and a swirling mass of gray hair.

ROV. Stands for *Remote Operated Vehicle.* A tethered underwater viewing system.

Rubin, Gary. Chief steward on Nebula Flight 106. Takes over the controls after Ammar parachutes out the hatch. One of three survivors of the crash.

Rufinus, Cuccius. Captain of the *Serapis.* Employed by Nicias, a Greek shipping merchant from the port city of Rhodes. Has a daughter named Hypatia who travels with him on his voyage to bury the Alexandria Library.

Ruger P-85. American-made semiautomatic 9-millimeter handgun that Ammar uses to shoot Pitt in the back.

Sadat, President Anwar. Former president of Egypt who was assassinated, mentioned by Kamil on page 237.

Salazar, Miguel. Mexico's director of foreign financing.

Sam Trinity Sand and Gravel Company. Front for the actual excavations of the Alexandria Library being carried out by Sharp.

Santa Inez Island. Island in Chile that has glaciers. Spot where Pitt concludes the *Lady Flamborough* is hidden. Described as sixty-five kilometers wide by ninety-five kilometers in length. The highest point is Mount Wharton at thirteen hundred twenty meters.

Sarapis. The Roman ship found by Pitt near Gronquist Bay Village. Thought to be from the fourth century. Pitt dives through the ice in a dry suit using surface-supplied air and examines the wreck. Pitt finds the wreck has no stern rudder and a lead-sheathed bottom. Asked to examine the stern post, Pitt finds a hardwood plaque with the Greek letters spelling *Serapis* and a face with curly hair and a heavy beard. Graham explains that the letters are not Classical but Eastern Greek and that it is the name of a Greek-Egyptian god. Pitt enters the hull and finds the galley in order but no bodies inside. Roaming through the ship, he examines the cargo hold and finds the crew, eight in all, perfectly preserved and crowded around an iron stove. Pitt theorizes they were killed by a buildup of carbon monoxide. After the ship is excavated from the ice, it is measured at just under twenty meters in length with a beam of seven meters.

Schiller, Julius. U.S. undersecretary for political affairs. Owns a beautiful thirty-five-meter motor sailer where poker games and politics occur with Soviet politicians. Married, he has a house in Chevy Chase, Maryland. Holds a clandestine meeting with Kamil at Senator Pitt's ski chalet in Breckenridge.

Severus, Domitius. The Roman centurion who runs the infantry unit that provides protection for Venator. Has the muscled arms of a soldier. Trained for the sword and the shield. Described as merciless, a savage. The personal symbol of the military detachment he leads is Taurus the Bull atop a lance. A Spaniard. Severus had volunteered for the Roman Legion when he was sixteen. He advanced from common soldier, winning several decorations for bravery in battles with the Goths along the Danube and the Franks along the Rhine. Fought against the Britons. Retired and became a mercenary. The last man to fall when the barbarians attack Venator's group.

Shark. Code name for Hollis in the assault on the *Lady Flamborough.*

Sharp, Lily. A professor of anthropology at the University of Colorado. Finds the Roman coin while excavating at the site near Ardencaple Fjord. Injured when Gronquist crashes one of the rescue snowmobiles into a severed wing from Nebula Flight 106. Saved by Pitt. She later shows up at Pitt's home dressed seductively. Pitt takes her into the bedroom and has sex with her. In the car chase with Ismail, she receives a bruised left cheek and a black eye on the right side.

Shaw, Elmer. Assistant secretary of the Navy.

Sherlock. A robot submersible operated from the *Polar Explorer.* Has two movie cameras and one still camera. Used to photograph the Alfa-class submarine located by Pitt.

Shiite. Sect of the Muslim religion most Iranians belong to. Said to be more bloody and revolutionary than the Sunni sect.

Simon, Lieutenant Cork. The leader of the *Polar Explorer*'s damage-control experts. Sent to the wreckage of Nebula Flight 106. Described as stocky.

Situation Room. Area in the White House where the president views all the assembled intelligence data and plans the recovery of the *Lady Flamborough*.

Slade, Lieutenant Colonel James. Air Force pilot of the SR-90 Casper who photographs Antarctica and Tierra del Fuego. Home base is in the Mojave Desert.

Sounder. NUMA research vessel assigned to a sonar mapping project of the continental slope off southern Brazil. The vessel's sonar gear can cut a swath two miles wide, and she carries a submersible. Pitt requests the ship to search for the *Lady Flamborough*. Launched at a Boston shipyard in 1961, the vessel spent three decades chartering out to oceanographic schools. Purchased by NUMA in 1990, she was completely overhauled and refitted. Her new 4,000-horsepower diesel engine was designed to push *Sounder* at a speed of fourteen knots. Stewart and the engineers managed to reach seventeen knots. Has twin cycloidal propellers, one forward, one aft. Arrives at Santa Inez Island and tows the *Lady Flamborough* away from the glacier.

Soviet Alfa-class submarine. A nuclear-powered, titanium-hull, nonmagnetic and noncorrosive Soviet submarine with the latest in silent-propeller technology. Said to be the deepest-diving and fastest submarines in either the U.S. or Soviet navy. Holds one hundred fifty men. *Sherlock* shows a gash down her side as if she tore her side out on a jagged edge of the crater she lies inside. What Pitt and Giordino on board the *Polar Explorer* are seeking. They have just found it when Nebula Flight 106 passes overhead.

Special Operations Force. U.S. military service integrated elite force. In the fall of 1989, the Army's Delta Force and its secret aviation unit named Task Force 160 were merged with the Navy's SEAL Team Six and the Air Force's Special Operations Wing. These soldiers are heavily trained in guerrilla tactics, parachuting, wilderness survival and scuba diving, with a special emphasis on storming buildings, ship and aircraft for rescue missions.

SR-90 Casper. Top-secret U.S. Air Force reconnaissance aircraft capable of reaching Mach 5 or just under five thousand kilometers an hour. The closest SR-90 to South America is based at an airfield in Texas. The president wants pictures of the *Lady Flamborough* and is told it will take five hours for the flight over and photographic development. The SR-90's fuselage is made of an incredibly tough, lightweight plastic skin that was tinted gray-white. Nicknamed Casper after the friendly comic-book ghost.

Stealth parachute. Special nondetectable parachute used by the Demon Stalkers.

Stewart, Frank. Captain of the *Sounder*. Described as narrow-shouldered, with slicked-down long, burnt-toast-brown hair. Looks like a small-town feed-store merchant and scoutmaster. A seasoned seaman, he can swim but refuses to learn how to dive.

Telmuk, Ibn. Ammar's servant and friend. Described as a swarthy type with a curly mass of ebony hair. He is present when Ammar parachutes from Nebula Flight 106. Later helps Ammar hijack the *Lady Flamborough.* After the shoot-out with Pitt, he helps Ammar escape Santa Inez Island and make his way back to Egypt. Later tries to kill Pitt in Roma with a pistolized shotgun, but Pitt cuts off his fingers with a Roman sword. Seconds later, he is blown to bits in the C-6 explosion.

Temple of the Magician. Pyramid temple in Uxmal where Topiltzin gives a speech.

Teotihuacan. Site of ancient pyramids, where Topiltzin preaches.

Terra-cotta amphora. Pitt sees an amphora on the sea bottom near the Soviet Alfa-class submarine. The Greeks and Romans used amphoras to transport wine and olive oil.

Texas A&M. University in Texas that translates the stone tablet Trinity finds. The tablet is from Venator and describes the location of the Alexandria Library.

Tezcatlipoca. One of the Aztecs' revered gods.

Theodosius. Emperor who orders the Alexandria Library destroyed. Venator instead leads a group that hides the library in a series of caves. Died in 395.

Thephilos. The patriarch of Alexandria who, along with Theodosius, ordered the Alexandria Library destroyed. Bishop of Alexandria.

Thompson submachine gun. Weapon of choice for Pitt on Santa Inez Island. Uses round drums that holds fifty .45-caliber shells.

Thule Air Force Base. U.S. Air Force base in Greenland that sends help to the site where Nebula Flight 106 crashes.

Tiber. Once-glorious city in the Roman Empire. Now a slum. Mentioned by Severus when talking to Venator.

Tierra del Fuego. Tip of Argentina cut off from the rest of the country by the Straits of Magellan.

Topiltzin. Described by Senator Pitt as a Benito Juarez/Emilio Zapata messiah who preaches a return to a religious state based on Aztec culture. Described as short, with long hair he ties at the base. Has a smooth, oval face that suggests Indian ancestry. Has dark eyes. Rivas describes him as not looking a year over thirty. Wants to take over Mexico and rename the country Tenochtitlan, its Aztec name. Nahuatl will be the official language. Population will be brought under control, foreign industry will become property of the state and only native-born people will be allowed to live in the country. No more goods will be bought from the United States, and no oil will be sold to the United States. Topiltzin also wants the return of California, Texas, New Mexico and Arizona. In actuality, he is Robert Capesterre and brother of Paul, who is acting as Yazid. Killed by Pitt in the excavation on Gongora Hill.

Trinity, Sam. Resident of Roma and proprietor of Sam's Roman Circus, a convenience store, gas station and Roman artifact museum. Has white hair and a dark calfskin-colored face. Very tall, skinny as a fence post, arms slender, shoulders narrow, but with a voice that has vigor and resonance. Loves to golf and dig for artifacts. Owns the twelve hundred acres of land surrounding where the Alexandria Library is buried. The land has been in his family since Texas was a republic. Is paid a tax-free ten million for the Alexandria Library by the U.S. government and takes off on a tour to play the top one hundred golf courses in the world.

TRIVMFATOR. Inscription on the coin found by Sharp.

Tula. Site of ancient pyramids where Topiltzin preaches.

Uncle Theodore's boat. One of the Capesterre uncles' yachts. Forty-five meters in length, the vessel is Dutch-built with aircraft-style lines. The vessel has transoceanic range and a cruising speed of thirty knots. Site of the meeting between Topiltzin and Yazid.

UNESCO. Acronym standing for *United Nations Educational, Scientific and Cultural Organization.*

University of Colorado. University located in Boulder, Colorado. Institution sponsoring the archaeological excavation near Ardencaple Fjord. The archaeologists find that the site contains proof that a band of hunters inhabited it nearly two thousand years ago. Radiocarbon dating on the excavated relics indicates the site was occupied from A.D. 200 to A.D. 400.

Vazquez, Lieutenant Eduardo. Works under Rojas's command.

Venator, Julius. Approaching his fifty-seventh year, with a gray, lined face, sunken cheeks and the tired, dragging steps that reflect the weariness of a man who has no more heart for life. A Greek wise man. In charge of the group that hides the Alexandria Library. Has a wife and daughter awaiting his return at the family villa in Antioch. Assembles a fleet of sixteen ships including the *Serapis* to carry the contents of the library. Described by Rothberg as the leading intellectual of his time. A renowned scholar and teacher who was hired away from one of the great learning centers of Athens to become the last of the Alexander Library's curators. Wrote more than one hundred books of political and social commentary. When the barbarians attack his soldiers and kill them, Venator attempts to swim out to the *Serapis* but is unsuccessful. He later describes what happens on the stone tablet found by Trinity. After escaping the barbarians, he made his way south, where he was taken in by a primitive pyramid people. Seven years later, he returned to Roma, then sailed for the Mediterranean but was never heard from again.

Vyhousky, Yuri. The Soviet Embassy's special advisor on American affairs.

Webster, Henry. Doctor aboard the *Lady Flamborough* who treats Pitt after the gunfight at the ore-crushing building. Described as a little bald-headed man.

Wismer, Harold. Present at the meeting at Lake of the Ozarks. An old crony and advisor to the president. Wears rimless glasses with pink lenses. A snarled beard almost hides his thin lips. Described as bald as a basketball. Has brown eyes.

Yazid, Akhmad. Leader of the fanatical mullahs who seek to overthrow the Egyptian government. An Islamic law scholar. Orders the murder of Kamil by destroying Nebula Flight 106. Fashions himself as a Muslim Gandhi. Described as young, no more than thirty-five. A small man whose face does not have the precise features of most Egyptians, the chin and cheekbones softer, more rounded. His eyes seem to shift in color from black to dark brown. Claims to have spent his first thirty years in the Sinai Desert talking to Allah. Claims to have been born in squalid poverty in a mud hut near the City of the Dead in the garbage dumps of Cairo. Claims his father and two sisters died from disease brought on by filthy living conditions. Claims his only formal schooling is what he received from Islamic holy men and also claims the Prophet Muhammad speaks through him. Linked to terrorism that includes the murder of a high-ranking Air Force general, a truck explosion outside the Soviet Embassy and the execution-style killing of four university professors who spoke out in favor of Western ways. In actuality, he is Paul Capesterre and brother of Topiltzin (Robert Capesterre). Killed with a carbon-composite knife by Ammar at his house in Egypt.

Yazid's house. Located twenty kilometers from Alexandria, the small villa squats on a low hill overlooking a wide sandy beach. Has an ornate doorway for honored guests and a small side door used by those who work for Yazid.

Ybarra, Eduardo. A member of the Mexican delegation on Nebula Flight 106. Once served as a mechanic in the Mexican Air Force. Described as having a round and brown face. His hair is thick and black with traces of gray. Has brown eyes. Helps Rubin in the cockpit of Nebula Flight 106 after Ammar parachutes out over Iceland. Killed in the crash of Nebula Flight 106. Is a suspect in the poisoning of the passengers because he didn't eat the in-flight meal, claiming to have an upset stomach. Later, the flight attendant notices him eating a sandwich taken from his briefcase.

Dragon

Acosta, Rico. A mining engineer attached to the Philippine security force looking for Yamashita's Gold. Described as tall for a Filipino, with eyes that indicate more than a trace of Chinese ancestry. His grandfather was in the 57th Philippine Scouts, captured by the Japanese and imprisoned at Fort Santiago. The grandfather never returned.

Ajima Island. Island in Japan that was later renamed Soseki Island. Location of the Dragon Center. About sixty kilometers off the coast due east of Edo City.

Akagi spy satellite. Japanese spy satellite.

Andersson, Olaf. The assistant chief engineer of the *Narvik*. Goes with the boarding party to the *Divine Star*.

Arizona. Code name for the operation to have Pitt place an atomic bomb on the fault line and wipe out Soseki Island.

Arnold, Lieutenant Joseph. Navigator on *Dennings' Demons* flight to Osaka.

Asakusa. An area northeast of Tokyo in a section known as Shitamachi. Part of the old city of Tokyo.

Atomic bomb. The one carried by *Dennings' Demons* is described as a gigantic overinflated football with nonsensical boxed fins on one end. The round ballistic casing was painted a light gray, and the clamps that hold the bomb together around the middle look like a huge zipper.

Avanti. Automobile produced by Studebaker and later other companies. Car used by Fox and Weatherhill when in Las Vegas.

Beanbag gun. A spring-powered piston tube with a wide-diameter barrel used to shoot the hedgehog. Used by Fox and Weatherhill as they break into the underground parking garage at the Pacific Paradise Hotel.

Big Ben. The DSMV, a later version than *Big John*, that Pitt uses to drive the atomic bomb from *Dennings' Demons* to the fault line to eradicate Soseki Island. Weighs thirty-five tons. The top speed has been increased over *Big John's*.

Big John. The DSMV Pitt is driving when he rescues the crew of *Old Gert. Big John* has tractor treads that can propel it at five kilometers an hour. On the front are a grappler and a scoop. The pilot sits behind a clear bubble shield. It is powered by a small nuclear reactor. Weight is fifteen tons. After Pitt drives *Big John* to Conrow Guyot, he is met by Giordino and Sandecker in a submersible. Giordino cuts off parts of *Big John* with an arc torch to allow it to rise to the surface. When the ascent begins to slow, Giordino grabs *Big John* with an arm from the submersible and pushes it to within ninety meters from the surface before the submersible begins to falter. There Pitt and Plunkett escape from *Big John* and swim to the surface, and *Big John* sinks again to the bottom.

Black Horse. Code name used by Frick's team.

Black Sky. Criminal organization that dominated Japan after the turn of the century. Korori Yoshishu and Koda Suma, father of Hideki, were members.

Black smokers. Oddly sculpted vents on the sea floor that emit 365-degree-Celsius clouds of black steam underwater. Pitt and Plunkett pass one on the way to Conrow Guyot. Around the vents are tube worms, white mussels and varieties of clams Plunkett has never seen before. They survive on bacteria that converts hydrogen sulfide and oxygen overflow from the vents into organic nutrients.

Blood Red Brotherhood. Japanese terrorist society described as fanatical butchers. A few are Japanese, but most are East Germans trained by the KGB. Tsuboi wants them to kidnap Smith and Diaz.

Blue Horse. Code name for the team that recovers a bomb car in New Jersey.

Bock's Car. Name of the B-29 that dropped the atomic bomb named Fat Boy on Nagasaki. Piloted by Major Charles Sweeney.

Brogan, Martin. Director of the Central Intelligence Agency.

Byrnes, Commander Hank. Weapons engineer on *Dennings' Demons* flight to Osaka. Is tasked with monitoring the atomic bomb. The only U.S. Navy officer aboard the plane.

Building C. Part of the National Security Agency at Fort Meade, Maryland. Location where Ingram studies pictures of the ocean bottom and locates *Dennings' Demons.*

Buson. Japanese poet who once wrote, "With his hat blown off/the stiff-necked scarecrow/stands there quite discomfited." Quoted by Suma on page 404.

C-8. Plastic explosive used by Mancuso at Soseki Island.

CAD/CAM. An acronym for Computer-Aided Design/Computer-Aided Manufacturing. Yaeger uses the system to help Pitt and Nash discover atomic bombs are being smuggled into different countries in the Murmoto's air conditioners.

Cain, Edward. Tourist on the beach at Marcus Island when *Big Ben* comes ashore. Married to Moira.

Central Command. Main base of operations for the MAIT. Housed in the Federal Headquarters Building.

Clausen, August. Farmer in Germany whose tractor falls into the underground cavern containing German jet fighters and expensive artwork. Lives near Bielefeld in North Rhine-Westphalia, West Germany. Described as a big, hearty man just past seventy-four. Has a wife and two daughters. Fought in World War II in the Panzer brigade.

Congressional Country Club. Where the president is playing golf when Jordan briefs him about the progress on Soseki Island.

Conrow Guyot. A seamount near Soggy Acres with a smooth summit that Pitt heads for in *Big John*. The sea floor rises up, and it is only three hundred ten meters to the surface.

Corregidor Island. Island at the mouth of Manila Bay in the Philippines. Where Mancuso believes Yamashita's Gold is buried. Corregidor was the location of General MacArthur's headquarters before he evacuated to Australia.

CPDA-1 red blood cell bags. What Pitt steals from the hospital on the fourth floor of Soseki Island. Uses the bags to drain his own blood. Later uses the blood to fool Katamori that he was killed.

Deep Quest. NUMA submersible that is sitting on the dock in Los Angeles Harbor. Sandecker wants to have the twelve-metric-ton *Deep Quest* air-dropped from a U.S. Air Force C-5.

Deerfield, Dr. Harry. Doctor who cares for Knox aboard *Shanghai Shelly*. Described as having graying bald hair and a warm twinkle in his eyes.

DEFCOM. Level of nuclear preparedness. DEFCOM One is a launch.

Delta One. The U.S. military team that is scheduled to remove the MAIT team from Soseki Island when they signal.

Delta watch. Special watch that beeps to alert the wearer that a coded message has been received. Labeled a Raytech so it looks ordinary. Jordan wears one.

DeLuca, Lieutenant David. The navigational officer on board *Tucson*.

Dennings, Major Charles. Pilot of the B-29 that takes off from Shemya Island bound for Osaka. Spent two years as one of the top bomber pilots in Europe, with more than forty missions to his credit. His plane and crew perish when they are shot down by a Japanese Zero and the B-29 bursts into flames.

Dennings' Demons. Boeing B-29 carrying the atomic weapon bound for Osaka. At takeoff, the plane is fully loaded at sixty-eight tons with her tanks filled to capacity with more than seven thousand gallons of fuel. With the forward bomb bay holding the six-ton atomic bomb and carrying a crew of twelve, the plane is seventeen thousand pounds overweight. It is powered by four 3,350-cubic-inch Wright Cyclone engines. The engines' combined power is 8,800 horsepower, and they spin sixteen-point-five-foot propellers. The fuselage is ninety feet long and made out of polished aluminum. The wings are one hundred forty-one feet, and the rear stabilizer is three stories tall. The insignia is a devil clutching a pitchfork in his right hand, a bomb in his left, with his feet clutching gold bars labeled "24K," a reference to the crew calling themselves goldbrickers after they are reprimanded for tearing up a beer hall in California.

Diaz, Senator Mike. U.S. senator who advocates stern measures against Japan. A widower in his late forties, his wife died of diabetes shortly after he was elected to his first term. Lives full-time in his office in Washington, D.C. No children. Was an army helicopter pilot in Vietnam who was shot down and wounded in the knee. Spent two years as a POW, but his jailers never properly attended to his wound, so he walks with a limp and the aid of a cane. Attended the University of New Mexico and became a lawyer. Hair is pure black and swept back in a high pompadour. His face is round and brown with dark umber eyes and a mouth that flashes perfect white teeth. Kidnapped by Suma's men from his fishing lodge and taken to Soseki Island. Later rescued by Pitt and group.

Divine Lake. Japanese cargo ship containing Murmoto automobiles that is five days out of Los Angeles.

Divine Moon. Japanese cargo ship containing Murmoto automobiles that off-loads in Boston.

Divine Sky. Japanese cargo ship containing Murmoto automobiles that is scheduled to dock in New Orleans within eighteen hours. Suma orders the vessel to divert to Jamaica.

Divine Star. Huge Japanese auto carrier. Her upper works stretch from blunt bow to a perfectly squared stern. The ship has five decks and a huge, completely automated wheelhouse. Seven hundred feet in length, it was delivered March 16, 1988. Owned and operated by Sushimo Steamship Company Limited. Her home port is Kobe, Japan. When found by the boarding party from the *Narvik*, she's loaded with 7,288 Murmoto automobiles due to be delivered in Los Angeles. Blown to bits when one of the boarding party from the *Narvik* shoots a bullet into the atomic bomb in a Murmoto.

Divine Water. Japanese cargo ship containing Murmoto automobiles that is off-loading in Los Angeles.

Dragon Center. What the detonation center for the Kaiten Project is called.

DSMV Acronym for *Deep Sea Mining Vehicle*. Also known as *Big John*.

Edo City. Set in a landscaped park and covered by a huge solar plastic dome, Edo City was named after the city renamed Tokyo. Designed and built by Suma, Edo City is a scientific research and think-tank community that supports sixty thousand people. Shaped like a giant cylinder around an atrium, the twenty-story circular complex contains living quarters for the scientific community, offices, public baths, convention halls, restaurants, a shopping mall, library and its own thousand-member security force. Smaller underground cylinders connected by tunnels to the main core hold the communications equipment, heating and cooling systems, temperature and humidity controls, electrical power plants and waste-processing machinery. The elaborate structures are constructed of ceramic concrete and reach fifteen hundred meters deep in the volcanic rock.

Enola Gay. The plane that dropped the atomic bomb on Hiroshima. As *Dennings' Demons* is settling onto the sea floor after being shot down, *Enola Gay* is just lifting off.

Enshu, Ashikaga. An investigator and art dealer who specializes in hunting down rare paintings. Described as having a perfect mane of silver hair, heavy eyebrows and a full moustache. Is actually a disguised Hanamura. When he goes to Suma's office to sell him a painting, he bugs the office.

Epee. Discipline in fencing.

Fat Boy. Code name of the atomic bomb dropped on Nagasaki.

Fazio, Lieutenant Commander Ken. Executive officer on board the *Tucson.*

Federal Headquarters Building. On Constitution Avenue in Washington, D.C., it is a shabby-appearing six-story building. It looks to be in disrepair, but that is a facade created to ensure secrecy. After taking the elevator up, Pitt and his group enter a giant gleaming control center manned by U.S. intelligence agents.

Five-oh-ninth Bomber Squadron. Squadron to which the *Enola Gay* belonged.

Foil. Discipline in fencing.

Ford Club Coupe. Pitt's maroon 1947 model was the first car in his collection.

Ford's Theater. Where President Lincoln was shot by John Wilkes Booth. In Washington, D.C., between E and F streets on Tenth. Where Meeker briefs Jordan that they are certain that the *Divine Star* blew up in an atomic explosion.

Foster, Brian. Tourist on the beach at Marcus Island when *Big Ben* comes ashore. Married to Shelly.

Fox, Stacy. Camera woman aboard *Old Gert.* Pretty, with long, straight blond hair that falls around her face. Looks younger than her thirty-four years. Her eyebrows are thick and her eyes wide apart, her irises a soft green color. Her lips sit above a determined chin and are almost always parted in a bright, even-toothed smile. Once a California beach girl, she majored in photographic arts at Chouinard Institute in Los Angeles. Twice married and twice divorced, with one daughter who lives with her sister. Is actually a covert U.S. intelligence agent working for the National Security Agency. After she arrives at Pitt's home and gives him a massage, they make love. Later, she breaks into the underground parking garage at the Pacific Paradise Hotel and disarms one of the bombs in a Murmoto. She later enters Soseki Island and is captured. A judo expert. Rescued by Pitt. After Pitt is believed dead, she has lunch with Smith.

Frick, Bill. Special agent with the FBI. Leads the group that storms the vault at the Pacific Paradise Hotel.

FSX fighter jets. Jets used by Japan's Self-Defense Forces. Built by a partnership of McDonnell Douglas and Mitsubishi.

Furukawa, George. Suma's agent in the southwestern United States. Vice president of the Samuel J. Vincent Laboratories. Known in intelligence circles as a sleeper. His family immigrated to the United States after World War II. Raised to be a leader of American business with help from mysterious funds wired from Japan. Received a Ph.D. in aerodynamic physics. Recruited for the Kaiten Project by Suma in Hawaii.

Gaijin. Japanese term for foreigners. Means *outside person.*

Galland, Adolf. One of the leading German aces in World War II. Said of the Messerschmitt 262, "It flew as though the angels were pushing."

Gentle Giant. The Lockheed C-5 that drops *Big Ben* with Pitt inside into the ocean near *Dennings' Demons*. Specially modified for aerial drops. Hit by a Toshiba surface-to-air missile, it lands at Naha Airfield on Okinawa.

Giordino, Alfred. What Kamatori calls Albert when he first meets Smith.

Glomar Explorer. Famous deep-sea recovery vessel constructed by Howard Hughes for the Central Intelligence Agency.

Golanov, Nickolai. Soviet counterpart to Jordan. Title is Director of Foreign and State Security for the Politburo.

Golden Dragons. A Japanese secret society begun after World War II.

Gray Horse. Code name for the team that recovers a bomb car in Minnesota.

Great Karnac. The latest in underwater visual technology. The *Tucson* is the first submarine to have the system. Karnac was developed by NUMA.

Groves, General Leslie. General in charge of the Manhattan Bomb Project.

Halder, Gert. German minister of historic works. Rewards Pitt for finding the missing artwork by giving him a Messerschmitt 262.

Hanamura, James. MAIT member of Team Honda and CIA field agent. Assigned to the internal Japan investigation. Lives in Redondo Beach, California, and drives a new Corvette. On the trail of the Kaiten Project, he impersonates an engineer to gain access to Edo City. Finds the blueprints that show the underground tunnel. Chased by guards, he races in his car over back roads to Tokyo. Hands the blueprints to a truck driver to deliver because he is shot and bleeding. When captured by Kamatori, he bites a poison capsule. Later beheaded by Kamatori and his head mounted on the wall in the study at Soseki Island.

Harper, Commander Wendell. Captain of the *Ralph R. Bennett*. Described as tall and beefy with a solid paunch.

Harris, Keith. NUMA project seismologist at Soggy Acres. Has a gray beard that matches his hair. Explains to Pitt that the explosion triggered the fault line near Soggy Acres and they need to evacuate.

Hatchetfish. Silver with deep bodies that flatten on the sides. Have slender tails and rows of light organs that flash along their lower stomachs. Their eyes are disproportionately large and protrude from tubes that rise upward.

Hauser, Lieutenant Commander Sam. U.S. Navy lieutenant commander who works for the Naval Radiological Defense Laboratory. Is on board the *Tucson* to measure the radioactivity from the atomic bomb explosion on the *Divine Star*.

Hedgehog. Nickname for a pulley device that attaches to the side of ductwork and used for covert entry to buildings. Used by Fox and Weatherhill when they break into the underground parking garage at the Pacific Paradise Hotel.

Henrico County Sheriff's Department. Helicopter with Giordino aboard that assists Pitt and Mancuso in chasing the limousine they think Smith is aboard.

Hispano-Suiza. A red 1926 drop-head cabriolet manufactured in Paris. Has an eight-liter six-cylinder engine. Features a flying stork radiator ornament. Car driven by Cussler in the race against Pitt in Richmond.

Hokkaido. One of the four main islands of Japan.

Honshu. One of the four main islands of Japan.

Hutcheson, Francis. A Scot philosopher quoted by Pitt on page 191: "Wisdom denotes the pursuing of the best ends by the best means." Or the more common bastardization: "The end justifies the means."

Ibis X-20. Ultralight power gliders that look like pint-sized Stealth bombers. They have a dark gray paint job and the same Buck Rodgers shape as Stealth bombers. Designed for one-man reconnaissance flights, they feature the latest in compact turbine engines that provide a three hundred–kilometer cruising speed with a range of one hundred twenty kilometers. Pitt and Giordino fly them from the *Ralph R. Bennett* to a crash landing on Soseki Island.

Ingram, Clyde. The director of science and technical data interpretation for the National Security Agency at Fort Meade.

Invincible. The British research vessel that is connected to *Old Gert*.

Itakura, Admiral. Japanese admiral assigned to the Japanese embassy in Washington, D.C.

Italian dueling saber. Weapon used by Pitt to defeat Katamori. A nineteenth-century sword with a ninety-centimeter blade.

Jordan, Raymond. Director of central intelligence and head of the National Security Service. Reports directly to the president. Has a photographic memory and speaks seven languages. Described as medium in height, late fifties, with a healthy head of silver-gray hair. He has a solid frame with a slight paunch and kindly, oak-brown eyes. Married for thirty-seven years, he has twin daughters who are in college. Consumes Maalox as if it were popcorn.

Junshiro, Prime Minister Ueda. Prime minister of Japan. Described as having short-trimmed white hair and defiant brown eyes. The president orders him to resign after the Kaiten Project.

Kaiser, Sonar Man First Class Richard. U.S. Navy sonar man assigned to the *Tucson*. Hears "Minnie the Mermaid" playing from *Big John*'s underwater speaker.

Kaiten Project. Suma's plan for Japanese domination of the world. One hundred thirty atomic warheads are placed in fifteen countries. Translated, means "a change of sky," but in Japanese it has a broader meaning: "a new day is coming, a great shift in events."

Kamatori, Moro. Suma's oldest friend and his chief aide. Meticulous and devious, he manages Suma's secretive projects. Has a stolid, resolute face flanked by oversized ears. Has heavy black brows and dark lifeless eyes that look through thick-lensed rimless glasses. He is a man without emotions or convictions whose greatest talent is hunting human game. Over the course of twenty-five years, he has killed two hundred thirty-seven people. His father was a fencing master at a university in Japan. Hobby is hunting people. After he decides to hunt Pitt but is eluded, Pitt returns and engages him in a sword fight. Pitt severs his hand, then pins him by his groin to the wall in the study on Soseki Island and kills him.

Kami. A Shinto word meaning "the way of divine power through various gods."

Kano, Daisetz. Top-level robotic engineer who works on Soseki Island.

Kappabashi. Street near the Tawaramachi subway station.

Kataginu. An Edo-period silk brocade sleeveless hunting jacket worn by Katamori when he hunts Pitt.

Katana. Japanese ceremonial sword.

Kawanunai Tours. Painted on the side of a small bus that picks up the crews from Soggy Acres and *Old Gert* after they are helicoptered to Hawaii.

Keegan, Dan. Wyoming rancher who dies when one of the Kaiten Project's atomic bombs is set off with a rifle shot. Married.

Kenjutsu. Japanese sword sport.

Kern, Donald. Jordan's deputy director of operations. Bony-thin, small and lean. Has intensely cool blue-green eyes that seem to reach into everyone's inner thoughts.

Kiai. Method of concentration used by Japanese sword masters. An inner force or power attributed to accomplishing miracles, especially among the samurai class.

Knox, Jimmie. *Old Gert*'s surface controller. Described as a jolly Scot. When the *Invincible* begins to sink, he leaps from the deck and grabs a piece of wood. Later picked up by the *Shanghai Shelly*. Dies from a superlethal dose of radiation before he can explain what happened.

Koror. Island in the Palau Republic chain that will house the U.S. intelligence information-gathering and collection point for the MAIT. The person in charge is Penner.

Korvold, Captain Arne. Captain of the Norwegian Rindal Lines passenger-cargo liner *Narvik.* Norwegian by birth, he is described as a short, distinguished man who never makes a hurried gesture. His ice-blue eyes seldom blink, and the lips beneath his short, graying, trimmed beard seem constantly frozen in a slight smile. Has spent twenty-six years at sea, mostly on cruise ships. Killed when the *Divine Star* blows up in the atomic blast.

Koyama, Masuji. Suma's expert technician in defense detection.

Kudan Hill. Hill in the middle of Tokyo atop which Yasukuni sits.

Kudo, Toshie. Suma's secretary. Much taller than her native sisters. Willowy, with long legs, jet-black hair falling to her waist and flawless skin enhanced by magical coffee-brown eyes. Boasts an IQ bordering on 165. The daughter of a poor fisherman and the fourth of eight children. Was a skinny, unattractive child until she blossomed. Suma noticed her fishing and bought her from her father. In time, she has grown to enjoy her role as Suma's secretary and mistress. Speaks English, French, Spanish, German and Russian. Removed from Soseki Island by Pitt and the group, she is later remanded into Giordino's custody.

Kurojima, Takeda. Chief director of the Dragon Center. The technical brain who headed the Kaiten Project from start to finish.

Kyoto. City in Japan that is the backup target for the atomic bomb carried by *Dennings' Demons.*

Kyushu. One of the four main islands of Japan.

Lange, Chancellor. Chancellor of Germany.

Langley Field. Airstrip near the headquarters of the CIA where the jet carrying Smith, Diaz, Suma and Toshie lands.

Liquid-metal fast breeder. Type of nuclear reactor in Japan. Along with power, it also produces plutonium and converts lithium into tritium, both essential ingredients for thermonuclear weapons.

Lockheed C-5 Galaxy. The largest cargo plane in the world. Built by the Lockheed Corporation. Maximum cruise speed four hundred sixty knots.

Lovin' Lil. B-29 that was in the air flying toward Japan when *Bock's Car* dropped the atomic bomb on Nagasaki.

Lowden, David. Chief vehicle engineer at Soggy Acres. Has a pretty wife and three kids. Wears rimless glasses. Pilots one of the submersibles to the surface.

Maglev. Short for *magnetic levitation.* Perfected by the Japanese and used to move trains and such. Works on the principle of repulsion between magnets.

MAIT. An acronym standing for *Multi-Agency Investigative Team.* A MAIT is assembled in the Federal Headquarters Building to combat the Kaiten Project.

Mancuso, Frank. U.S. government intelligence officer working with Philippine intelligence in an attempt to locate Yamashita's Gold. Described as forty-two with the long-limbed, thin body of a basketball player. Has brown hair and a soft, round, Germanic face. Has blue eyes. Smokes a pipe. Graduated from the Colorado School of Mines and spent his early years prospecting and working mines in search of precious gems such as opals in Australia, emeralds in Colombia and rubies in Tanzania. He also did a fruitless three-year hunt on Japan's northern island of Hokkaido for the rarest of rare gems, Red Painite. Shortly before he reached thirty, he was courted by an obscure Washington intelligence agency and appointed a special agent under contract. Once inside the tunnel on Corregidor, Mancuso finds a number of trucks and a small auto house trailer made of aluminum. That convinces him that the Japanese returned for Yamashita's Gold. When he meets Pitt at the Federal Headquarters Building, he is described as a thin older man with shoulder-length hair. Enters Soseki Island but is taken prisoner. Freed by Pitt, he returns to the United States.

Manganese nodules. Black and round-shaped like cannonballs. They are littering the bottom of the ocean in a thick layer where *Old Gert* lands. A swath is cut through the field of nodules in a straight line like a vacuum cleaner would make. The swath is where Pitt and crew used *Big John* for underwater mining.

Manhattan Project. The code name for the project based in Los Alamos, New Mexico, that resulted in the atomic bomb.

Marcos, Ferdinand. Former leader of the Philippines who found several hundred tons of Yamashita's Gold.

Marcus Island. Island 1,125 kilometers southeast of Japan. Turned into a resort by a Japanese developer. Location where Pitt drives *Big Ben* ashore.

Marmon. Famous American automobile. A 1931 Marmon V-16 town car is at the race in Richmond. Pitt has a Marmon in his collection.

Mauser bolt-action. Type of rifle carried by Keegan.

McCurry, Bill. One of the National Security Agency's top investigators. Described as having long, sun-bleached hair and skin darkened by the California sun.

McGoon. What Pitt and Giordino call the robot guard that watches them after they are captured on Soseki Island.

McGurk. One of the robots guarding Pitt and Giordino.

Meeker, Curtis. Deputy director of advanced technical operations. Basically a shy man but acknowledged as the best satellite photo analyst in the world. A nice-looking man, black hair sprinkled with gray, kind face, easy smile and eyes that reflect friendliness.

Mendicino Fracture Zone. Location near Soggy Acres that Pitt and Plunkett must pass through on their way to Conrow Guyot. Said to dwarf the famous tourist site in northern Arizona, its steep escarpments average three thousand meters high.

Messerschmitt 262. The German Luftwaffe's first turbojet airplane. Also called Swallows. Has a slim cigar shape to its fuselage, a vertical stabilizer and ungainly jet pods that hang from knifelike wings. Has four 30-millimeter cannon for armaments. Pitt is given one by Halder. Pitt arranges to ship it to his home. After Pitt is feared dead, Giordino vows to restore the plane.

Metcalf, General Clayton. Chairman of the Joint Chiefs of Staff.

Midgaard, Arne. Seaman from the *Narvik* who is on the boarding party that enters the *Divine Star.* Alerts Steen to the automobile in the cargo hold with its hood up. Dies from radiation poisoning.

Midway. Island in the Pacific that sends rescue units to the site of the *Divine Star* explosion.

Miller, William A. Name on the dog tags of a skeleton Mancuso and Acosta find in the excavation of Corregidor.

"Minnie the Mermaid." Famous B. G. DeSylvia song. Played by Pitt over *Big John*'s underwater speaker when he rescues the crew of *Old Gert.*

Mitsubishi A6M Zero. Plane Okinaga is flying. Powered by an 1,130-horsepower Sakae engine. Armed with two machine guns and two 20-millimeter cannons.

Mitsubishi Ravens. Jet interceptors in the Japan Air Self-Defense Forces that are dispatched to shoot down the tilt-rotored airplane carrying Pitt and the group from Soseki Island.

Miwa, Suboro. Person who detonates the atomic bomb on Keegan's ranch. Claims to be an engineer with Miyata Communications. Married, with three sons. Member of the Golden Dragons.

Miyata Communications. Company Miwa claims to work for.

Miyaza, Jiro. One of Suma's chief structural engineers at Edo City. Has a wife and two children. Resembles Hanamura in face and body, so Hanamura impersonates him to gain access to Edo City and find the blueprints that show the underground tunnel. Miyaza recognizes he is being impersonated when he notices Hanamura wearing his security badge. Alerts the guards, who chase Hanamura.

Monroe, Roy. Secretary of the Navy.

Morrison, General Harold. Special deputy to General Leslie Groves who is head of the Manhattan Bomb Project. Briefs Dennings and his crew before their mission. Was both a master flight mechanic and aircraft engineer during his early Army Air Corps career. As

Dennings' Demons lifts off the runway, he can hear one of the cylinders in one of the engines not firing.

Morse, Clayton. Geophysicist at the National Earthquake Center.

Morton, Commander Beau. U.S. Navy commander and skipper of the *Tucson.*

Mosely, Sergeant Robert. Flight engineer on *Dennings' Demons* flight to Osaka.

Mother's Breath. Code name for the atomic weapon carried by *Dennings' Demons.* Morrison believes that President Truman came up with the name. Measures nine feet in length and five feet in diameter. An implosion-type bomb.

Mother's Pearl. Nickname for the atomic bomb loaded on *Lovin' Lil* at Guam. After Fat Boy was dropped on Nagasaki, the bomb was shipped back to Los Alamos.

Muraski. Name of the robot guard that watches Pitt and Giordino after they are captured on Soseki Island. It means "purple."

Murmoto four-wheel-drive. Pickup truck Hanamura drives in Japan. Powered by a V-6 engine.

Murmoto limousine. Type of automobile Suma owns. Black and custom-built, it is powered by a twelve-cylinder 600-horsepower engine.

Murmoto Motor Distribution Corporation. Located in Alexandria, Virginia. The building is described as modern red brick with large windows. Giordino goes there to find out where the Murmotos carrying bombs were shipped.

Murmoto SP-500 sports sedans. Model of car that contains the atomic bombs. To be identifiable, the bomb-laden cars are painted a putrid brown color.

Murmoto sports car. Automobile Furukawa drives. Powered by a 400-horsepower, 5.8-liter, thirty-two-valve V-8, it has a six-speed transmission.

Murphy, Owen. Owner of *Shanghai Shelly*. An old man with snow-white hair in a windblown mass and a long, curling white moustache. Went to Annapolis with Sandecker, then resigned from the Navy and started an electronics company. Sandecker claims Murphy has more money than the U.S. Treasury.

Narvik. Norwegian Rindal Lines passenger-cargo ship. Scheduled cruise is Pusan, Korea, to San Francisco. Carrying one hundred thirty passengers when it comes upon the abandoned *Divine Star*. Total of two hundred fifty passengers and crew. Blown to bits when the atomic bomb on the *Divine Star* ignites.

Nash, Dr. Percival. Nicknamed "Payload Percy." He is Pitt's uncle on his mother's side. Eighty-two years old. Nash was one of the scientists on the Manhattan Project which built the first atomic bomb. Former director on the Atomic Energy Commission, now retired. Has a great white beard, a knuckle for a nose and squinting eyes. A lifelong bachelor and gourmand who owns a wine cellar that is the envy of every society party thrower in town. The Motor Vehicle Department recently took away his motorcycle license, but he still drives his Jaguar XK 120.

Natalie. Chef at the Maryland retreat where Suma is being debriefed by Jordan.

National Earthquake Center. Located at the Colorado School of Mines in Golden, Colorado, the center monitors earthquake intensity worldwide.

Nichols, Dale. Special assistant to the president. Smokes a pipe and wears old-style reading glasses. Nicknamed "the Protector of the Presidential Realm." Has a thicket of coffee-brown hair.

Nippon. Another name for Japan. Means "source of the sun."

Nogami, Josh. Described as a young, smiling Japanese. Doctor on Soseki Island. Tells Pitt he was born and raised in San Francisco and served his internship at St. Paul's Hospital in Santa Ana, California. Actually a British deep-cover agent who is against Suma. Father was a British subject, mother was from San Francisco. Attended medical school at UCLA. Escapes aboard the tilt-rotored aircraft to the *Ralph R. Bennett.*

Oba. Nurse who works in the hospital on Soseki Island. Knows karate.

Ocean Mother. Code name of an atomic bomb that was on Midway Island.

Okinaga, Lieutenant Junior Grade Sato. Japanese pilot who shoots down *Dennings' Demons.* Described as young and inexperienced.

Okinawa. Island between Japan and Taiwan where *Dennings' Demons* was due to refuel after it dropped its bomb.

Okuma, Ubunai. Top-level robotic engineers who work on Soseki Island.

Old Gert. The British deep-sea submersible that is near the *Divine Star* when she blows apart. Constructed by a British aerospace company, *Old Gert* is on her maiden test dive to survey the Mendocino fracture zone. The design of *Old Gert* is unique; instead of the single cigar-shaped hull, she features four transparent titanium and polymer woven spheres connected by circular tunnels that give her the appearance of a jack from a child's game.

Orita, Roy. MAIT member of Team Honda and CIA field agent. In reality, he was born in the United States, a third-generation American. His father won the Silver Star in the Italian campaign in World War II.

Osaka. City in Japan that is the primary target for the atomic bomb carried by *Dennings' Demons.*

Oscar Brown's Hardware Emporium. After being chased by Suma's men, Pitt, with Giordino and Sandecker aboard, crashes the Jeep Wagoneer into the store, and they head for the gun display to arm themselves.

Otokodate. Another name for Taiho.

Pacific Paradise Hotel. Hotel in Las Vegas owned by Suma. Fox and Weatherhill trace the shipment of bomb-laden Murmotos to the hotel's underground parking lot. The hotel is constructed of concrete painted light blue with round porthole windows on the guest rooms.

Penner, Mel. U.S. intelligence agent who is director of field operations for the MAIT on Koror. Described as having a corduroy-red face. His cover is that he is a UCLA sociologist studying native Palau culture.

Phosgene. Poison gas that must be inhaled to kill. Found by Pitt booby-trapped in the cavern holding artwork under Clausen's farm.

Photonics. Fiber-optic transmission that allows people to see one another while talking over the telephone.

Pillow lava. Wormy-looking rocks Fox views on the bottom of the ocean. Made when fiery lava strikes the cold ocean.

Plunkett, Craig. Chief engineer and pilot of *Old Gert*. Described as a man of forty-five or fifty, with graying hair combed forward to cover his baldness. His face is ruddy and his eyes a medium brown with a bloodhound droop. An old confirmed bachelor.

President of the United States. Described as having a lean build and bright blue eyes with a warm, outgoing personality. Formerly a senator from Montana.

Pyramider Eleven. Newest version of U.S. spy satellite. Reveals subterranean and suboceanic detail.

Ralph R. Bennett. U.S. Navy detection and tracking ship. Features a giant box-shaped phased-array radar six stories tall. Was on station off the Soviet Union's Kamchatka Peninsula when it was ordered off Japan to launch Pitt and Giordino in the Ibis X-20s.

Red Horse. Code name for the director of the FBI's field operations.

Reinhardt, Lieutenant Helmut. German dive officer who works with Pitt at Clausen's farm. Tall and well muscled. Speaks English with only a trace of an accent.

Remington 1100 shotgun. Type of weapon selected by Giordino for the shoot-out at Oscar Brown's Hardware Emporium. Giordino loads the shotguns with No. 4 Magnum buckshot.

Robot dogs. Machines built in Suma's factory. Used by Katamori to track Pitt on Soseki Island. Able to detect human scent, heat and sweat.

Rokota. Coastal town in Japan where there is a nuclear waste dump.

Saber. Discipline in fencing.

Sakagawa, David. Communications man on the *Narvik.* Joins the party that goes aboard the *Divine Star* because he's the only crewman who can speak Japanese. A Norwegian-born Asian.

Salazar, Dr. Raul. *Old Gert*'s marine geologist, from the University of Mexico. A small dynamo with a huge mass of curly hair. His movements are quick, black eyes darting constantly, never staring at one person or object for more than two seconds. Married, with a son. His family is in Veracruz.

Samuel J. Vincent Laboratories. Furukawa is vice president of the company. The laboratory is situated in a tall glass building hidden from the street by a grove of eucalyptus trees. The company is a research and design center owned by a consortium of space and aviation companies. The work performed at Vincent is highly classified, and much of its funding comes from government contracts for military programs.

Sang, Kim. Tourist on the beach at Marcus Island when *Big Ben* comes ashore. Married to Li.

Sarah. A pretty red-headed lady in her early twenties. One of the scientists working in Soggy Acres. Works part-time as a marine equipment engineer and as a marine biologist. She took first in a Miss Colorado bodybuilding competition and can bench-press two hundred pounds.

Sawa 5.56-millimeter. Fifty-one-shot automatic rifles used by Suma's men in the shoot-out at Oscar Brown's Hardware Emporium.

Sea Vulcan. Thirty-millimeter air defense weapon that can shoot forty-two hundred rounds a minute with a range as far as eight kilometers. A modern Gatling gun. Weapon on the *Ralph R. Bennett* that shoots down one of the Mitsubishi Ravens.

Senzu Air Base. Base in Japan that dispatches the pair of Mitsubishi Ravens to shoot down the tilt-rotored aircraft carrying Pitt and the group after they escape from Soseki Island.

Seppuki. Japanese term for belly cutting. What Americans refer to as *hara-kiri.*

Shanghai Shelly. Classic Foochow-type junk or Chinese sailing ship. Three-masted with a high ovoid stern. Slams into the submersible piloted by Giordino when escaping Soggy Acres and sinks it. Owned by Murphy. Custom-built in Shanghai. Murphy and his crew are sailing it to Honolulu, then on to San Diego. When Sandecker arrives by flying boat, he asks his old friend Murphy if he can make the *Shanghai Shelly* the fleet command ship.

Shemya Island. One of the Aleutian Islands, which are part of Alaska. Where *Dennings' Demons* took off for the flight to Osaka.

Shikoku. One of the four main islands of Japan.

Shimzu, Masaki. A revered sixteenth-century Kano school landscape artist. Painted a series of thirteen island seascapes featuring the Hida Mountains. The perspective of the paintings is from above looking down, and Shimzu allegedly painted them from sketches he took while hanging from a kite.

Shintoism. Primary religion in Japan.

Shokonsha. Another name for Yasukuni. Means "spirit-invoking shrine."

Showalter, Marvin. Assistant director of security for the U.S. Department of State. Operates Team Cadillac from the U.S. Embassy in Tokyo and handles diplomatic problems. Has a wife and two young children. Abducted by Suma's men.

Simmons, Jesse. U.S. secretary of defense.

Simpson, Lieutenant Commander Raymond. Navy officer who briefs Pitt and Giordino on the Ibis X-20s. Described as a man on the young side of thirty with sun-bleached blond hair. Later coordinates Pitt and group eluding Mitsubishi Ravens and landing safely on the *Ralph R. Bennett.*

Soggy Acres. Nickname of the NUMA underwater mining project Pitt is working on when the *Divine Star* explodes. Earthquakes triggered by the explosion crush Soggy Acres.

Soseki Island. Formerly known as Ajima Island.

Sounder. NUMA ocean survey vessel. *Sounder* is sonar-mapping the ocean floor off the Aleutians when Soggy Acres collapses.

SR-90 Casper. A stealth reconnaissance aircraft that replaced the famous SR-71.

Stanton, Captain Irv. The bombardier on *Dennings' Demons* flight to Osaka. A jolly, round-faced man with a walrus moustache.

Steen, Oscar. Chief officer of the *Narvik*. Has a sculpted Nordic face. His eyes are a darker blue than Korvold's, and he stands as lean and straight as a light pole. His skin is tanned and his hair bleached blond from exposure to the sun. Talks Korvold into letting him lead the search party to the *Divine Star*. When he finds his boarding party and himself becoming ill, he fires the Steyr into the front end of the car with the raised hood. That triggers the atomic reaction that destroys *Divine Star, Narvik* and *Invincible* and damages *Old Gert* and Soggy Acres.

Stevenson, Roger. Director of the National Earthquake Center.

Steyr. Austrian-made 9-millimeter double-action pistol Steen finds under the desk in the captain's quarters of the *Divine Star*.

Stromp, Captain Mort. Copilot on *Dennings' Demons* flight to Osaka. Described as a complacent Southerner who moves with the agility of a three-toed sloth.

Stutz. Famous automobile maker. Pitt has a 1932 Stutz LeBaron-bodied turquoise-colored town car in his collection. Stutz cars were produced from 1911 until 1935 in Indianapolis, Indiana. The Stutz has an eight-cylinder five-liter engine featuring twin overhead camshafts with four valves per cylinder. Has a sun goddess radiator ornament. At the appearance judging at Richmond, Pitt's Stutz finishes third in its class. He beats Cussler's Hispano-Suiza in the race by half a car length.

Suhaka, Dennis. Director of transportation for the Murmoto Motor Distribution Corporation in Alexandria, Virginia. Giordino, posing as an employee of the Commerce Department, questions Suhaka. Described as round and jolly with a grand smile.

Suma, Hideki. Has brushed-back white hair. At forty-nine years of age, he is short for a Westerner but slightly on the tall side for a Japanese. The irises of his eyes are a magnetic blue.

Suma, Koda. Father of Hideki. The son of an ordinary seaman in the Imperial Navy. His father forced him to enlist in the Navy, but he deserted and joined the Black Sky. The Black Sky later fixed his desertion record and placed him in the Army as an officer. Rose to the rank of captain and worked with Black Sky to loot and steal from Navy vessels. When he realized that Japan was doomed to lose the war, he and Yoshishu traveled by submarine to Valparaiso, Chile, and lived out the rest of the war and five years after in comfort. Returning to Japan, he resumed his criminal activities. Died in 1973 and left his son Hideki in charge.

Sweeney, Major Charles. Pilot of *Bock's Car*.

Taiho. One of the robot electrical inspectors on Soseki Island. The name means "big gun." Also referred to as Otokodate; a term for a sort of Robin Hood.

Tawaramachi. Stop on the Tokyo subway that Showalter exits from after eluding the Japanese agents following him.

Team Buick. MAIT code name for Fox and Weatherhill. They are handling the domestic end of the investigation. Their cover is that they are journalists for the *Denver Tribune*.

Team Cadillac. MAIT code name for Showalter's team.

Team Chrysler. MAIT code name for Penner's team.

Team Honda. MAIT code name for Orita and Hanamura. They are in charge of the investigation in Japan and detecting the source of the bombs and the location of the command center that can detonate the bombs.

Team Lincoln. MAIT code name for the group at Central Command.

Team Mercedes. MAIT code name for Sandecker and Giordino. They are tasked with searching and salvaging the ocean floor for wreckage from the *Divine Star.*

Team Stutz. MAIT code name for the team of Pitt and Mancuso. They are assigned to act as a support team.

Tibbets, Colonel Paul. Pilot of the *Enola Gay.*

Tinian. Island in the South Pacific where *Dennings' Demons* was to fly after refueling at Okinawa.

Toshiba surface-to-air missiles. Missiles Yoshishu orders to be fired at *Gentle Giant.*

Toyama. Japanese painter who in 1485 painted *The Legend of Prince Genji,* in Suma's collection on Soseki Island.

Tsuboi, Ichiro. The chief director of Kanoya Securities, which is the largest securities company in the world. Described as short and slender with a jolly face. Is as ruthless as he is shrewd. A member of the Golden Dragons since age fourteen.

Tsunami. A seismic sea wave. One of these wipes out Soseki Island.

Tucson. U.S. Navy attack submarine that arrives at the site of the Soggy Acres collapse.

Turner, Major Marcus. Pilot of *Gentle Giant.* Described as a big ruddy-featured Texan.

Wake Island. Island in the South Pacific. Location of famous battle in World War II. Pitt and the group that escaped from Soseki Island are taken here when they depart the *Ralph R. Bennett.*

Weatherhill, Timothy. MAIT member of Team Buick. A nuclear scientist who specializes in radioactivity detection.

"We May Never Pass This Way Again." Song by Seals and Crofts that Fox heard at her senior prom. She is running out of air in *Old Gert* as the song plays in her head.

Yamashita's Gold. Named after General Yamashita Tomoyuki, who was commander of Japanese forces in the Philippines after October 1944. The treasure is an immense hoard consisting of thousands of metric tons of exotic gems and jewelry, silver and gold bullion, along with Buddhas and Catholic altar pieces encrusted with priceless gems and cast in solid gold. The hoard was taken from China, the Southeast Asian countries, the Dutch East Indies and the Philippines, then collected in Manila, Philippines. Because of heavy Japanese shipping losses, less than twenty percent of the hoard ever reached Tokyo. Faced with no place to stash the loot, the Japanese hid it in more than a hundred different sites on and around the island of Luzon. Conservative estimates place the value of the hoard at between four hundred fifty and five hundred billion dollars.

Yasukuni. The revered memorial in Japan that honors those who died fighting for the emperor's cause since the revolutionary war of 1868. No foreigners are allowed to pass through the huge bronze gateway leading to the war heroes' shrine.

Yoshishu, Korori. The grand old thief and leader of the Golden Dragons. Ninety-one years old. Was in the Black Sky organization until he founded the Gold Dragons. The son of a temple carpenter in Kyoto. Kicked out of the house by his father at age ten, he joined Black Sky. In 1927, when he was eighteen, the leaders of Black Sky arranged for him to join the Army, where he rose to the rank of captain. Helped the Black Sky dominate heroin smuggling in Southeast Asia. When he realized Japan was doomed to lose the war, he and Koda Suma traveled by submarine to Valparaiso, Chile, where they lived out the war and five years afterward in comfort. Later returned to Japan to resume his criminal activities. After Koda Suma's death, he split the group with Hideki Suma and concentrated on the criminal end.

Sahara

Across the Sahara Safari. Backworld Explorations' twelve-day tour.

Adar des Iforas. Extension of mountainous Ahaggar Range in the Sahara Desert.

Adrar. City in Algeria where Hadi takes Pitt and Giordino after they escape from Tebezza and cross the Sahara.

Air Afrique. French civilian aircraft emblazoned with light and dark green stripes. Used by UNICRATT to land at Gao and rescue Gunn.

Airbus Industrie A300. Kazim's plane. A gift from Massarde. Electronically fitted as a military communications command center.

Air France Concorde. Supersonic jet Gunn takes back to Washington, D.C., after he is rescued by UNICRATT at the Gao International Airport.

Alden, Captain James. Commander of the *Brooklyn.*

Algeria. Country in northern Africa that borders Mali on one side and the Mediterranean to the north. When Pitt and Giordino escape from Tebezza and ride *Kitty Mannock* across the desert, they end up in Algeria.

Ali, El Haj. Fourteen-year-old tribesman who rides a camel from his village of Araouane to see the railroad leading to Fort Foureau. He inadvertently mentions that the gates to the old fort are locked to security guards, who include it in a report that leads Kazim's troops to the fort.

Apache helicopter. Army attack helicopter Giordino and Steinholm come across in Mauritania. The airship is mounted with a 30-millimeter Chain gun, two pods of thirty-eight 2.75 rockets and eight laser-guided antitank missiles.

Aquifer. A geological stratum that allows water to penetrate through pores and openings. Pitt thinks the Oued Zarit is probably an aquifer.

Archival Safekeeping Depository. Near the town of Forestville, Maryland, it is the huge underground storage area that hides U.S. government secrets. The bodies of Amelia Earhart and Fred Noonan, her navigator, along with the Japanese records of their execution on Saipan, are hidden there along with other secrets such as the Kennedy assassination files.

Army Special Forces. Crack U.S. combat team.

Arsenic. Substance found in the blood of the villagers at Asselar.

AS-332 Super Puma. Helicopter Pitt and Giordino see on the ground when they meet the UNICRATT team.

ASD. Acronym for the *Archival Safekeeping Depository.*

Asselar Oasis. Village-oasis in Mali. Contains a sprawl of mud huts clustered around a well. Was once the cultural crossroads of western Africa. Located two hundred forty miles from Gao.

"Atchison, Topeka and the Santa Fe." The hit song Judy Garland sang in *The Harvey Girls.* Part of the conundrum Pitt sends to Sandecker.

Atlanta. Former Confederate ironclad ram captured by the Union. Patrols the river above Newport News.

Rammed by the *Texas*. The only Confederate ironclad known to try to cross open waters. She was captured during a fight with two Union monitors on Wassaw Sound in Georgia. Later sold to the king of Haiti for his navy. After leaving the Chesapeake Bay for the Caribbean, she vanished.

Atzerodt, George. Alleged conspirator with Booth.

Austin, Commander John. Captain of the *Onondaga.*

Automated micro-incubator. Device used by Gunn aboard the *Calliope* to test for river pollution.

Avions Voisin. French-made 1936 sedan owned by Kazim. A rose-magenta-painted car whose body is a combination of pre–World War II aerodynamics, cubist art and Frank Lloyd Wright. Powered by a six-cylinder sleeve-valve engine that provides smooth silence and simple endurance. The vehicle has unique door handles, three wipers mounted on the glass of the windshield, chrome struts that stretch between the front fenders and the radiator and a tall winged mascot atop the radiator shell. Has a Cotal gearbox. Kazim's belonged to the governor-general when Mali was a territory of French West Africa. Voisins were built between 1919 and 1939 by Gabriel Voisin.

Avro Avian 9. Biplane with an open cockpit and 80-horsepower Cirrus engine. First plane owned by Mannock.

Azauad. A barren region of dunes and nothingness in northern Mali.

Babanandi, Lieutenant Abubakar. Malian Air Force pilot who replaces real WHO pilot and lands the WHO scientists at Tebezza. Might be Djemaa.

Bamako. Capital city of Mali.

Batutta, Captain Mohammed. Malian Army officer who meets Hooper and the WHO group as they land at Timbuktu. Batutta and a team of ten men accompany the WHO team on their inspection trip in Mali.

Beecher, Clarence. Claimed to be the only survivor from the *Texas.* Gave a deathbed statement to a British reporter in a small hospital outside York. After the *Texas* sailed up a river, the level dropped and the ship grounded. Beecher and four others were selected to row down the river in a small boat and seek help. He was the only one to survive. Quite ill, he was nursed back to health at a British trading post, then given free passage to England. He eventually married and became a farmer in Yorkshire. He never returned to his native state of Georgia because he thought he would be hung for what the *Texas* did.

Benin. Country in Africa, the People's Republic of Benin. A tight dictatorship. President Ahmed Tougouri rules by terror.

Benue. River in Africa that empties into the Niger River delta.

Beretta automatic. Silenced handgun used by Levant in the liberation of Tebezza.

Beretta NATO Model 92SB. An older 9-millimeter automatic carried by Kazim aboard Massarde's yacht. Kazim wants to shoot Pitt with the Beretta, but Massarde stops him.

Beta-Q clearance. Level of government clearance once held by Perlmutter.

Bionic booster. Device Batutta uses to listen to the WHO search party's conversations.

Bock, General Hugo. Senior commander of UNICRATT. A former German Army officer, he is described as a born killer. Has great shrubs of gray eyebrows. Leads the group to liberate the prisoners at Tebezza and the defense of Fort Foureau. Resigns from the UN tactical team at the height of his reputation and retires to a small village in the Bavarian Alps.

Bordeaux. Code name for the operative who meets with Yerli to pass information to Massarde. Described as having slicked-down sandy hair with a razor part on the left side. Has pale blue eyes. He is the head of Massarde Enterprises' commercial intelligence operations in the United States. A Frenchman.

Bourem. City in Mali on the Niger River, where, nearby, the contamination from Fort Foureau enters the river.

Brooklyn. Union wooden frigate. Porter's flagship. Fights the *Texas.*

Brown, Neville. Confederate captain who made a deathbed confession to a doctor in Charleston, South Carolina, in 1908. He claimed his troops captured Lincoln and delivered him to the *Texas.*

Brunone, Captain Charles. Chief of security at Massarde's plant at Fort Foureau. A product of the French military establishment.

Burkina Faso. Country in Africa.

Calliope. Vessel Pitt, Giordino and Gunn use to travel up the Niger River. Described as a masterpiece of aerodynamic balance in fiberglass and stainless steel. Designed by NUMA engineers and built in tight secrecy in a boatyard up a bayou in Louisiana. Length is eighteen meters. Draws only one and a half meters of water. Powered by three V-12 turbo-diesel engines. Top speed seventy knots. Blown to bits by Pitt so it doesn't fall into Kazim's hands.

Cape Tafarit. Location on the Atlantic Ocean in Mauritania where the railroad track from Fort Foureau ends.

Catacomb. A subterranean cemetery for the dead. Pitt and Giordino find one at Tebezza when they are escaping. Giordino thinks there are more than a thousand dead bodies inside.

Chapman, Dr. Darcy. Chief toxicologist at the Goodwin Marine Science Lab in Laguna Beach, California. Briefs Pitt and Giordino aboard the *Sounder.* A black man at least twenty years older and slightly more than two meters tall. Has a doctorate in environmental chemistry. Used to play basketball for the Denver Nuggets. After the red tide epidemic is contained, he and Gunn are nominated for a Nobel Prize but do not win.

Chauvel, Sergeant. Female UNICRATT sergeant involved in the liberation of Tebezza.

Cheik, Colonel Sghir. Malian Army officer who is Kazim's chief-of-staff. Described as having a wedge-shaped beard.

Chesapeake Bay. Large bay bordered by Virginia and Maryland. The *Texas* fights her way through the Union fleet there.

Chickasaw. Union monitor recently returned from Mobile Bay, where she pounded the *Tennessee.* Fights the *Texas.*

Chronosport dive watch. Type of watch worn by Gunn.

Clipperton Island. Island the French assume control over in 1979. Formerly used by the pirate John Clipperton as a lair in 1705. It measures about five square kilometers. Where Massarde hid the gold mined from Tebezza.

Cobalt. Mineral found in the blood of the villagers at Asselar.

Coleridge, Samuel Taylor. Poet who wrote "The Rime of the Ancient Mariner."

Colorado. Union ship that fights the *Texas.*

Confederation of French African Francs. Currency Pitt removes from the soles of his shoes to pay for beers at the bar in Bourem.

Conundrum. A riddle. Pitt uses a conundrum to explain to Sandecker which direction the group from Tebezza is headed.

Cooper, Gary. Actor who starred in the 1939 movie *Beau Geste.* Part of conundrum Pitt sends Sandecker.

Craven, Lieutenant Ezra. First officer of the *Texas.* Described as a big, brusque Scotsman who speaks with a peculiar combination of brogue and Southern drawl.

Crosby, Commander John. First officer of the *New Ironsides.*

Croydon, England. A suburb of London where Mannock began her flight.

Dark-skinned man. After Pitt rescues Rojas from attackers on the beach, the dark-skinned man tries to torch Pitt's Jeep Cherokee. When Pitt stops him and begins to question him, he bites down on a cyanide capsule concealed in his false tooth and kills himself.

Davis, Jefferson. President of the Confederate States. Before he died, he claimed the gold from the Confederate Treasury was loaded aboard the *Texas* so he could form a government in exile.

Delta Team. Also known as Delta Force. A special unit of the Army's Special Forces.

Diatoms. Tiny plant forms such as algae that live in the sea. They create seventy percent of the new oxygen on earth through photosynthesis.

Digna, Mohammed. A young man no more than eighteen. He is tall and slender with a slight hunch to his shoulders. He has a gentle oval face with wide, sad-looking eyes. His complexion is almost black, his hair thick and wiry. He attended primary school in Gao and college in Bamako, where he finished first in his class. Can speak four languages, including his native Bambara tongue, French, English and German. Attempts to rob Pitt and Giordino in the bar at Bourem.

Dinoflagellates. Tiny organisms that contain a red pigment that gives ocean water a reddish-brown color when they proliferate. The cause of red tides.

Djellaba. Long-skirted garment with full sleeves and a hood that Gunn fashions out of a bed sheet so he can pass through Gao unnoticed.

Djemaa, Lieutenant. Malian Army officer who impersonates the WHO pilot he replaces. Speaks English. His mother was from South Africa.

Djerma, Messaoud. Mali's foreign minister.

Donlevy, Brian. Actor in the 1939 movie *Beau Geste.* Part of the conundrum Pitt sends Sandecker.

Drewry's Bluff. Location on the James River that the *Texas* passes.

Ecureuil. The brand of late-model, French-built, twin-turbine helicopter Pitt and Giordino steal from Massarde's yacht.

Egyptian Organization of Antiquities. Group to which Pitt turns over the coordinates of the location of Menkura's funeral barge.

El Alamein. Location of famous World War II battle. Site one hundred and ten kilometers from Alexandria, Egypt, where Rojas sunbathes.

Exotic organometallic compound. Substance Gunn believes is causing the red tide. He guesses it consists of an altered synthetic amino acid and cobalt. He believes the synthetic amino acid came from a biotechnology laboratory.

Fairchild FC-2W. Type of airplane flown by Mannock. A high-winged monoplane with an enclosed cockpit and cabin. Powered by a Pratt and Whitney Wasp 410-horsepower radial engine. Has a one hundred and twenty–knot cruising speed. A four-passenger airplane formerly owned by American-Grace Airways. Later recovered after it is missing in the desert. The plane is restored and placed in the Military Museum in Canberra, Australia.

Fairweather, Major Ian. Tour leader of the Across the Sahara Safari. Described as a tall, lean ex–Royal Marine. Originally from Liverpool, England. Smokes cigarettes. Only survivor of the attack on the tourists at Asselar, he wanders in the desert until rescued by a French oil exploration party. He is taken to a hospital in Gao. Later taken to Tebezza. Rescued by UNICRATT. Killed in the assault on Fort Foureau.

Falcon One. Radio call sign Batutta uses when calling Mansa from the WHO's jet at Asselar.

Fisher 1265X. Brand and model of metal detector used by The Kid/Cussler.

Five-five-six French automatic rifles. The all-plastic and fiberglass general military issue rifles Pitt and Giordino steal during their escape from Tebezza.

Floyd Bennett Field. Airfield on the shore of Jamaica Bay, New York, where the NUMA jet carrying Sandecker and Chapman lands after returning from Africa.

Fort Foureau. Long-abandoned French Foreign Legion fort near the Massarde solar waste detoxification plant. Also the nickname of the Massarde plant. A dumping ground for nuclear waste.

Fox. Confederate blockade runner standing by off Bermuda to recoal the *Texas* for the second leg of the journey.

Fredricksburg. Confederate navy vessel scuttled at Drewry's Bluff.

French AMX-30-type tanks. Tanks used by Kazim in the attack on Fort Foureau. They fire SS-11 battlefield missiles.

Gao. City in Mali on the Niger River.

Gao International Airport. Main airport in Mali. Where Gunn hides as he waits to sneak out of the country.

Garland, Judy. Famous singer in the conundrum Pitt sends to Sandecker.

Gas chromatograph/mass spectrometer. Device used by Gunn aboard the *Calliope* to test for river pollution.

Gashi, Seyni. The chief of Kazim's military council.

Gauloise Bleu. Brand of French cigarettes smoked by Massarde.

GeoSat. New satellite used by the United States.

Gowan, Sid Ahmed. Kazim's personal intelligence officer. The only officer on Kazim's staff who was educated in France. Graduated from Saint Cyr, France's prestigious military academy. Discovers the report from Ali and the guards that the gate is locked at Fort Foureau and alerts Kazim that the group that escaped from Tebezza might be inside.

Greenwald, Major Tom. U.S. Air Force officer assigned to the Pentagon. Analyzes the GeoSat film from Webster.

Grimes, Dr. Warren. Chief epidemiologist of the WHO project to find the source of illness in Africa. A New Zealander, he is an older man who is tall, heavy, with iron-gray hair and light blue eyes. Taken to Tebezza, later rescued by UNICRATT.

Hadi, Ben. Arab truck driver who rescues Pitt and Giordino and takes them to Adrar.

Halverson, General. Commander of the U.S. Special Forces. Based in Tampa, Florida.

Hampton Roads. City near Newport News and site of the battle between the *Monitor* and the *Merrimac.*

Hargrove, Colonel Gus. Commander of the Army Ranger covert attack helicopter force sent by the president to rescue the defenders of Fort Foureau. A hardened professional soldier, he has directed helicopter assaults in Vietnam, Grenada, Panama and Iraq. Has blue eyes.

The Harvey Girls. A movie that starred Judy Garland. Mentioned in the conundrum used by Pitt to communicate with Sandecker.

Heckler & Koch MP5. Submachine guns carried by the UNICRATT team that liberates Tebezza.

Herold, David. Alleged conspirator with Booth.

Hiking. A condition experienced by land sailors where the wind tilts the craft on two wheels. Similar to a sea sailor heeling his sailboat over.

Hoag, Dr. Muriel. NUMA's director of marine biology. Described as quite tall and built like a starving fashion model. Her jet-black hair is brushed back in a neat bun. Her brown eyes peer through round spectacles, and she wears no makeup.

Hodge, Keith. NUMA's chief oceanographer. Described as in his sixties with dark brown eyes and a lean, high-cheekboned face. With the right clothes, he looks as if he could have stepped from an eighteenth-century portrait.

Holland, Dr. Evan. NUMA's environmental expert. An environmental chemist who looks like a basset hound contemplating a frog in its dish. His ears are two sizes too large for his head, and he has a long nose that is rounded at the tip. His eyes stare at the world as if they were soaked in melancholy.

Hopper, Dr. Frank. Canadian leader of the WHO medical team. Described as big, humorous, red-faced and heavily bearded. One of the two finest toxicologists in the world. Taken to Tebezza, later rescued by UNICRATT.

Houdini. New-generation American spy satellite.

Inductively coupled plasma/mass spectrometer. Device used by Gunn aboard the *Calliope* to test for river pollution. Its purpose is to identify all metals and other elements that might be present in the water.

International Geological Institute. International body that assigns names to geological landmarks.

Invicta silencer. Type of noise suppressor used by Fairweather on the *Patchett.*

Jerome, Arizona. City where The Kid would go to hit his favorite watering hole.

Johnson, Andrew. Seventeenth president of the United States. Was vice president under Lincoln and became president after Lincoln disappeared. Was unaware of Stanton's plot. Was scheduled to be assassinated the night of the Ford's Theater incident, but the assassins bungled the effort.

Jolly Roger. The pirate flag flown by the *Calliope* after it leaves Niamey.

Kaduna. River in Africa that empties into the Niger River delta.

Kazim, General Zateb. True leader of Mali. His face bears the dark cocoa shade and sculpted features of a Moor. His eyes are tiny topaz dots surrounded by oceans of white. Has a sparse moustache that stretches off to the side of his face. Looks like a benign villain out of a Warner Brothers cartoon. Massarde pays him fifty thousand American dollars a month to operate the solar detoxification plant. Attended Princeton University.

Ketou, Commander Behanzin. Captain of the Begin Navy riverine attack craft that attempts to stop the *Calliope.*

The Kid. What everyone calls the prospector Cussler.

Kingsford-Smith, Sir Charles. Famed Australian pilot.

Kitty Mannock. The land yacht built by Pitt and Giordino from parts of Mannock's plane. They sail the yacht to freedom.

La Manche. Location of a French radioactive waste depository.

Land Rover. Sport utility vehicle used by Backworld Explorations.

Landsat. Older-model American spy satellite.

Lansing, Mrs. A Canadian tourist on the Across the Sahara Safari. Described as comely.

"The Last Time I Saw Paris." Song the blond-haired woman is playing on the piano when Pitt and Giordino board Massarde's yacht.

Levant, Colonel Marcel. Second-in-command of UNICRATT. A highly decorated veteran of the French

Foreign Legion. A graduate of Saint Cyr, France's foremost military college. Described as having an intelligent, even handsome face. Thirty-six years old, he has a slim build, long brown hair, a long but neatly clipped moustache and large gray eyes. Is involved in the escape from Tebezza and the defense of Fort Foureau. Promoted to general, succeeds Bock as head of UNICRATT.

Lincoln, Abraham. Sixteenth president of the United States. Taken prisoner and transported aboard the *Texas.* Described as seeming older than his years. His face is drawn and hollow under a gaunt pallor, a man used up and exhausted by years of stress. Body discovered by Pitt aboard a gaunt pallor, a man used up and exhausted by years of stress. Body discovered by Pitt aboard the *Texas.* Later buried inside the Lincoln Memorial in Washington, D.C.

Lincoln, Mary Todd. Abraham Lincoln's wife. Drugged so she was unaware of the deception at Ford's Theater.

Madani, Dr. Haroun. Doctor who cares for Fairweather at the Gao hospital. Described as coal-black with Negroid features, deep-set ebony eyes and a wide flattened nose. A big, beefy man in his late forties with a wide square-jawed head. His ancestors had been Mandingo slaves. He was a major in the French Foreign Legion and educated and schooled in Paris.

Madeline. Nickname for the Vulcan gun used in the defense of Fort Foureau. Named after a girl whose favors the gun crew enjoyed in Algeria.

Mali. Republic of Mali. Country in northwestern Africa. Formerly known as French Sudan until 1960, when it declared its independence.

Malian Security Forces. Forces that question Fairweather and the French oil-prospecting team that rescues him. Later they kill the French.

Manhattan. Union monitor that fights the *Texas.*

Mannock, Kitty. Considered one of the three greatest female pilots. A lovely woman with deep blue eyes and black flowing hair that falls to her waist. She is the daughter of wealthy sheep ranchers outside Canberra, Australia. Aviatrix who set the long-distance record from Rio de Janeiro to Madrid in 1930. She is on a long-distance flight from Croydon to Cape Town, South Africa, when she disappears. Crashes in the desert on October 10, 1931. Remains missing until Pitt and Giordino stumble across the plane's wreckage after their escape from Tebezza. From the wreckage of her plane, they build a land yacht and sail to freedom. Later, her body is recovered by an Australian crew and buried in Australia.

Mansa, Colonel Nouhoum. Malian Army officer who checks the passports of Hooper and the WHO team at Timbuktu.

Marrakech, Morocco. City in Morocco that was to be the last stop for the Across the Sahara Safari.

Marx, Gary. NUMA pilot of the research boat Pitt and Giordino use to locate Menkura's funeral barge. A tall blond with limpid blue eyes.

Massarde Enterprises de Solaire Energie. Company that operates a solar-energy hazardous-waste treatment facility in Mali. Actually an underground dumping ground for nuclear waste.

Massarde, Yves. Head of Massarde Enterprises. Formerly the head of France's overseas economic agency. His wealth is estimated to be between two and three billion dollars. Described as having blue eyes, black brows and reddish hair. His nose is slender and his jaw square. His body is thin and his hips trim, but his stomach protrudes. Nothing about him seems to match. Called the Scorpion because a number of his competitors and business partners disappeared. One of his ships carrying carcinogenic chemicals broke up in a storm off Spain four years ago and sank. Hodge thinks it was scuttled as an insurance scam. After the assault on Fort Foureau, Pitt and Giordino bake him in the sun, then give him water poisoned by the waste from his plant. He dies a horrible death in Tripoli, Libya.

Massarde's yacht. A self-propelled three-story houseboat that features a flat bottom for cruising upriver. Has a glass-domed spiral staircase that ascends from the spacious master suite to the heliport. Has ten sumptuous staterooms furnished in French antiques, a high-ceilinged dining room, steam rooms, sauna, Jacuzzis and a cocktail bar in a revolving observation lounge. Has a worldwide communications system. The design and shape remind Pitt of an old Mississippi side paddle-wheeler except there are no paddle wheels and the superstructure is more modern.

Matabu, Admiral Pierre. Chief of the Benin Navy. Brother of President Tougouri. Described as short, squat and in his mid-thirties. He commands a fleet of four hundred men, two river gunboats and three oceangoing patrol crafts.

Mauritania. Country in western Africa. The railroad carrying the toxic wastes to Fort Foureau runs east from Mauritania to the fort.

Melika. Female black straw boss at the Tebezza mines. Described as being built like a gravel truck whose bed is fully loaded. Her hair is wooly, and she has high cheekbones, a rounded chin and a sharp nose. Her eyes are small and beady, and her mouth stretches nearly the full width of her face. She has a cold look, enhanced by a broken nose and a scarred forehead. Served ten years as the chief of guards at the Women's Institution in Corona, California. Later shot and killed by Giordino.

Memphis. Ancient capital of Egypt.

Menkura. A pharaoh of the Old Kingdom. He reigned during the Fourth Dynasty and built the smallest of the three pyramids at Giza. NUMA finds his funeral barge in the Nile River.

Mercedes four-wheel-drive. Malian military vehicle used by the WHO team.

Mirage 2000 delta-wing fighters. Planes Pitt and Giordino see on the ground when they go to meet the UNICRATT team.

Modified M-16 rifles. Weapons used by Gunn when the crew of the *Calliope* attacks the Benin Navy.

Monitor. Class of Union ironclad named after the famous vessel that fought the *Merrimac.* More than sixty were built, some as late as 1903.

Monteux, Louis. One of the French engineers who constructed Fort Foureau, was later imprisoned by Massarde at Tebezza.

Moore, Frank. Archivist-curator at ASD.

Morrison, Lieutenant. UNICRATT officer in the liberation of Tebezza. In charge of Unit Four.

Mr. Periwinkle. Cussler's burro. Found roaming free in the Nevada desert eight years ago. Shipped by Cussler to Africa to help in the search for the *Texas.*

Mycerinus. Greek spelling of *Menkura.*

"My Darling Clementine." Song Cussler is singing when Pitt and Giordino first see him.

Nahant. Union monitor that fights the *Texas.*

Nelson, Ernie. U.S. agent who picks up Perlmutter in Forestville and drives him to the ASD. Described as a dark-brown-skinned African American.

New Ironsides. Union vessel with a conventional iron-clad hull. Has a complement of eighteen heavy guns. Fights the *Texas.*

Niamey. Capital of Niger. Has a bridge named for John F. Kennedy.

Niccolite. A mineral often associated with cobalt. A common arsenic.

Niger. Country in Africa. The head of state is propped up by Libya's Muammar Qaddafi, who is after the country's uranium mines. Capital is Niamey.

Niger River. The third-longest river in Africa behind the Nile and the Congo. It begins in the nation of Guinea only three hundred kilometers from the sea. Flows northeast and then south for forty-two hundred kilometers before emptying into the Atlantic Ocean at its delta on the coast of Nigeria.

Nigeria. Country in Africa. Described as Africa's most populous, with one hundred twenty million people. The new democratic government was overthrown by the military, the eighth successful coup in twenty years. The country is torn apart by ethnic wars and bad blood between Muslims and Christians.

Nile Hilton. Hotel in Cairo where Pitt and Rojas have dinner.

Nile River. River in Africa that winds sixty-five hundred kilometers from its headwaters in central Africa to the Mediterranean. The only one of the great rivers that flows north. The Nile between Khartoum and the delta has more shipwrecks per square kilometer than anywhere else on earth.

O'Bannion. Chief engineer of the Tebezza mining operations. Described as a thin, towering man. His face is heavily scarred and disfigured from a premature dynamite explosion during his younger mining days in Brazil. Pitt places him in a mine shaft and blows off explosives, killing him by imprisoning him inside.

O'Hare, Angus. Chief engineer of the *Texas.* Discovered by Pitt inside the *Texas* next to a page from his log book.

Onitsha. City in Africa on the Niger River across from Asaba.

Onondaga. Union Navy dual-turreted monitor. Has eleven inches of armor on her turrets and five and a half inches on her hull. Guns include two powerful fifteen-inch Dahlgren smooth-bores and two one-hundred-fifty-pound Parrott rifles. Fights the *Texas.*

Organometallic. A combination of metal and an organic substance. What Chapman believes is causing the proliferation of red tide off the coast of Africa.

Oued Zarit. A legendary river that ran through Mali until one hundred thirty years ago, when it began to sink in the sands. Used to flow from the Ahaggar Mountains six hundred miles to the Niger River.

Paine, Lewis. Alleged conspirator with Booth.

Paleozoic upheaval. Phenomenon that happened during the earth's development that formed geological structures.

Palisades. Area above the Hudson River where Yerli meets with Bordeaux.

Patchett. A submachine gun used by Royal Marines. Fairweather uses one to try to fight off the savages who attack the Backworld Explorations tour. Shoots nine-millimeter one-hundred-weight-grain round-nosed bullets.

Pembroke-Smyth, Captain. UNICRATT officer who briefs Pitt and Giordino on the assault of Tebezza. Is involved in the liberation of Tebezza and the defense of Fort Foureau. Afterward, he is promoted to major and returns to the British Army. Awarded the Distinguished Service Order by the queen of England. Currently posted with a special commando unit. Drives a Bentley.

Pergamon. Code name for Yerli.

Peugeot 605 diesel sedan. French Air Force staff car Pitt and Giordino ride in to meet the UNICRATT team.

Photosynthesis. Process by which plants create oxygen.

Photovoltaic energy. Process used to create electricity at the Fort Foureau waste plant. It uses a system of flat-plate solar cells made from polycrystalline silicon to convert sunlight to electricity.

Plutonium 239. Radioactive substance with a half-life of twenty-four thousand years.

Polaris. Star Pitt uses for navigation in the desert after the escape from Tebezza.

Polycythemia vera. What Hooper diagnoses killed the villagers at Asselar. Symptoms include a massive increase in red blood cells. It is as though the victims have been injected with a massive dose of vitamin B-12.

Port Etienne. Port in Mauritania where the train to Fort Foureau begins and ends.

Port Harcourt. A seaport on the Niger River in Nigeria.

Porter, Rear Admiral David. Union naval officer in charge of the Union fleet. His flagship is the *Brooklyn.* Described as thickset and bearded.

Powhatan. Union wooden-sided, old side-wheel steam frigate. Hit by a shell from the *Texas* that causes great loss of life.

President of the United States. A former senator from Montana. Described as long and lean. Speaks in a soft drawl and has blue eyes. Has a ranch on the Yellowstone River not far from the Custer battlefield. Was president when Pitt aborted the Kaiten bomb incident in *Dragon.*

Preston, Robert. Actor who starred in the 1939 movie *Beau Geste.* Part of conundrum Pitt sends Sandecker.

Pyramider. New-generation American spy satellite.

Quinn, Ned. Australian who leads the effort to recover Kitty Mannock's body and remove her plane.

Rapier. A new all-purpose weapon designed to engage subsonic aircraft, seagoing vessels, tanks and concrete bunkers. Can be fired from the shoulder or mounted in quad to a central firing system. Weapon used aboard the *Calliope.*

Rasmussen, Master Sergeant Jason. Army Ranger from Paradise Valley, Arizona. In the attack on Fort Foureau, he singlehandedly changes the course of history in Mali by killing Kazim.

Rat-faced Man. Assassin who, along with his partner, attempts to kill Rojas on the beach. Pitt kills him instead by twisting his neck.

Red tide. Microorganisms that threaten the world's oxygen supply. NUMA finds they cannot reproduce if a one-part-per-million dose of copper is placed in seawater.

Remington TR870 automatic shotgun. Weapon carried aboard the *Calliope.*

Renault truck. What the French oil-prospecting team that finds Fairweather is driving.

Richmond. Confederate Navy vessel scuttled at Drewry's Bluff.

Riverine attack crafts. Russian-built riverboats used by the Benin Navy. They are armed with twin thirty-millimeter guns with a rate of fire around five hundred rounds per minute.

Robotic transporter. Mechanical device used at Fort Foureau. Look like squat bugs. They have four wheels with no tires, flat, with a level cargo bed. On the front, they have a boxlike unit that contains lights and a bug-eyed lens.

Rocky. Cartoon character Pitt claims to be when captured by Massarde's guards at Fort Foureau.

Rojas, Eva. Works with the World Health Organization. Described as having a firm body with slim, tanned limbs. Has red-gold hair and Dresden-blue eyes. With smooth skin and high cheekbones, she is age thirty-eight but could easily pass for thirty. Her family home is in Pacific Grove, California. Taken to Tebezza, later rescued by UNICRATT.

Ruins of Pergamon. Code message Yerli uses to reach Massarde's messenger in New York.

Sakito Maru. Japanese passenger-cargo ship that was carrying V-2 rockets to Japan when it was sunk by the American submarine *Trout.*

Saugus. A Union single-turreted monitor. Has twin fifteen-inch Dahlgrens. Fights the *Texas.*

Schonstedt Gradiometer. Instrument that detects iron by measuring deviation in the earth's magnetic background. Used by Pitt, Giordino and Perlmutter to locate the *Texas.*

SeaSat. U.S. satellite that monitors the world oceans and seas.

Second Division of the National Defense Staff. Division of the French government for which Yerli works.

Semmes, Admiral Raphael. Famous Confederate admiral and captain of the *Alabama.* Later commander of the James River Squadron. Described as having a heavily waxed moustache and a small goatee. With Mallory, delivers Lincoln to Tombs.

Seward, William Henry. Secretary of State under Lincoln. Was unaware of Stanton's plot. Targeted to be killed the night of the Ford's Theater incident, but the assassins bungled the effort.

Shaw, Stan. One of the NUMA crew flown in to replace Pitt and Giordino after Gunn pulls them off the Menkura Project.

Sikorsky H-76 Eagle. Type of helicopter that Hargrove uses. Pitt and Giordino are flown in it to meet with Massarde after the assault on Fort Foureau.

Smith & Wesson .38-caliber. Snub-nosed Bodyguard-model revolver carried by Gunn in Gao.

Society of French Historical Exploration. The group Pitt claims to be working for after he is captured aboard Massarde's yacht.

Society Islands. Series of islands in the South Pacific where Pitt tells Giordino he thinks Massarde hides his money and gold. Some of the islands include Tahiti, Bora Bora and Moorea.

Sounder. NUMA research ship, one hundred twenty meters long and built at the cost of eighty million dollars. The vessel is loaded with the most sophisticated seismic, sonar and bathymetric systems afloat.

Southern Cross. Sir Charles Kingsford-Smith's airplane. Now on display at the Military Museum in Canberra, Australia.

Special Operations Command. Command of U.S. Special Forces, located in Tampa, Florida.

Special Operations Forces. Another name for U.S. Special Forces.

Stain-teethed Man. Assassin who, along with Rat-faced Man, attempts to kill Rojas on the beach. Pitt shoots him through the temples with a spear gun.

Stanton, Edwin McMasters. Secretary of war under Abraham Lincoln. After Lincoln is kidnapped by the Confederacy, he forms a plot to fake the death of

Lincoln at Ford's Theater and then have Vice President Johnson and Secretary of State Seward killed, leaving himself next in line as president.

Steinholm, Lieutenant. UNICRATT officer in the liberation of Tebezza. In charge of Unit Three. Described as a big, blond, handsome Austrian. Once drove in the Monte Carlo Rally. Drives from Fort Foureau with Giordino to bring back help.

Supreme Military Council. Malian group that is bleeding the country dry. Led by Kazim.

Surratt, Mary. Alleged conspirator with Booth.

Tahir. President of Mali. A puppet head of state, as Kazim actually wields the power in Mali.

Takaldebey. Town in northern Africa in the former French Sahara where the French Foreign Legion has a post. The French Foreign Legion searches for Mannock.

Tamarisk shrubs. Plants that Pitt and Giordino hide the Voisin under when Malian search planes pass overhead.

Tanezrouft Desert. Location where Djemaa, after bailing out, crashes the UN Boeing 737 to make it appear the WHO scientists were killed. Described as a huge, sprawling badlands with almost two hundred thousand square kilometers of bleak, grotesque wasteland broken by only a few rugged escarpments and an occasional sea of sand dunes. Pitt and Giordino have to cross the area to bring back help to liberate Tebezza.

Taoudenni. Location in Mali that has salt mines mined by prisoners.

Teach, Edward. Also known as Blackbeard the Pirate. Captain of the *Queen Anne's Revenge.* Name Pitt gives Kazim over the radio when the *Calliope* is making the run toward Gao.

Tebezza. Location of a gold mine mined by the prisoners at the penal colony there. Location Kazim orders Fairweather to take. He later orders the WHO team taken there and imprisoned. The French engineers who built Fort Foureau, along with their families, are also imprisoned there.

Tessalit. Town in northern Africa that sends out searchers looking for Mannock.

Texas. Confederate Navy ship. Built at the Rocketts Naval Yard in Richmond. Specially constructed for a single voyage, she is one of the finest ships in the Confederate Navy. A twin-screw (propeller), twin-engined vessel one hundred ninety feet in length with a forty-foot beam that draws only eleven feet of water. Her sloping twelve-foot-high casemates are angled inward at thirty degrees and covered with six inches of iron plate backed by twelve inches of cotton compressed by twenty inches of oak and pine. Iron shutters can be closed over her gunports. Mounted with four guns, two one-hundred-pound Blakely rifled guns mounted fore and aft on pivots and two sixty-four-pound guns covering port and starboard. Her machinery is brand new with the boilers lying below waterline. She has twin nine-foot screws that can push her through the water at fourteen knots. Leaves the pier in Richmond on April 2, 1865. Journeys to Africa with the Confederate Treasury and Lincoln aboard. Later runs aground in a river in the desert and is lost to time. Later discovered by Pitt, Giordino and Perlmutter. Removed from the Malian desert and transported back to the United States. Now on display at the Washington Mall. Her crew was buried in the Confederate Cemetery in Richmond, Virginia.

Timbuktu. Fabled city in Mali that was to be the Across the Sahara Safari's next stop after Asselar.

Togo. Country in Africa.

Tombs, Commander Mason. Confederate naval officer in charge of the *Texas.* Described as ambitious and energetic and one of the finest naval officers in the Confederacy. He is a short, handsome man with brown hair and eyebrows, a thick red beard and a flinty look in his olive-black eyes. He commanded small gunboats at the battles of New Orleans and Memphis. He was gunnery officer aboard the famous *Arkansas* and first officer on the infamous raider *Florida.*

Tougouri, Ahmed. President of the Republic of Benin.

Trans-Sahara Motor Track. Road that leads through the Sahara Desert.

Traore, Lieutenant Moussa. Army officer who removed Mali's first president in a coup. Was then president. Overthrown by then-Major Kazim. Now a general.

Trastero. A nineteenth-century cabinet in Massarde's yacht office that contains communications gear.

Tuaregs. Tribesman who live in the desert near Fort Foureau. The men wear indigo veils around their heads and eyes. They speak the Berber language.

Tukulor. African tribe that speaks the Fulah dialect. The nurse who tends Fairweather in the hospital at Gao is a Tukulor.

UN Boeing 737. Plane used by the WHO team investigating the outbreak in Mali and western Sahara.

UNICRATT. Acronym that stands for *United Nations International Critical Response and Tactical Team.* The soldiers of UNICRATT are called "unicrazies" by other special forces teams.

UNICRATT all-terrain vehicle. Used in Gunn's rescue at Gao International Airport. Described as a maze of tubular supports welded together. Powered by a supercharged V-8 Rodeck 541-cubic-inch engine used by American drag racers. Has a wicked-looking six-barrel, lightweight Vulcan-type machine gun manned by a gunner sitting slightly above the driver. Over the rear axle, another gunner faces backward with a 5.56-millimeter Stoner 63 machine gun.

United Nations Environment Program Organization. United Nations group that promotes the environment.

United Nations International Intelligence Service. United Nations organization that provides intelligence to the UNICRATT team.

Verenne, Felix. Massarde's personal aide. Described as a slender bald-headed man in his forties.

Victor, Dr. Marie. One of the WHO doctors taken to Tebezza. Described as a vivacious lady and one of the finest physiologists in Europe. Murdered by Melika, who beats her to death.

Virginia II. Confederate Navy vessel scuttled at Drewry's Bluff.

Wadilinski, Corporal. One of the UNICRATT team that liberates Tebezza.

Washington Arsenal Yard. Where the Lincoln conspirators were hung.

Watkins, Captain Joshua. Captain of the *New Ironsides.*

Webster, Chip. NUMA's satellite analyst.

White, Dick. One of the NUMA crew flown in to replace Pitt and Giordino after Gunn pulls them off the Menkura Project.

WHO. Acronym for the *World Health Organization.*

Willover, Earl. The White House Chief of Staff. Described as a balding, bespectacled man of about fifty. Has a large red moustache.

Winchester rifle. Lever-action rifle carried by Cussler.

World Health Laboratory. Located in Paris. Hooper explains to the Babanandi that it is where the samples are to be taken.

World Health Organization. Group headquartered in Geneva, Switzerland, with which Rojas works. Part of the United Nations.

Yerli, Ismail. Coordinator and logistics expert for the WHO team looking into the outbreak in Africa. Lean, stringy and immensely efficient. His home is in Antalya, Turkey. Described as having a massive thicket of coarse black hair complemented by bushy eyebrows that meet over his nose. Has a huge moustache. Smokes a meerschaum pipe. Actually a French intelligence agent working undercover. Had an affair with Kamil. He was recruited by the French at Istanbul University.

Inca Gold

Adams, Frank. Senior editor at Falkner and Massey. Was Bender's editor. Age seventy-four.

Aldrich, Judge. The judge in Chicago from whom Pottle receives a search warrant for Rummel's apartment.

Alhambra. Passenger-car ferry that originally plied San Francisco Bay until 1957. She was later sold and used by the Mexicans on a run from Guaymas across the Sea of Cortez to Santa Rosalia. Taken out of service in 1962. Built in 1923, she was one of the last walking-beam steamboats to be built. In her heyday, the two-hundred-thirty-foot vessel could carry five hundred passengers and sixty automobiles. Her long black hull is topped with a two-story white superstructure whose upper deck mounts one large smokestack and two pilothouses, one on each end. The power train is a radial type similar to the old waterwheels used to power flour and sawmills. Strong cast-iron hubs mounted on a driveshaft have sockets that attach to wooden arms that extend outward to a diameter of thirty-three feet. Vessel leased by NUMA for the expedition to find Huascar's treasure.

Allard J2X. One of Pitt's automobiles. His is a bright red 1953 model powered by a Cadillac engine.

Altar Desert. Desert just south of the Arizona border that the Mexicans and Zolar use as a staging area for the expedition to recover Huascar's treasure.

Alvarez, Admiral Ricardo. Mexican admiral who is alerted that Pitt has been rescued by the *First Attempt.*

Amaru, Tupac. Leader of the Shining Path terrorists in the City of the Dead. Takes his name from the last of the Inca kings to be tortured and killed by the Spanish. Described as short and narrow-shouldered with a vacant brown face devoid of expression. Wears a thick moustache and long sideburns. Has a thick mass of straight hair as black as his empty eyes. Has narrow, bloodless lips that cover a set of teeth that would make an orthodontist proud. Attended the University of Texas at Austin. After he shoots Miller in the City of the Dead, Pitt appears, puts his Colt .45 down his pants and pulls the trigger. After Pitt emasculates him, he reappears at the underground cavern. Pitt shoots him in the lung, then drowns him. His body is later found in the Sea of Cortez by the crew of the *El Porquería.*

Amauta. An educated Inca who could understand *quipu* text.

Amphora. Jar or vase with two handles. Ortiz mentions divers occasionally find Roman and Greek amphoras in the waters off Brazil, bucking the idea that pre-Columbian civilizations did not visit the Americas.

Angel de la Guarda. Island in the Sea of Cortez.

Atahualpa. Brother of Huascar. Son of Hauyna. Usurped his brother after a lengthy civil war.

Aztec Star. Zolar-owned modified crude-oil tanker used to smuggle stolen artwork.

Baffin CZ-410. Twin turbo-prop-engined sea plane used by Zolar International to try to locate Huascar's treasure. Most frequently seen in the Canada lake country.

Bender, Nicholas. Journalist-explorer who published twenty-six books, including *On the Trail of El Dorado* in 1939. Perlmutter tracks down Bender, who is now eighty-four years old. Still mentally sharp, but his health is failing. He lives on a farm in Vermont. After talking to Perlmutter, Bender offers to Federal Express his journal which contains clues to the whereabouts of the *Concepción.*

Bingham, Hiram. Explorer who rediscovered Machu Picchu.

Birns Oceanographic Snooper. Dive light Pitt uses when he dives the sinkhole.

Boeing 747-400. Large jet Zolar plans to fly Huascar's treasure to Morocco aboard. Micki Moore diverts the plane to El Paso, Texas, instead, where it is captured by American authorities.

Boeing Chinook. Heavy-lift helicopter. Can lift fifty troops or twenty tons of cargo.

Bolivia. Country in South America. Portuguese explorers reported they found a tribe in Bolivia with magnificent beards, contrary to the fact that most Indians lack abundant facial hair.

Boriego Springs. Springs near the Box Car Café.

Box Car Café. Café near the Mexican border with California. Built out of old Southern Pacific Railroad freight cars sometime around 1915. Where Pitt and Smith meet Clive Cussler.

Brunhilda. What Yaeger calls his computer terminal.

Burgundy topaz. Precious gem found in the second sculpture inside the cavern on Cerro El Capirote. The gem is not indigenous to the United States and was probably mined east of the Andes in the Amazon.

Burley, August. NUMA's chief engineer aboard the *Deep Fathom.* Described as a powerfully built man with a portly stomach.

Cahuilla. Indian tribe that resides in Mexico and the United States.

Calexico. Town on the California side of the border with Mexico.

Callao de Lima. City in Peru. Founded by Francisco Pizarro in 1537, it quickly became the main shipping port for gold and silver plundered from the Inca empire. The last of the Spanish forces surrendered to Simon Bolivar in 1825 in Callao, and Peru became a sovereign nation. Combined now with Lima; the twin cities boast a population of six and a half million people.

Campos, Colonel Roberto. Commander of northern Mexico's military forces on the Baja Peninsula.

Cano Island. Island off Ecuador where Drake intends to bury treasure from the *Golden Hind* to lighten the load.

Canyon Ometepec. The Montolo village where Yuma lives.

Capac, Huayna. A great Inca king. Father of Huascar. Ordered an immense gold chain to be cast in honor of the birth of Huascar, which was later smuggled out of Peru.

Capital Concours de Breaux Moteurcar. Classic car show in East Potomac Park, where Pitt shows his Pierce-Arrow Berline with matching 1936 Pierce-Arrow Travelodge house trailer.

Carabiner. Used in climbing. An oblong metal ring with a spring-loaded closing hatch that hooks the climbing rope to the piton.

Carter, Howard. Famed archaeologist who discovered King Tut's tomb.

Caxanarca. Ancient Inca city.

Cenote. A deep limestone sinkhole.

Cerro El Capirote. Mountain where Huascar's treasure is buried. *Capirote* in English means "a tall, pointed ceremonial hat," or what used to be called a dunce cap.

Cerro El Capirote sculpture. Sitting atop the mountain, it is carved after the legend of a condor laying an egg that was eaten and vomited by a jaguar. A snake was hatched from the regurgitated egg and slithered into the sea, where it grew fish scales. The beast was so ugly it was shunned by the other gods, who thrived in the sun, so it lived underground where it eventually became the guardian of the dead.

Chachapoyas. A town in Peru fifty-six miles from the limestone sinkhole.

Chachapoyas Culture. A vast confederation of city-states that encompassed almost four hundred square kilometers. The tribes were conquered by the Inca Empire around A.D. 1480. Known as the Cloud People, they were a pre-Inca civilization that flourished high in the Andes from A.D. eight hundred. The culture was highly stratified but did not have royal elite like the Inca. The Chachapoyan people were fair-skinned with blue and green eyes.

Chaco, Juan. Inspector general of Peruvian archaeology and director of the Museo de la Nacion in Lima, Peru. Involved with the Solpemachaco. When the attack is bungled on the City of the Dead, he is thrown from a tilt-rotored plane into a potato field in Ecuador. He strikes the ground in the middle of a small corral, just missing a cow, and dies instantly.

Chiclayo. Town in Peru north of Trujillo to which Pitt informs the *Deep Fathom* he is flying. It's a fake, however, to throw off pursuers.

City of the Dead. Also known as Pueblo de los Muertos. It is a magnificent lost city recently rediscovered by the Shining Path terrorists.

Colorado School of Mines. Location in Golden, Colorado, where Gaskill borrows a ground-penetrating radar detector unit to search the Zolar warehouse in Galveston.

Colt .45. Handgun made by Colt Arms Corporation. Pitt's was carried by his father in World War II from Normandy to the Elbe River and then presented to Dirk when he graduated from the Air Force Academy.

Colt Combat Commander. A 9-millimeter handgun used by Swain in the undercover stake-out of Rummel.

Corporacion Estatal Petrolera Ecuatoriana. The state oil company of Ecuador. NUMA steered the company to a natural gas find in the Gulf of Guayaquil. The company loans NUMA a helicopter to search for the *Concepción.*

Cortina, Rafael. Police commandante of Baja Norte who is bought off by the Zolars at the price of ten million dollars. At age sixty-five, his career has spanned forty-five years. Described as having a square, brown-skinned face. Has a wife, four married sons and eight grandchildren.

Cuthill, Thomas. Sailing master of the *Golden Hind.* Originally from Devonshire, England. Later placed by Drake in charge of the *Concepción.* When the *Concepción* is swept inland in a tsunami, Cuthill survives and lives with the local Indians. He writes of the tsunami in a journal that Perlmutter later recovers. The journal gives the approximate location of the *Concepción,* which Pitt and Giordino later find.

Cutting, Patty Lou. Name on the gravestone near the Spanish mission close to the Montolo village. Her date of birth and death are listed as 2/11/24–2/3/34. To those readers who wonder about the unexplained significance of this in *Inca Gold,* good luck. Clive is silent on the issue.

Cuzco. Location of the Inca capital.

De Anton, Captain Juan. Skipper of the *Nuestra Señora de la Concepción.* Described as a brooding man with Castilian green eyes and a precisely trimmed black beard.

De Avila, Bishop Juan. A Jesuit historian and translator who, between the years of 1546 and 1568, recorded many mythical accounts of early Peruvian cultures.

De Orellana, Francis. Spanish explorer who searched for El Dorado.

De Silva, Numa. Portuguese pilot whom Drake captures off Brazil and presses into service on the *Golden Hind.*

Deep Fathom. NUMA research ship. A state-of-the-art scientific boat. Officially called a super-seismic vessel. Primarily designed for deep-ocean geophysical research, she can also undertake a myriad of other subsea duties. Her hull is painted in NUMA's traditional turquoise and white superstructure with azure blue cranes. She stretches the length of a football field. Her dining room is fitted out like a fine restaurant, and the galley is run by a first-rate chef.

Demonio de Muertos. Also known as the demon of the dead. A Chachapoyan god who was the focus of a protective rite connected with the cult of the underworld. Part jaguar, part snake, he sinks his fangs into whoever disturbs the dead and drags them back into the black depths of the earth.

Derringer, .38-caliber. Weapon Sarason has strapped to his leg when Pitt appears in the underground cavern.

Diaz, Don Antonio. Original owner of La Princesa. A peon who struck it rich mining the Huachuca Mountains in Arizona.

Diego, Captain Juan. Mexican captain who is informed that the guard post inside Cerro El Capirote is not reporting.

Diffusionism. Pre-Columbian travel to and from other continents.

Di Maggio, Anthony. U.S. Customs Service agent who tells Gunn that Pitt was picked up alive by the *First Attempt.*

Doc Miller's ring. Used by Pitt to identify the body he finds during his first trip into the sinkhole. The ring has a sixty-million-year-old piece of yellow amber with the fossil of a primitive ant inside.

Douglas, Arizona. City near the border with Mexico. Where Joseph Zolar has a hacienda.

Downing, Wick. Author of a paperback mystery novel that Stucky is reading aboard the *Deep Fathom* when Pitt calls over the radio.

Drake Quipu. *Quipu* that was taken in the cedar-lined jade box from the *Concepción* by Drake. Holds the key to the location of Huascar's treasure. Lost when the Concepción is washed into the mountains in a tsunami. Located by Pitt aboard the *Concepción.* Made from different metals, mostly copper, some silver and one or two gold. Appears they were hand-formed into wire and then wound into tiny coillike cables, some thicker than others, with varied numbers of strands and colors.

Drake, Francis, later Sir. Famous British pirate captain. Captain of the *Golden Hind.* Described as a beady-eyed gamecock of a man with dark red curly hair complemented by a light sandy beard that tapers to a sharp point under a long, swooping moustache. A gifted navigator and amateur artist. After returning from an around-the-world cruise, was knighted by Queen Elizabeth. Later served as admiral-of-the-seas, mayor of Plymouth and a member of Parliament. During an expedition to plunder ports and harass Spanish shipping in 1596, he died of dysentery and was sealed in a lead coffin and dropped into the sea near Portobelo, Panama.

Duncan, Dr. Peter. A U.S. Geological Survey hydrologist who dives into Satan's Sink with Giordino and confirms the underground river.

EG&G Geometrics G-813G magnetometer. Used by Pitt and Giordino to locate the *Concepción.*

Einstein Museum of Renaissance Art. Museum in Boston that has a fake Michelangelo statue of King Solomon.

El Centro Regional Medical Center. Hospital just north of Calexico where Gunn is taken after being rescued in the underground cavern.

El Porquería. The unofficial name of G-21, a Mexican patrol boat. Means "piece of trash." A two-hundred-twenty-foot-long modified U.S. minesweeper.

Estala, Maria. Last surviving member of the Diaz clan. Died at age ninety-four in 1978. Sold La Princesa to Zolar.

Estanque Peak. Peak in the Sea of Cortez that the *Baffin* circles.

EXO-26. Full face mask that uses an exothermic air regulator. Manufactured by Diving Systems International. Worn by Pitt when he dives on the sinkhole.

Fairchild Museum. Museum in Scarsdale, New York, where Ragsdale recently solved a theft of Sung Dynasty jade carvings.

Falkner and Massey. Publisher of Bender's books. Located in New York City.

First Attempt. The Hagens' fifty-foot oceangoing ketch. Based in Newport Beach, California. Has a Capri-blue hull.

Fluorescein yellow with optical brightener. Dye that Duncan asks Pitt to toss in the underground river so the outflow can be targeted.

Foreign Activities Council. An obscure government agency that operates out of a small basement room in the White House. Tasked with carrying out the assassinations of foreign terrorist leaders. Once employed by Henry and Micki Moore.

Forty-millimeter rocket. People's Republic of China made. Fired from a Type 69 launcher. Used in the attack on the City of the Dead and the helicopter Pitt and Giordino steal and fly out to sea. One of the rockets, designed for hardened steel like tank bodies, passes easily through the body of the Mi-8.

Francisco, Corporal. Mexican corporal guarding Cerro El Capirote who is reported missing.

Fujimori, President. President of Peru.

Gadsen Purchase. U.S. purchase of the Mesilla Valley from Santa Ana.

Galapagos Islands. Islands off South America.

Galveston. City in Texas on the Gulf Coast south of Houston. Location of the Zolar stolen art headquarters.

Gardner Museum. Museum in Boston that was robbed in April 1990 of artwork valued at two hundred million dollars.

Gaskill, Davis. U.S. Customs Service special agent. Works undercover specializing in the smuggling of antiquities. An eighteen-year veteran of the Customs Service, he looks more like a football coach than a government agent. An African American, he has gray hair, and his skin is more doeskin-colored than dark coffee. His eyes are a strange mixture of mahogany and green. Has a massive bulldog head. Was once an all-star linebacker for the University of Southern California. Originally from South Carolina. Married for twenty years; his wife died from hemochromatosis. Has a getaway cabin on a Wisconsin lake. Lives in the town of Cicero outside Chicago.

Gato. One of the deckhands on the *Alhambra.*

Geographic Information Systems. Part of the NUMA supercomputer data bank Yaeger uses to help try to find the *Concepción.*

Golden Body Suit of Tiapollo. Considered the most prized artifact ever to come out of South America because of its historic significance. A cast of the Chachapoyan general known as Naymlap. Spanish conquerors discovered Naymlap's tomb in a city called Tiapollo high in the mountains. The body of the suit is covered with hieroglyphics that give the location of the treasure of Huascar. The suit was stolen from the Museo Nacional de Antropología in Seville, Spain, in 1922. The suit is later traced to Rummel's secret apartment in Chicago but is stolen before Customs agents can recover it. Originally stolen by Zolar's father, who sold it to a wealthy Sicilian mafioso who kept it until his death in 1984 at age ninety-seven. The mafioso's son later sold it to Rummel.

Golden Hind. British pirate ship. Formerly named the *Pelican.* Described as a stout and sturdy vessel with an overall length of about thirty-one meters (one hundred two feet) and a displacement tonnage of one hundred forty. Has eighteen guns. After a sail around the world, she returns to Plymouth on September 26, 1580, her hull bulging with spoils. Queen Elizabeth's share of the plunder in her holds forms the foundation for future British expansion throughout the world. The second ship to circumnavigate the world. For three generations, she remained on view in the Thames River until she either burned or rotted away to the waterline.

Granados. Mexican inspector Sandecker usually deals with. Matos tells Sandecker that Granados is working on a case in Hermosillo.

The Great Zolar. Name of a dumb kid in the eighth grade whom Giordino saw performing a corny magician's act at school assemblies.

Guaymas, Mexico. Location that is the starting point for the Zolar team trying to find Huascar's treasure. Located midway across the Sea of Cortez on the Mexican mainland side.

Hagen, Claire. Wife of Joe Hagen. Described as having a face free from wrinkles and with breasts still large and firm.

Hagen, Joe. Runs a family auto dealership in Anaheim, California. Is fishing aboard his boat, the *First Attempt,* when he comes across Pitt and rescues him. Described as a big man with a well-rounded stomach.

Heckler & Koch. A 9-millimeter automatic Amaru uses to shoot Miller.

Hemochromatosis. Iron-overload disease that led to Gaskill's wife's heart attack.

Hidalgo, Lieutenant Carlos. Executive officer on *El Porquería.* Described as tall and lean with a narrow face. He looks like a well-tanned cadaver.

Highway Five. Highway running from San Felipe to Mexicali.

Huaqueros. Tomb robbers. A local Peruvian term for the robbers of ancient graves.

Huascar. An Inca king who was captured in battle and murdered by his brother Atahualpa, who was in turn executed by the Spanish conqueror Francisco Pizarro. Huascar possessed a gold chain that was two hundred fourteen meters long and estimated to weigh twenty thousand pounds. It's worth today would be in the neighborhood of one hundred million dollars.

Huascar's Golden Chain. Coiled, it measures thirty-three feet in height. Each link is as large as a man's wrist. It is conservatively valued at three hundred million dollars.

llano Colorado. Village near Canyon Ometepec that has a mission church that contains a pure gold chalice.

Inca Highway Network. Highway that ran from the Colombia-Ecuador border almost five thousand kilometers to central Chile.

Inca seagoing vessel. Raft constructed of reed bundles bound and turned up at both ends. Six of the bundles make up one hull, which is keeled and beamed with bamboo. The raised prow and stern are shaped like serpents with dogs' heads, their jaws tilted toward the sky as if baying at the moon.

Inca weavings. Considered the finest in the world, they contain five hundred threads per inch as opposed to the weavers of Renaissance Europe, who used eighty-five threads per inch. The Spanish mistook the weavings for silk, so fine was the quality.

Incas. Ancient tribe of South America.

Iridium. Portable, digital, wireless phone made by Motorola and used by Gunn. Works off a satellite enhancement network.

Isla Bargo. Island in the Sea of Cortez that the *Baffin* flies over.

Isla Carmen. Island in the Sea of Cortez eliminated by the Zolar team in the *Baffin* as too large to be the island that hides Huascar's treasure.

Isla Cholla. Island in the Sea of Cortez that is skipped by the crew of the *Baffin.*

Isla Danzante. Three-square-mile island in the Sea of Cortez south of Loreto, flown over by the *Baffin.*

Isla Gruapa. Island in the Sea of Cortez that the *Baffin* flies over.

Isla San Ildefonso. Island in the Sea of Cortez that is skipped by the crew of the *Baffin.*

Jade box. Carved from jade with the mask of a man for a lid. The lid seals so perfectly that the inside is nearly airtight. Inside are multicolored tangles of long cords of different thickness with more than a hundred knots.

Jaguar/Serpent. What the Incas chisel using bronze bars and chisels on the island in the forgotten sea.

Jeep Grand Wagoneer. Pitt's example is a 1984 with a Rodeck 500-horsepower V-8 engine taken from a wrecked hot rod.

Jesús. One of the deckhands on the *Alhambra.*

Juarez, Enrique. The oldest Montolo tribal elder and one of the few who still remember the old stories and ancient ways.

Julio. One of Amaru's Peruvian guards who is selected to rape Smith. First, she claws his eyes out instead.

Kammer, Cindy. Wife of Sidney Kammer.

Kammer, Sidney. A high-level corporate attorney Rummel uses. The lease on the secret apartment below Rummel is in Kammer's name. He and his wife, Cindy, actually live in the posh suburb of Lake Forest and have never been inside the apartment they have leased.

Karst. A limestone belt that is penetrated by a system of streams, passages and caverns. What Duncan thinks is the underground river.

Kelsey, Dr. Shannon. Archaeologist who specializes in Chachapoyan culture. Funded by a grant from Arizona State University. Described as having straight soft blond hair and tanned skin. Has an hourglass figure with an extra twenty minutes thrown in for good measure. In her late thirties. Has big, wide hazel eyes under dark brows. Drives a Dodge Viper she bought with her grandfather's inheritance.

Kermantle communications and safety line. Thick nylon line with emergency release buckle that hooks Pitt to Giordino when he dives in the sinkhole.

Key West. Island in the Florida Keys and home to one of NUMA's research labs.

Lake Cahuilla. Ancient sea in the desert of California that dried up between A.D. 100 and 1200.

Lake Cocopah. Lake southeast of Yuma, Arizona, where a fisherman disappeared and later turned up in the Sea of Cortez.

Lake Salada. An area of wetlands and mud flats less than a kilometer from the border between the United States and Mexico in California.

La Princesa. Zolar's hacienda near Douglas, Arizona.

Las Tinajas Mountains. Inland mountains where Pitt believes Cerro El Capirote is located.

Library of Congress. Vast repository of information in Washington, D.C. Perlmutter does research on the Drake *quipu* there.

Lima. Capital of Peru.

Limestone. A sedimentary rock composed of calcium carbonate, a sort of blend of crystalline calcite and carbonate mud, produced by lime-secreting organisms from ancient coral reefs. The type of rock surrounding the sinkhole.

Logan Storage Company. Front company for Zolar's stolen art empire in Galveston.

Loreto. Resort town in Mexico on the Sea of Cortez.

Lost Horizon Era. Era from which Henry Moore explains the Golden Body Suit of Tiapollo comes.

Macapa. City in Brazil. The survey team that recovered Cuthill's journal dropped it off there to the viceroy.

Madame LaFarge. What Pitt names the machete he uses to hack through the forest above the *Concepción.*

Maderas, Commander Miguel. Skipper of *El Porquería.* Described as having a round, friendly face under long, thick black hair. His teeth are large and white. He is short and heavy and solid as a rock.

Magdalena, Sophia. Wife of Don Antonio Diaz.

Magellan Strait. Strait on the tip of South America. Runs through what is now Chile.

Magic Castle. Pitt's answer to the radio call trying to establish the location of the stolen Mi-8.

Mandrake Pitt. What Pitt calls himself on page 109. After an old cartoon character.

Manta. Port city in Ecuador fifty-five kilometers from the wreckage of the Concepción.

Manuel. One of Amaru's killers who is shot and killed by Pitt aboard the *Alhambra.*

Matos, Ferdinand (Fernando). Mid-level official with the Mexican National Affairs Department who meets with Starger and Sandecker in Calexico. Described as bald and wearing thick horn-rimmed glasses with a black moustache exactingly trimmed. He is a tall, complacent man. On the Zolars' payroll, he is due to receive five percent of Huascar's treasure.

McDonnell-Douglas Explorer helicopter. Type of helicopter that NUMA borrows from the Peruvian national oil company to search for the *Concepción.* A big red twin-engined craft with no tail rotor. Costs two point seven-five million.

Mesoamericans. Indians in Panama with whom the Incas traded.

Mexicali. Town on the Mexican side of the border with California.

Mi-8 assault-transport helicopter. Nicknamed the Hip-C by NATO during the Cold War years. A twenty-year-old ugly craft powered by twin 1,500-horsepower turboshaft engines. Can carry four crew and thirty passengers. Has a five-bladed main rotor. Giordino and Pitt steal it from the Peruvian mercenaries and fly it toward the *Deep Fathom* and safety. Top speed approximately two hundred forty kilometers an hour. Giordino sets his speed at one hundred forty-four kilometers to save fuel.

Michigan Avenue. Street in Chicago where Rummel's office is located.

Miller, Dr. Steve. Archaeologist from the University of Pennsylvania. Described as a tall, slender man in his sixties with a silver-gray beard that covers half his face. Helps Kelsey with the dive on the limestone sinkhole.

MK1-DCI. Diver radio manufactured by Ocean Technology Systems. Worn by Pitt when he dives on the sinkhole.

Montolo. Indian tribe that resides in Mexico and the United States.

Montolo ceremonial artifacts. Ceremonial idols carved from the wood of cottonwood trees. Stolen by Zolar's men and offered for sale to Vincente, who turns them down. Later recovered by Pitt and returned to Yuma and the Montolo tribe.

Montolo Village. Where Yuma resides. Population of the village is one hundred seventy-six. The villagers survive by raising squash, corn and beans; others cut juniper and manzanita to sell for fence posts and firewood.

Montolos. Ancient cave dwellers who lived in the Sonoran Desert near the Colorado River.

Moore, Henry. Professor of anthropology at Harvard who has made pre-Columbian ideographic symbols his life's work. Zolar forces him to decode the etchings on the Golden Body Suit of Tiapollo. Lives in a condo in Boston. Described as aging gracefully with a slim body, a full head of shaggy gray hair and the complexion of a teenage boy. Worked for the Foreign Activities Council for twelve years as a political assassin. Doctorate from University of Pennsylvania.

Moore, Micki. Wife of Henry Moore. An archaeologist. Handles the computer end of the decoding of symbols with her husband. Lives in a condo in Boston. Described as a good fifteen years younger than her husband. Has a thin figure like a seventies fashion model, which she once was. Her skin is on the dark side, and her high rounded cheekbones suggest American Indian heritage. Worked for the Foreign Activities Council for twelve years as a political assassin. Doctorate from Stanford.

Moran. Director of the FBI.

Morganthaler, Jacob. Attorney known as Jury-rig Jake. Rummel hires him to try to recover his artwork that was seized.

Mr. Periwinkle. Cussler's burro.

Mysterious intruders. Described as having white skin, blond hair and blue eyes. They wear ornate embroidered tunics.

Nador. City in Morocco where Zolar intends to take Huascar's treasure.

National Heritage Museum. Museum in Guatemala that reported an eight-million-dollar theft.

Nuestra Señora de la Concepción. The largest and most regal of the Pacific armada treasure galleons. Displaces five hundred seventy tons. Extremely rugged and seaworthy, her gun decks hold ports for nearly fifty-four-pound cannon. Attacked and taken by Drake and the *Golden Hind* en route to Callao de Lima in March 1578. Later swept away in a tsunami.

Olmec. Ancient people who lived in Mexico about 900 B.C.

One-eyed Guard. Described as enormous with an entirely repulsive face, thick lips, flat nose and one eye. The empty eye socket is left exposed, giving him the brutal ugliness of Quasimodo. Starts to rape Smith but is stopped by Pitt. Pitt later shoots him in the neck and kills him.

Ortiz, Dr. Alberto. A Peruvian doctor with the National Institute of Culture in Chiclayo. Peru's most renowned expert on ancient culture. Described as a lean, wiry old bird in his early seventies. Has a long, flowing white moustache and bushy white eyebrows.

Oxley, Charles. Legal name of Charles Zolar. Described as having medium brown hair clipped short in a military crew cut. His cheeks and chin are closely shaven. Has shamrock-green eyes.

Padilla, Gordo. Engineer on the *Alhambra.* Has sleek, well-oiled hair as thick as marsh grass. Has brown eyes in a round face. Devoid of body hair and tattoos. Diminutive; his height and weight would easily qualify him to ride race horses. Married to Rosa.

Pembroke, Nathan. Retired Scotland Yard inspector who wrote a manuscript titled *The Thief Who Was Never Caught,* about the Specter. Pembroke is now in his late eighties.

Peruvian Investigative Police. Police force that shows up at the City of the Dead after Pitt and group along with their kidnappers escape.

Phony conquistador. Pitt finds a planted body in the sinkhole dressed like an old Spanish conquistador.

Pierce-Arrow Berline. One of Pitt's cars. His is a twelve-cylinder sedan with a divider window and is hitched to a 1936 Pierce-Arrow Travelodge house trailer painted a matching shade of dark, gleaming blue.

Pike. A sharp-pointed spear used for fighting.

Piton. A metal spike with a ring on one end used in climbing.

Pizarro, Francisco. Explorer of South America who removed valuable treasures.

Pottle, Winfried. Customs Service special agent and second-in-command of the surveillance team led by Gaskill. Described as a slim, handsome man with sharp features and soft red hair.

Pueblo de los Muertos. Also known as the City of the Dead.

Punta El Macharro. Also known as Macharro Point. On the Sea of Cortez two or three kilometers above San Felipe.

Quechan. Indian tribe that resides in Mexico and the United States.

Quetzalcoatl. A feathered serpent that was the most important deity of Mesoamerica.

Quipu. An Inca system for working out mathematical problems and record keeping. A kind of ancient computer that uses colored strands of string or hemp with knots placed at different intervals.

Quipu-Mayoc. A secretary or clerk who works with the quipus to record information.

Ragsdale, Francis. The FBI's chief of interstate stolen art. Age thirty-four. Described as clean-shaven with black wavy hair and a reasonably well-exercised body. Has the handsome face, pleasant gray eyes and bland expression of a soap-opera actor.

Ramos, Lieutenant. Mexican lieutenant who is at Cerro El Capirote.

Rappeling. Descending a rope that wraps under a climber's thigh, across the body and over the opposite shoulder.

Rimac River. River that runs through Callao and Lima.

Rio Pitt. The name later given to the underground river beneath the desert.

River of Gold. What the legend of Hunt's underground river became.

Rodgers, Miles. Photographer who is shooting footage of the dive on the limestone sinkhole in the jungle. Described as a year shy of forty with luxuriant black hair and a beard.

Rojas. Chief of the Northern Mexico Investigative Division. Person Sandecker usually deals with, but Matos appears instead. Matos tells Sandecker Rojas is ill.

Ruiz, Bartolomé. Pizarro's pilot. Mentioned seeing large rafts equipped with masts and great square cotton sails. Other sailors mentioned seeing rafts with hulls of balsa wood, bamboo and reed carrying sixty people and forty or more large crates of trade goods. Besides sails, the crafts were powered by teams of paddlers. The rafts featured stern posts with carved serpent heads similar to the dragons gracing Viking long ships. Yaeger believes they may have been the ships that transported Huascar's treasure.

Rummel, Adolphus. A noted collector of South American antiquities who lives in a plush penthouse apartment twenty floors above Lakeshore Drive in Chicago, Illinois. Described as a short, stringy man with a shaven head and an enormous walrus moustache. In his mid-seventies, he looks more like a Sherlock Holmes villain than the owner of six huge auto salvage yards. Unmarried and reclusive. In the 1950s, he smuggled a cache of Nazi ceremonial objects across the Mexican border and used the money from the sale to found a string of auto junkyards that netted him two hundred fifty million when he sold out. Became interested in South American antiquities in 1974 and began to buy from all sources, legitimate or not. Paid one-point-two million dollars for the stolen Golden Body Suit of Tiapollo.

Saint John. Radio call sign from the person who calls Chaco to inform him that Pitt has overpowered Amaru's group at the City of the Dead.

Saint Peter. Chaco's radio call sign.

Salton Sea. Artificially created sea in California made when the Colorado River overflowed the banks of a canal and flooded the desert floor.

San Felipe. Where the *Alhambra* takes off.

San Lorenzo. The large offshore island that protects Callao's natural maritime shelter.

San Pedro de Paula. A ship de Silva claims is the *Golden Hind* when they engage the *Concepción.*

Santa Ana, Antonio Lopez de. General and later president of Mexico. Deeded the land where La Princesa was built.

Sapa Incas. Inca supreme rulers who were encased in gold and used as objects in religious ceremonies.

Saponification. The process in a dead body whereby the meaty tissue and organs are turned into a firm soaplike substance. Pitt notices that the process is starting in the most recent body he finds in the sinkhole.

Sarason, Cyrus. Man who impersonates Doc Miller. Described as heavily bearded.

Satan's Sink. Sinkhole where two divers disappear. Their bodies later turn up in the Sea of Cortez. The sinkhole lies in Mexico at the northern foot of the Sierra El Mayor Mountains.

Sea of Cortez. Also known as the Gulf of California. The body of water that divides Baja California from mainland Mexico.

Sedona. Town in Arizona where Pitt and Smith spent the night with the Pierce-Arrow.

Sendero Luminoso. Known as the Shining Path. A Maoist revolutionary group that has terrorized Peru since 1981. Terrorists who capture the group at the sinkhole and cut Pitt's Kermantle safety line.

Seville. City in Spain where the *Concepción* is based.

Shang Dynasty. Twelfth-century Chinese dynasty. A museum in Beijing reported forty-five drinking vessels were stolen recently.

Sic Parvis Magna. Drake's motto: "Great things have small beginnings."

Silver reflectors. Highly polished silver reflectors found inside the cavern on Cerro El Capirote. Sun striking the reflectors bounces from reflector to reflector, lighting the cavern without the smoke and soot given off by oil lamps.

Solpemachaco. What Amaru calls his group. A combination Medusa dragon myth that comes from the local Peruvian ancients. An ancient serpent with seven heads who lives in a cave. One myth claims he lives in the City of the Dead. Later, the Solpemachaco is shown to be the Zolar family.

Sonoran Desert. The desert in Mexico on the border with California.

Sonoran Waterway Project. The project to use the water from the underground river for irrigation.

Specter. Infamous art thief who leaves a calendar at the scene of his thefts with the date of his next theft circled. Last-known theft was in London in 1939; the stolen art consisted of a Joshua Reynolds, a pair of Constables and three Turners. The Specter was actually Mansfield Zolar.

Starger, Curtis. Customs agent in Calexico whom Pitt calls from Yuma's village. A veteran of sixteen years with the Customs Service. Described as a trim, handsome man with sharp features and blond hair.

Stewart, Frank. Captain of the *Deep Fathom.*

Straight, Dr. Bill. Head of NUMA's marine artifact preservation department. Described as a bald-headed, cadaverous man with a scraggly Wyatt Earp moustache.

Stucky, Jim. Communications technician on the *Deep Fathom.*

Summer. Pitt's one and only true love. Pitt met her during the *Pacific Vortex* affair. Mentioned on page 561.

Swain, Beverly. Customs Service undercover agent on Gaskill's team. A smart blonde, she was a California beach girl before joining the Customs Service.

Temple of the Sun. Temple in Cuzco.

The Thief Who Was Never Caught. Title of a manuscript by Nathan Pembroke.

Thomas. Director of the Customs Service.

Tiburon. Island in the Sea of Cortez.

Torres, Luis. Chief pilot and second-in-command of the *Concepción.* Described as a tall, clean-shaven Galician.

Trujillo. City in Peru.

Twenty-man flotation unit. What the life rafts aboard the Mi-8 are labeled. Pitt tosses one into the rotor blade of an attacking helicopter, and it crashes.

Type 56-1. Chinese-manufactured assault rifles.

"Up a Lazy River in the Noonday Sun." Tune Pitt starts to hum after he finds the remains of the *Wallowing Windbag* and starts down the underground river again.

Valley of the Kings. Area in ancient Egypt. Location of King Tut's tomb.

Valley of Viracocha. Valley that contains the City of the Dead.

Valparaiso. City in Chile.

Vancouver Island. Island off British Columbia, Canada, that Drake and the *Golden Hind* sail to after leaving Cano Island.

Victorio Peak. Legendary peak in New Mexico where Spanish gold was discovered by civilians in the 1930s. The gold was allegedly stolen by the U.S. Army.

Vincente, Pedro. Drug dealer to whom Zolar sells the Chachapoyan artifacts taken from the City of the Dead. His cover is that he is a Costa Rican coffee grower. Owns the second-largest coffee plantation in Costa Rica. Described as having straight slicked-back black hair, partridge-brown eyes, smooth olive complexion and a sharp nose. His height and weight show a short man on the thin side whose age is forty-four. A fastidious dresser whose clothes look as if they come right out of *GQ* magazine. His ex-wife and four children live on a farm outside Wichita, Kansas.

Vincente's DC-3. Beautifully restored fifty-five-year-old cargo plane powered by two 1,200-horsepower Pratt and Whitney engines. Flown by Vincente from Nicoya, Costa Rica, to Harlingen, Texas, then on to Wichita, Kansas, to purchase the stolen art from the City of the Dead from Zolar. The plane began life as a commercial airliner for TWA shortly before the war. Vincente found the plane hauling cargo for a mining company in Guatemala and had it restored.

"Waiting for the Robert E. Lee." Song that Pitt claims he wants to hear when he surfaces from the sinkhole. Giordino has a mariachi band playing the song when Pitt is dropped off by the *El Porquería*.

Wallowing Windbag. The specially modified NUMA Hovercraft that Pitt and Giordino use to travel on the underground river. Known as a water rescue response vehicle, it is ten feet in length and five feet wide. It has eight air chambers and features a four-cycle, 50-horsepower engine that can propel it at forty miles an hour.

Wichita, Kansas. City where Zolar meets with Vincente to sell him the artifacts from the City of the Dead. Vincente's ex-wife and kids live there on a farm.

Yuma, Billy. Native American from the Montolo tribe. A small man of fifty-five. Won a bronco-riding contest in Tucson, Arizona, and was once the fastest cross-country runner in his tribe. He has a round, brown face with a strong jaw, straggly gray eyebrows and thick black hair. Drives a Ford pickup truck. His wife's name is Polly. He speaks native Montoloan and Spanish along with some English.

Yuma, Polly. Wife of Billy. A large woman who carries her weight better than any man. Her face is round and wrinkled with enormous brown eyes. Despite being middle-aged, she has hair as black as a raven's feathers.

Zavala. The one-hundred-fifty-year-old steamship that belonged to the Republic of Texas Navy. NUMA found the ship under a parking lot in Galveston.

Zolar International. Zolar's company. Its corporate jet is painted a golden tan with a bright purple stripe running along its fuselage.

Zolar, Charles. Brother of Joseph, Marta and Samuel. Tracked down the Golden Body Suit of Tiapollo and had it stolen from Rummel. Legal name is Charles Oxley.

Zolar, Joseph. Owner of La Princesa. A rich financier, antiquarian and fanatical collector. Described as having surgically tightened eyelids. Has a pinched, constantly flushed face that complements his thin, receding, brushed-back, dull red hair. He is somewhere in his late fifties. His body is small.

Zolar, Marta. Sister of Charles, Joseph and Samuel.

Zolar, Samuel. Brother of Charles, Joseph and Marta. Helps steal the Golden Body Suit of Tiapollo with Charles. Legal name is Cyrus Sarason.

Shock Wave

Adams, Marion. A convict and one of the survivors of the raft from the *Gladiator.* Convicted of stealing food from her master's pantry. She dies giving birth to a daughter named Mary.

Agusta Mark II. British-built type of helicopter Giordino pilots from the Dorsett yacht with Sean and Michael Fletcher aboard.

Aleksandr Gorchakov. Russian factory ship Gorimykin is based aboard. When he returns to the ship from a flight, Gorimykin finds everyone aboard dead from the effects of an acoustic convergence.

Ames, Dr. Stanford Adgate. Called the soundmeister by his fellow scientists, he is to sound what Einstein was to light. Once a trusted advisor to the Department of Defense, he was forced to resign after protesting ocean noise tests designed to measure global warming. Described as having a long, scraggly beard that covers his mouth and comes down to his chest and looking like a desert prospector. He is in his late sixties. If he hadn't gone into physics, he'd have entered the PGA tour as a professional. Wears blue-tinted bifocals. Helps NUMA come up with the idea for the underwater reflector that redirects the sound beam back to Gladiator Island.

Amy & Jason. Whaling ship that takes Dorsett and Fletcher's two sons as well as Adams and Winkleman's daughter, Mary, to Auckland, New Zealand, where they book passage on a ship bound for England.

Anderson, Dave. A cook for the miners on Kunghit Island. Described by Mason Broadmoor as a decent guy who drinks too much beer.

Angus, Lieutenant Samuel. Second officer of the *HMS Bridlington.*

Aqualand Pro. Type of dive watch worn by Giordino.

Argentinian Research Station. Located on Seymour Island. Pitt and Giordino visit the site by helicopter and find all the inhabitants dead.

Avondale, Lieutenant Commander Roger. First officer of the HMS *Bridlington.*

Bakewell, Dr. Charlie. NUMA's chief undersea geologist. A balding man who wears rimless glasses.

Basil. What Maeve calls the sea serpent that lives in the lagoon on Gladiator Island. Maeve classifies him as a mega-eel. He has a cylindrical body thirty meters long, ending in a tail with a point. His head is slightly blunt like a common eel's but with a wide canine mouth filled with sharp teeth. He is bluish with a white belly, and his jet-black eyes are as large as a serving dish. He undulates in the horizontal like other eels and snakes.

Bass Strait. Strait between Tasmania and the southern tip of Australia.

Baxter, Admiral. Admiral with the Joint Chiefs of Staff who told Sandecker he could use the *Enterprise.*

BOFORS. A pair of the twin 40-millimeter guns aboard the HMS *Bridlington.* They open fire on the sharks feasting off the dead bodies of the crew of the *Aleksandr Gorchakov.*

Botany Bay. An inlet south of the present city of Sydney, Australia, that housed a penal colony where the convicts aboard the *Gladiator* were due to be imprisoned.

Brandsfield Strait. Strait near Seymour Island where the *Polar Queen* heads to ride out the storm as the passengers go ashore on Seymour Island.

***Bridlington,* H.M.S.** British Navy Type 42 destroyer. En route from Hong Kong to England, the vessel picks up a Russian helicopter pilot who spots whales for the Russian fishing fleet.

Briscoe, Captain Ian. Captain of the HMS *Bridlington.* Described as having a precisely trimmed red beard.

Broadmoor, Irma. Wife of Mason. Described as a woman of grace and poise, stout yet supple. Has haunting coffee eyes and a laughing mouth.

Broadmoor, Mason. A member of the Haida tribe who lives on the Queen Charlotte Islands of British Columbia. Carves totem poles for a living. Posey refers Pitt to him to assist in the investigation into the Dorsett mining operations on Kunghit Island. Described as having long straight black hair and a round face. Has coal-black eyes. His uncle was killed by the Dorsett security forces.

Bushmaster M-16 rifles. Customized assault rifles with noise suppressors carried by the Dorsett security forces on Kunghit Island.

C. Dirgo & Co. New York diamond brokers who estimated that the Dorsett mine on Kunghit Island could bring in as much as two billion dollars in diamonds.

Cadillac STS sedan. Automobile driven by the Dorsett security guards following Maeve. Has a 300-plus-horsepower engine that propels the car upward of two hundred sixty kilometers an hour. Pitt loses them in the Allard.

Callahan, Steve. A yachtsman who survived seventy-six days at sea after his sloop sank off the Canary Islands, the longest record for one man in an inflatable raft.

Calvert, Irene. Former wife of Arthur Dorsett. Daughter of a professor of biology at the University of Melbourne. Committed suicide. Was walking along the cliffs of Gladiator Island with her husband when she fell to her death in the surf below. Maeve thinks she was murdered by Arthur Dorsett.

Cape Farewell. The cape on the tip of New Zealand's South Island. The Dorsett yacht passes it after the security people capture Pitt, Giordino and Fletcher.

Carlisle, Abner. One of the partners who owns Carlisle & Dunhill. A thin, wiry man who is completely bald. He has kindly eyes and walks with a noticeable limp caused by a fall from a horse when he was younger. A respected shipping magnate. Besides his shipping company, he also owns a mercantile business and a bank. Scaggs calls Carlisle to his deathbed and explains to him the true story of the wreck of the *Gladiator,* then asks him to have the diamonds sent by Betsy Dorsett appraised.

Carlisle & Dunhill. The shipping company that owned the *Gladiator* and employed Scaggs.

Cassidy, Admiral George. Commanding officer of the San Francisco Naval District who remands the orders giving Sandecker the use of the *Enterprise.*

The Castle. A group of rocks above the cliffs on Gladiator Island where there is a guard station.

Center for Disease Control. The branch of the world organization located in Melbourne, Australia, concludes that the deaths aboard the *Polar Queen* were caused by a rare form of bacterium similar to the one that causes Legionnaire's disease.

Central Selling Organization. The body the South African diamond cartel uses to sell its diamonds.

Chinook Cargo Carriers. The company featured on the side of the strawberry-red float plane that Pitt flies aboard to Kunghit Island.

Chirikof Island. Island near the Aleutians where three thousand sea lions and five fishermen are killed by the acoustic waves.

Cochran, Thomas. The *Gladiator*'s carpenter. Survives the raft and lands on the island, later leaves with Scaggs and returns to England. Prefers the company of men. Dies when the *Zanzibar* sinks in the South China Sea in 1867.

Colored gemstones. Dorsett Consolidated controls eighty percent of the world market. Including rubies, emeralds, sapphires, topaz, tourmaline and amethyst along with tsavorite, red beryl or red emerald and the Mexican fire opal.

Commodore Island (Komandorskiye Ostrova). Island off the Commonwealth of Independent States that is one corner of the Acoustic Convergence. Located off the Kamchatka Peninsula in the Bering Sea.

Converse, Garret. Hollywood actor and box-office action hero. Aboard his ship, the *Tz'u-hsi,* when it is hit by an acoustic wave.

Cross-shaft. A method of determining latitude devised by the ancient mariners. With one end of a shaft held to the eye, a crosspiece is calibrated by sliding it back and forth until one end fits exactly between either the star or sun and the horizon. The angle of latitude is then read on notches carved on the staff. Once the angle is established, the mariner is able by crude reckoning to establish a rough latitude without using published tables for reference.

Crutcher. One of the Dorsett security guards on Kunghit Island. Described as a cold-faced, arrogant young man of no more than twenty-six or twenty-seven.

Dancing Dorothy. The Bermuda ketch found by Pitt, Giordino and Fletcher on the Tits. Her upperworks are painted a light blue with orange undersides. Was owned by Rodney York, who wrecked her on the rocks off the Tits.

Danger Islands. Three small islands that are little more than pinnacles of exposed rocks near mainland Antarctica. They lie near the Drake Passage. Site where Pitt finds the *Polar Queen* and saves it from destruction on the rocks.

De Beers. The famous South African diamond cartel. Named for the South African farmer who sold his diamond-laden lands to Cecil Rhodes for a few thousand dollars.

De Havilland Beaver. Type of bush plane in which Stokes flies Pitt to Kunghit Island. The plane was built in 1967. Features a Pratt and Whitney R-985 Wasp engine with 450 horsepower.

Deep Abyss Engineering. Undersea exploration company that hosts the party where Maeve Fletcher is reunited with Pitt. Also the company that leases the *Glomar Explorer* to NUMA.

Dempsey, Paul. Captain of the *Ice Hunter.* Dempsey grew up on a ranch on the Wyoming-Montana border and ran away to sea after graduating from high school and worked on the fishing boats out of Kodiak, Alaska. Later became a captain on an ice-breaking salvage tug. When the salvage company he worked for became debt-ridden, he was hired by NUMA. He is described as broad-shouldered and thick-waisted, habitually standing with his legs wide set. Gray-haired and clean-shaven with a briar pipe perpetually jutting from the corner of his mouth.

Diamonds. Stones that formed the basis of the vast Dorsett fortune. Merely crystallized carbon, they are chemically the sisters to graphite and coal. Arthur Dorsett claims their only practical application is that they happen to be the hardest substance known to man, and that alone makes them essential for the machining of metals and drilling through rock. The word *diamond* comes from the Greek and means "indomitable." The Greeks and later the Romans wore them as protection from wild beasts and human enemies. The first diamond engagement ring was given by Archduke Ferdinand of Austria to Mary of Burgundy in 1477.

The notion of a diamond engagement ring did not take hold until the late 1800s.

Dorsett, Anson. Son of Charles Dorsett and Mary Winkleman. Grandfather of Arthur Dorsett. Died in 1910.

Dorsett, Arthur. Maeve and Deirdre's father. Head of a diamond empire second only to De Beers and the sixth-richest man in the world. Chairman of Dorsett Consolidated Mining Limited. A recluse. Only child of Henry and Charlotte Dorsett. Born on Gladiator Island in 1941. At the age of eighteen, he entered the Colorado School of Mines in Golden, Colorado. After graduating with a degree as a mining engineer, he worked for De Beers in South Africa for five years. Was married to the former Irene Calvert. A giant of a man with the hairy muscular build of a professional wrestler. Has coarse and wiry sandy-colored hair. His face is ruddy and as fierce as the black eyes that stare from beneath heavy, scraggly brows. His skin is rough and tanned by long days in the sun. A huge moustache curls downward past the corners of lips that are constantly stretched open like a moray eel's revealing teeth yellowed from long years of pipe smoking. When Pitt meets him, he notices Arthur has weathered lines in his face and rough, scarred hands. His moustache is long and scraggly, and his teeth look like the ivory keys of an old piano, yellowed and badly chipped. Before being set adrift in *Marvelous Maeve,* Pitt uses his thumb to poke out Arthur's eye. On Gladiator Island, Pitt shoots off the tip of his ear, smashes and breaks his shinbone with a floor lamp, then crushes his windpipe with the soles of his shoes, killing him.

Dorsett, Boudicca. Sister of Maeve and Deirdre. Described by Maeve as the devil incarnate. Age thirty-eight. Far taller than her sisters, with black eyes and a flood of reddish-blond hair that falls to her hips. She has definite underlying masculine qualities. Known as "The Emasculator." Maeve claims not to know her well, as she is eleven years older. Said to favor handsome young men and to sleep around. Giordino fights her, then crushes her neck and chokes the life out of her. After lifting her silk robe, he finds out she is a man.

Dorsett, Charles. One of the two sons of Betsy Fletcher and Jess Dorsett. Educated at Cambridge in England. Later married Mary Winkleman.

Dorsett, Deirdre. Sister of Maeve Fletcher. Discovered by Pitt still alive aboard the *Polar Queen.* Described as having wide brown eyes and a flawless facial complexion with an unmistakable pallor and just a hint of gauntness. Her hair is the color of red copper, and she has the high cheekbones and sculpted lips of a fashion model. Hired to sing and play piano aboard the *Polar Queen.* Thirty-one years old. Was once married to a professional soccer player, but after he wanted a divorce and a large property settlement, he conveniently fell from a Dorsett family yacht to his death. Pitt charges her aboard the Dorsett yacht at Gladiator Island after she shoots him, and he snaps her spine in three places.

Dorsett, Henry. Son of Anson Dorsett. Brother of Mildred Dorsett.

Dorsett, Jess. Notorious highwayman who is being sent to Australia aboard the *Gladiator.* A fashionable dresser who has every hair on his head fastidiously in place. He is described as six feet four inches tall with long copper-red hair. His head is long-nosed, with high cheekbones and a heavy jaw. Married Betsy Fletcher on Gladiator Island. Later died when a sudden squall upset his fishing boat.

Dorsett, Jess Jr. One of the two sons of Betsy Fletcher and Jess Dorsett. Educated at Cambridge in England along with his brother Charles.

Dorsett, Mildred. Daughter of Anson Dorsett. Sister of Henry Dorsett.

Dorsett Consolidated Mining Limited. Based in Sydney, Australia, and owned by the Dorsett family, it is second only to De Beers as the world's largest diamond producer.

Dorsett headquarters. A Trump Towers–like building in Sydney, Australia, paid for in cash. Arthur Dorsett's office is a gigantic vault with a steel door and walls two meters thick. Hundreds of precious stones are displayed in black velvet cases, and the estimated worth of the stones is one-point-two billion dollars. His desk is a huge monstrosity of polished lava rock with mahogany drawers.

Dorsett manor house. Built and designed by Anson Dorsett, who tore down the original log structure topped by a palm frond roof. The style is based on a classic layout—a central courtyard surrounded by verandas from which doors open into thirty rooms, all furnished in English colonial antiques. The only visible modern conveniences are a large satellite dish rising from a luxuriant garden and a modern swimming pool in the center courtyard.

Dorsett Rose. A D-grade flawless diamond with tremendous luster that was discovered by a Chinese worker at the Gladiator Island mine in 1908. Weighed 1,130 carats before cutting. Weighed 620 carats after. Double-rose cut in ninety-eight facets to bring out the brilliance. Arthur Dorsett has it inside his office.

Dorsett yacht. Wilbanks estimates the length to be somewhere in the neighborhood of thirty meters with a beam of about ten meters. Probably powered by a pair of Blitzen Seastorm turbodiesels, most likely BAD 98s, which combined would produce more than 2,500 horsepower. Estimated cruising speed is in the neighborhood of seventy knots. A sleek sports cruiser with twin hulls and a smooth rounded design. Built by Jusserand Marine in Cherbourg, France. Has a sapphire-blue hull. Merchant later discloses that the yacht has four turbocharged diesel engines connected to water jets that produce a total of 18,000 horsepower and enable the eight-ton craft to cruise at one hundred and twenty kilometers an hour. The yacht has Casale V-drives.

Dunhill Alexander. One of the partners who own Carlisle & Dunhill.

Duo 300 WetJets. Type of personal watercraft owned by Mason Broadmoor made by Mastercraft Boats. The craft feature a V-hull and a high-torque, modified big-bore long-stroke engine with a variable-pitch impeller. Their estimated top speed is close to sixty knots.

Duse Bay. Location of a British research station where the survivors of the *Polar Queen* are to be transferred. From there, they are to take a jet to Sydney, Australia.

Easter Island (Isla de Pascua). Island off South America that is one corner of the Acoustic Convergence.

Elmo. One of the sadistic security guards at the Kunghit Island mine. Pitt punches him when he first escapes from Kunghit Island with Stokes. He later smashes a rifle muzzle into Pitt's stomach.

Environment Canada. The Canadian equivalent of the U.S. Environmental Protection Agency. Located in the Ottawa city of Hull.

The Executioner. A great white shark estimated to be twenty-two to twenty-four feet in length that circles the raft from the *Gladiator,* eating those who fall into the water.

Faraday, Molly. NUMA's intelligence agency coordinator. A former analyst with the National Security Agency who joined NUMA at Sandecker's request. Described as having soft toffee-colored hair and brown eyes. She is all class. In her forties.

Ferguson, Jack. The superintendent of the Dorsett mines. Dorsett has him baby-sit the Fletcher twins.

Fletcher, Betsy. Convicted of stealing a blanket for her sick father, she is aboard the *Gladiator* when the typhoon hits. From a small village in Cornwall, she was arrested in Falmouth. Described as nearly as tall as most men. Her legs are long and smooth, and she has a narrow waist and a nicely shaped bosom. She was waist-length yellow hair that is well brushed and eyes as blue as an alpine lake. Married Dorsett on Gladiator Island. Later dies from a stomach malady.

Fletcher, Maeve. Described as towering above most women and taller than most men. Her hair, which she braids into twin pigtails, is as yellow as a summer iris. She has eyes as blue as the deep sea and a strong face with high cheekbones. She has a warm smile that reveals a tiny gap in her front teeth. She is three years shy of thirty and has a master's degree in zoology. She was halfway through her doctoral dissertation at the University of Melbourne when she took a job as a naturalist with Rupert & Saunders to earn extra money. She has two sisters. Her mother committed suicide when Maeve was twelve years old. She has twin six-year-old sons named Sean and Michael, from an affair with the son of a sheep rancher she met at college. Age twenty-seven. Shot by her sister Deirdre on the Dorsett yacht at Gladiator Island, she dies in Pitt's arms.

Fletcher, Sean and Michael. Twin six-year-old sons of Maeve Fletcher. After she is killed, they are united with their father. They later inherit Dorsett Consolidated and the Dorsett fortune.

Ghoster. A sailing ship that needs very little wind to sail.

Gladiator. Clipper ship built in Aberdeen, Scotland, in 1854. Owned by Carlisle & Dunhill of Inverness and captained by "Bully" Scaggs. Her measurements are 1,256 tons, one hundred ninety-eight feet in length, with a thirty-four-foot beam. A ghoster, she can sail on the barest breath of wind. She has three masts. She is fitted out by her owners for the Australian trade, but it is found she can make more money hauling convicts. Sets the England-to-Australian sailing record, a record that still stands, by making the run in sixty-three days. During her last voyage, she makes an incredible twenty-four-hour run of four hundred, thirty-nine miles. On that last voyage, she holds a total of two hundred thirty-one—one hundred ninety-two convicts, eleven soldiers and twenty-eight in the crew. Wrecked in the great typhoon of 1856 in the Tasman Sea.

Gladiator Island. Island where the raft of the *Gladiator* lands. Later forms one corner of the Acoustic Convergence. Described as the exposed tip of a deep ocean range of volcanic mountains that surfaces midway between Tasmania and New Zealand's South Island. Privately owned by the Dorsett family.

Glomar Explorer. Deep-sea salvage vessel built by the CIA, Global Marine and Howard Hughes in the 1970s. The ship is two hundred twenty-eight meters long with a twenty-three-story derrick rising in the middle. The vessel has a helicopter pad, and the high bridge superstructure sits on the stern. The raised house on the forecastle shows no sign of ports, only a row of skylightlike windows across the front. The hull is faded, chipped and rusted but is painted a marine blue with a white superstructure. The ship originally was proposed by Davis Packard of Hewlett-Packard fame while he was deputy director of defense. Based on an earlier design by Willard Bascom called the *Alcoa Seaprobe.* Built in secrecy in a fast forty-one months at the Sun Shipbuilding & Dry Dock Company in Chester, Pennsylvania, and launched in the fall of 1972. Became famous for raising an entire Russian Golf-class submarine from a depth of five kilometers in the middle of the Pacific Ocean. After that, no one knew quite what to do with the ship, and she was mothballed in the backwaters of Suisun Bay northeast of San Francisco. Five months ago, she was leased to Deep Abyss Engineering to mine copper and manganese two hundred kilometers south of the Hawaiian Islands. The vessel is chartered by Sandecker to drop the underwater reflector off Hawaii.

Gorimykin, Fyodor. Chief pilot in command of locating whales for a Russian whaling fleet from the port of Nikolayevsk. Lands his helicopter on the HMS *Bridlington.*

Gorman, Otis. Surgeon-superintendent assigned to the *Gladiator.* Tends to the prisoners' general health. A compassionate man.

Greenberg, Dr. Moses. Ship's doctor aboard the *Ice Hunter.* Described as tall and slender, he wears his dark brown hair in a ponytail. He has twinkling blue-gray eyes.

Gulfstream V. Type of jet in the hangar on Kunghit Island. The latest development in business jets, it is spacious with a cabin tall enough for most men to stand up inside. Capable of cruising nine hundred twenty-four kilometers an hour at an altitude of just under eleven thousand meters with a range of sixty-three hundred nautical miles. Powered by a pair of turbofan engines built by BMW and Rolls-Royce. Costs upwards of thirty-three million dollars.

Halawa Bay. The harbor on the island of Molokai where the *Lanikai* delivers the reflector to the *Glomar Explorer.*

Halley Bay. Site of the British station on Seymour Island.

Harbor Tours. Name painted on the side of the Toyota van that picks up Pitt, Fletcher and Giordino in Wellington.

Haynes, Trevor. First officer of the *Polar Queen.* Described as quiet and quite handsome.

Heinklemann Specialty Boat Builders. Boat constructor in Kiel, Germany, which Wilbanks mentions as a possible builder of the Dorsett yacht. It turns out not to be the case, however. An engineer from the firm has spotted the boat in Monaco nine months prior and alerts Wilbanks to the true builder.

Herradura Silver tequila. Tequila Pitt drinks on the Dorsett yacht when he is first introduced to Boudicca.

Holden Automobiles. Australian-made automobiles that are on Gladiator Island. They are painted a bright yellow and are customized by having all the doors removed for easy entry and exit.

Hollender. Name of the teacher and his wife in Perth who care for Maeve's sons until they are taken by her evil father and returned to Gladiator Island.

House of Dorsett. Chain of nearly five hundred retail jewelry stores owned by the Dorsett family that sells the gemstones produced by Dorsett Consolidated Mining Limited.

Howard Hughes. Reclusive billionaire who, along with the CIA, built the *Glomar Explorer.*

Hudson, George. Second officer of the *Rio Grande.*

Huggins, Jake. A convict on the *Gladiator.* Called the murdering Welshman. Described as short and squat with a barrel chest. He has long, matted, sandy hair, an extremely large flattened nose and an enormous mouth with missing and blackened teeth, which combine to give him a hideous leer. Leads the attack on the crew of the *Gladiator* when they are aboard the raft. After he attacks Dorsett, he slits his throat.

Hutton, Wilbur. The U.S. president's chief of staff. Described as a man not easily intimidated, as big and beefy as a Saturday night arena wrestler. He keeps his thinning blond hair carefully trimmed in a crew cut. His head and face are colored like an egg dyed red, and his limpid smoke-blue eyes always stay fixed ahead. A graduate of Arizona State University with a doctorate in economics from Stanford, he is known to be testy with anyone who brags of coming from an Ivy League college. He enlisted and was an infantryman in the Army and served in the Gulf War.

Ice Hunter. NUMA research vessel. No mere garden-variety research ship, she was designed entirely by computers by marine engineers working with oceanographers. She rides on twin parallel hulls that contain her big engines and auxiliary machinery. Her space-age rounded superstructure abounds with technical sophistication and futuristic innovations. The quarters for the crew and scientists rival those of a luxury cruise ship. Her radically designed triangular hulls can crush an ice floe four meters thick. She has a gleaming white superstructure and turquoise hull.

J2X Allard. One of Pitt's cars. Built in England in 1952, the roadster is low and red in color. It features twin bucket seats and a small curved windscreen. Powered by a Cadillac V-8 engine with dual four-barrel carburetors and an Iskenderian camshaft. Pitt estimates its top speed at two hundred ten kilometers an hour.

Joseph Marmon Volcanic Observatory. Location in Auckland, New Zealand, where Bakewell phones Sandecker and discloses that the volcanoes on Gladiator Island will probably blow as a result of the redirected sound waves.

Ka-32 Helix. Gorimykin lands a smaller version of the Russian Navy helicopter aboard the HMS *Bridlington.* The craft is used for light transport duty and air reconnaissance. The one Gorimykin is flying is used to spot whales for hunting.

Kaumalapau. Port on the island of Lanai where the parts of the reflector are loaded aboard a cargo ship.

Kea. Species of parrot that lives on New Zealand and the surrounding islands. One is spotted by the remaining survivors on the raft of the *Gladiator* when they are near the island later to be known as Gladiator Island. Later, one is spotted by Pitt just before they reach land. He describes it as having a wing span of about a meter, with feathers a mottled green with specks of brown. The upper beak is curved and comes to a sharp point. It appears to Pitt to be an ugly cousin of the more colorful parrot family.

Kelsey, Jason. Captain of the *Rio Grande.*

Kimberlite Pipes. A mixture of liquid rocks and diamonds. Named for the South African city of Kimberly.

King George Island. Location where the survivors of Seymour Island are taken.

Krakatoa. Volcano that erupted in 1883. Located south of Java, the eruption created huge tidal waves and upset the world's weather for months.

Kunghit Island. Island off British Columbia that is one corner of the Acoustic Convergence. Location of the Dorsett Consolidated Mining Limited diamond mine. The southernmost island in the Queen Charlotte chain. Part of the Moresby National Park Reserve but leased by the Canadian government anyway. Dorsett then closed off the island to all visitors and campers.

Lanai Satellite Information Collection Facility. Faraday explains that the NSA has a parabolic reflector inside the extinct Palawai volcano on the island of Lanai that is eighty meters in diameter. NUMA removes the reflector without permission and hangs it from the *Glomar Explorer.*

Lanikai. The freighter Faraday charters to move the reflector.

Larsen Ice Shelf. Famous location on Antarctica that is the source of most of the icebergs in the Weddell Sea.

Lim, Poon. The Guiness World Record holder for survival at sea. Poon, a Chinese steward, was set adrift on a raft after his ship was torpedoed in the South Atlantic during World War II. He survived one hundred thirty-three days before being picked up by Brazilian fishermen.

MacIntyre, Commandant. Commander of the U.S. Coast Guard.

Macquaries. Islands south of New Zealand that Pitt hopes the *Marvelous Maeve* can hit.

Marvelous Maeve. The small semi-inflatable boat that Fletcher, Pitt and Giordino are set adrift on from the Dorsett yacht. Three meters in length by two meters wide, it has a fiberglass V-hull that appears sturdy but later cracks. Pitt, Giordino and Fletcher pilot the boat to Gladiator Island. It is later recovered by Giordino and placed in Pitt's aircraft hangar/home.

Marvin, Carl. Claims to be a photographer from the *Ocean Angler* but is quickly found out as a fake by Giordino. Actually works for the Dorsett security force. Giordino chokes him, then throws him out of the Toyota van.

McDonnell-Douglas 530 MD Defenders. A military designed aircraft built for silent flying and high stability during abnormal maneuvers. A pair of the blue-black helicopters mounted with 7.62-millimeter guns are inside the hangar at Kunghit Island.

Mentawai. An Indonesian freighter bound from Honolulu to Jayapua to New Guinea.

Merchant, John. Head of security for Dorsett mining operations on Kunghit Island. Known as "Dapper John." He is described as small, thin and fastidiously dressed. He has deep-set gray eyes. Smokes cigarettes. Broadmoor cracks him on the head with a wrench when he and Pitt escape Kunghit Island, giving him a hairline skull fracture. When Pitt storms Gladiator Island, he shoots him in the knee, then ties him up and leaves him in the closet.

Misery Islands. See The Tits.

Moon Pool. Located in the center of the *Glomar Explorer,* it is an open area where salvage recoveries can take place. Rectangular in shape, it is 1,367 square meters and takes up the middle third of the ship.

"Moon River." Famous Henry Mancini song that Fletcher and Pitt dance to at the party thrown by Deep Abyss Engineering. The song Maeve is whispering as she dies.

Moresby Island. Island across the Houston Stewart Channel from Kunghit Island.

Motorola Iridium. Wireless telephone used by Sandecker.

Mount Scaggs. One of the volcanic peaks on Gladiator Island. It last erupted between A.D. 1225 and 1275. Described as a shield volcano. Explodes first when the acoustic wave hits Gladiator Island.

Mount Winkleman. One of the volcanic peaks on Gladiator Island. It last erupted between A.D. 1225 and 1275. Described as a shield volcano. Explodes second, with the roar of a hundred freight trains rolling through a tunnel, when the acoustic wave hits Gladiator Island.

Mulholand, Hugo. Perlmutter's chauffeur. A taciturn character.

Multilateral Council of Trade. Known to insiders as the Foundation, it is an institution dedicated to the development of a single global economic government. They meet inside a modernistic all-glass structure built in the shape of a pyramid that sits on the outskirts of

Paris. The board of directors is made up of fourteen men including the man who runs the South African diamond cartel, a Belgian industrialist from Antwerp, a real estate developer from New Delhi, India, the billionaire head of a German banking firm and the sheik of an oil-rich country on the Red Sea. Other members of the board include the Japanese head of a huge electronics firm, the French head of one of the world's largest fashion houses, an Italian owner of cargo ships, the CEO of a major Asian airline, a Russian entrepreneur who operates aluminum and copper mines, a British subject who owns a publishing empire and the former U.S. secretary of state from one of the United States' wealthiest families who is the founding father of the Foundation. Clive may have made a mistake here: There are only twelve men listed here, but at the end of the chapter, on page 448, fourteen voices give an affirmative *yea.*

National Science Board. Group that advises the president on the Acoustic Convergence problem. They downplay the danger.

Natural Resources Canada. The Canadian governmental agency that oversees mining. Posey tells Pitt he should be coordinating the investigation of Dorsett Consolidated operations on Kunghit Island with them. Pitt disagrees.

Nimitz. U.S. Navy aircraft carrier Pitt falsely claims is going to attack Kunghit Island.

O'Toole, Major. A major in the Australian Army who leads the rescue efforts after the explosion on Gladiator Island.

Occam's razor. Mentioned by Ames. It states: Entities should not be multiplied unnecessarily.

Ocean Angler. NUMA research vessel on a deep-sea survey project in the Bounty Trough, west of New Zealand.

Oppenheimer, Sir Ernest. Former legendary chairman of De Beers.

Overmeyer, Admiral John. Admiral based at Pearl Harbor from whom Sandecker attempts to borrow the *Enterprise.* Served with Sandecker on the *Iowa.*

Pacific Gladiator. Dorsett-owned company that mines colored gemstones.

Pahoehoe. Thin lava flows, usually basaltic in composition.

Pendleton, Inspector. Stokes's superior in the Royal Canadian Mounted Police.

Petrels. Giant birds described as the vultures of the sea which attack the dead penguins on Seymour Island.

Pier 16. Pier in Wellington where the *Ocean Angler* is tied up.

Pitt, Colonel Thadeus. What Pitt refers to himself as when he builds a pair of sun goggles from a board taken from York's berth.

Polar Queen. Rupert & Saunders–owned cruise ship that is visiting Seymour Island when the acoustic wave hits. Quite small by cruise-ship standards, she measures seventy-two meters with a twenty-five-hundred-gross rated tonnage. Built in Bergen, Norway, she is specially constructed to cruise polar waters and can function as an icebreaker if the need arises. Her superstructure and a broad horizontal stripe below her lower hull are painted glacier-white. The rest of her hull is a bright yellow.

Posey, Edward. Works for Environment Canada in Hull. A short man with glasses and a beard. Worked with Pitt in 1989 on the *Doodlebug* project.

Pryor, John. A convict and one of the survivors of the raft from the *Gladiator.* Dorsett beats his brains in with a rock when he attempts to rape Betsy Dorsett.

Pulse Excavator. Dorsett mining innovation that uses high-energy pulsed ultrasound to carve through the blue clay that contains the major deposits of diamonds. Beam that creates the Acoustic Convergence.

Punta Arenas. Chilean port to which Pitt and Giordino fly the NUMA helicopter from the *Ice Hunter.*

Pygoscelis Adeliae. Adelie penguins that are one of seventeen true species. They have a black-feathered back and hooded head with a white breast and beady little eyes. Their ancestors evolved forty million years ago and were then as tall as a man.

Queen Charlotte Islands. String of about one hundred fifty islands off the coast of British Columbia. The total area of the islands is ninety-five hundred eighty-four square kilometers. The population is fifty-eight hundred ninety people, mostly Haida Indians who invaded the islands in the eighteenth century.

Quick, Captain James. Captain of the *Glomar Explorer.* Described as a short, plump man a few years over forty.

Ramsey, First Officer. First officer of the *Gladiator.* Suffers severe contusions in the first fight aboard the raft from the *Gladiator.* Killed in the second fight aboard the raft from the *Gladiator.*

Reed, Alfred. An able seaman and one of the survivors of the raft from the *Gladiator.* Murdered by Winkleman in a dispute over Marion Adams.

Rhodes, Cecil. Founder of De Beers.

Rio Grande. A U.S. container carrier bound for Sydney, Australia, with a cargo of tractors and agricultural equipment. Receives a distress call from the *Mentawai.*

Rolls-Royce Silver Dawn. Car owned by St. Julien Perlmutter. A 1955 model with coachwork by Hoopers & Company. The engine is a straight-six with overhead valves. The automobile is painted silver and green.

Roosevelt. U.S. Navy nuclear aircraft carrier Sandecker wants to use to hang the underwater reflector.

Currently docked at Pearl Harbor. He is rebuffed in his efforts to use the vessel.

Ross, Joe. Captain of the *Ocean Angler.*

Rostron, Captain Arthur. Captain of the *Carpathia,* the ship that rescued the survivors from the *Titanic.* According to Maeve, he reported seeing a sea serpent.

Rudolf, Surgeon. Doctor aboard the H.M.S. *Bridlington.* Speaks Russian. Described as a short man with blond hair.

Rupert & Saunders. The cruise line that employs Maeve Fletcher. Based in Adelaide, Australia, it specializes in adventure tours.

Ryan, Ian. Captain and chief of operations for Rupert & Saunders. Receives the *Polar Queen* from Dempsey. Described as big and ruddy.

Saint Francis of Paola. Known as the patron saint of mariners and navigators. Pitt discovers a medal with Saint Francis that has fallen from the pocket of the captain of the *Polar Queen* onto the ship's controls and is making the ship steam in circles.

Sandecker's whaleboat. An old navy double-ender whaleboat Sandecker bought surplus and rebuilt. The vessel was built in a small New Hampshire shipyard in 1936, then transported to Newport News, Virginia, where she was loaded aboard the newly launched aircraft carrier *Enterprise.* She served as Admiral Bull Halsey's personal shore boat until the *Enterprise* was decommissioned and scrapped. After being left to rot in a storage area behind the New York shipyard, the craft is purchased and restored by Sandecker. Powered by a four-cylinder Buda diesel engine. Sandecker uses the boat to cruise on the Potomac River on Sundays for relaxation. Clive owned a similar boat in Newport Beach, California, before he began writing.

Scaggs, Charles "Bully." The hard-driving captain of the *Gladiator.* Described as a giant of a man with the physique of a stonemason. He stands six feet two inches tall, with olive-gray eyes that peer from a face weathered by the sea and sun. Has a great shag of ink-black hair and a magnificent black beard that he braids on special occasions. At the time the *Gladiator* is struck by the typhoon, he is thirty-nine years old. Suffers two broken ribs on the first fight aboard the raft of the *Gladiator.* Later lands safely on the island, leaves on a raft and reaches Australia. Once he returns to England, Carlisle & Dunhill offer him the command of their newest clipper, and he makes six more voyages to China before retiring to his cottage in Aberdeen at the early age of forty-seven. Was married to Lucy, who preceded him in death. After catching a cold from sailing his small ketch to visit his grandchildren in Peterhead, he dies at age fifty-nine.

Scaggs, Jenny. Daughter of "Bully." Cares for her father before he dies.

The Serpent. Inhabits the lagoon on Gladiator Island and saves the survivors on the raft from the Executioner. Described as an enormous eel-like creature with a blunt head and long, tapering tail. The length of the body is estimated to be sixty-five feet, with the circumference that of a large flour barrel. The mouth has short fanglike teeth. The serpent's skin appears smooth and colored dark brown, almost black on the top, with an ivory white belly.

Seymour Island. Island near Antarctica that makes up the largest nearby ice-free surface. A singularly ugly place inhabited by only a few varieties of lichen and a rookery of Adelie penguins. A group of Norwegian explorers survived two winters on the island after their ship was crushed in the ice in 1859. First sighted by James Clark Ross in 1842. There is a historic whaling station aboard the island still maintained by the British that the passengers of the *Polar Queen* visit.

Sheppard, Lieutenant Silas. Commander of the ten-man detachment from the New South Wales Infantry Regiment that guards the prisoners aboard the *Gladiator.* Garroted and killed by two convicts in the fight aboard the raft. His parents reside in Horsby.

Sherman, Hank. First officer of the *Rio Grande.* Leads the boarding party to the *Mentawai* and is aboard when she sinks, killing the entire boarding party.

Sherman, Martha. Sandecker's longtime secretary.

Southern Cross. A constellation of stars that is not visible above thirty degrees north latitude, the latitude running across the tip of Florida and North Africa. Its five bright stars have steered mariners and fliers across the immense reaches of the Pacific since the early voyages of the Polynesians. Pitt uses it to navigate aboard the *Marvelous Maeve.*

Stokes, Inspector Malcolm. Royal Canadian Mounted Police inspector in the Criminal Intelligence Directorate who flies Pitt to Moresby Island where Broadmoor lives. Questions Pitt about the *Empress of Ireland* project Pitt worked on in *Night Probe.* After escaping in the *Beaver* with Pitt from Kunghit Island, he is wounded in the left lung by a metal splinter when the *Beaver* crashes. Married, with five children.

Strouser, Gabe. Head of Strouser & Sons. Has known Arthur Dorsett since childhood. Still bitter at Dorsett for firing his company without an explanation. After being fired by Dorsett, he moved his company's headquarters to New York City from Sydney, Australia, and aligned the company with the South African cartel. Described as a strikingly attractive man in his early sixties. Has a head of well-groomed silver hair, a narrow face with high cheekbones and a finely shaped nose. He is trim and athletically built with evenly tanned skin. Several centimeters shorter than Arthur Dorsett, he has dazzling white teeth and a friendly mouth. He has blue-green eyes. Arthur and Boudicca Dorsett kill him by pouring D-grade flawless diamonds into his mouth through a funnel, suffocating him. They later decapitate him and send the head to the Multilateral Council of Trade.

Strouser, Levi. Jewish gem merchant to whom Scaggs asks Carlisle to take the stones Betsy Dorsett sent to him for appraisal. His gem shop, Strouser & Sons, is in the Castlegate section of Aberdeen. Married twice;

his second wife bore him four sons and two daughters. Explains to Carlisle that the stones Betsy Fletcher sent are diamonds worth somewhere in the neighborhood of fifty million dollars on today's market.

Summer. Pitt's only true love. Mentioned on page 163. Described by Pitt on page 372 as having gray eyes and red hair but still looking much like Maeve.

Tantoa, Ramini. A native of Cooper Island in the Palmyra Atoll chain, he finds the *Tz'u-hsi* after she washes ashore in the lagoon on his island.

Tasman Sea. Location of the *Gladiator* when she is abandoned and the convicts and crew take to the raft.

Thurston lava tubes. Hollow tubes in lava beds that are resonating and radiating the sound from the Dorsett Consolidated mines into the oceans.

The Tits. Also known as the Miseries, the small rock islands Pitt, Giordino and Fletcher find, as well as the location of Rodney York and the wreck of the *Dancing Dorothy.* Nine hundred sixty-five kilometers southwest of Invercargil, New Zealand.

Toft, Jason. The *Glomar Explorer*'s chief engineer. Described as a man with a huge stomach and short legs. He is responsible for repairing the *Glomar Explorer*'s engines in record time so she can be deployed to drop the deflector.

Tucson. U.S. Navy missile cruiser that was Sandecker's last command.

Tz'u-hsi. Ningpo-design Chinese junk named after the last Chinese dowager empress and owned by Converse. Twenty-four meters in length with a beam of six meters and built from top to bottom of cedar and teakwood. Converse is sailing the ship on an around-the-world cruise when it is hit by an acoustic wave.

Ultrasonic drilling equipment. Used by Dorsett Consolidated. Uses sound pulses with acoustic frequencies of sixty thousand to eighty thousand Hertz or cycles per second.

Underwriting Room of Lloyd's of London. Area in the famous ship insurer where lost ships are recorded.

U.S. Navy F-22A. Type of jet fighter that transports Sandecker from Hawaii to Tasmania. A two-place jet that can operate at Mach 3+ speeds.

U.S. Navy SH-60B Sea Hawk. Helicopter with NUMA markings that Ames lands on the *Glomar Explorer.*

Van Fleet, Robin. Wife of Roy Van Fleet.

Van Fleet, Roy. NUMA marine biologist who is aboard the helicopter piloted by Giordino when Pitt visits Seymour Island. Married, he has three children.

Vega Island. Location mentioned by Pitt as the site where fifty or more dead seals washed ashore.

Weddell Sea. Location mentioned by Pitt as site of a huge school of dead dolphins.

Wellington, New Zealand. Capital city of New Zealand. Enclosed by a huge bay and a maze of islands, along with low mountains with Mount Victoria the highest peak. Lush, green vegetation surrounds the port, which boasts one of the finest harbors in the world. Pitt, Fletcher and Giordino land there with the intention of boarding the *Ocean Angler* but are kidnapped by Dorsett security forces and taken aboard the Dorsett yacht.

Wilbanks, Wes. Marine architect in Miami, Florida, who helps Giordino identify the yacht seen leaving the area near the *Mentawai.* Described as in his early thirties and quite tall. Has a soft Southern drawl. His handsome face is framed by an abundance of fashionably slicked-back hair that is graying at the temples.

Winkleman, John. A convict and one of the survivors of the raft from the *Gladiator.* Murders Reed in a dispute over Marion Adams, then later marries her. Goes mad when Adams dies giving birth to a daughter and tries to kill the baby. Later gets hold of his senses but is never the same again.

Winkleman, Mary. Daughter of Marion Adams and John Winkleman. Educated at a proper girls' school in England. Later marries Charles Dorsett.

York, Rodney. Yachtsman who entered a solo around-the-world sailboat race that began in Portsmouth, England. The race was sponsored by a London newspaper, and the prize was twenty thousand pounds for the winner. He left Portsmouth April 24, 1962. Lived in Falmouth in Cornwall. Survived on the Tits for one hundred thirty-six days before dying. Had a wife and three daughters. York's widow is still living in Falmouth Bay, a sweet little lady in her late seventies. Giordino has York's log books delivered to her by courier.

Zodiac. A versatile rubber craft designed by the late Jacques Cousteau and used by the passengers of the *Polar Queen* to visit Seymour Island.

Flood Tide

Aserma Bulldog. Twelve-gauge self-ejecting shotgun Pitt uses against assassins inside his aircraft hangar.

Bamboo VI. Code name Han uses when he calls Hong Kong during the INS raid on Orion Lake.

Bartholomeaux Landing. The area where the sugar mill is located.

Bayou Kid. Name Cussler uses for his appearance. Described as an older man, in his mid-sixties. Plays the role of the loner but has a humorous and friendly grin in his blue-green eyes. His hair is gray, and it matches a moustache that falls and meets a beard around his chin. Said to own a fleet of fishing boats and a big catfish farm. You wouldn't know to look at him, but he's a wealthy man.

Benthos AUV II. Used in Louisiana, it is three times the size of the one Pitt used in Orion Lake. Features twin horizontal thrusters and imagery equipment that includes a video camera with low-light sensitivity and high resolution, a video still camera and a ground-penetrating radar unit.

Benthos Inc. AUV. Autonomous Underwater Vehicle that has a high-resolution underwater camera. Remotely operated. Pitt uses it to search Orion Lake. He controls the AUV by means of a joystick mounted on a small remote handbox. After Pitt views the videotape shot by the AUV, he sees bodies strewn on the bottom of Orion Lake.

Black, Charles. Canadian anatomist who discovered the Peking Man.

Boone, Sam. Mississippi River pilot assigned to navigate the S.S. *United States* upriver. Described as a heavy man with a beer belly. Hung-chang orders him taken prisoner and locked up belowdecks.

Butterfield Freight Corporation. Company the guard at the Bartholomeaux Sugar plant claims he works for. Most likely a Shang-owned front company.

Cabrillo, Chairman Juan Rodriguez. Leader of the group that operates the *Oregon.* Described as a handsome man in his mid-forties with blue eyes and blond hair in a crew cut. His parents immigrated from Mexico in 1931 and became American citizens five years later. His leg is amputated after the battle with the *Chengdo.*

Campbeltown. British World War II vessel loaded with explosives and rammed into the drydock at Saint-Nazaire to thwart the Nazis.

Carr, Robin. Receptionist in the West Wing of the White House. Described as an attractive lady in her late thirties with auburn hair tied in an old-fashioned bow.

Charlie's Fish Dock, Seafood and Booze. Location in Louisiana where Pitt and Giordino meet the Bayou Kid. The inside is described as like walking back in time. The ancient air conditioning long ago lost its war with human sweat and tobacco smoke. The wooden floor is worn smooth and scarred by hundreds of cigarette burns. The tables are cut and varnished from the hatch covers of old boats. The tired captain's chairs look patched and glued. The walls feature rusty advertising signs.

Chau, Lei. Deputy minister of internal affairs who succeeds Tsang.

Chengdo. Chinese Luhu Type 052 Class destroyer that orders the *Oregon* to stop. ID number 116. Launched in the late 1990s, the vessel displaces forty-two hundred tons and features two gas turbine engines rated at 45,000 horsepower. Carries two Harbine helicopters and has a complement of two hundred thirty men, forty of them officers. Her armaments include eight sea-skimming missiles and a surface-to-air octuble launcher, twin 100-millimeter guns in a turret aft of the bow, eight 37-millimeters mounted in pairs along with six torpedoes in two triple tubes and twelve antisubmarine mortar launchers. Sunk by the *Oregon.*

Cherokee Oil Company. Oil company based in Baton Rouge, Louisiana, that owns the concrete pier where Pitt and Giordino stop the shanty boat. There they are accosted by a security force from Sungari that arrives in a Hovercraft and films them.

China Maritime. Chinese government-owned shipping company Miang tells Shang will replace Qin Shang Maritime.

Ching, May. Works for the Dragon Triad and is with Loo at Bartholomeaux Sugar. Described as looking Eurasian. Her shiny black hair falls in a long cascade down her back. Her shoulders are broad, her breasts nicely rounded, and her slim waist neatly merges with her trim legs. She wears makeup with skill, and her nails are incredibly long. Her eyes are unusual, one nearly black and the other light gray. Her father was British. Held by Pitt for the INS agents.

Chong, Kung. Han's second-in-command. Has a quiet, competent voice. Formerly an agent with the People's Republic of China's intelligence service.

Chris-Craft Runabout. Boat owned by Foley. A 1933 twenty-one-footer that features a gleaming mahogany hull and double cockpits. The boat has a tumble-home stern, curved gracefully from the transom forward to the engine compartment, which sits between the forward and aft cockpits. Powered by a big, straight-eight, 125-horsepower Chrysler marine engine.

Chu, Lin Wan. Cook on the *Sung Lien Star* whom Lee impersonates. The real Lin grew up on a farm in

Jiangsu Province, then ran away to sea. She is drugged with a shot from a hypodermic needle and taken aboard the *Weehawken*.

Cochran, Chief Mickey. Chief aboard the *Weehawken* who helps Lee make the identity switch. A burly man with a walrus moustache and deep-set gray eyes.

Colburn, Dick. The owner of the general store at Orion Lake. Sells Pitt provisions. Explains that Shang has bought most of the property surrounding Orion Lake.

Crabtree, Monica. Supply and logistics coordinator on the *Oregon*. Described as six feet tall and weighing two hundred pounds.

Daniels, Harry. Colburn tells Pitt that Daniels hunts and camps along the Orion River and has seen a strange work boat traveling the lake after midnight and never under a moon.

Davis, Charles. Special assistant to the director of the Federal Bureau of Investigation. Davis is present after Pitt and Lee escape Shang's assassins and are debriefed. Described as a tall man with the look of a Saint Bernard coming across a garbage can at a barbecue restaurant.

Dean Hawes. U.S. Navy salvage vessel that assists in the recovery of the artifacts from the *Princess Dou Wan*. Described as new, only two years from her launch date, and constructed especially for deep-water work, particularly the recovery of submarines.

Deng, Chu. Captain of the black catamaran that dumps the bodies in Orion Lake. Also supervisor in charge of transporting illegal immigrants from the mother ship and responsible for the execution of those who are unfit for slave labor.

Divercity. Boat Pitt hires to search for the *Princess Dou Wan* on Lake Michigan. Described as a twenty-five-foot Parker with a cabin and powered by a 250-horsepower Yamaha outboard. Electronics include NavStar differential global-positioning system interfaced with a 486 computer, a Geometrics 866 marine magnetometer, a Klein side-scan sonar and a Benthos MiniRover MKII underwater robotic vehicle.

Dragon Lady. Code name Lee uses over the radio to the security team when she attends the party at Shang's home in Chevy Chase with Pitt.

Dragon Triad. Qin Shang's partner. They buy what Shang imports: people, drugs, weapons. Loo from the Triad meets with Wong at Bartholomeaux Sugar.

Du Gard, Marie. Chef on the *Oregon.* From Belgium, she plans to open a restaurant in Midtown Manhattan after two more undercover operations.

Duesenberg. One of Pitt's cars. His is a 1929 convertible sedan with orange body and brown fenders. The Model J Duesenbergs were the finest examples of American automaking. Produced from 1928 until 1936, they are considered by many collectors as the handsomest cars ever built. Pitt's car was custom-bodied by Walter M. Murphy Company in Pasadena, California. The straight eight-cylinder engine displaces four hundred twenty cubic inches. The engine produced two hundred sixty-five horsepower. Under the right conditions, the car can reach speeds of one hundred forty miles an hour. Has big 750-by-17-inch tires.

Elder, Cindy. Colburn tells Pitt she tends bar over at the Sockeye Saloon and gives a great massage.

Farrar, Jack. The deputy director of the Immigration and Naturalization Service region that encompasses Orion Lake.

Felix Bartholomeaux Sugar Processing Plant Number One. Established in 1883, it is used in Shang's smuggling operation. Location where Lee is taken prisoner by Wong, who wants to trade her to Loo.

Ferguson, Dale. Commandant of the Coast Guard. Described as a large, ruddy man with a ready smile. Married to Sally. Has boys in college.

Foley, Sam. An old friend of the Pitt family. Loans his cabin on Orion Lake to Pitt so he can relax and recuperate. The only person who has not sold Shang his cabin on Orion Lake.

Fort McNair. Base in Washington, D.C., where Sandecker and Gunn meet with President Wallace. Because of terrorist threats, the president and the first family only rarely visit the White House and live here.

Fritz. The dachshund dog owned by Katrina Garin. Drowns aboard the *Princess Dou Wan.* Pitt recovers the dog's bones and presents them to the Gallagers for burial.

Gallager, Ian "Hong Kong." Chief engineer on the *Princess Dou Wan*. Described at the time of the sinking as an ox-shouldered, red-faced, hard-drinking, heavily-moustached Irishman. Perlmutter finds accounts of Gallager rescuing the passengers and crew of a sinking tramp steamer off the Philippines in 1936. After 1948, he seemed to drop off the face of the earth. Yaeger learns he became an American citizen in 1950. After that, he worked as a chief engineer with the New York–based Ingram Line. Married Katrina Garin in 1949 and raised five children. Later retired to a lakefront town named Manitowoc on the Wisconsin side of Lake Michigan. When Pitt and Lee visit him, he reveals the location of the *Princess Dou Wan*.

Garin, Katrina (Gallager). Girlfriend and later wife of Ian Gallager. Described at the time of the sinking as having long blond hair. Her complexion is smooth and flawless with high cheekbones. Her body is long and beautifully proportioned, and her eyes are the vivid blue of a late-morning sky.

Gavrovich, Pavel. Shang's chief enforcer. Formerly one of the finest and most ruthless undercover agents in all of Russia. Described as a tall, medium-built man with Slavic features. He has thick black hair that he greases and combs back across the head with no part. Attempts to kill Pitt at his aircraft hangar/home but is killed instead.

George B. Larson. Army Corps of Engineers survey boat that inspects the Mississippi River.

Gibbs, William Francis. Famed ship designer who designed the S.S. *United States.*

Giraud, Lucas. Captain of the *George B. Larson.* Looks like one of the Three Musketeers with French hawklike features and flowing black moustache waxed and twisted at the ends. A big man with a big belly.

Greenberg, Sam. NUMA driver who drops Pitt off at his aircraft hangar/home after returning from searching the S.S. *United States.* Young, no more than twenty, a student studying oceanography at a local university while earning extra money under a marine educational program created for NUMA by Sandecker. Pitt tells him to call Sandecker and a security force.

Grosse, Erich. One of the fake identities used by Pitt and Giordino when they search the S.S. *United States* at the dock. Said to work for the German shipbuilding firm of Voss and Heibert.

Hall, Wes. One of the crew of the *Divercity.* Described as an easygoing, soft-spoken and smoothly handsome man who could double for Mel Gibson.

Han, Lo. Chief of compound security for Shang's Orion Lake facility. Described as a big bull of a man built like a beer keg with a massive, square-jawed head and eyes that are always bloodshot. After Pitt escapes on the Chris-Craft and the Orion Lake compound is raided, Han commits suicide in his mobile security vehicle.

Hanley, Max. Corporate vice president of operational systems aboard the *Oregon.* Has a red face with no trace of a tan. Has alert brown eyes, a bulbous nose and only a wisp of auburn hair splayed across his head.

Harper, Peter. Executive associate commissioner for field operations for the Immigration and Naturalization Service. Has thinning blond hair and gray eyes and wears rimless spectacles.

Hill, Wilbur. A director with the Central Intelligence Agency. Hill is present after Pitt and Lee escape from Shang's assassins and are debriefed. A blond man with a moustache and pale blue eyes set wide apart.

Hispania. A country of Spanish-speaking people that will spread from Southern California across Arizona, New Mexico and the lower half of Texas.

House of Tin Hau. Shang's mansion. Located on an island about a mile in diameter in Repulse Bay near Hong Kong. Originally a Taoist monastery built in 1789, it was abandoned in 1949 and purchased by Shang in 1990. Protected by a high wall and well-guarded gates, the enclosed gardens contain many rare trees and flowers. The inside is furnished with rare works of art, and the dining room is massive with a huge circular table. Guests arrive by helicopter or aboard Shang's two hundred-foot ship.

Hovercraft. Used by Shang's security force at Sungari. An amphibious craft that can ride on both water and land. Propelled by twin aircraft engines with propellers at the stern. The Hovercraft is supported by a cushion of air contained within a heavy rubber structure and produced by a smaller engine attached to a horizontal fan.

Hudson Bay. Canadian salvage ship owned by Deep Abyss Systems Limited out of Montreal. An older vessel converted from a powerful oceangoing salvage and tugboat. Assists in the recovery of artifacts from the *Princess Dou Wan.*

Hui, General Kung. General with the Nationalist Chinese Army who supervises the hiding of the Peking Man and the priceless art treasures aboard the *Princess Dou Wan.* During the sinking, he boards a life raft with Gallager and Garin but dies before they reach land.

Hui, Wang. Guard at Shang's Orion Lake facility.

Hung-chang, Captain Li. Captain of the *Sung Lien Star.* In his late forties. His hair is gleaming salt-and-pepper, though his narrow moustache is still black. Has kindly-grandfather dark-amber eyes. After the *Sung Lien Star,* he is assigned to captain the S.S. *United States.*

Hunt, Captain Leigh. Captain of the *Princess Dou Wan.* Described as a thin man with graying hair and sad, vacant eyes. Served eighteen years with the Royal Navy and eighteen more as an officer with three different shipping companies. Originally from Bridlington, England. Dies aboard the *Princess Dou Wan* when the vessel sinks.

Indigo Star. Vessel that has the appearance of a typical cruise ship but is instead used to smuggle twelve hundred illegal aliens to the United States. Her hull is painted white from the waterline to the funnel.

Jade Adventurer. Shang-owned research vessel constructed in his shipyards at Hong Kong. A marvel of undersea technology. Has a sleek superstructure and twin catamaran hulls that give her the look of an expensive yacht. Has an A-frame crane on her stern. Her hulls are painted blue with a red stripe running around her leading edges. The upperworks are painted white. She measures 325 feet in length. At the site of the wreck of the *Princess Dou Wan.*

James, Pete. One of the *Oregon* crewmen. Diver and former Navy SEAL. Shot in the legs when the *Oregon* attacks the *Chengdo.*

Jiang, Chen. Captain of the *Jade Ad enturer.* Has worked for Qin Shang Maritime for twenty of his thirty years at sea. Described as tall and thin with straight white hair, he is quiet and efficient in the operation of his ship.

Jingzi International Passages. Shang front company located in Beijing, China, that Lee pays thirty thousand dollars to be smuggled to the United States.

Kai-shek, Generalissimo Chiang. Head of the Nationalist Chinese Army and leader of Nationalist China. Orders the artwork and the Peking Man to be loaded aboard the *Princess Dou Wan.*

Kalashnikov AKM rifle. Used by the Chinese on the S.S. *United States.*

Kasim, Hali. The *Oregon*'s vice president in charge of communications.

Klein & Associates Systems 2000 Sonar. Sonar unit on the *Divercity* used to locate the *Princess Dou Wan.* Has a high-resolution color video display unit mounted in the same console as a thermal unit that records the ocean floor in 256 shades of gray.

Kwan, Zhu. Seventy-year-old scholar who is one of China's most respected historians. Described as a little man with a smiling face and small, heavy-lidded brown eyes. He is helping Shang search for the art treasures that disappeared on the *Princess Dou Wan.* Perlmutter leaks information to Kwan about the wreck of the *Princess Dou Wan* being found to lure Shang to the site.

Kwong, Wu. Premier of China. Contributes to President Wallace's campaign.

Laird, Morton. The U.S. president's chief of staff. Described as a tall, balding man with rimless spectacles. Has fox-brown eyes with heavily thicketed eyebrows. Formerly a professor of communications at Stanford. Wears three-piece suits with vests and has a pocket watch with a gold chain. After Shang meets with the president in the White House, Laird resigns in disgust. He moves to an island off the Great Barrier Reef in Australia and begins to write his memoirs.

Lampack School of Oceanography. Where the *Marine Denizen* is to be donated. Clive is having fun here; Peter Lampack is Clive's longtime agent.

Lee, Julia Marie. Special undercover agent with the Internal Affairs Division of the U.S. Immigration and Naturalization Service. Born in San Francisco, California. Her father had been an American financial analyst based in Hong Kong who married the daughter of a wealthy Chinese banker. Has dove-gray eyes, beautiful blue-black hair and Asian features. Books passage on the *Indigo Star* to investigate the smuggling of illegal aliens. When her true identity is discovered, she is bound and tossed into Orion Lake to drown before being rescued by Pitt. Later attends Shang's party with Pitt and is nearly killed in the Duesenberg chase. Then she sneaks aboard the *Sung Lien Star* and is captured. At the end of the book, Pitt invites her to Mazatlan, Mexico, for a romantic vacation.

Lewis, Captain Duane. Captain of the *Weehawken.* Has deep-set brown eyes.

Lin, Ming. First officer on the S.S. *United States.* Lin pilots the ship up the Mississippi River after training on a computer simulator.

Loo, Jack. Chief executive officer for the Dragon Triad. Eurasian, suntanned, with vapid black eyes. His hair is long and black and tied in a ponytail. His face looks like that of a party animal, and he has had more than one facelift. Hit by Pitt in the head, he dies at Bartholomeaux Sugar.

Lotus II. Code name for the person Han calls in Hong Kong after the INS raid begins at Orion Lake.

Louisiana & Southern Railroad. Name on the diesel-electric locomotive inside Bartholomeaux Sugar.

Loyang, Lin. President of China.

M1A1 tanks. Tanks used by the Louisiana National Guard. Mounted with 105-millimeter guns.

Mahler, Karl. One of the fake identities used by Pitt and Giordino when they search the S.S. *United States* at the dock. Said to work for the German shipbuilding firm of Voss and Heibert.

Manitowoc, Wisconsin. Town where the Gallagers retired. Located thirty-five miles south of Green Bay.

Marchand, Sheriff Louis. Sheriff of Iberville Parish. Described as trim and smartly dressed in a tailored uniform. He is polished, urbane and extremely street-smart.

Marine Denizen. NUMA research vessel. The oldest ship in the NUMA fleet and soon to be retired. Assigned to the Mississippi River project.

Mazatlan. Mexican resort town where Pitt invites Lee for a romantic vacation.

McDonnell-Douglas Explorer. Fast, no-tail rotor, twin-engined helicopter with a top speed of 170 miles an hour. Giordino and Gunn use the helicopter to attack the ultralights and help Pitt and the immigrants aboard the Chris-Craft escape.

Meadows, Bob. One of the *Oregon* crewmen. Diver and former Navy SEAL. Shot in the legs when the *Oregon* attacks the *Chengdo.*

Mercado, Juan. A naval archivist from Panama whom Perlmutter asks to search the Panama Canal records for ships passing through the canal from November 28 through December 5, 1948. He finds that the *Princess Yung T'ai* passed December 1, 1948.

Miang, Qian. China's ambassador to the United States. A portly man with short hair styled in a crew cut whose face is fixed in a constant little grin. Was schooled for three years at Cambridge.

Monroe, Duncan. Commissioner of the Immigration and Naturalization Service.

Montaigne, Major General Frank. President of the Mississippi River Commission and head of the Army Corps of Engineers for the entire Mississippi Valley from the Gulf up to where the Missouri River joins the Mississippi near St. Louis. Described as late-fiftyish with steel-gray hair. His eyebrows stayed black and sat on top of gray-blue colored eyes. Born below New Orleans to a fisherman father, Montaigne has served a distinguished career in both Vietnam and the Gulf War and has a Ph.D. in hydrology. Married, with three daughters. Present when the S.S. *United States* runs upriver.

Morgan City, Louisiana. Town closest to Sungari. With a population of fifteen thousand, the city is the largest in St. Mary Parish. The city faces west, overlooking a wide stretch of the Atchafalaya River called Berwick Bay.

Mosby underwater rifles. An underwater weapon that fires a missile with a small explosive head through water. Used by the Chinese who attack the *Sea Dog II.*

Mystic Canal. Dredged by Shang to divert the Mississippi River.

Nanchang Investments. Holding company based in Vancouver, British Columbia, that Shang hides behind when he purchases the Orion Lake property.

National Gallery of Art. Where the artifacts removed from the *Princess Dou Wan* are to be exhibited.

Newtsuits. Deep-water atmospheric diving system that enables the diver inside to work for long periods of time at the four-hundred-plus depth without concerns over decompression. Bulbous, constructed of fiberglass and magnesium and self-propelled.

NUMA Marine Science Center. NUMA facility at Bremerton, Washington, where Giordino and Gunn borrow the helicopter used to help Pitt on the Orion River.

Ocean Retriever. NUMA vessel that was working off the coast of Maine but was diverted to Lake Michigan to help with the recovery of the artifacts from the *Princess Dou Wan.*

Olson, General Oskar. Commander of the Louisiana National Guard. Attended West Point. Old friend of Montaigne's. A man in his late fifties, youthful-looking, confident and buoyant. He is about the same size as Pitt but has a slight paunch at the waist. Has olive-brown eyes.

Operation Iberville. The operation at Morgan City.

Operation Orion. The operation at Orion Lake.

Oregon. Formerly a Pacific Coast lumber hauler, the vessel sailed between Vancouver and San Francisco for close to twenty-five years before being retired. When Pitt boards her in Manila, he guesses her length at just under three hundred feet, with a forty-five-foot beam, and figures the vessel displaces between four and five thousand tons. Flies an Iranian flag. Powered by twin diesel turbine engines; her twin screws can push the ship past forty knots. For armaments, the vessel features sea-to-sea and sea-to-air missile launchers along with Harpoon surface-to-surface missiles and Mark 46 torpedoes. Owned by the covert intelligence corporation that helps Pitt search the S.S. *United States.*

***Oregon's* launch.** A big, double-ender powered by a 539-cubic-inch, 1,500-horsepower engine.

Orion Lake. Lake on the Olympic Peninsula where Shang's compound is located. Shaped like a slender teardrop whose lower end gently tapers into a small river.

Orion River. Starts at Orion Lake. Runs sixteen miles through a canyon before emptying into the upper end of a fjordlike inlet called Grapevine Bay. Grapevine Bay opens into the Pacific Ocean.

Paladin Self-Propelled Howitzer. Used by the Louisiana National Guard to attack the S.S. *United States.* Shoot a 155-millimeter high-explosive fragmentation shell.

Pecorelli, Harold. President Wallace's new chief of staff after Laird resigns.

Peking Man. *Sinanthropus pekinensis.* A very ancient and primitive man who walked upright on two feet. His skull was discovered in 1929 by Canadian anatomist Charles Black digging in a quarry that had once been a hill with limestone caves near the village of Choukoutien. In December 1941, when invading Japanese troops were closing in on Peking, officials at the Peking Union Medical College, where the bones were stored, decided they should be moved to a place of safety. The bones were packed in two Marine Corps footlockers and put aboard a train bound for the port city of Tientsin, where they were to be placed aboard the S.S. *President Harrison,* an American ship belonging to the American President Line. They never arrived. Recovered from the wreck of the *Princess Dou Wan.*

People's Republic Ministry of Internal Affairs. Obscure Chinese government agency that is involved in everything from foreign espionage of scientific technology to the international smuggling of immigrants to relieve population overcrowding.

Po, Li. Second mate on the *Princess Dou Wan.*

Princess Dou Wan. Carries the treasures ordered removed from China by Chiang Kai-shek. Launched in 1913 by shipbuilders Harland & Wolff. Gross tonnage of 10,758. Length of 497 feet with 60-foot beam. The ship had triple expansion engines that could generate 5,000 horsepower. Her twin screws could power her to seventeen knots. Her accommodations were designed to carry 55 first-class passengers, 85 second-class and 370 third-class. She was normally crewed by 190 officers and men, but on her final voyage she was manned by only 38. Originally named *Lanai.*

Princess Yung T'ai. Sister ship of the *Princess Dou Wan.* Launched into service the year after the *Princess Dou Wan.* According to records, the *Princess Yung T'ai* was broken up six months before the *Princess Dou Wan* was due to be scrapped.

Project Pacifica. Chinese government plan to split the United States into three countries. Pacifica would stretch from Alaska to San Francisco.

Qin Shang Maritime Limited. Shang-owned shipping company based in Hong Kong. Operates a fleet of more than a hundred cargo ships, oil tankers and cruise ships.

Qingdao, China. Port from which the *Indigo Star* left.

Reflecting Pool. 160-foot-long pool in Washington, D.C., that Pitt drives the Duesenberg through to elude Shang's assassins.

Rolls-Royce. Cabrillo borrows a 1955 Silver Dawn with Hooper coachwork and has Seng drive Pitt and Giordino to where the S.S. *United States* is docked for an inspection.

Romberg. Fish-eating bloodhound the Bayou Kid loans to Pitt and Giordino. Described as incredibly lazy with floppy ears. Enjoys sniffing.

Ross, Linda. Surveillance analyst on the *Oregon.* Had been chief fire-control officer on board a U.S. Navy Aegis guided-missile cruiser.

Russell, Arthur. Director of the INS's San Francisco office and Lee's boss. Described as gray-haired and reasonably trim from daily workouts.

SA-7 missile. Russian-made, man-portable infrared homing antiaircraft missile used by one of the Chinese Special Forces commandos on the S.S. *United States* to shoot down the helicopters.

San, Li. Guard at Shang's Orion Lake facility.

Sappho IV submersible. NUMA submersible Pitt and Giordino use for recovering artifacts from the *Princess Dou Wan.*

Sea Dog II. NUMA submersible used to survey the hull of the S.S. *United States* at Kwai Chung north of Kowloon. Has the appearance of a fat Siamese cigar with stubby wings on each side that curve to vertical on the tips. The twenty-three-foot long, eight-foot-wide, 3,200-pound vehicle may look ungainly on the surface, but she dives with the grace of a baby whale. Three thrusters in the twin tail section impel water through the front intakes and expel it out the rear. Can dive to a depth of two thousand feet.

Sea Jasmine. Shang-designed submersible built as a backup to *Sea Lotus.*

Sea Lotus. Shang-designed submersible. Built at a company in France that specializes in deep-undersea vehicles.

Selby, Norman. Colburn tells Pitt he is the real estate agent who sold Shang the old fish cannery he converted to his compound on Orion Lake.

Seng, Eddie. Part of the crew of the *Oregon.* Was the CIA's agent in Beijing for almost twenty years until he was forced to return to the United States and retire. Shot twice in the right arm when the *Oregon* attacks the *Chengdo.*

Shang, Qin. A Chinese shipping magnate who operates out of Hong Kong. Owns the compound on Orion Lake. Born on the same day in the same year as Pitt. President Wallace's chief fund-raiser in Asia. Described as tall for most Asian men at five feet, eleven inches. Heavy around the waist, chubby, he weighs

210 pounds. His black hair is thick and cut short with a part down the middle. His head and face are not round but narrow and almost feline, and match his long and slender hands. His mouth, oddly and deceptively, seems fixed in a permanent grin. His eyes are the color of the purest green jade. As an orphan, he begged on the streets of Kowloon across Victoria Harbor from the island of Hong Kong. By age ten, he had saved enough money to buy a sampan; two years later, he operated a fleet of ten. Before he was eighteen, he sold the sampans, bought an ancient intercoastal tramp steamer and built his fleet from there. Likes to drink American coffee with chicory. Owns an island near Hong Kong as well as a house in Chevy Chase, Maryland. Orders Pitt killed, but the assassins are foiled. Dies aboard the *Sea Lotus* on the site of the *Princess Dou Wan* when he encounters Pitt and Giordino.

Shantyboat. Also called campboats. The Bayou Kid loans one to Pitt and Giordino to use. Described as broad and flat like a barge. A square box atop the deck with windows and doors is the house. Inside is a wood-burning potbellied stove. The vessel is powered by a 427-cubic-inch Ford V-8 engine, with dual carburetors that produces close to 425 horsepower.

Sikorsky S-76 Eagle. Type of helicopter that attacks the S.S. *United States.*

Simmons, George. Assistant district director of the Immigration and Naturalization Service who meets the Chris-Craft when it reaches safety. A tall, jovial-looking man with twinkling eyes.

Skyfox Flying Boat. Built by Lockheed, the two-seater jet aircraft were originally designed as jet trainers. Modified by NUMA, the plane can make water landings, Has twin jet engines mounted on the fuselage behind the wings and cockpit.

Smith & Wesson First Response knife. Brand of knife Lee straps to her leg before going aboard the *Sung Lien Star.*

Smith, John. Fake identity assumed by Cabrillo when he picks up Pitt and Giordino at the Manila Airport. In disguise, he appears as a great slob of a man with a big belly. He has a hook nose that looks as if it has been broken a few times, and his lip and chin are covered with stubble. Has greasy black hair and yellow irregular teeth. His biceps and forearms are covered with tattoos. Pitt and Giordino see through the disguise.

Stephen Miller. Cargo ship that recovers a body in a life raft that came from the *Princess Dou Wan.*

Stewart, Frank. Captain of the *Marine Denizen.* Has brown hair cut short and slickly combed with a precision part on the right side. Slim and tall with deep-set blue eyes. He is unmarried.

Stingray. Compact, battery-powered diver propulsion unit that Pitt uses on Orion Lake.

Stowe, Lieutenant Jefferson. Lieutenant on the *Weehawken.* Described as tanned, blond and tall, with the boyish good looks of a tennis instructor.

Straight, Tom. Bartender at Charlie's Fishdock, Seafood and Booze.

Sungari. Huge port facility built by Shang on Atchafalaya Bay near Morgan City, Louisiana. Covers two thousand miles and stretches over a mile on both sides of the Atchafalaya River. The area is dredged to an operational depth of thirty-two feet. The port consists of one million square feet of warehouse space, two grain elevators with loading slips, a six hundred-thousand-barrel-capacity liquid bulk terminal and three general-cargo-handling terminals that could load and unload twenty container ships at one time. The warehouses and office structures are constructed in the shape of pyramids and are covered by a gold galvanized material that blazes like fire when struck by the sun.

Swordfish. Laird's code name with the Secret Service.

T'ai, Ling. Fake identity assumed by Lee. T'ai is said to hail from Jiangsu Province, where she lived until age twenty and finished her studies. She then allegedly went to Canton and became a schoolteacher. Her father is said to be a professor of chemistry at Beijing University. Her great-grandfather was a Dutch missionary.

Tien, Yu. Captain of the *Chengdo.*

Ting, Quan. Chairman of China & Pacific Lines. A competitor of Shang's, Tsang explains that he will be taking over immigrant smuggling for the Chinese government. Shang has Ting and his wife killed in an auto accident.

Tsang, Yin. Chief director of the People's Republic Ministry of Internal Affairs. A short man with dense gray hair. His eyes bulge as they protrude from fleshy pouches. After Shang gives him drugged tea, he suffers a fatal heart attack.

Tsung. Helmsman on the *Princess Dou Wan.*

Turner, Colonel Bob. Commander of the battle group of Louisiana National Guardsmen who try to stop the S.S. *United States.* A veteran of the Gulf War.

Ultralights. Used by the Chinese to chase the Chris-Craft. Powered by a lightweight reduction-drive, 50-horsepower pusher engine. Pitt estimates their top speed as 120 miles an hour. The pilot sits forward out in the open with the passenger behind and slightly elevated.

Underground Washington. A series of tunnels that connect the White House with the Supreme Court, Capitol Building, State Department, under the Potomac River to the Pentagon, the Central Intelligence Agency in Langley, Virginia, and about a dozen other strategic government buildings and military bases around the city.

***United States,* S.S.** Former cruise liner that was taken out of service and laid up in Norfolk, Virginia, for thirty years before being sold to a Turkish millionaire. Towed from Norfolk across the sea to the Mediterranean, past Istanbul and into the Black Sea to Sevastopol. On her maiden voyage, she set the speed record between New York and London, averaging thirty-five knots knots or about forty-one miles an hour. The brainchild of famed ship designer William Francis Gibbs. Her keel was laid in 1950 by the Newport News Ship Building & Dry Dock. In an effort to build the fastest and most beautiful passenger liner afloat, Gibbs specified aluminum wherever possible. From the 1.2 million rivets in her hull to the lifeboats and their oars, the stateroom furnishings, bathroom fixtures, babies' high chairs, even the coat hangers and picture frames, all had to be made from aluminum. A huge ship, she measures 990 feet with a beam of 101 feet. Her gross tonnage is 53,329. Designed to carry 694 passengers, the ship featured air conditioning, nineteen elevators, three libraries, two cinemas and a chapel. Powered by eight massive boilers creating superheated steam, her four Westinghouse-geared turbines could put out 240,000 horsepower or 60,000 for each of her four propeller shafts, and could drive her through the water at more than fifty miles an hour. In 1952, she won the prestigious Blue Riband, awarded for the fastest time across the Atlantic. No liner has won it since. By 1969, she was retired and laid up at Norfolk, Virginia, for thirty years. Her hull was painted black, her superstructure white and her two magnificent funnels red, white and blue. Used by Shang in an attempt to flood the Lower Mississippi River Basin.

Valparaiso, Chile. City where a radio operator reported a distress call from the *Princess Dou Wan.*

Wallace, Dean Cooper. President of the United States. Was vice president. A former two-term governor from Oklahoma. Sleeps three hours a night between four and seven A.M. He looks sixty-five but is only in his late fifties. Has premature gray hair, red veins streaming through his facial skin and beady eyes that always look red. An intense man with a round face, low forehead and thin eyebrows.

Wan-Tzu, Han. Fake identity Seng assumes when he delivers Pitt and Giordino to the dock where the S.S. *United States* is located. Wan-Tzu is said to be chief of dockside security.

Weehawken. Coast Guard Cutter that drops Lee off on the *Sung Lien Star.*

Welland Canal. Canal that separates Lake Erie from Lake Ontario. Perlmutter finds the *Princess Yung T'ai* passed through the canal on December 7, 1948.

Wen, Chu. Second engineer on the *Princess Dou Wan.*

Wheeler, Doug. Old friend and neighbor of the Bayou Kid. Owner of Wheeler's Landing. A portly man with a thick moustache.

Wheeler's Landing. Where Pitt and Giordino pick up the Bayou Kid's shantyboat and buy supplies for their trip. Raised off the ground on short pilings, has a long porch that runs around the building. The walls are painted a bright green with yellow shutters framing the windows.

Wiay, Hui. Former Nationalist Chinese Army colonel. Now lives in Taipei. Fought against the Communists until forced to flee to Formosa (now Taiwan). Ninety-two years old, but his mind is still sharp. Perlmutter contacts him, and he discloses that he followed Chiang Kai-shek's orders, rounded up artwork and delivered it to the Shanghai docks and an old passenger liner commanded by Hui.

Willbanks, Ralph. One of the crew of the *Divercity.* Described as a big, jolly man in his early forties with expansive brown eyes and a bristling moustache.

Wong, Ki. Chief enforcer on the *Indigo Star.* A thin, neatly attired man. Has a smooth brown face that is intelligent but expressionless. Has narrow lips. Discloses to Lee that he knows she is not T'ai and sentences her to die. Later captures Lee at Bartholomeaux Sugar but is shot and killed by Giordino.

XM4 command-and-control vehicle. Location where Turner directs fire onto the S.S. *United States.*

Yokohama Ship Sales & Scrap Company. Based in Japan, the front company Shang uses to purchase his competitors' ships so his shipping company could grow.

Zhong, Su. Shang's private secretary. Moves with the grace of a Balinese dancing girl.

Answers to Advanced Pitt Trivia

1. Al Capone.
2. British Sterling.
3. Omega.
4. Serial number 19385628.
5. "Alexander's Ragtime Band."
6. Miss Gosset.
7. Celestial Seasonings Red Zinger.
8. Abercrombie & Fitch.
9. "Yankee Doodle Dandy."
10. The complex is SKIQUEEN. The unit number is 22B.
11. "TRIVMFATOR."
12. Asakusa Dude Ranch.
13. Susan.
14. The Algonquin Hotel.
15. Bentley.

16. "Alkali Sam's Tequila: If your eyes are still open, it ain't Alkali Sam's."
17. Aqualand Pro.
18. Dodge Viper.
19. Managua, Nicaragua.
20. Ninety-five miles.

ATLANTIS FOUND

by

CLIVE CUSSLER

IMPACT

6120 B.C.
In what is now
Hudson's Bay, Canada

The intruder came from beyond. A nebulous celestial body as old as the universe itself, it had been born in a vast cloud of ice, rocks, dust and gas when the outer planets of the solar system were formed more than four and a half billion years ago. Soon after its scattered particles froze into a solid mass one mile in diameter, it began streaking silently through the emptiness of space on an orbital voyage that carried it around a distant sun and halfway to the nearest stars again, a journey lasting two million years from start to finish.

The comet's core, or nucleus, was a conglomeration of frozen water, carbon monoxide, methane gas and jagged blocks of metallic rocks. It might accurately be described as a dirty snowball hurled through space by the hand of God. But as it whirled past the sun and swung around on its return path beyond the outer reaches of the solar system, the solar radiation reacted with its nucleus and a metamorphosis took place. The ugly duckling soon became a thing of beauty.

As it began to absorb the sun's heat and ultraviolet light, a long coma formed that slowly grew into an enormous, luminous blue tail that curved and stretched out behind the nucleus for a distance of ninety million miles. A shorter, white dust tail more than one million miles wide also materialized and curled out on the sides of the larger tail like the fins of a fish.

Each time the comet passed the sun, it lost more of its ice, and its nucleus diminished. Eventually, in another two hundred million years, it would lose all its ice and break up into a cloud of dust and become a series of small asteroids. This comet, however, would never orbit outside the solar system or pass around the sun again. It would not be allowed a slow, cold death far out in the blackness of space. Within a few short minutes, its life would be snuffed out. On this, its last orbit, the comet passed within nine hundred thousand miles of Jupiter, whose great gravitational force made it veer off on a collision course with the third planet from the sun, a planet its inhabitants called Earth.

Plunging into the Earth's atmosphere at one hundred twenty thousand miles an hour on a forty-five-degree angle, its speed ever increasing with the gravitational pull, the comet created a brilliant luminescent bow shock as its two-billion-ton mass began to break into fragments due to friction from its great speed. Seven seconds later, the misshapen comet, having become a blinding fireball, smashed into an ocean with horrendous effect. The immediate result from the explosive release of kinetic energy upon impact was to gouge out a massive cavity the size of today's Hawaiian island of Maui as it vaporized and displaced a gigantic volume of water.

The entire Earth staggered from the seismic shock

of an 11.0 earthquake. Millions of tons of sediment from the ocean bottom burst upward, thrown through the hole in the atmosphere above the impact site and into the stratosphere along with a great spray of pulverized, fiery rock that was ejected into suborbital trajectories before raining back to earth as blazing meteorites. Firestorms destroyed forests throughout the world. Volcanoes that had been dormant for thousands of years suddenly erupted, sending oceans of molten lava spreading over millions of square miles, blanketing the ground a thousand or more feet deep. So much smoke and debris were hurled into the atmosphere and later blown into every corner of the land by terrible winds that the sun was blocked out for nearly a year, sending temperatures plunging below freezing and shrouding the earth in darkness. Climatic change in every corner of the world came with incredible suddenness. Temperatures at vast ice fields and northern glaciers rose until they reached between ninety and one hundred degrees Fahrenheit, causing a rapid meltdown. Animals accustomed to tropical and temperate zones became extinct overnight. Many, such as the woolly mammoths, turned to ice where they stood in the warmth of summer eating grasses and flowers still undigested in their stomachs. Trees along with their leaves and fruit were quick-frozen. For days, fish that had been hurled upward from the impact fell from the black skies.

Waves thousands of feet in height were thrown against the continents, surging over shorelines with a destructive power that was awesome in magnitude. Water swept over low coastal plains and swept hundreds of miles inland, destroying everything in its path. Endless quantities of debris and sediment from the ocean floors were spread over low land masses. Only when the great surge smashed against the base of mountains did it curl under and begin a slow retreat, but not before changing the course of rivers, filling land basins with seas where none existed before and turned large lakes into deserts.

The chain reaction seemed endless.

With a low rumble that grew to the roar of continuous thunder, the mountains began to sway like palm trees under a light breeze as avalanches swept down their sides. Deserts and grassy plains undulated as the onslaught from the oceans reared up and struck inland again. The shock from the comet's impact had caused a sudden and massive displacement in the Earth's thin crust. The outer shell, less than forty miles thick, and the mantle that lay over the hot fluid core buckled and twisted, shifting crustal layers like the skin of a grapefruit that had been surgically removed and then neatly replaced so it could move around the core of fruit inside. As if controlled by an unseen hand, the entire crust then moved as a unit.

Entire continents were shoved around to new locations. Hills were thrust up to become mountains. Islands throughout the Pacific Ocean vanished, while others emerged for the first time. Antarctica, once west of modern-day Chile, slid more than two thousand miles to the south, where it was quickly buried under growing mountains of ice. The vast ice pack that once floated in the Indian Ocean west of Australia now found itself in a temperate zone and rapidly began to melt. The same occurred with the former North Pole, which had spread throughout what is now northern Canada. The new pole soon began to produce a thick ice mass in the middle of what once had been open ocean.

The destruction was relentless. The convulsions and holocaust went on as if they would never stop. The movement of the Earth's thin outer shell piled cataclysm on cataclysm. The abrupt melting of the former ice packs, combined with glaciers covering the continents having suddenly shifted into or near tropical zones, caused the seas to rise four hundred feet, drowning the already destroyed land that had been overwhelmed by tidal waves from the comet's impact. In the time span of a single day, Britain, once connected to the rest of the European continent by a dry plain, was now an island, while a desert that would become known as the Persian Gulf was abruptly inundated. The Nile River, having flowed into a vast fertile valley and then on toward the great ocean to the west, now ended at what had suddenly become the Mediterranean Sea.

The last great ice age had ended in the geological blink of an eye.

The dramatic change in the oceans and their circulation around the world also caused the poles to shift, drastically disturbing the Earth's rotational balance. Earth's axis was thrown off by two degrees as the north and south poles were displaced to new geographical locations, altering the centrifugal acceleration around the outer surface of the sphere. Because they were fluid, the seas adapted before the Earth made another three revolutions. But the land mass could not react as quickly. Earthquakes went on for months.

Savage storms with brutal winds swirled around Earth, shredding and disintegrating everything that stood on the ground for the next eighteen years, before the poles stopped wobbling and settled into their new rotational axis. In time, sea levels stabilized, permitting new shorelines to form as bizarre climatic conditions continued to moderate. Changes became permanent. The time sequence between night and day changed as the number of days in a year decreased by two. The earth's magnetic field was also affected and moved northwest by more than a hundred miles.

Hundreds, perhaps thousands of different species of animals and fish became instantly extinct. In the Americas, the one-humped camel, the mammoth, an ice age horse and the giant sloth all disappeared. Gone also were the saber-toothed tiger, huge birds with twenty-five-foot wingspans and most other animals that weighed one hundred or more pounds, most dying by asphyxiation from the smoke and volcanic gases.

Nor did the vegetation on land escape the apocalypse. Plant life not turned to ashes by the holocaust died for lack of sunlight along with the algae in the seas. In the end, more than eighty-five percent of all life on Earth would die from floods, fires, storms, avalanches, poison from the atmosphere and eventual starvation.

Human societies, many quite advanced, and a myriad of emerging cultures on the threshold of a progressive golden age were annihilated in a single horrendous day and night. Millions of Earth's men, women and children died horribly. All vestiges of emerging civilizations were gone, and the few pathetic survivors were left with nothing but dim memories of the past. The coffin had been closed on the greatest uninterrupted advance of mankind, a ten-thousand-year journey from the simple Cro-magnon man to kings, architects, stonemasons, artists and warriors. Their works and their mortal remains were buried deep beneath new seas, leaving few physical examples and fragments of an ancient advanced culture. Entire nations and cities that stood only a few hours before had vanished without a trace. The cataclysm of such magnitude left almost no evidence of any prior transcendent civilizations.

Of the shockingly low number of humans who survived, most lived in the higher altitudes of mountain ranges and were able to hide in caves to escape the furies of the turbulence. Unlike the more advanced Bronze Age peoples who tended to cluster and build on low-lying plains near rivers and ocean shorelines, the inhabitants of the mountains were Stone Age nomads. It was as though the cream of the crop, the Leonardo da Vincis, the Picassos and Einsteins of their era had evaporated into nothingness, abruptly leaving the world to be taken over by itinerant hunters and backwoods trappers, a phenomenon similar to the glory of Greece and Rome cast aside in favor of centuries of ignorance and creative lethargy. A neolithic dark age shrouded the grave of the highly cultured civilizations that once existed in the world, a dark age that would last for two thousand years. Slowly, very slowly, did mankind finally walk from the dark and begin building and creating cities and civilizations again in Mesopotamia and Egypt.

Pitifully few of the gifted builders and creative thinkers of the lost cultures survived to reach high ground. They had erected mysterious magaliths and dolmens of huge upright stones across Europe, Asia, the Pacific Islands and into the lower Americas. Their only visible legacy consisted of these monuments commemorating the frightful destruction and loss of life, which also acted as warnings to future generations of the next cataclysm. Within two hundred years, they had been assimilated into the nomadic tribes and ceased to exist as a race of advanced people.

For hundreds of years after the convulsion, humans were afraid to venture down from the mountains and reinhabit the lower lands and coastal shorelines. The technically superior seafaring nations were but vague thoughts of a distant past. Ship construction and sailing techniques were lost and had to be reinvented by later generations whose more accomplished ancestors were revered simply as gods.

All this death and devastation was caused by a hunk of dirty ice no larger than an average shopping mall. The comet had wreaked its unholy havoc, mercilessly, viciously. The Earth had not been ravaged with such vehemence since a meteor had struck sixty-five million years earlier in a catastrophe that exterminated the dinosaurs.

For thousands of years after the impact, comets were associated with catastrophic events and thought to be portents of tragedies. They were blamed for everything from wars and pestilence to death and destruction. Not until recent history were comets considered nature's wonders, like the splendor of a rainbow or clouds painted gold by a setting sun.

The biblical flood and a host of other calamity legends all had their ties to this one tragedy. The ancient civilizations of Olmecs, Mayans and Aztecs of Central America had many traditions relating to an ancient cataclysmic event. The Indian tribes throughout the United States passed down stories of waters flooding over their lands. The Chinese, the Polynesians and the Africans all spoke of a cataclysm that decimated their ancestors.

But the legend that was spawned and flourished throughout the centuries, the one that provoked the most mystery and intrigue, was that of the lost continent and civilization of Atlantis.

ALSO BY

CLIVE CUSSLER

Blue Gold
A Novel from the NUMA Files

✸

Clive Cussler
and Dirk Pitt® Revealed

✸

Cyclops

✸

Deep Six

✸

Dragon

✸

Flood Tide

Iceberg

✷

Inca Gold

✷

The Mediterranean Caper

✷

Raise the Titanic!

✷

Sahara

✷

The Sea Hunters

✷

Serpent
A Novel from the NUMA Files

✷

Shock Wave

✷

Treasure

 POCKET BOOKS